# LISTEN TO MOTHER

## L J SMITH

First published in 2025 by Blossom Spring Publishing
Listen to Mother Copyright © 2025 L J Smith
ISBN 978-1-0685693-6-4
E: admin@blossomspringpublishing.com
W: www.blossomspringpublishing.com

"Then I will come to my mother by and by"
William Shakespeare, Hamlet

# One

When she dropped the phone into the Arno, she knew it made her look guilty, but she didn't know what else she should have done with it. It had rested beside the dead man. The dead man who hadn't yet been found.

As she sat quietly on the edge of the bridge staring out between the two stone pillars towards the cleaned and pristine facade of the Uffizi, the phone felt cold in her hand. She held it tightly, so tightly she thought she might not be able to let it go. She wondered if anyone would notice her hand slipping over the edge of the bridge and hugging the stone. She wondered how much noise it would make as it hit the Arno, shining green in the early spring sunshine. She wondered if anyone would be looking over the edge as she let it go, and would they watch it fall from her hand; would they speak to her and commiserate over her lost phone? Or would they look at her soft white face and wonder why she was dropping her phone? She couldn't draw attention to herself. She wanted no questions later.

It was very warm for April. It was all a new experience for Lesley. Scotland could still be cold in April. A good day at home would be the opportunity not to wear a coat but to luxuriate in wearing only a jumper with a t-shirt underneath. Here she had been wearing cropped trousers for two weeks, and today was no different. She still wore the customary April jumper, but it was lighter and it required no t-shirt to add to its weight. Even January and February had felt warm to her. Four months in Florence.

Everyone at home had thought Florence an odd choice since she had some grasp of French but no understanding of Italian. She had always loved France, seeking it out at every opportunity. Its varied landscape and climate always pleased her, while the ability to be in the countryside without having to meet a town or city for long periods made it very attractive to her. No people to contend with or worry about, and now she sat surrounded by hundreds of people from across the globe, drawn to Florence for its history, architecture, beauty and fine foods. She had been drawn there for other reasons. The need to do something unexpected, the need to surprise others and hope they would be surprised, but at this distance it was hard to tell.

Japanese tourists stood in a group close to her discussing in a language that was today simply a jumble of sounds where they would stand for a photo and who would stand where. She sat quietly looking at the river, staring into the middle distance at the weir and waiting. She knew she should wait for them to form a group before dropping the phone; their chatter would cover the noise as it sped through the air to the water. She would get up immediately she dropped it and walk away as if there were no connection between her and the phone. She could use the huddled group as an excuse, an appropriate apology for her sudden movement. They would understand English and she could be on her way unnoticed. But if she did this, she would never see the phone hit the water and disappear under the green surface. And she knew she couldn't do that. If she didn't see it go, she would never believe it was gone, and the overwhelming knowledge that what she was doing was wrong would reside with her until she couldn't live with it any longer and confession would be her only cure.

She felt the same about the body. At first, she had

found it hard to leave. It was partly shock and partly curiosity. Lesley had always been curious. As an infant, she would sit perfectly still in the garden and watch the grass. Just a small area of grass, small enough that you would notice every bug and creature that passed through it. If you sat very still, garden birds would land, dig for worms and be blissfully unaware of your presence. They would let you be part of their world for seconds and moments that made you feel privileged, special. The body had made her feel the same way.

He was a young man, younger than twenty-five, she thought. She had seen him once or twice before, but she knew now that she would see his face forever. His face was intact; it was perfect. His eyes were shut, his skin still bronzed, his lips closed tightly but peacefully. He lay on his back as if he might be lying on the grass in the warm spring sunshine, anticipating the heat to come when the weeks would pass and summer would arrive. The only distraction from this picture was the large pool of dark red blood that circled the back of his head. It was a perfect circle; it could have been painted on the concrete of the stairwell. Nothing else was wrong or unusual. At his side lay the phone. It was on and lit, with the first four numbers of a phone number staring out from the screen. All this could only have happened minutes before. She had heard nothing before leaving her flat, and she couldn't see what had caused this massive injury. She pondered whether he had simply fallen and hit his head. But so much blood. She wondered how he could have fallen so perfectly on his back. She wondered why the phone would be out of his pocket. She wondered whether or not it was his phone.

She didn't think to listen for breath; it was clear that

his chest wasn't lifting. There was no noise from his body. She thought this must be what he always looked like. His family would say, *he looks just like himself.* That's what she had said with her mother and sister when her father died. He could have been in his own bed, asleep and peaceful, not a patient in a hospice for the living dead. The stairwell was very quiet, unusually quiet. No noise from the other flats, front doors firmly shut. Even the street seemed quiet at that moment. The Via Porta Rossa always had noise in it. Tourists and shoppers through the day, students and Florentines by night. She should have been more alert. She should have been aware of the strangeness and reacted accordingly. Instead she picked up the phone and left the scene, unsure why she had done that. Doctors could do nothing else for him and neither could she. Someone else would find him and call the authorities. Someone with good Italian, someone who understood the customs for such an event.

As soon as the sunlight hit her when the large wooden entrance door was opened, she realised her mistake. She should have left the phone with the dead man. She wondered why she'd picked it up. She knew there was no rational explanation. But as she bathed in the warmth of the sun, she realised quite suddenly that the phone didn't belong to the dead man. It couldn't have. He couldn't have dialled as the blood seeped from his head. His energy would have gone instantly. It belonged to someone else, someone who had been at the scene before her. Someone who might be watching her now, realising they had left their phone and the implications of that.

*

The noise of the street hit her at the same time as the sunlight. People were speaking quickly and loudly as they admired the street, consulted tourist maps, discussed today's business or chatted to friends as they walked away from or towards the city. She looked straight ahead to see if someone was watching her. She looked left, then right in the search to seek out a person. She couldn't. There were too many people and too many thoughts as she realised the silence of the stairwell had only been in her head. She knew now she had to get rid of the phone.

The walk to the Ponte Vecchio was different today though everything looked the same. The buildings were just as old, the cobbles causing her feet to slide now and again from the direction she placed them in just the same. But she felt different. She couldn't concentrate on admiring the buildings, the shapes they made, the intricate order of the bricks making each building turn a corner or curve away down a small alley towards the Arno. Things she noticed every time she walked along these streets were gone from her mind. Her wonder at living in a city with such history was gone from her mind. All her thoughts were focused on the phone. It was in her hand in her trouser pocket, causing her hand to sweat. She worried it would ring and she would be drawn to answer it, forced to show herself as the thief. She wanted to look at it and determine whether or not it belonged to the dead man. Panic was rising in her. It would have been best to do nothing, touch nothing. It would have been best to call the police when she found the body. It would have been best to have nothing more to do with it than be the person who called the police. She knew now that when she returned to the Via Porta Rossa, when the police were there and the building was cordoned off, she would have to lie. She would have to say she had left twenty minutes before she did. The body couldn't have been there long. The blood had still been oozing out, slowly and determinedly, into a circle, a halo.

The Japanese tourists were all in place now, ten to fifteen of them. No one else on the bridge could see her. She was completely hidden. This was her best chance. She pulled the phone from her pocket and slowly slid her hand over the edge of the bridge, just a foot from the ledge. Then she let it go. She looked over and watched it fall quickly towards the water. It was gone.

The group of tourists slowly dispersed from in front of her and the space they had occupied was filled by other tourists. Another language, another photo opportunity. She stood up and turned to look across the Arno towards the Uffizi. Everyone was doing it. She felt relief that it was gone. Lying wouldn't be so difficult now. No one had noticed her. She would do some shopping, then return to the flat. She turned to leave, making her apologies as she passed the tourists.

As he stood outside the Uffizi looking towards the Ponte Vecchio, Paolo removed the stolen camera from his eye, holding the lens in one hand before lifting the strap from around his neck and placing the camera on the ground next to the wall. He removed his black leather gloves and put them in his pocket. The phone was gone. That in itself was a relief, but the girl knew more than he wanted anyone to know. A decision on her fate should be agreed with others.

## Two

Paolo couldn't remember a time when he didn't kill people or plan their deaths. It wasn't a career choice but one that had chosen him after he killed Father Rossi one Monday evening following a visit to confession with his mother.

Paolo had grown up in a family where money was never an issue, but they lived a modest life. His father worked at the Fiat factory near Turin, and Paolo's life in Cesate was unremarkable. He attended school, always arriving on time, striving to ensure his behaviour was unremarkable and that all the reports received by his mother were positive. The family attended Mass twice a week, his parents participating in the Latin service, he saying nothing but following all the ritual moves to avoid attention. He played no sport and he had few friends. He liked it that way. He liked having distance from people, being able to watch them and understand their thinking simply from their behaviour. Reading was his escape, adventures penned on a page removing him from his situation, allowing him to experience the world through the eyes of a writer, allowing him to experience feelings he thought he may never have the opportunity to experience in reality.

Paolo knew his home was a quiet home where little was said. On summer evenings when windows of houses nearby were open to let the cool air of the evening waft through the rooms, he could hear families laughing, chatting, singing, crying. His home wasn't like that. Before and after school, he and his mother would talk at length about what they had heard on the radio, the books they were reading, Paolo's day at school and his mother's outings to the local shops or occasionally into Milan for new clothes. But when his father came home, silence would descend on the house, broken only by the noise of cutlery as they ate their evening meal and the occasional question from his father, which was duly responded to by either Paolo or his mother without any eye contact being made. He and his mother never spoke about the absurdity of this when they were alone.

Only two evenings in the week were different. Every Tuesday and Thursday evening, Paolo's father would come home around six thirty, eat his meal with the family as usual, then leave the house, not returning until the early hours of the morning. Paolo looked forward to those evenings. As soon as the meal was over, he and his mother would remain at the table while his father carefully put his suit jacket back on, collected his car keys, said a brief farewell from the hall and left the house. The noise of the car crunching the pebbles on the drive as it sped out through the gates brought smiles to the faces of Paolo and his mother, and they would start to clear the table. Once the table was cleared, the dishes done and everything back exactly where it should be, he and his mother would agree how they would spend their evening. Sometimes they played board games, sometimes they watched television, sometimes they read their books, and sometimes they sat out on the terrace that went round three sides of the house. They would look out towards the Parrochia San Alessandro e San Martino, where the bells would ring on the hour and every half hour. When night descended, the church would come alive with lights shining on its façade and on its bell tower. His mother would admire it every time and cross herself while mumbling prayers of forgiveness. Paolo felt she had nothing to seek forgiveness for.

This Monday evening was different. His mother usually went to confession in the afternoon, but she knew her husband would not be home, attending instead the Fiat AGM — an event he always attended and rarely came home from. So she decided to wait and take Paolo with her to church in the evening. Paolo never went to confession. He would sometimes be sent out to take part in it, but he would instead walk through the lanes and alleys of Cesate, ensuring an adequate amount of time had passed before he returned home. He knew it was a private contract between sinner and priest never to be discussed outwith that moment, so he felt confident his mother would never find out, and he wasn't sure what he should seek forgiveness for anyway.

The Bianchi house was on two floors, with living quarters on the top floor and the garage and utility areas on the ground floor. Usually they would leave the house via the garage, using the internal stairs, so Paolo was surprised when his mother said they would leave by the front door and the external stairs. He wasn't going to question her decision — he never did — until they passed the door to the garage and he realised it was open just slightly. He moved quietly towards the door to shut it and secure the house, when his mother explained why it was open. *There was a snake in the garden this afternoon and I'm sure it got into the garage. I shouldn't have left the door open while I was working, but it was just easier. I looked for it in the usual places but couldn't find it. I thought if I left the door open, it might find its way out. Papa wouldn't be happy if he knew I had left the door open.* She stopped speaking but continued to look at Paolo. She knew he would understand her discomfort and her need to solve the problem before her husband found out. Paolo nodded and left the door exactly where it was. They crunched across the pebbles and left by the side gate that took them straight onto the path leading to the church. They said nothing as they walked, but Paolo planned to look for the snake on his return, and even if he didn't find it, he would say it was gone.

The Parrochia San Alessandro e San Martino was very quiet. The evening light shone through the stained glass, casting a yellow haze on two elderly ladies kneeling in prayer with their heads raised upwards towards a crumbling statue of Christ. Paolo followed his mother up the main aisle. She curtsied as they neared the altar, while Paolo crossed himself before sitting down in the row indicated as his destination by his mother's pointing finger. She walked on towards the confessional. He focused on the fading frescoes which adorned many areas of the building. They always made him feel sad. Sad for their loss as the paint faded with the centuries and small pieces of masonry crumbled to dust. Sad for the suffering depicted in each painting. Sad that such suffering should bring solace to the worshippers when this isn't what suffering resulted in, in his experience. Suffering resulted in silence, hidden thoughts, lies and deceit. As he was thinking this, he heard a muffled moan but was unsure where it came from. He looked around at the two old ladies praying. They seemed oblivious to the noise and continued to pray as they had been. He recognised it as a familiar noise, but he could see no one else. The moan died and its echo disappeared from the church, only to be replaced by mumbled sobbing. He knew now where it was coming from. This was the noise he would hear when he was in bed and his father was talking to his mother, the noise he would also hear sometimes when his mother was on her own. He stood up, unsure what he should do. He waited.

When she appeared from the confessional, Paolo's mother was covering her face with one hand but continuing to sob. She didn't speak as she passed him, but he knew to follow. Just as he turned to follow her, he saw Father Rossi come out from the confessional and close all the doors as if nothing had happened. His eyes did not follow the sufferer, nor did he look concerned by what had just occurred. He closed the doors quietly and turned to leave the church, confessions complete. Job done.

Paolo hated to hear his mother crying; he didn't want her to suffer. They both suffered so much. He followed her back up the path towards the house, a few steps behind, unable to comfort her or reassure her that things would be fine. The feeling of helplessness was not unfamiliar to him, but usually, he heard the crying from the safety of his bedroom; he was never in the same space as it. He hated it. Once in the house, he made his mother coffee. She sat quietly now in a chair with her head bowed, unable to say anything. Then they both sat quietly, each comforted by the company of the other until the church bells chimed nine. *Bed time, Paolo. Good night.*

He didn't question this instruction and was happy to escape to the familiar noises and surroundings of his bedroom. He didn't know why, but he didn't change; he simply lay down on the bed and hoped that sleep would overcome him. It didn't. The sound of his mother crying continued to overwhelm him even though the house was now silent and she had long ago gone to bed. He wanted to silence this echo in his head. He wanted things to be as they had been before their trip to the church.

Killing Father Rossi would restore order to his brain.

There was no plan when he left his bedroom and pondered how he would leave the house without his mother hearing. Then he remembered the garage door. It was open. They hadn't shut it on their return. The internal door to the garage stairs was next to his bedroom and furthest from his mother's room. This was his quickest means of escape. Gently, he pressed down the handle of the door and pushed it open only as far as was needed for him to slink out. Once in the garage, he walked purposefully to the middle, where the car was usually parked. No tools or garden equipment to bump into. The door was still open, and with just a little nudge, he was able to squirm his way out onto the driveway. Instead of heading straight to the gate, he balanced on the cobbles that edged the driveway and slowly made his way to the side gate and the path. The path that would take him back to the church. He liked being out when no one else was. He liked the cool air on his face, the deafening silence helping him focus on what he was about to do.

Father Rossi lived in a small house just behind the church. He lived alone. He had lived there for twenty years, following the routines of the church: Mass, funerals, christenings, weddings, confessional, confirmation. He carried out all his duties as required but without feeling. He rarely smiled, and he rarely engaged his flock in conversations outwith the expected and anticipated formalities. It was a job and not a calling, a predictable life. Predictable until now.

Once he was outside Father Rossi's house, Paolo realised he had no plan, he just had an end game. Gaining entry to the house was his first priority, but he knew he didn't want to do that next to the path. Although he felt alone, he was aware that there could be someone else out walking, enjoying the solitude for other reasons. He needed cover. There was a gap at the rear of the house between the end of the church and Father Rossi's house. He put his back flat against the wall and sidestepped through the space until he reached the small garden of the house. There were no lights on; there was no sound. But there was a window open. No doubt Father Rossi felt safe enough to do this, to make this mistake. The window needed to be pulled open, and Paolo was unsure what this would result in. The house was as old as the church, and the windows were rotting. He removed his shirt to use it as a makeshift glove and began pulling the window until it was wide enough for him to climb through. It groaned rather than creaked, and once open, Paolo waited to see what would happen. Nothing. No noise, no lights, no calling out. He climbed through and found himself in the living room of the house: sparsely furnished and easily negotiated. He removed his shoes and left them neatly together just under the window, his escape route. Although old and cracked, the tiles allowed his walking to be silent. He had perfected this skill at home, where silence was highly valued and kept you safe. He climbed the stairs, slowly keeping his eyes fixed on each step to prevent any trips. Father Rossi's snoring drew him towards his ultimate goal.

At the top of the stairs, both doors were open, and for the first time, he could see Father Rossi. Although short in stature, his girth made him look like a ball tucked in a bed, inflating and deflating as he snored. Paolo stood perfectly still and contemplated what he would do next.

Two discarded pillows lay on the floor next to the bed. He would smother him; he had no other means of killing him. For some minutes, he did nothing. He considered the weight ratio he would need in order to carry out this task. He considered the importance of the element of surprise in preventing his victim from moving. He considered how he would use his shirt to prevent his hands touching the pillow. He never considered the act and its consequences. It seemed the right thing to do.

Once he had tied knots in the sleeves of his shirt at the cuffs and pushed his arms back into the sleeves, he stepped forward to the side of the bed. Father Rossi continued to snore. Paolo picked up a pillow and the tussle began. With speed and force, he pushed the pillow down onto Father Rossi's face, at the same time sitting astride his fat stomach and pushing his feet firmly into the mattress for extra force. He expected more of a fight. Father Rossi's arms flapped around, trying to grab any part of the bed or the bed clothes, but he couldn't. Paolo's knees were pinning his arms at the elbows. Paolo continued to push.

It took a long time, longer than Paolo had anticipated, but finally the muffled sounds and the flapping stopped. Everything was still and everything was silent. Paolo stood up slowly, dropped the pillow and looked at his victim. The noise of his mother's crying had gone from his head now. He felt nothing.

# Three

Lesley was annoyed she had left the flat so early that morning but knew she couldn't return too soon. She needed someone to have found the body, and she wasn't certain how long that would take. Mainly students lived in the flats, and they were always away early in the morning. Signora Conti lived on the ground floor and wouldn't see the body even if she went out. Her only hope was that Signor Alfonsi, her taxi-driving neighbour, would get up around mid-morning and head out for a beer. This was his usual routine.

Lesley liked her flat. She had chosen it without viewing prior to her departure from Scotland. Although it turned out to be very different to the image portrayed in the photographs, she grew to like it and learnt the joy of limited space. It was positioned on the third floor of the building, which meant light. The sun would welcome her in the morning as she made breakfast, and by evening her bedroom would be filled with the fading light of the day. Every room was small and sparsely furnished, but this lack of furniture gave her the feeling of space, space that belonged only to her. The windows didn't allow you to look straight down to the street, so when they were open, it was as if nothing else existed.

She had come to Florence for a number of reasons, but the chief one was to write. She had tried many times in her life to complete a novel, but work and life's events had taken over. When her marriage ended, she knew it was her opportunity to do things differently. She had her share of the money and felt, against the wishes of everyone, that this was her chance to complete a novel and make decisions from there. At first her family agreed it was a good idea — until it entailed leaving her job and then leaving the country. She knew it was a gamble not having a steady income, but she knew teaching was something she could return to if things didn't work out quite as she wanted, so it didn't frighten her to leave. She wasn't quite forty yet, so plenty of time to return and establish herself once again. But now she wasn't sure she could ever return.

Her mother understood Lesley's need to live elsewhere and knew her objections to Lesley leaving were about her own loneliness since the death of her husband some years before. She relied on her daughters for help, comfort and company, and didn't want that to change. In particular, she relied on Lesley for optimism and cheer. If Katy, Lesley's sister, had said she was leaving for a year, she knew she wouldn't have been as upset. Katy relied on both her and Lesley for help, comfort and strength, and she didn't want to have to do this alone now. But she wanted the best for Lesley, who had survived her loveless marriage without complaint although she had often looked unhappy. And so Lesley went to Italy with her mother's blessing and her suspicion that Lesley would never return.

To ensure the body would be found before she got back, Lesley decided to walk to the church of Santa Croce before having some breakfast at Le Vespe and returning to her flat via the small supermarket on Via dei Servi. Signora Conti would be able to confirm that doing her shopping was Lesley's usual routine in the morning, even though they hadn't spoken that morning. It would sound a plausible story; Lesley would just change her timings.

Although it was only after nine, the square at the Santa

Croce was already very busy. Bus parties from the cruise liners always arrived early and were today standing in large groups, appearing to listen to their guide while taking photographs of the glorious white façade. Lesley walked around the side of the church and entered the building. She always enjoyed looking at the Giotto frescoes. She was amazed to think of the centuries of people who had come to this place to admire their detail, composition and colours. How they had survived seemed a miracle to her and something to be admired. As she sat in the church quietly and peacefully, she realised she hadn't thought of the body for some time. She felt this wasn't right but was relieved that his face and the blood could be forgotten. She hoped that would continue to be the case.

It was warm when she came out, and she could feel the warmth of the sun seeping through her as she navigated her way to Le Vespe, one of her favourite cafes. Getting vegetarian food in Florence wasn't an issue, but not everywhere had such a range of dishes. She settled on avocado on toast, then took out her Kindle and began to read. The staff knew her well, and although her Italian was improving, carrying out a conversation of any length in Italian was still a challenge for Lesley. She was happy to be quiet today, and using a Kindle had a way of ensuring others ignored you. Now that she had learnt to take life at a slower pace, a difficult lesson for Lesley, taking an hour over breakfast was no longer an issue.

Once her day's supplies had been purchased, she began the walk back to the Via Porta Rossa and the body. Lesley thought she knew what to expect: the road cordoned off, the police in situ, a van for the removal of the body. She would admit to being a resident in the street and ask what she should do. She would look for her neighbours and ask them what had happened, pretending to have no knowledge of events. She would tell them where she had been; she would reaffirm her story with others. This would become the truth.

From the supermarket, she headed down the Via dei Calzaiuoli towards the Arno and the Via Porta Rossa. Her anxiety levels grew; she repeated her plan in her head over and over. She looked for the flashing lights and the tape. She kept looking. But she could see neither. They must have cordoned off only the building, not the street. She would see the lights when she turned the corner. She didn't. The Via Porta Rossa was exactly as it had been when she left two and a half hours earlier. People were speaking quickly and loudly as they admired the street, consulted tourist maps, discussed today's business or chatted to friends as they walked away from or towards the city.

Lesley didn't know what to do now. She stood outside the chemist's some distance from the entrance to her flat, her back firmly against the wall. She looked up and down the street for anything unusual, but there was nothing. Everything was as it always was. What should she do? If she entered the building, she would have to report the body which would still be lying there, surrounded by its blood. She would have to speak to Signora Conti or Signor Alfonsi and ask them to call the police. She would have to take action and her story would have to change.

She considered her other options. She could carry on along the street and not return for hours, spending the day in a park. But questions would be asked. She had bought frozen food and allowed it to defrost? Why would she do that? She always returned mid-morning to write before venturing back out later in the day. Signora Conti would confirm that was the case. She had to keep to her routine; only this would be a reasonable alibi. She would return to her flat.

She turned her key in the lock of the outside door, still expecting to be met by a policeman on the other side. Instead, Signor Alfonsi was descending the last flight of stairs towards the door, smiling as he saw her. *Ciao, Lesley. How are you this morning? Been shopping as usual, I see.* She responded as she would normally and held the door ajar as they kissed on both cheeks. She wasn't sure she should be kissing Signor Alfonsi; she hadn't known him long enough, she thought, but it felt comfortable. As he disappeared into the noise of the street, she closed the door and slowly began to walk up the stairs. She knew the body couldn't be there now. When she reached the second floor, the place where the body had been half strewn over the landing and the stairs was both empty and clean. There was no sign of blood; there was no stain where it had been. She kept climbing until she reached her front door. She turned the key, entered her flat and sat down. The frozen food melted as she didn't move for hours.

Paolo continued to watch the door to the flats to see what her next move would be.

# Four

This had been an unusual assassination for Paolo. He had always preferred those committed at a distance — a bomb, a shooting, a staged crash. He didn't like to see their pain when death hit them suddenly without warning. But work had been limited, and although he had a considerable amount of money saved and he lived a modest life, he always felt he couldn't turn down a job. He was fussy for whom he would work. Franco understood his need for anonymity, with no trail leading to his door.

He had carried out only one other murder in Florence in the past twenty years, so didn't know the place well. This had meant a lot of surveillance and research before planning Pepe's murder. He always worked with photographs and a Christian name when carrying out a job: this was one of his rules. He didn't want to know too much about the person. He didn't want to have to make judgements about them, something his limited understanding of human behaviour would make very difficult. He was happy to agree to the murder without any knowledge of the crime. Nothing had really changed for him since the murder of Father Rossi.

Pepe was a young man living as a student in Florence. He had a very fixed routine: he rose early to attend classes, spent most of the day on the campus of the university, sometimes returned home late afternoon and generally went out to meet friends later in the day. He was studious without being isolated. He enjoyed the company of his friends. Paolo understood that and watched him in various locations chatting freely and openly. This had never been part of Paolo's life, but he could see it in others and wondered what had gone wrong for him. Pepe's father owned the flat, and his son made good use of it to enjoy life, unconcerned about what might happen next. He was two hundred miles from his father's businesses and the underhand practices that were their trademark. No one turning up late at night to discuss things with his father, no hushed whispers between his parents when he might be within earshot, and no concerns for his safety. No need for a chaperone.

Paolo realised that killing Pepe, a revenge killing, he assumed, wasn't going to be easy. Pepe was rarely alone, nor did he spend time in isolated places where an attack could be considered. He didn't drive a car; he walked amongst the seething masses wherever he went. Occasionally, he would walk home late on his own, but that was unpredictable, and Paolo had no way of knowing when this might occur. He decided the assassination would have to take place in the flat. A gun with a silencer. Early morning would be best. No neighbours to be concerned with. He knew the taxi driver on the top floor slept late and left his flat mid-morning most days and the girl on the top floor rarely went out before nine thirty. The old lady on the ground floor was always up early, but her routine did not involve leaving the house until all her daily chores had been done. The students left about eight, so he could be in and complete his task between 0700 and 0730.

His main concern was the age of the property and the difficulties he would have gaining access from the street. The main door was big and heavy, with deadlocks providing the security everyone craved. He had done it before but knew he would need to practise to ensure he could get in and that all would run smoothly.

Paolo still lived in Cesate, alone now since his mother's death two years previously. His father had long ago left the family home when he finally took up residence with a fellow worker he had been seeing for many years. They had bought a flat in Turin but had left him and his mother with the house in Cesate. He was glad about that. It was familiar and comfortable. Nothing needed to change; his routines could remain as they always had. His mother was less happy. He didn't understand this. Although they could speak whenever they wanted to, go where they wanted and no longer live with their rigid routine, his mother changed nothing. Every aspect of their routine continued: meals eaten at the same time every day and the same dishes being made according to the day of the week, attendance at Mass unchanged. Even the need to ensure doors were always closed as you left a room and lights switched off was strictly adhered to.

He had expected his mother to develop friendships and had worried about how he would cope with visitors in the house. But he needn't have. No friendships were developed. She spoke to neighbours and shopkeepers just as she always had, but nothing further. She kept the house clean and tidy and looked after Paolo just as she had always done. They spent their evenings playing cards, watching television or discussing their day. He liked that, and he liked not having to worry about when his father might appear and spoil their tranquillity.

After Father Rossi's death, Paolo's mother continued to attend church, but she never went back to confessional. He didn't know why, and she was never keen to impart any aspect of her decision-making. And, in reality, he didn't really want to know.

As the years at school passed, Paolo wasn't sure what he would do when he left. His mother wanted him to attend university in Milan, and his father was happy to pay. And so this was what he did. He studied maths. He met people who were as clever as he was and whose interest in puzzling out problems was as great as his. His mother worried less once he was at university. He no longer mixed with the young people in Cesate, and she no longer had to contend with the knowing glances from other parents who found Paolo hard to understand.

He also met Franco.

Paolo was nearing the end of his course at university when they met. He thought he had enjoyed his four years of study and assumed this was what happiness felt like. His mind was busy with problems that needed solving but always had an answer. No ambiguity. He knew like-minded people, and although he wouldn't have called them friends, he enjoyed their company within the confines of university life. Paolo used his breaks to be alone, and he enjoyed eating lunch outside on a bench that looked over the gardens towards the university buildings. It was predictable and quiet. People rarely came as far as this bench. But Franco did.

The sun was shining the day Franco sat down beside him as he ate the lunch provided by his mother. He mirrored Franco's smile but was uncomfortable with his presence on the bench. He wouldn't have minded if he'd sat down to read or carry out some other task, but he just sat there staring ahead as if waiting for Paolo to finish his lunch and start a conversation. Paolo didn't want to speak, and the anxiety induced by this expectation meant he took longer to finish his lunch than usual. As soon as he had finished eating, Franco spoke. *Your mother spoke*

*to me last week and asked me to have a chat with you.*
*I'm Franco.*

Paolo had never seen Franco before, and he wondered how he knew his mother. She had never mentioned Franco; she had never mentioned the possibility of such a conversation arising. She knew he hated surprises; she knew he would find this very hard to cope with. Paolo said nothing and waited for Franco to speak. This wasn't what Franco had expected or how he had anticipated this conversation would go. So he just kept speaking. *She told me you killed the local priest when you were sixteen and have kept it a secret all this time. An unsolved crime. A perfect hit.* He waited for Paolo to respond, but he said nothing and remained stationary on the bench, staring straight ahead. Paolo didn't know what to do. He wanted to be out of the situation and far away from the words uttered by this person. He quietly put the lid back on his lunch box, placed it on the top of his rucksack, picked it up and walked away from Franco towards the library. He felt instinctively that Franco wouldn't be able to follow him; he guessed he wasn't a student.

For the next few days, Paolo ate his lunch in the library. The long glass panes next to the study benches gave him a perfect view of his preferred lunch bench. Every day, Franco arrived at 1230 and left at 1330, knowing Paolo would not change his eating habits. He was right.

Franco looked very out of place in the university. He was tall, with shoulder-length dark hair that always shone brightly in the sunshine. His clothes were modern and expensive. He wore heavy gold jewellery popping out from the neck of his shirt and encircling four or five of his fingers. His watch dangled carelessly from his wrist, always looking like it would suddenly fall to the ground. He carried no bag or books. He would drape his arm along the back of the bench, turning his body to cross his legs in order to have a better view of everything around him. He would sit for the hour in the hope that Paolo would appear. Paolo found his persistence disturbing.

At home, he mentioned nothing of his meeting with Franco but was certain his mother would know about it and the fact that he had not engaged in conversation with him. He discussed his day with his mother as he always did and looked for suggestions in her face that would tell him she was puzzled by his change in habits. He told her about eating in the library and abandoning his favourite bench. She still said nothing. This lasted for a week. Then she spoke.

*You need to speak to Franco tomorrow, Paolo. He has a job offer for you which I think will suit you perfectly. You won't be able to work with others when you finish at the university. That has always been difficult for you. And Franco may have the perfect solution.*

Paolo was unsure what he should say. He always agreed to do what she wanted, but he had so many questions he wanted to ask, he wasn't sure whether he would simply be able to say *yes, mother.* But he did.

It was a perfect day of blue skies and warm sunshine when he returned to the bench to eat his lunch. It was 1215, and he knew Franco would turn up at 1230 just as he had done every other day. He began eating. He saw Franco walking towards him as his watch turned to 1230. Franco sat down on the bench but remained securely in the corner, looking forward across the grass towards the university buildings. Paolo knew his mother must have spoken to him. He felt more comfortable now with a distance between them and no threat of his coming nearer. Franco waited patiently for Paolo to finish his lunch, knowing he wouldn't have his attention until that task was complete.

Franco spoke quietly and determinedly without emotion and without looking at Paolo. He explained that he worked for a number of businessmen across the north of Italy who would ask him from time to time to recruit someone to carry out a planned assassination. He said this generally helped their business interests. Paolo understood immediately what he was being asked and didn't really care to hear anything further. He had given no thought to the murder of Father Rossi for a number of years, and although he often considered how he might murder again, there had been no reason to try out any of his plans.

*It pays well, Paolo, and you wouldn't have to deal with people. You could work when you wanted to and stop whenever you wanted. My business partners would not know who you are, they would only know you worked for me. I'm sure we could work out a way to make it work. We would split the fee forty-sixty. Sixty to you, of course.*

Paolo said nothing. He needed time to consider whether it was something he wanted to undertake. He needed to know the rules of the game and he needed to feel in control of these. He turned towards Franco. *Thank you for the offer. We should meet here next Wednesday at the same time, when I will give you my answer.* Paolo stood up immediately and walked towards the library. He knew he would accept the offer; his mother would want that. He just had to consider how it would work.

# Five

Lesley remained in her flat. She expected something to happen. She expected a knock at the door. She expected someone would have reported her strange behaviour. She expected someone to know the young man was dead. But nothing happened.

She wanted her day to pass as it usually did, with several hours of planned writing before a light lunch and several hours of planned writing after lunch. She sat at her desk staring at the computer, writing a few words before the strangeness of the day would fill her mind again and nothing more would be typed. She sat for longer than she would normally. She heard Signor Alfonsi return to his flat, whistling as he ascended the stairs, followed by the resounding thud of his door closing. He would have an early meal, then go to work. She heard the students return from classes, chattering as they climbed the stairs and laughing at the things that had happened during the day. This was usually her cue to go for a walk, exploring different parts of Florence she hadn't yet visited.

Lesley knew it would be odd if she didn't follow her usual routine. Someone might notice and comment on it to a policeman when the death of the young man finally came out. Despite her anxiety, she knew she had to leave the flat and have a walk. So she did.

Paolo was still standing hidden in the alley next to the Hotel Davanzati when Lesley opened the door and stepped out into the bright sunshine and the noise. He looked at her more carefully now as she headed west along the Via Porta Rossa and he followed her. She moved easily among the crowds, smiling briefly at people as she passed them or squeezed through gaps. Her build was slight and her soft white face when combined with her blonde hair made him think she wasn't Italian. He knew this would be an advantage since her Italian would most likely not be fluent and she may not want to be involved with the police. She stopped every now and again to look at a building or to admire a shop window. He kept his distance.

When she reached the Arno, she kept walking west until she reached the Parco delle Cascine. It was quieter now and harder for Paolo to remain unseen. He slowed his pace and kept a greater distance from her as she walked up the treelined avenue towards the cascading fountain. Lesley felt tired, the strain of the day having taken its toll. She looked eagerly for an empty bench and sat with her back to the families playing games on the grass but facing the Arno and the gently flowing water. A sound of calm. Paolo stopped some way back and sat on a bench. She took a small book out of her bag and began reading. More waiting.

Lesley found it hard to concentrate on reading. She finally gave up and replaced the slim volume in her bag. She felt she should do something, but it was the most relaxed she had felt all day, so she placed the back of her head on the curve of the bench and thought she might sleep. She put her bag across her body and placed both her hands around it. The sun was warm, and she very quickly began to drift off.

Paolo remained at first on the bench he had occupied further down the avenue. He was puzzled by the girl's behaviour. He could see she was sleeping, and he wondered how she could erase what she had found and what she had done from her memory. This, he felt from his knowledge of others, was not typical behaviour. He knew he should have left Florence the minute he saw her drop his phone into the Arno. He should have let Franco decide what should happen to the girl. But he didn't. He hadn't completed the job. He hadn't murdered Pepe. His plan had not, for the first time, worked.

He had followed Pepe for the whole day prior to his death. There had been nothing remarkable about the day. Pepe had left his flat to attend university just as he always did, chatting excitedly to the other students who lived downstairs from him as they walked along the road. They all appeared to be speaking at the same time, and Paolo wondered how they understood what was being discussed. Pepe attended classes all morning, ate lunch in the sun-drenched gardens of the university with a different group of friends and returned to his flat late afternoon, leaving again around 1800. Paolo had followed him throughout the evening. Pepe met friends at a restaurant near the church of the Santa Croce, then left with a girl around 2200. Paolo recognised the girl; he had seen Pepe with her on other occasions. She was as tall as Pepe, but she was as blonde as he was dark. She held Pepe's hand tightly as they walked close together along the road, gently stroking his arm every so often as they spoke. Paolo knew they were heading for the girl's flat, and once they were safely inside, Paolo returned to the Via Porta Rossa to enter Pepe's flat and finalise his plan.

It was quiet now in the Via Porta Rossa. Paolo walked quickly along the street, donning his black leather gloves as he neared the building. Along the street, there were some windows open and some lights illuminating the darkness, but Paolo remained in the shadows, walking close to the buildings, brushing against the stone. He fumbled in his pocket for the keys Franco's fixers had made for him and held them tightly in his hands. This was the first time he had tried the key, and it worked. He was in. He climbed the stairs with his back to the wall, quietly placing his feet on each stone step and listening for any noise that might alert others to him. No one appeared.

When he reached the door of the flat, he stopped and waited. No sounds. The key turned easily in the lock. He was in. He illuminated the darkness with a small torch and began looking around to ensure he had a map of the flat in his head. Killing had to be done swiftly and quietly. It needed thought and planning. He enjoyed this part of his job; an efficient death was simply a consequence of good planning. It was a small flat, six steps from the front door to the bedroom. Ten steps from the front door to the living area. Eight steps from the front door to the bathroom. His victim would be accessible in all areas of the house.

Paolo knew that Pepe would be his youngest victim, and this had bothered him ever since Franco had asked him to carry out the job. He had never had a rule about age, but he realised once he had spent time watching Pepe that the age of his victim did matter to him. More than that, their behaviour mattered to him. He could see nothing in the many places he had observed Pepe that made him feel justified in killing him. This hadn't been the case for most of his victims. He understood that a revenge killing was different since the murder of a son would strike at the heart of a family, but he wasn't sure he was the person to carry this out. However, he had agreed to the contract, and he had never reneged on an agreement. Not yet anyway.

The flat was very tidy, he thought, for a young man. The bed was made and no clothes lay strewn across the floor. A volume of Dante's work lay under the bedside lamp, with a scarlet bookmark sticking out of the top. The kitchen had no dishes waiting to be washed, and work surfaces looked clear and clean. A red sofa draped with a turquoise throw faced a large television screen, and a small set of shelves held more books and folders. The bathroom was also tidy and clean. For a moment, Paolo wondered if Pepe intended bringing the girl back here, hence the tidiness, but as he took a seat on the red sofa, he had a sense that this was the way Pepe lived. Paolo felt very comfortable and enjoyed imagining how different his life as a student might have been if he had not remained at home. He might have learnt to be part of the world, although more likely, he would have created another solitary world of order and limitations.

As he sat, he realised he didn't want to move. And he didn't. He slept for a while before taking a book about frescoes from the shelves and reading it through. Daylight was filling the small room by the time he decided he should leave, though he knew from his observations that if Paolo went to the girl's house on a Friday night, he rarely returned home until lunchtime on the Saturday. He felt safe and secure to sit as long as he wanted. It was just after 0730 when Paolo decided he should leave. He placed the book carefully back on the shelves in exactly the position he had taken it from, slightly in front of the books on either side of it. He ensured the throw on the sofa was securely in place, then he headed for the front door. He would return on Wednesday morning to carry out his task.

He was looking back down the hall when he heard the

key turning in the lock. There was no place to hide; the flat was too small. He had no gun with him. He had made a mistake. He didn't like making mistakes. He should never have stayed. He should have considered that Pepe's plans could change. People's plans often did. He moved back down the hall to give himself the best chance of charging at Pepe and surprising him. It worked.

As Pepe gently pushed the door open, Paolo began running towards him. It was only at the last minute that Pepe looked up. It was too late to react. His hand was still firmly on the door handle when the palms of Paolo's two hands hit his chest, and he lost his balance. His hand slipped from the door handle and he began to fall backwards. As he fell, he tried in vain to regain his balance by throwing his arms and upper body forward, but it had no effect. His head glanced against the edge of the metal bannister and his six-foot frame fell back down the stairs, sliding at speed until his head lay on the landing at the bottom. Swiftly, Paolo shut the door of the flat and locked it. He descended the stairs, avoiding the halo of blood emanating from Pepe's head. He needed to phone Franco; he would clear things up.

Just as Paolo took a phone from his pocket and began dialling, he heard the door of an upstairs flat. He knew he should walk quietly and deliberately down the stairs, but he stared instead at the phone and turned to leave the building. But he turned too quickly. The phone fell from his hand, hitting Paolo's chest area and sliding to the floor. The footsteps were getting closer. He fled. He knew this was what people called panic, and he didn't like it. His hands tingled while his brain kept silently repeating unhelpful phrases. In the street, he waited in the shadow of the alley beside the Hotel Davanzati, upset at his behaviour, upset that there were now loose ends. He used a second phone to call Franco and get things tidied up. Franco knew what to do; his fixers had been following Paolo to make sure he carried out the assassination as agreed. Franco had for the first time had his doubts that this would happen. And so the body disappeared swiftly and silently from the building, and all evidence of Pepe's death was erased.

Except the phone.

Paolo didn't tell Franco about the girl, about seeing her with his phone in her hand, about the fact she had seen the body. He knew now this was the end of the killings.

# Six

While Lesley slept, Paolo walked up and down the broad avenue several times, checking each time whether she was still asleep. After the third time, he donned his black leather gloves and sat down on the opposite end of her bench. He thought this would wake her, but it didn't. She remained perfectly still, breathing evenly as she slept. He knew how to remain still and silent; he had learnt it as a child and had never lost the skill. She slept for what seemed a long time, but he waited patiently, unsure why he wanted to be there when she woke up.

Most benches had at least one if not two people sitting on them either together or separately. Paolo watched; he enjoyed watching. He always had. Those who were alone all had tasks to complete: reading, drawing, texting, surfing the web. Those who were together chatted and watched those who were alone. He was concerned that he stood out. His lack of activity seemed to stand out. But he was unsure what to do about it, so he just sat still, surveying the scene in the park.

Lesley slept for at least half an hour, and as she woke from her stupor, she smiled briefly to herself before remembering her day and its strangeness. She was aware of the outdoors and her slumped position on the bench. She slowly raised her head and pushed her body upwards to regain her composure. As she did this, she became aware of someone else on the bench who wasn't moving. She thought they too must have fallen asleep and readjusted her position more sensitively so as not to wake them. She pushed her fingers through her hair and looked across to see who was sitting next to her.

To her surprise, she realised the person was awake and

sitting perfectly still, staring blankly into the middle distance. She turned her body slightly so she could look more carefully at the man on the bench. He wasn't tall, probably about her height. He had dark, neatly cropped hair which didn't move in the breeze. His face was smoothly shaved, and she thought he looked to be in his forties. His clothes were simple and plain: jeans, black trainers, black socks, a white shirt and a leather jacket. Then she noticed his gloves, a pair of perfectly black leather gloves. She thought this odd but no less odd than his sitting position. Not since she worked as a teacher had she seen anyone hold such a stationary position and hold such a fixed stare. For a moment, she wondered if he was feeling unwell, but he was one of the few people she had met who could look relaxed in their rigidity. She decided to speak to him; she felt sorry for him.

*It's a lovely evening, isn't it, and the park looks so nice.* He didn't respond, and she wondered if her Italian was incorrect. But she tried again. *Are you okay? I was saying it's a lovely evening.* And she leaned along the bench towards him. He turned suddenly and looked at her without smiling. Initially, she felt disturbed by this, but once she smiled at him, he returned her smile and began talking about the weather. She was aware it was the weather he was talking about, but she couldn't understand most of what was being said due to its speed. Her face had changed, so he stopped speaking. Lesley thought she should make her excuses and leave. She was aware that her presence was increasing this man's anxiety. So she moved forward to perch on the edge of the bench before saying goodbye and heading back towards the gates of the park. She walked slowly, wanting to turn round on numerous occasions to see what the man had done, but she didn't. The park was quiet now as dusk fell and she didn't want him to notice her looking, so she continued to look straight ahead and concentrated on her walk home.

Paolo watched her all the way to the gates. He was aware that any movement by him to follow her would be noticed, and he didn't want to be noticed; he had made himself vulnerable enough by speaking to her and sitting in plain sight for so long. So he sat. He felt confident she would not go to the police, and he felt confident she would continue with her routines in order to banish the memories and control her anxiety. That's what he would have done. He would watch her again tomorrow to make sure he was right.

It was a lovely time to be walking in Florence, and Lesley enjoyed looking at the different colours of the buildings as the evening sun changed and moved the shadows. It was a time of day to look upwards, where the last of the daylight would catch the tops of the buildings, accentuating every angle of the masonry. When she got back to the Via Porta Rossa and pushed open the front door, Lesley was greeted by Signora Conti, who was standing at the open door of her flat. *Ciao, Lesley, how are you today?* Signora Conti leant forward to kiss her on one cheek. *I've been looking for you, but I knew you would be out for your afternoon walk. It was a lovely day for a walk. I hope you're discovering all the wonders of Florence. You must come in for a coffee one day and we can discuss where you haven't been.* She smiled. *I was just wanting to ask if you know the young man living in the flat above me?*

Although Lesley smiled and she was sure her face looked exactly as it always did, her brain was working hard to understand why this question was being asked. Signora Conti's fixed gaze spurred her on to reply. *I've seen him a few times and said hello, but I didn't know him, I'm afraid. Is there a problem?*

*No, no. It's just that I haven't seen him today and I do usually when he returns with the other students. He wasn't with them, and I thought that was strange. I didn't hear him in the flat last night, and I usually do. He sings a lot, and all has been silent. Not to worry, maybe he's gone home for a few days. I'll speak to the students tomorrow. They may know. See you again soon, no doubt. Ciao.* She turned to close her door and return to what she had been doing. Although Lesley liked Signora Conti and had appreciated her help when she first arrived in Florence, she was aware that very little of what happened in the building got past her. She heard everyone come in and out. She kept her small window next to her front door open in order (Lesley suspected) to overhear the occasional conversation or disagreement.

Lesley walked slowly up the stairs to her flat, panicked by the conversation. She hadn't thought anyone would notice he was gone so soon. She hadn't expected others to question his disappearance. She checked her watch to make sure she would know the exact time she had spoken to Signora Conti. She knew now Signora Conti would be both the reporter of the disappearance as well as being Lesley's alibi. She needed to stick to routines.

Paolo sat on the bench for longer than he should after Lesley left. It took him some time to decide what to do next. He was angry with himself for not having stayed in the shadows. She would remember his singular movements and his obsessive talk of the weather. She would remember his black leather gloves. He slowly stood up, took off his gloves and placed them back in the pockets of his leather jacket. The park was quiet now. He would return to his rented flat for some supper before deciding how long to stay in Florence and when next to phone Franco. If he didn't call him soon, he knew Franco would come looking for him.

## Seven

Signora Conti had lived in the Via Porta Rossa for almost 40 years. It had changed a great deal in that time, as had she. The flat had been the first and only home she and her husband had known. They had expected to move because they had expected to have children, but that didn't happen despite many consultations with doctors and priests in the hope a miracle might occur. And, although her husband died ten years after their wedding, she had never had any desire to move elsewhere. Her friends often suggested she move to the suburbs, somewhere quieter, but she liked the noise of the city and its convenience. She also couldn't bear the thought of living surrounded by old people. She wanted to continue to feel alive.

When she had retired from her job at the local police station five years previously, she considered using the lump sum from her pension to travel across Europe and discover all the places she had thought and read about for so long. But she worried about travelling alone, and it had been such a long time since she had last left Italy that she decided instead to holiday at Lake Como, as a marker of her life changing and moving on. It had been a lovely holiday, which she enjoyed very much despite being alone. Her work on the reception desk of the police station had been a very busy and often a very stressful job. She had spent all her time speaking to others, whether they be members of the public or policemen based in that station. Rarely in her working day had she been silent or alone, and she thought she would miss that. She didn't.

The two weeks in Lake Como were spent at a bed and breakfast in Bellano on the eastern shore of Lake Como.

Although a small town, it provided her with opportunities to take trips sailing on the lake or to walk in the hills. She embraced the silence of her days and revelled in deciding what she would do without having to consider others. The hosts were most helpful and happy to chat if you wanted to, but if not, you could sit quietly on the terrace and read your book or admire the view without any disturbance. It had established a new pattern to living which she continued on her return to Florence.

The block of flats had changed a great deal over the years. Only she and Signor Alfonsi had lived there for any length of time. The others were mainly either rented to students or they were short-term lets. When she first moved into her flat, the others had been occupied by people who were also working in the city. Most had been young, and she had made many friends. There had been regular parties and outings at weekends to the surrounding Tuscan countryside. But most of her friends had moved to the suburbs when they had children, and now she visited them in retirement flats or in the small area allocated to them in their child's home. She knew that that life would never be for her.

She liked the young man who lived in the flat above her. He was very polite when he met her on his way in and out, and he always seemed to be smiling. He looked like he enjoyed life. He lived quietly, and although he rarely played music, he would often sing, and she enjoyed listening to him. He had many friends who came and went, and he enjoyed the company of the other students in the block. Today, she was worried that she hadn't felt his presence; there had been something reassuring about that.

She wanted to do something about her unease, but she

knew it was too soon to call the police; they would just laugh at her. A student not in his flat! He could be anywhere doing anything or could simply have gone home. They would do nothing. But it wasn't just the young man's absence that made her uneasy. The small man standing in the alley next to the Hotel Davanzati made her more uneasy. She noticed he had been standing there on a number of occasions over the last few days but had disappeared from time to time — she was unsure where. And he had returned again today. It was hard to see his face. He pressed his body hard up against the wall in the shadow of the building, but the black leather gloves would occasionally flash in the light of the street as he shifted to a different position. They seemed so out of place. She knew she must remember to mention him when she eventually reported the young man missing.

*

Not since his mother's death had anyone spontaneously smiled or spoken to Paolo. He wasn't sure what he had expected the girl to do when she woke up on the bench, but speaking to him had not been a factor he had considered. She had smiled so warmly and had persisted in trying to speak to him. His interactions with others were always controlled and on his terms, but they hadn't been this time. He wished now he hadn't replied, and more importantly, he wished he hadn't spoken so animatedly about the weather. He knew she would remember him. The weather was one of his favourite topics, but his enthusiasm in relation to it was strange to others. His mother had told him this often, and even she would ask him to stop when she got bored with his observations.

He promised himself he would watch the girl for only one more day. He had never done this before. Once the murder had taken place and things had been cleaned up, he always left the city, town or village and returned to the security of Cesate and his routine life, waiting for the next job. He wasn't worried about her contacting the police; he felt she would have done this yesterday if she was going to, but he hoped he might be able to speak to her again and feel that warmth that had been missing from his life for so long. Then he would return to Cesate and end his links with Franco, choosing instead a quiet life filled with routine. He had cleaned the rented flat early this morning, loaded his suitcase into his car, and would set off for Cesate as soon as he had spoken to the girl once again.

*

Franco was concerned. Paolo always called after a hit to give him all the facts and to ensure the agreed fee had been transferred to his account. The money had not yet been transferred, and there had been no call. He hated botched jobs; it left all of them vulnerable. Too many people involved, too many possibilities for evidence to be left or mistakes to be made.

The family who paid for the hit expected reports of Pepe's murder on national television, but there was nothing, and they were reluctant to pay despite Franco's reassurances. The body had been taken by sea to Palermo before being thrown overboard in the Straits of Sicily in its heavily weighted black bag. Pepe would never be found. His disappearance would get publicity eventually but not the publicity those taking out the contract had wanted. He would have to negotiate a lesser fee once they had proof of Pepe's death. Everyone would have to settle for less.

In Paolo, Franco knew all those years ago that he had found a reliable and meticulous assassin: the best assassin on his books. They only spoke when there was a job to be done, and the rules were always very simple: Paolo needed photographs of the victim, their Christian name, details of their place of residence and a date by which the assassination needed to be completed, and then he did all the legwork himself. His planning was always exact and his ability to lurk in the shadows unnoticed, his real trademark. His solitary life in Cesate was never questioned, and his lack of contact with others meant that he never aroused suspicion. Prior to this job, Paolo had never questioned why the person should be killed. He had carried out his side of the bargain in exchange for his fee.

But when Paolo called him two days before the agreed date for the assassination, Franco had been concerned. Paolo had asked questions about why Pepe should be killed and who had requested this. He had never done this before. He rambled at length about how young Pepe was and gave Franco details of Pepe's student life. Then he stopped speaking. There was a long silence which he knew Paolo was more comfortable with than he was. *I can't give you those details, Paolo, you just need to carry out the job. Can you do that?* Silence. *If you can't, tell me and I'll get someone else to do it.* Silence. *What's wrong?* Silence.

*I'll do it, Franco, I agreed to do it. I'm not sure I'll want to do this again.* The phone went dead.

Franco thought he would call him tonight.

# Eight

Lesley woke early, earlier than usual, and felt the weight in her limbs of an unsettled night. As she wondered how long Signora Conti would wait to contact the police, she started her daily routines in the certain knowledge that routines would see her, once again, through a difficult phase in her life. The sun was shining into her kitchen as she prepared a simple breakfast, which she ate sitting at the small table parked in front of her living room window. Usually, she read a book as she ate, but today she stared at the clear blue sky, opening the window to freshen the stale air of the flat.

Lesley knew she had an inner resilience that few people have. She knew she could recover from the worst of events as long as she could understand her actions and live with them in her head. Life had been good to Lesley despite the isolation of her marriage and the emotional toll it had taken. She often wondered now why for ten years, she had stayed in a marriage that she knew from before her wedding day was inevitably going to fail. But it was a complicated picture.

Without an overt statement ever being made, Lesley knew from an early age that making a choice meant sticking with it. A commitment meant being in it for the long haul, whether that was joining the tennis club, choosing your friends or establishing a career. Supporting others and doing good were important attributes, not to be shied away from. Her parents valued good decision-making and perseverance, and she recognised as she sat through twelve years of Sunday school, Bible class and Presbyterian church services that these were valued by many more people than just her parents. She also knew that losing face was something she found extremely difficult to deal with. She didn't want to explain her actions or the feelings that were behind her choices. These would be outwith the understanding of those around her, so she kept them to herself. She conformed.

Now she wished she hadn't. She should have ended the marriage after six months. It would have been easier. Without saying anything, they both knew they had made the wrong decision, but neither of them felt able to end it. It would be hard to justify and hard to explain to others. There were no arguments, but emotionally, he was shallow and without feeling. They spoke about daily tasks, planned events and a myriad of other things of no consequence, but never of feelings. It was a relationship of routines. Sometimes she would cry about it, but she would rationalise her feelings by believing she had nothing to complain about. She shouldn't cry. She could live with the silence and emptiness and compensate for it through her friends. And she did.

The problem was that each year, it got harder to deal with. Her father's death and her mother's grief only highlighted her own unhappiness. She had always known her parents loved each other very much. Every day when he came home from work, her father would kiss her mother, then swing her round like a child before kissing both her and her sister. She knew this was unusual and always enjoyed the spectacle. Her parents laughed a great deal and often smiled secretly to each other when they thought no one else was looking. They always had something to speak about. They argued infrequently and it was always over quickly. None of these things were part of Lesley's marriage. She felt only relief when her husband wasn't in the house and rejoiced when his shifts meant that apart from a few hours here and there, they didn't see each other for days.

As their ten-year anniversary approached, she knew she would have to leave. But she didn't; he did. She woke to the phone ringing. She knew it was early, but she turned over in the bed and he wasn't there. He should have been. She felt confused and suddenly troubled as she moved slowly towards the noise of the phone. She looked briefly in the kitchen and saw his keys and his wallet lying on the table. She looked in the living room and he wasn't there. Finally, she picked up the phone. She said nothing. *It's me, Lesley.* She knew the voice but not the tone. It was flat and dead. She said nothing. *I've decided to leave. I'm heading south. I don't need anything, I'll find work. I'm not coming back.* She didn't know what to say and found herself saying nothing at all. There was a long silence. *I have no more money to put in the phone, Lesley. Goodbye.* She started talking, but the line was dead.

Her first thought was how she would explain this to others. What would she say? She was angry that he had left and wanted him back in some strange way so that the other questions wouldn't have to be answered or explained. At the same time, she was relieved and glad she hadn't had to be the one to leave. She spent months trying to find him, contacting those she knew were his friends, but she got no leads. She visited her solicitor to seek advice about reporting him missing. He was missing as far as she was concerned. He told her not to report him missing but to wait. This was very hard for Lesley, who liked solutions and wanted to be able to rationalise the panic that woke her frequently at night, gasping for breath. In contrast, her days were quiet and predictable.

She liked that and knew now that she could never have him back. But she needed to end it, and she could only do that if she could find him. And she did.

Several months after he left, a letter came through the door from the insurers of his motorbike. She opened it expecting no clues as to his whereabouts, but instead it was a renewal letter. There was no new address on it, but she knew they would know where he was. He must have kept the bike. So she called them. It was much easier than she would have anticipated. She said her husband had asked her to call them because he wasn't sure if they had the correct address for him now that he was working away from home. And, without any other questions, the girl gave her the address and she wrote it down. Although surprised, she knew now she could find him.

Her mother and sister were unsure that she should go to London alone, but they didn't suggest going with her. Lesley knew it was the only way she could bring things to a conclusion and move on with her life, even if it would result in more anxiety and uncertainty. And so she arranged a weekend in London.

As she stood outside the house in St Mark's Road, South Norwood, she questioned the sanity of what she was doing, but there seemed no other option if she wanted things to change. The elderly lady who answered the door smiled when she asked for him by name. *He never gets visitors, you know. I'm sure you'll be a very nice surprise.* She showed Lesley into a small living room, which seemed to be entirely brown, then went off to find him. Just as if the last five months had never happened, Lesley and her husband said nothing to each other at first. Nothing had really changed. The old lady lingered at the door, eager to know what was happening, but before she could say anything, Lesley's husband suggested that he and Lesley go to his room.

It was a tiny, depressing bedsit which made Lesley feel even more sad than she was already feeling. She sat on the one chair in the room and stared at this man who had been part of her life for more than ten years. She realised she had never known him at all. They discussed what he had been doing for the past five months and she explained her predicament in terms of the house. *I want none of it, Lesley. I'm happy to give it all to you. Just get your solicitor to send the paperwork and I'll sign it all over to you. It makes sense now.* She agreed she would do that. They had nothing else to say; the divorce could be discussed later now she knew where he was. They sat silently for some time. Lesley said she would go, and as she moved towards the door, she said, *I hope you find whatever it is you're looking for.* Later, she often remembered the look on his face, but she didn't wait for an answer then. It was done.

\*

The divorce followed two years later, and Lesley felt stronger for confronting so many fears and finding a way to move on. She felt young again and able to make independent decisions without answering to anyone. She knew now it was more important to do what you felt was right rather than trying to make others happy all the time. And so she had ended up in Florence, happy to be following her own path.

\*

As she headed down the stairs to go out for her shopping, she could hear a brush scraping the wood of the stairs and knew she would again meet Signora Conti. They greeted each other as usual and commented on the lovely day. Lesley moved to turn the handle on the outside door. *I think I'll contact the police about Pepe today. I spoke with the other students this morning and they haven't seen him either. They said his girlfriend was concerned too. He hadn't come back to her flat when he said he would. Do you think I should?*

Lesley knew she had to be careful and chose her words carefully. *I don't know anything about him, Signora Conti, but if it will make you feel better, then I think you should. Do you want me to help in any way?* Lesley smiled.

*No, no, I'll probably pop along to the station. It's easier to explain in person. Enjoy your shopping trip. Ciao.*

# Nine

Paolo spotted her immediately. He moved backwards into the shadows of the alley, waiting for her to decide on which direction she would walk. She went west, and he followed her. She walked more slowly today, and he thought she looked more relaxed. She stopped at different shops to look in the windows and occasionally went in to browse before emerging into the sunlight without having made a purchase. Once in the Piazza della Signora, she found a table tucked in the corner of a café, ordered a coffee and sat looking out across the square.

It was easy for Paolo to remain unnoticed in the thronging crowds who had just arrived from the cruise liners for their organised march around the sites of Florence. But he wanted her to see him. He wanted to be noticed.

As he walked towards the café, he removed his black leather gloves; they wouldn't be needed. There was a table free next to the girl's, and he headed straight for it. He didn't allow his gaze to move from the table. She would have to be the one to recognise him, otherwise he would simply have a coffee, then leave. Getting into the table was difficult. Everything was tightly packed, and customers were too busy speaking to move for him. He always chose a table on the edge of a café to avoid contact with others, and he was still unsure why he was willing to compromise this to be noticed.

She recognised him instantly. There were few people in Florence that she had started conversations with, and her ability to remember faces rarely failed her. He was wearing the same jeans, shirt and jacket. They looked clean and bright, and she wondered if his wardrobe consisted only of these identical items. The only things missing were the black leather gloves. Then she noticed the edge of them sticking out of his jacket pocket. Lesley wasn't sure if she wanted to speak to him since she knew how difficult the conversation would be, but she felt sorry for him. She could see his anxiety as he made his way through the tables with his arms unnaturally high in order that he made no contact with others. He ordered a coffee. She waited.

*Excuse me.* She touched his arm. It felt like a metal bar touching him. *Didn't we meet in the park yesterday evening? You were there when I woke up.* She smiled directly at him, and Paolo, on this occasion, didn't avoid her gaze. *I'm Lesley.* And she put out her hand to shake his. His smile changed and she pulled her hand away, realising that this was a step too far for him. After a few minutes he said, *I'm Paolo. It's nice to see you again.*

Although he smiled and maintained eye contact with her, Lesley was aware that she would need to be the facilitator of the conversation. He said nothing. She commented on the weather, and just as he had done the previous evening, he gave her a detailed account of the expected weather for the rest of the day. She continued to smile, explaining, once he had finished, that she was enjoying the weather and how different it was from Scotland. Although she might have expected him to ask her about Scotland and why she was now in Florence, she knew he wouldn't, so she simply gave him the information without a prompt. She finished by saying, *do you live in Florence?*

Paolo always had a cover story, so without a pause, he was able to explain his presence in the city. *No, no. I live on Lake Como and am just here on business. I have an antiques business and was down here to sell a couple of items. I'm going back home today.* He knew now he would have to leave Florence; the story decided it. Then she spoke. She spoke about the beautiful buildings in Florence, its history and how much she enjoyed being in what she regarded as a living museum. Paolo listened and thought of his mother. He had always enjoyed when she spoke and the detail she would give him about how she felt. He never reciprocated and he wouldn't today either. He could think of nothing else to say. It was time to leave.

*It's been lovely meeting you, Lesley, but I will need to leave now and head back to Lake Como.* Lesley thought about extending her hand once again but decided from his stiff position and the formality of his language that it was best they part simply on *ciao*. He made his way slowly through the tables with his arms aloft, and Lesley ordered a second coffee. Her shopping could wait a few minutes.

Paolo donned his gloves and walked purposefully back to his car. He thought he had enjoyed his time with Lesley, and he thought he felt happier than he had in a long time. He decided he was ready to call Franco. Once in his car, he dialled the number and waited. Franco answered very quickly, as if he had been anxiously waiting for this call. *I am just about to leave Florence, Franco. My apologies for the way things worked out. It wasn't my intention. I want no more jobs, Franco; it is over for me.* He could hear Franco breathing, and he waited for his response. *We have a problem, Paolo. The family won't pay. I might be able to negotiate a lesser fee, but I can't promise it. They wanted publicity, not this emptiness.*

*I don't want any money, Franco. I failed. It's over*

*now. I won't call again, and please don't call me.* Paolo ended the call, removed the SIM card from the phone and tucked it in his pocket to be destroyed once he was home. He started the engine and headed north, out of the city.

*

Signora Conti had completed all her morning chores, a routine she rarely altered. She was ready to go to the police station. As she locked her door, she thought she should go up to Pepe's flat and knock on his door just in case he was there. She didn't want to look foolish. She rarely went upstairs and had forgotten how many steps there were to get from one floor to the next. She knocked loudly on the door to ensure it would be noticed if he was in there. She looked through the letter box and even tried the door handle to convince herself that no one was there. There was no response.

The nearest police station was in the Via Delle Terme, and although it wasn't the one where she had worked, Signora Conti knew the girls on the desk and felt comfortable about speaking to them. In her experience, mid-morning was a good time to go to the station since the early morning rush was over and there was a slight lull in the chaos of the day. As she pushed the outside door shut, she looked across at the Hotel Davanzati to see whether the man with the black leather gloves was still there. He wasn't.

It was a short walk to the police station, but she was wrong about it being a good time to report her concerns. There were people sitting on the steps and a small queue at the front desk. Lucia spotted her when she walked in and waved. They had worked together for a short time a number of years ago before Lucia got promotion and took charge of the desk at the Via Delle Terme station. Signora Conti found an empty seat and sat down to wait. It seemed that those in the station were mainly tourists reporting thefts or asking directions. She guessed this was the main trade for a police station so near the centre of Florence. After most of the queue had been dealt with, Lucia signalled for Signora Conti to follow her to a small office just off the main reception.

Signora Conti had often interviewed members of the public in a similar small office, but she hadn't realised how intimidating it could feel until now. There was no natural light, and apart from a table with two chairs, there was nothing else to make the room welcoming. *It's lovely to see you, Signora Conti, it has been a while. How is retirement?* They kissed on both cheeks. Signora Conti confirmed her pleasure at not working, then swiftly moved on to the reason for her visit. She explained about the young man living upstairs from her and her concerns about his whereabouts. It had been three days since she had last seen him and three days since anyone else could confirm they had seen him. She could only give Lucia his first name, but Lucia said this wasn't a problem; they would be able to find out who he was. Lucia took notes.

The two women smiled at each other. Lucia looked again at her notes before she spoke. *I'll pass on the information, Signora Conti, and someone will be in touch once we have decided on a course of action.* Lucia stood up and opened the door. Signora Conti was glad to leave the stale air of the room and be welcomed by the warmth of the April sunshine as she re-emerged into the chaos of a busy Florence. She had no commitments today, so she decided to take a walk along the Arno before returning to her flat for lunch. It seemed strange to her that she had felt so anxious in the police station.

# Ten

Paolo arrived back in Cesate in the late evening. Everything was, as always, quiet and still. Once in the driveway, he closed the gates, removed his luggage from the boot of the car and headed up the outside stairs to the front door. The ivy crawling its way up the wall was needing a trim. His mother had always kept it from encroaching on the bannister, and he did likewise. He would not work now, so the many jobs he had squirreled away in his head to complete once he finally retired could be started on, and this job could be added to the list.

He opened the two locks and pushed the door firmly before stepping inside. The house smelt a little stale. He realised then that he had been away for three weeks, longer than he would normally. He knew he had definitely delayed the hit on Pepe much longer than he should have. He wondered if he had simply lost his nerve or whether his assertion that Pepe was too young and too innocent to be killed had been his motivating factor. He knew he didn't like the idea of losing his nerve, but he was unsure if this was what that would feel like.

After placing his suitcase on his bed and emptying it immediately, he surveyed every room in the house to ensure everything was just as he had left it. The house seemed particularly brown this evening. The dark furniture and the beige tiled floors seemed to merge into each other, with the lamps casting a dim light across everything. Nothing had changed since his father left, and even though he would occasionally suggest to his mother that they change aspects of the house from the lucrative proceeds of his job, she would refuse to do so. She clung to the past, as did he despite his concerns about this. He knew he would soon settle back into the routines of his life in Cesate, and changes to any aspect of the house would then become impossible.

The last room he entered was his mother's bedroom. It was as if she had just popped out to the shops or was still sitting in the living room watching television before retiring to bed. The striped bed cover was in place, with plumped pillows tucked neatly underneath. Her red slippers sat side by side next to the bedside table, where her heavily thumbed Bible rested sadly under the lamp. He sat down on the small red chair at the bottom of the bed. This was one of his favourite places to sit when things seemed outwith his control. He could always find a way back to his normality if he sat here. And he simply sat. Motionless. When the clock on the bedside table read 2130, he left the room, switched off all the lights and retired to his own bedroom for the night. He thought he felt better already although Lesley was still in his head, smiling at him and chatting as if she had always known him.

The next day was filled with jobs for Paolo. He put his car in the garage. He destroyed the SIM card he had been using in Florence and ensured all his guns were replaced in their underground chest beneath the floor of the garage, along with the additional mobile phones he used when on a job. If he never worked again, he wouldn't need any of these things, but he had to consider how he might dispose of them. They would be clues to unsolved murders over the last 20 years, and he wanted no trail leading back to him. He now considered more mundane jobs that needed to be done.

*

Although he had brought enough with him to eat breakfast, doing some shopping was his priority. The walk to the supermarket allowed him to see if anything in Cesate had changed while he'd been away. As always, nothing had, but he liked to discover this for himself rather than assuming it would be the case. He walked by the main roads but returned via the path behind the Parrochia San Alessandro e San Martino. The wildflowers that grew annually along the length of the path were beginning to emerge as the days got longer and the sun gradually got warmer. The only change was that the fence put up after the murder of Father Rossi to prevent anyone getting into the garden was now being replaced. Four workmen were dismantling the old fence to replace it with new, stronger posts and slats. Paolo did not acknowledge the greetings of the workmen and carried on back to the house. He thought how well built the fence had been that it had lasted more than 20 years, but he didn't take his memory back to the events of that night and the path it had taken him on. If he had, he knew he would again wonder how his mother had known what he had done, and then he would wonder how she had known Franco. These were too difficult to think about and there were no answers. He liked answers.

Lunch was a plate of bread, cheese and fruit: his favourite kind of lunch. He ate it on the terrace, working out the numerous jobs that needed to be done in the garden. He would need to prioritise these, and he spent some time deciding how he would do this. Absurdly, he usually did this according to what visitors to the house would see first, even though visitors were rare indeed. And so he started by trimming the ivy on the stairs, preventing it from encroaching on the railing. It was a warm day, and he enjoyed feeling the sun on his back as he worked his way round the garden. He wondered what Lesley would be doing and where she would be. His mother wouldn't like him thinking like this; she always worried about his obsessions.

*

Lesley had been surprised to see Paolo again. It seemed quite a coincidence given the number of people roaming the streets of Florence. She had been surprised at his desire to sit at the back of the café when his anxiety getting through the crowd was so pronounced. But he was gone now, away from Florence and no longer her concern. After her second coffee, she left the square to visit the supermarket and gather together her provisions for the day. Lesley never tired of making her daily food purchases. It was a new way of living she particularly liked since it removed her from the weekly shop which was such a feature of her life in Scotland. Her day was now punctuated by different activities that took her out and about rather than being dominated by being in school from 8 until 4.30. There had never seemed to be time to do anything other than work.

As she turned into the Via Porta Rossa, a young girl begging in a doorway caught her eye. She hadn't seen her there before. She was struck by the girl's youth and beauty and wondered how she had ended up in such a situation. Generally, Lesley found it easy to walk past beggars, but as she passed her, she felt a need to give her something. She reached into her shopping bag and pulled out a basket of cherries. The girl was staring at the ground, her long hair making eye contact impossible, forcing Lesley to bend down and speak to her. *I wondered if you would like these cherries?* The girl looked up, smiled broadly and took them. She grasped Lesley's hand and said thank you.

As Lesley stood up and turned, a Carabinieri police car drove slowly into the street — no blue lights, no need for speed. She stayed where she was to let it pass, then continued to walk along behind it. As she watched it, she noticed it slowing as it neared her house. She knew then that Signora Conti must have been to the police station.

When Lesley arrived at the main door, a uniformed policeman was standing outside, while a man in plain clothes was inside speaking to Signora Conti. She smiled at the policeman, but he didn't smile back. He put his arm out, preventing her from entering. Signora Conti quickly spoke up on her behalf. *This is my neighbour. She lives on the top floor.* She looked quickly from the uniformed policeman to the man in plain clothes. He nodded, and the arm preventing her from entering was lowered. Lesley walked in and moved towards the stairs.

Without looking up, Detective Diego Borroni said, *we'll need to speak to you. Your name is?* Lesley turned to look at him. His face was angular, and his penetrating grey eyes, which were now looking straight at her, were without sparkle. He held his small notebook tightly in his hand, the pen poised ready to write. *Lesley Hamilton.* Signora Conti again came to her aid, spelling the names for Detective Borroni and explaining where Lesley was from. *Thank you, Ms Hamilton, we'll be up to speak with you this afternoon.* She could feel him watching her as she began to climb the stairs.

Lesley carried on with her daily routines: shopping put away, writing, lunch, writing. All the while, she could hear noise everywhere. Feet going up and down the stairs, voices chattering loudly, doors being knocked on. She just had to wait for it to be her door.

# Eleven

It was late afternoon before there was a knock on Lesley's door. It had seemed a long wait.

While speaking to Signora Conti, Detective Borroni hadn't seemed very tall, but as she opened her front door, Lesley noticed he had to duck slightly for his face to be visible. He smiled straight at her and gestured that he would want to come in. She stood aside, holding out her arm as an invitation to enter. With the confidence of someone whose working life involves speaking to many different people in many different places, he understood the gesture and strode forward purposefully into the main living area. Lesley took a moment to join him since she expected the accompanying policeman to come in as well. But he didn't.

For the few moments he had to wait for Lesley, Detective Borroni scanned the room, taking in all the details and making assumptions. Everything was in its place; there was no untidiness. But he guessed the lack of space made a tidy room essential. There were few personal items, and it seemed clear to him she hadn't been living there long.

In perfect Italian, Lesley invited him to sit down and asked if he would like coffee or tea. He declined any refreshment and sat down in one of the two wooden chairs either side of the small table in the window. Lesley sat in the other. As he fumbled in his pocket for his notebook, Lesley looked carefully at his face. *So, Ms Hamilton, I need to speak to you about your neighbour who was living in the flat below you.* His English was perfect. He had had no need of Signora Conti's help earlier. *Would you rather speak in Italian?* She realised she must have looked surprised but pleasantly so.

*No, no, English is perfect. I have been trying to improve my Italian, but I haven't been here long and it is taking me longer than I expected to get more fluent. I find it particularly hard if people speak quickly but ...* Her voice trailed off as she realised that she could end up saying far more than she meant to. *My neighbour: how can I help?*

Detective Borroni explained that the young man in the flat below, Pepe Poccini, hadn't been seen for a few days and there were concerns regarding his whereabouts. He was hoping Pepe's neighbours might be able to shed some light on his disappearance. While relating all this information, Detective Borroni had been looking at his phone and now turned it towards Lesley. It showed a photo of Pepe. Apart from the pool of blood at the back of his head, he looked exactly as he had looked when she found him lying on the floor. She took the phone and looked carefully at the photo before speaking, concerned not to look for too long or not long enough. Then she spoke.

*I met him on the stairs a couple of times, but I did not know him or know his name. Signora Conti said he is a student, but I wasn't aware of him really at all. I did hear him singing sometimes but nothing else. He was a quiet neighbour. I have only been here since January, and because of my daily routine, I've really only got to know Signora Conti and Signor Alfonsi. I usually go out in the morning before eight for some shopping and sometimes my breakfast, then back home to write. I'm a novelist. Then lunch, more writing and a walk to a new part of the city. I haven't made any friends yet, so my evenings are generally spent at home. What do you think might have happened to him?*

Detective Borroni never liked to speculate with potential witnesses or suspects and chose to say very little. *He may simply have gone away for a few days and nothing has happened to him, but now that his family are aware of his disappearance, they are keen we try to trace him. What made you come to Florence, Ms Hamilton?*

She smiled. *My personal circumstances changed, and I had the opportunity to have a year abroad to concentrate on my writing and thought Florence would fit the bill. My resources would allow me to live here comfortably without a need to get a job. And I'm enjoying it very much. It is a beautiful city and an easy place to live. Inspirational for a writer.* She could have continued but felt uneasy giving too much information. Her guilt was weighing heavily on her now.

*Did you see Mr Poccini at all this week?*

She paused before answering. *No, I'm fairly certain I haven't seen him this week, but as I said earlier, if I had, it would only have been in passing.*

Detective Borroni smiled at her and maintained eye contact for what felt like an unusually long time before speaking. *What are you writing, Ms Hamilton?* And he turned to look at the computer with its cold black screen. *Have you been writing today?*

*I write historical sagas, I suppose. So Florence is perfect. I feel steeped in history every time I go out. Yes, I write every day, although some days more than others.* She realised it had been hard to write today and that her computer would show only 500 words had been added to the text when her aim was 2000 every day, and generally, she made that target. She smiled to cover her rising sense of panic. She could hear his voice, but she wasn't listening. Irrationally, she was wondering if he would ask to see her computer. Then she remembered he didn't know Pepe was dead; only she did and the person who murdered him. He wouldn't look at the computer. Detective Borroni was standing now, and he was surprised Lesley was still sitting. *Thank you, Ms Hamilton. If there is anything else you remember or think may be important, this is my card and the number where I can be contacted.* Lesley took the card, stood up and walked towards the front door.

*Goodbye, Detective Borroni.*

As she closed the door behind him, Lesley could hear him speaking to the policeman who had remained outside her door while his superior was doing the questioning. The voices were muffled and gradually disappeared as they went down the stairs once again. Unexpectedly, she felt better for having spoken to the police and was pleased someone was now looking for the young man. It was after four and she knew there was little chance of her writing anything else today. She looked out of the window at the blue sky and the warm sun and decided she would go for her afternoon walk just as she always did. She would head north today towards the Giardino della Gherardesca, where she could have a coffee, then wander through the manicured lawns and parterres, admiring the modern sculptures. She grabbed her shawl and bag and headed out.

The stairwell was quiet, and she was certain the police had gone. She could leave the worrying about the young man to someone else now. As she reached the main entrance, Signora Conti's door opened and out came Detective Borroni. *Off out for your walk, Ms Hamilton? A lovely day for it. Routine is such a helpful thing.* Lesley smiled and nodded while opening the door and entering the noisy world of the Via Porta Rossa.

*Thank you again, Signora Conti, you have been most helpful. All those years in the police station have honed your instincts, I think. If you think of anything else, just give me a call. I left my card on your table.* He turned to leave and had his hand on the handle of the main door when she spoke.

*There is something else, Detective Borroni. I meant to tell Lucia when I went to the police station, but I forgot. And I nearly forgot again just now. I'm not sure if it's important or relevant, but it seemed strange. For a few days around the time of Pepe's disappearance, I saw the same man standing in the alley next to the Hotel Davanzati on several occasions. He seemed to be watching our building. Unfortunately, I couldn't see him clearly but was aware that he always had on a pair of black leather gloves. It seemed unusual now the weather is warmer. I'm so glad I finally remembered to tell someone.*

Detective Borroni made a note of it in his book. He was glad there was something unusual to note since no one had reported anything out of the ordinary. He wished he had had this information when questioning everyone; maybe someone knew the man or had also noticed him. Someone, probably not him, would be back to ask more questions so they could make enquiries then. He thanked Signora Conti again for this information and took his leave.

\*

Detective Diego Borroni, like Lesley, hadn't been in Florence long. But, unlike Lesley, he hadn't chosen to move there. He had worked in the Milan Carabinieri for twenty years, and until last year, had enjoyed every moment of it. It was never the same two days in a row, and there was always something new to discover about human nature. When he first joined, his work revolved around violent crimes — murders, armed robbery. He had shown a talent for solving these crimes and had been highly praised for his work. Promotion came, and ultimately, he joined the ROS, the Raggruppamento Operativo Speciale, with a focus on organised crime. He felt he had found his niche. It involved him using all aspects of his detection skills and gave him now and again the excitement of taking part in armed operations. But more than all of this, he felt he was doing a service for his country, where many poor people were at the mercy of these gangs and were made all the poorer as a consequence. Finally, he became an inspector and took charge of the Organised Crime Squad in Milan.

His work filled his life. Although others had families and enjoyed a life outside their work, Detective Borroni had not chosen that path. All his energies were channelled into his work. Relationships fell by the wayside and were never prioritised. Tanya knew that better than most. Then things changed.

The Poccini family had long been a target for Diego Borroni's team, but with little success. Marco Poccini was head of the family, running his large textile factories in the Milan suburbs with the help of his two eldest sons, Luca and Lorenzo. They lived lavish lives, with luxurious houses on the outskirts of Milan as well as an extensive estate overlooking Lake Como. They mixed with the great and the good — royalty, Hollywood celebrities, international tycoons. A lifestyle that couldn't be funded by textiles alone. Rumours had long suggested drug trafficking supplemented their livelihoods, but no proof could þe found. The family didn't appear to associate with any of the known mafia groups, and how they managed their drug dealing was very hard to detect. Diego Borroni and his team worked tirelessly to find links between the drug world and the Poccinis. Marco, Luca and Lorenzo were kept under constant surveillance for many months. They lived their lives just as they always had, and nothing could be found to link them to any form of criminality. Their finances were investigated, and again, nothing could be found that didn't come from the profits of the factories. Even their taxes were paid promptly, and it appeared, in full.

Marco's youngest son, Pepe, arrived 15 years after Lorenzo and to a second wife. His life was very different. He worked hard at school, played football at regional level, achieved highly and rarely went near the factories. Both Pepe and his father were keen that he spread his wings and attend university away from Milan. Florence was his first choice: it was far enough but not too far for his parents to visit, the art history degree he was undertaking was highly regarded, and Marco thought he knew enough people in Florence who could ensure his son's safety if it was needed. And so Marco purchased the flat on the Via Porta Rossa and Pepe made the move.

As is often the case with policemen enthralled by their work, Diego Borroni felt driven to prove that the Poccini family were not the law-abiding citizens they appeared to be. It became an obsession that would lead to his demise rather than the family's. Following harassment claims and court appeals, Diego and his team had been directed to end the surveillance of the family and turn their attention to other matters. Diego knew that doing this sometimes resulted in a breakthrough with a case you had previously been investigating and that he should wait for a mistake to be made, but he could not let it go. And so his evenings and weekends were taken up with studying his files for the smallest of leads and watching the family members as best he could. Still, nothing surfaced.

Time passed, but instead of lessening Diego's obsession, it simply increased it. The Poccinis weren't going to make a mistake, but he would. One Saturday afternoon a few months after the court ruling, he followed Lorenzo to the Lake Como estate, and instead of parking up and watching from afar, he decided to venture into the grounds and feign that he was lost if he was discovered. He parked a mile away and walked quietly through the woods bordering the estate. When he reached the boundary, he momentarily wondered if he was making the right decision but continued with his plan. It wasn't a fence for keeping people out, so he was soon over it and walking towards the house which he could see vaguely through the trees. His focus was so concentrated on reaching the house that the cracking of twigs did not alert him to what was about to happen.

Suddenly, a dog started barking and was coming at him through the trees, closely followed by a young man dressed entirely in black and carrying what Diego thought was a taser. He knew there was no point in running since the dog would catch him and bring him to the ground, so he stood as still as he could and waited to see what the dog would do. It didn't attack him but waited in front of him barking loudly, showing its teeth and awaiting further commands. As the young man reached him, Diego saw others coming through the trees towards them and raised his arms. It was now that he made his mistake. Instead of staying silent, he apologised for being in the grounds and said he had been walking and didn't realise he was now in the grounds of a house. He said he would simply go back the way he'd come and turned as if to go. Instantly, the dog started barking again and moved towards him. As did the men. There were three of them now. One took his arm and asked him to walk towards the house. The other two walked behind them with the dog, who no longer seemed interested in his presence. Diego guessed the dog knew his part of the job was over.

When they emerged from the trees, the full grandeur of the house was laid out before him. Its Palladian facade adorned with CCTV cameras went round three sides of the building, with stone steps leading to the lawns and the lake. Standing at the top of these steps was Lorenzo, smoking a large cigar and carrying a glass of red wine in his hand. Diego still felt confident that Lorenzo wouldn't remember him and was working out his story as they strode across the lawn. He was wrong, however.

*Hello, Detective Inspector Borroni. I wasn't aware you enjoyed walking?* Lorenzo turned his back on them and moved towards a small table on the corner of the terrace and sat down. *Do join me. I've contacted my father to let him know you are here, and I'm sure he will now be speaking to whoever needs spoken to. Would you like something to drink?* Diego declined the offer, realising there was no point in speaking since anything he said may simply make things worse. Now he needed a story for his bosses. *I think they call this harassment, Detective Inspector, but we'll no doubt find out once my father calls back.* They sat in silence.

After some minutes, a young lady emerged from the house carrying a phone, which she handed to Lorenzo. *Ah, Commissar Pontini, how nice of you to call ... Yes, he's right next to me. I'll pass the phone over to him.*

Diego reluctantly took the phone. *Get out of there, Borroni, and report to me at the station. This is highly irregular. We can't have this.* Diego simply said yes, handed the phone to Lorenzo and stood up to leave.

*We can't have you in danger on the road, Detective Inspector, so two of my men will escort you back to your car the way you came. I can't say it's been a pleasure seeing you, but I trust I won't be seeing you again.* He stood up, glass in hand, turned away and walked back into the house.

And he didn't see Diego again. Within the week, the detective inspector was transferred to Florence and demoted to detective, and he returned to mundane policing. He was certain he wouldn't be continuing the investigation into Pepe's disappearance, although he wanted to.

## Twelve

Paolo's life had now returned to a routine he liked. Early morning walks to the shops before too many people were out, doing jobs around the house, lunch, having a walk or a drive in the afternoon, dinner, then reading or TV. It made things simple for him and meant there was no need to wonder what he should be doing or if he was doing the right things. He didn't miss his work at all and was surprised at that. It had been part of his life for such a long time that he would have expected to be sorry it was over. In fact, it removed many things he found unsettling: contact with strangers, buying food in unknown shops, living in flats or houses where cleanliness could not be guaranteed, ensuring he remained anonymous.

Now he wanted to rid himself of the trappings of his occupation and began thinking of ways to dispose of them. Firstly, there were the guns. He knew people who would buy them, but he couldn't run the risk of someone passing on the name of their previous owner. He decided he would dismantle them into their component parts, then bury them in various places around the country. He had no facility to melt the metal and did not want to engage the assistance of anyone else in his plans, so scattering and burying them seemed the best way forward.

As he did when all decisions were made, Paolo put his plan into action as soon as possible. So the next day he began doing all the work in the garage to ensure there was no need to move the items far from their hiding place. It was the kind of work he enjoyed. Small tools needed to be used for the dissections and parts grouped together so that if ever discovered, they didn't match and couldn't tell a story. He used four plastic boxes to put them in, ensuring he wore gloves at all times and washing each tiny part in bleach before placing them in the similarly decontaminated boxes. The phones were easier to get rid of. He had always shredded his SIM cards, put the remains in the regular bin and enjoyed watching them being taken off to the local landfill along with his more mundane rubbish. The phones themselves could tell no story, but he knew he would feel better if they were in pieces rather than simply sending them off to the landfill site with the shredded SIMs. And so he broke each one into tiny little shards, swept up the remains and distributed them equally into the boxes of gun parts.

It took almost a week for Paolo to complete this job and be happy with his work. Deciding where to bury them was more problematic. He wanted to ensure a good distance between each burial site but didn't want to be away longer than a few days so that no suspicion was aroused in his neighbours. They had never been suspicious before, but it was a possibility every time Paolo went away and one he always took into account. He also didn't want to stay in hotels or any other accommodation in case he was remembered at some future date, but sleeping in the car or a tent was something he could only tolerate for two or three nights.

After much deliberation, he settled on the two national parks located in Liguria and Emilia-Romagna. Hiking alone would not seem unusual, and it was something he'd done before. He decided he would go the next day. He used the dining room table to gather together all the things he would need. And, as with everything he did, Paolo was meticulous in his planning, considering everything he might need for every eventuality. His biggest concern was a car breakdown where he might need the help of someone else who would have to see inside the car. And so he packed three manuals relating to car maintenance, and in particular, the manual relating to his model of Alfa Romeo. Once he was happy, he packed two identical rucksacks — both contained all his camping essentials, two boxes of gun parts, a collapsable spade and several pairs of black gloves.

It was 2130. Time for bed. He switched off all the lights and retired to his bedroom, where he removed the small pistol from his bedside drawer in order that he remembered to take it with him tomorrow. Although content with all his planning, Paolo knew that at his last chosen burial site in Emilia-Romagna, he would be less than an hour's drive from Florence, which meant less than an hour's drive from Lesley. He had thought about her every day since his return to Cesate, and although he would sit in his mother's room to rid himself of those thoughts, he couldn't help but feel tempted to drive on to Florence. He decided to make the decision once he was rid of the gun boxes and hoped his desire to see her and speak to her had lessened by then.

The Regional Park dell'Antola was a familiar place for Paolo and his first stop. As a child, he had gone there every summer with his grandfather to hike and camp for a couple of weeks. Those were times of respite for Paolo, away from the strain of his parents' relationship. His grandfather was a quiet man who spoke little and never — in Paolo's presence anyway — raised his voice. They would wander across different areas of the park admiring the landscapes and the animals and enjoying some wild camping. Although it was hard for Paolo, the escape from the tension of home more than made up for the other stresses camping caused him. And so Paolo knew how to enter the park without parking in the designated car parks where CCTV protected the wilderness from the masses.

Once away from the car, Paolo headed into the national park via a small wood that filled the narrow valley and led him on to the mountains. He started to climb. It was harder than he remembered, and the weight of the metal in his rucksack added to the challenge. He thought he should go to the top first and then decide where would be a good spot to bury the first two boxes. If he had been seen, it would also make him seem like the other visitors to the park. The view was stunning, unhindered by either buildings or people. Around a mile down the other side of the mountain, Paolo could see a cluster of trees that had probably seeded themselves but were unlikely to be wandered through by either the park rangers or the public. The first location was identified. Further on, Paolo reckoned about 5 miles away, he could see another small wood which he hoped would suffice for the second box as well as a place to camp for the night.

Paolo liked when a plan came together, and this one did. He met no one and felt sure no one had seen him. The ground in both woods was slightly damp due to recent rain in the area, so digging deep enough holes wasn't too onerous. He dug down over a metre before being happy to place a box in each of the holes. Once filled in, the holes were covered with the top layer of soil and debris that he had meticulously removed before starting to dig. He looked at the area from a number of angles and felt no one would be able to identify it as a dig site.

As predicted, night had fallen by the time he completed the second dig. Paolo found the darkness comforting and quietly put up his small tent some distance from the area where he had been digging. He had the meal of cold pasta he had packed that morning, then crept into his sleeping bag and waited for sleep to overcome him. And it did.

Although it was raining gently when he woke, he quickly packed up his tent and started the walk back to his car. He was confident now that he could bury the other two boxes with the same stealth. Everything had gone according to plan. The grey clouds covered the tops of the mountains, crowding the horizon and affording him more cover than he had anticipated.

Emilia-Romagna was less familiar to Paolo. He had been there only twice before with his grandfather. He was relying on memories from 30 years ago to ensure he wasn't seen, but his memory rarely failed him, and it didn't on this occasion either. He followed the same pattern as for the first two boxes and completed his task without any difficulties. A second night under canvas was completed, and now a decision had to be made. He should return to Cesate without delay, but his proximity to Florence meant that Lesley was in his thoughts virtually all of the time. He tried very hard to think of his mother and what she would say, but he found it hard when he didn't have her room to sit in or the oppressive sense of her presence that existed in the house. She would say he shouldn't go, but her voice in his head wasn't as strong as it had always been and he found it easy to dismiss her objections. As he put his rucksack in the boot of the car, he saw the third rucksack he'd brought with him. In it was his usual attire — black trousers, socks and shoes, a white shirt, a black leather jacket and his black gloves.

He would go.

## Thirteen

For a couple of weeks, life returned to normal for Lesley. There was no further mention of the young man when she spoke to Signora Conti, and no policemen visited the flats. Then things changed.

*

It was a perfectly still May morning, with a clear blue sky accentuating the angles of the buildings and brightening the colours of the plants that hung down from the many balconies and terraces in the city. Lesley had enjoyed a walk along the banks of the Arno and was about to enter the supermarket when she saw a photograph of the young man, Pepe, on the front cover of La Nazione. She took the newspaper from its wire rack and studied it as best she could. From what she could understand, he was now officially a missing person. His father and brothers were pictured underneath the story, and their determination to find him was evident from their steely expressions. She felt uncomfortable knowing she was one of the few people who knew what had happened to him and more uncomfortable at the prospect that she might be asked questions by the family. How well could she lie then? She returned the newspaper to the rack, got her daily shop and returned more quickly than she intended to her flat.

As she turned into the Via Porta Rossa, she noticed, once again, the young girl sitting in the empty doorway begging. Lesley wanted to stop and give her some food, but her increasing sense of anxiety drove her to keep walking. She lifted her head abruptly, and there in front of her was Detective Diego Borroni smiling straight at her. She stopped, fearing her face showed all the guilt and anxiety she was feeling.

*How nice to see you, Miss Hamilton. I was just at your flat.* She kept smiling, but the noise of her heart beating loudly in her head made it hard to hear what he was saying. *I was showing my colleague, Detective Francesco, where the flats are and introducing him to some of the residents now that he is taking over the case. He specialises in missing people. No doubt you were out doing your morning shop, hence the reason we didn't see you.* And he pointed at her bag. She had said nothing and felt her fixed expression must be disturbing Diego. She needed to change it.

*Yes, I am so predictable, really. No doubt I'll see Detective Francesco when I get back. I thought things must have changed when I saw the young man's face on the front of La Nazione this morning. My Italian isn't good enough to read the papers, but I managed to work out that he was now a missing person. How sad.* She hoped she sounded sincere and continued to maintain eye contact with Detective Borroni.

*Now that I'm no longer on the case, I guess we could have a coffee if you aren't in a hurry to get back. There's a nice cafe on the corner of the Piazza Davanzati.* Silence. She hadn't expected him to say this and wasn't sure how to react. Did he want to have a coffee with her or was he still on duty, looking for more information to pass on to his colleagues? Equally, she didn't want to say no. She liked his smiling face, she liked the thought of speaking to him, and she was flattered. Something she hadn't felt for a long time.

*It's just a coffee, Miss Hamilton.*

*Yes, that would be nice. Please call me Lesley; I feel like I'm a teacher again when I'm called Miss Hamilton.* She smiled broadly and genuinely for the first time. She would have the coffee and speak about anything apart from Pepe. It would be fine.

*I'm Diego.* He extended his hand towards her, and they laughed as they shook hands. Diego guided her towards the café, which was still quiet at this early hour. They sat down at a table on the edge of the terrace, which gave 180-degree views along the street. People watching was a full-time job in Florence no matter what time of day it was. They each ordered an espresso and a glass of water. She started the conversation.

*Where did you learn to speak such beautiful English?*

*I learnt it first at school and had an exchange month with a family in Cambridge when I was 16. That really improved my language skills. Just like you, I found it hard to understand everything when people spoke quickly and had to work hard to overcome that. But I was young and keen, so I did.* He leant his arms on the edge of the small table and smiled at Lesley, eager to find a connection with her. *Then I went to university in Milan and completed an English degree, which meant I had the opportunity to live in England for a year as part of that. I lived and worked in London for the year as an exchange student in four different schools. It was quite tough since learning Italian wasn't really the young people's favourite thing, but I persevered and enjoyed every minute of it. I met lots of interesting people and was able to travel a bit. I never made it to Scotland, I'm afraid, but guess I should have made more of an effort.*

Lesley was very surprised at how open and forthcoming Diego was. He was nothing like the policeman she met in her flat. She guessed there was no longer a focus for his interest in her and therefore he could be himself. He seemed keen to speak. And she felt herself keen to listen.

*You'll be pleased to hear that Detective Francesco also speaks English.* He slowly leant back in his chair, crossing his legs and looking along the street. *It isn't as good as mine, but then you can't have everything.* They both laughed.

*The police seems an odd choice after all that. Did you choose it, or did it choose you?*

*My father had been a policeman and I'd always been interested in his work. I guess I didn't know what I wanted to do, and the opportunity to be a fast-tracked graduate came up and I took it. It was a good move and not one I regret. I have had lots of interesting experiences, met really interesting people, and it has been quite exciting at times, so all in all, the right choice for me.* He didn't want to give any more details at this point and needed to switch the conversation, but he was too slow.

*Is your father still in the police? Do they live in Florence?*

*No, he's retired now. I was brought up just outside Milan in a small town called Cesate. My parents still live there. I don't see them as often as I should, but we speak on the phone two or three times a week. Thankfully, my sister lives nearer and is much more dutiful than me. Cesate was a great place to grow up — safe and quiet. I miss Milan but am getting used to Florence. I still find it amazing to live in a place where history hits you in the face every time you walk out your front door. There are plenty of places to escape the crowds, and the Tuscan scenery is so near at hand.* He paused. *Anyway, what brought you here?*

Lesley's story was a long one and one she rarely imparted when she first knew people, and Diego would be no different. She would give him the abbreviated version that she was comfortable with. She never understood why people needed to know every detail of each other's lives since the details were often hard to explain and even harder to understand. And so Diego got the simplified version. *It's not nearly as interesting as your story, I'm afraid. I got divorced and suddenly had money available to me that I didn't have before. So I saw it as my opportunity to finish the novel I've been writing for far too long. I knew I couldn't do that as long as I was teaching. It's a very all-consuming job, I'm afraid, although the holidays do compensate slightly for that. So I decided to have a year away from Scotland and simply write until I was finished and then work hard to get the book published. The cost of living in Florence meant that I would be able to do this without working as long as I didn't expect a lavish lifestyle, and so here I am.* He realised it explained the tiny flat and limited comforts.

*What did you teach? Not Italian, obviously?* She laughed and suddenly looked more relaxed.

*I taught children with autism. I had started out as an English teacher but realised early on that I couldn't see myself doing that forever. Autistic people are very interesting, and once I gave it a go, I knew it would keep me interested for years to come. Strangely, though, I haven't found myself missing it since I got here, but maybe that's just because I was needing a sabbatical of some description.*

*Where did you live in Scotland?* His phone vibrated on

the table, where he had placed it when they sat down. He apologised, picked it up and reverted to speaking in Italian. Lesley realised that would be the end of their conversation, and she thought she was sorry about that.

She was right.

*I'll have to go, Lesley, I'm afraid. I enjoyed speaking to you. Could we do it again?* He pushed the phone back into the inside pocket of his jacket, placed a 10 Euro note in the tray next to the bill and stood up.

She smiled up at him and confirmed she would like that. *I have your mobile number in my notebook. I'll call you tomorrow.* They shook hands, holding on to each other slightly longer than they would normally, and he left. Although the mention of his notebook had caused her a moment of anxiety, she was glad he was going to call.

Slowly but deliberately, Paolo came out from the dark entranceway where he'd been watching Lesley. And instead of walking towards her, he turned away from the cafe and disappeared into the crowds, staring determinedly at the cobbles, which were making it difficult for him to walk as quickly as he would have wanted to. He needed to leave Florence for now. Why was Diego Borroni there, and how did Lesley know him?

## Fourteen

Paolo was tired when he got back to Cesate. It was dark and late, later than he would have wanted. Driving had been difficult for him with so many muddled thoughts in his head, so he had stopped several times at motorway services. As always, he was careful to park under the trees in the unlit picnic area, where he could sit in the darkness and gather his thoughts. He wanted to walk in the fresh air but knew it would be hard to avoid the CCTV cameras, so he chose instead to remain in his car. His mother's voice was pounding in his head, reminding him of the need to remain alone and isolated and laughing at his attraction to Lesley. *What made you think she would want to hear about the weather again?*

It was too late to clear out the car on his return, so he drove it carefully into the garage, ensuring there was enough room for him to empty it in the morning without having to open the garage doors. The stairs took him up to the house, which was as he had left it. He went immediately to his mother's room and sat in the small chair, staring at the neatly made bed, hoping it would banish the multitude of thoughts in his head and give him the focus she had always been able to give him when he felt troubled. Although he felt calmer in the familiar surroundings and the pain at the front of his head was receding, he couldn't stop thinking about Lesley and what her relationship with Diego was. He wondered if he was jealous and tried to remember from books he'd read how people feel when they are jealous. It helped him a little, but not entirely, since he was certain anger was mixed up in his feelings. Anger that Lesley wasn't alone and anger that the one person who had made his young life bearable was now a friend of the only girl he had ever enjoyed speaking to.

The clock in the hall chimed 11, and he knew he needed to get back into his routine; it was his only means of coping with life. He straightened the cushion on the chair, switched off the lights, closed the door and went directly to bed. Sleep didn't come easily, but he did finally fall into a deep sleep, which was only broken when the alarm on his phone rang, indicating it was now 0730 and time to get back to a routine way of living.

For several days, Paolo immersed himself in the routines that he had become used to. He shopped early, ate at regular times, cleared out the car, washed everything he had taken with him, cleaned the car thoroughly and then returned to the routine jobs around the house. His sleeping pattern returned, and he was aware that his anxiety levels had fallen. He was able to cope with the thoughts in his head and box them up when he wanted to, unleashing them only when he felt it was safe to do so. Then he met Mrs Borroni.

It was an ordinary morning. The sun was warm for early in the day, so Paolo had taken his hat with him just in case he felt the need for shade. He walked to the supermarket via the path behind the Parrochia San Alessandro e San Martino. It was quiet, and with no wind blowing, the sun felt hot for eight in the morning. So he donned his hat and kept walking, smelling the scent of the many flowers that grew along the sides of the path. He did his shopping in the almost empty supermarket and was exiting via the automatic doors when a hand touched his shoulder. Over the years, he had learnt not to jump when someone touched him, and he understood that the pain he felt on his skin when the hand was removed wasn't how other people felt in the same situation. It was peculiar to him and people like him. He turned to see who had touched him, trying to ensure that his face remained neutral, the best he could do in this situation.

*Paolo Bianchi?* Initially he didn't recognise this elderly lady smiling up at him. She was smartly dressed, slim and upright, with a kind face. He smiled at her because he knew that was expected and was working hard to go through names and faces in his memory, trying to select the right one.

*Mrs Borroni. You went to school with my son, Diego. I'm sorry to have surprised you like that. It has been a long time since we've spoken, but I always spoke to your mother. It must be lonely for you on your own now.* She smiled straight at him, waiting for a response.

*How nice to see you, Mrs Borroni. Yes, it's been a long time. My mother used to tell me about your conversations. I'm doing fine, thank you.* Paolo was always aware that his responses sounded formulaic and contrived, but it was the only way he knew how to respond. What fascinated him was how the person receiving the words would react. Sometimes people just cut the conversation short, sometimes they just kept talking in the hope that Paolo wouldn't have to say anything else, and sometimes they carried on as if Paolo's responses were perfectly normal. Mrs Borroni fell into the last category since she knew of Paolo's difficulties and had always treated him just as she treated other schoolchildren her son knew.

*It's going to be a hot one today. I'm glad I decided to come out early. My husband doesn't like being left alone since his stroke, so I find it's always best to get all the jobs done as early in the day as possible.*

*I just like to be out when it's quiet.* Mrs Borroni knew that would be the case and was surprised she hadn't seen him more often since she generally completed all her shopping chores by 9.00 am. She was aware then that Paolo was speaking, catching the odd word here and there about today's weather forecast, and she smiled to herself as she remembered the many times she had had to reprimand Diego for complaining as Paolo regaled the family with the details of the weather forecast. *He doesn't know it's boring; it's what interests him, just as your interest in football is what you mainly want to talk about. The problem is it's his only interest, and so we must be patient.* Diego was never sure why his mother occasionally invited Paolo over to the house for the afternoon. He knew his mother felt sorry for Mrs Bianchi and her situation — a husband who spent as little time as possible at home and a son who found fitting in impossible. But Diego found those afternoons very difficult. Paolo was a star at school, particularly when it came to maths and science, but he never initiated conversations, nor did he want to take part in any games. He was, strangely, most comfortable in the company of the adults. Diego guessed they were more predictable.

*Well, it was lovely seeing you, Paolo. I better get back and see how Mr Borroni is.* All the time he had been speaking, Paolo was weighing up whether or not he should ask about Diego. He wanted to know why he was in Florence, but he knew it would seem strange if he were to ask such a personal question. Lesley was back in his head again, and the need to know more drove him on to speak. *How is Diego? Is he still in Milan?*

She had already turned to go off in the direction of her house when he spoke, and her surprise at him asking such a personal question was written all over her face. *Thank you for asking, Paolo. No, he is working in Florence now and has been since the start of the year. We don't see him as often as we used to, but his work keeps him very busy — there are always lots of crimes to solve, it would seem. I'll tell him you were asking for him. You take care, Paolo, and maybe we'll meet here at the supermarket again.*

She smiled at him, and he knew he was expected to smile back. So he did. He started his walk home, thinking about why Diego would have moved to Florence. But thinking about Diego also meant thinking about Lesley, and he didn't want to do that. He walked more quickly in an effort to clear his mind, but he knew it would be impossible.

He had always liked Diego, or at least he appreciated the fact that Diego was the one child at school who always spoke to him. They had attended the same schools and often found themselves in the same classes. Diego had stood up for him when others made fun of him, not knowing that it was of no consequence to Paolo when things were said about him. He knew it had been hard for Diego when he visited his house and he had to entertain him for the afternoon. But Paolo always appreciated the effort he made. He particularly appreciated his support when Diego's father, then Detective Borroni, had been investigating Father Rossi's murder.

It had been a very difficult case for the police and high profile, given Father Rossi's position in the community. The police knew from forensics that the person who murdered him couldn't be very tall nor very heavy. They just appeared to have an excellent technique and much determination. They knew there had been no break in, and nothing was disturbed in the house.

Although Father Rossi had been the priest in Cesate for many years, Detective Borroni knew that he wasn't liked in all quarters. He lacked empathy, and many people felt it was a job of routine for him rather than a vocation. Many people resented his abrupt manner, and he was certain that many in his congregation would have been happy to see the back of him. Happy enough to murder him? That was the question, but few answers were ever found.

With few answers to their many questions, the police started looking through the files for locals with a history of violence. Most didn't fit the profile. Most were grown men with a history of domestic violence or those who might get into a fight after drinking too much. But one name that came up and could fit the profile was that of Paolo Bianchi. Detective Borroni was surprised when he found the boy's file since no charges had ever been brought against Paolo. But someone must have been concerned enough about his actions to keep the file in case it was needed in the future.

Paolo was ten when the incident happened. Although he never considered it his fault, the killing of the cat had been both violent and sudden when described by both Paolo and the other children who witnessed it. It was lunchtime at school, and Paolo never ate with the other children. He preferred to sit outside alone, enjoying the fresh air and the quiet. The dinner hall was too noisy for him. He had noticed the cat sitting in the corner of the playground watching him but gave it very little thought. He continued eating, making sure that every part of his packed lunch was consumed. He always remembered the packed lunch had seemed bigger than usual that day and therefore took him longer to eat. Children were beginning to come out into the playground before he finished his lunch. This never happened, and he could feel his anxiety levels rising. Although no one came near him, he didn't want to eat with people looking at him, but he knew he had to finish it. That was what he always did.

As he reached out his hand to get the last piece of fruit from his box, the cat, who had made his way round to the bench and was sitting next to the lunch box, was frightened by the sudden movement and scratched him. The pain was both excruciating and surprising to Paolo. Unexpectedly, the cat remained sitting, and with a sudden lunge, Paolo grabbed it by its red collar and held it up in the air in front of him. He pulled and pulled on the collar, twisting it at the same time, driving all the air out of the cat until it was limp and still. He laid it on the ground and continued eating his lunch.

Those in the playground stood either in stunned silence or were screaming as they watched the killing unfold. The head teacher was summoned, and along with two staff who had responded to the commotion, they stood in front of Paolo, astonished that he would continue eating. He didn't look up until he had finished eating and was spoken to.

Although an investigation was undertaken within the school, the owners of the cat called the police, who also carried out an investigation. Paolo's condition was much discussed, and given the nature of the incident and the fact that he readily admitted to the killing, no charges were brought. But the nature of the killing had a dramatic effect on how others viewed Paolo and how he was supervised in the future. He was never alone eating his lunch again. And his mother spent many months ensuring he learnt what he could and could not do. He attended a child psychiatrist to help him understand his condition, how that was viewed and how to deal with the unexpected, even if it caused him physical pain. He was a good learner and had continued his daily life in Cesate with few other problems.

It was six months after he murdered Father Rossi that Detective Borroni visited him at home in his capacity as a policeman. He came just after school and spoke to him in the presence of his mother. It wasn't a formal interview — he would have needed more evidence for that — but it felt formal to Paolo's mother and to Paolo himself. He was asked lots of questions about the day Father Rossi had died, most of which he was unable to answer. His mother kept saying, *it's been six months. How could you expect him to remember?*

It was easy to forget. As long as he didn't open that box neatly tucked away at the back of his mind, he wouldn't remember. He told Detective Borroni the things he did remember about the day but nothing else. His mother remained silent on their evening visit to the church for confession. The interview passed and Mr Borroni never revisited the conversation. Father Rossi's murder remained an open case.

*He's very timid, Dad. He doesn't speak to anyone. I'm the only one who looks out for him and the only one who has to have him round to their house.* Diego looked directly at his mother when he said this, and she smiled. *He's not that strange, just quiet and keeps himself to himself.* It had been a general conversation, and Diego hadn't even been aware he was defending a suspect. It was a detective's conversation — suck them in and get them talking. Diego would have known exactly what his father was doing now, but not then.

## Fifteen

As promised, Diego phoned Lesley the following day and dinner arrangements for later in the week were made. Agreeing to go hadn't been difficult, but she was surprised at the anxiety it induced. It had been a long time since she last went out on a date, and she was no longer sure of the rules, if such rules existed. Although she continued with her usual routines, she found herself thinking often about what she would wear, what she would talk about and what she would do at the end of the evening. But despite this anxiety, she was also excited and pleased to find she could still make connections with others that might be more than friendship. She wrote furiously, passing her daily word target every day.

Although Pepe's disappearance continued to feature in the local newspapers, Lesley now thought infrequently of the events of that day. Although she felt she should have behaved differently, several weeks had now passed and nothing else had happened. Detective Francesco had spoken to her as part of his enquiries, but nothing additional had come of that and she was glad to retell her story, the same story she had told Diego. It almost seemed to be the real story now, and she rarely ventured back to the exact details of the day in her mind. Detective Francesco did not appear to doubt any aspect of her story and confirmed what she said matched with that of others. He smiled a great deal, and she felt safe. And, although his English wasn't as good as Diego's, they got through the interview by helping each other with a bit of English and a bit of Italian. She was glad it was done.

Diego called for her as agreed at 8.00 pm. He looked pleased to see her and smiled as she came through the door into the Via Porta Rossa. They kissed on both cheeks before turning away from the city and walking down towards the Arno. Diego, with a confidence that was escaping her, put his hand in his trouser pocket and linked her arm through his. It felt comfortable and safe, and Lesley liked that. The conversation started slowly as she had expected, but soon, Diego was giving her a brief history of the buildings they were passing and other aspects of the city. Lesley enjoyed listening. Diego was conscious of speaking too much but didn't know what else to do. He was aware Lesley was still smiling and appeared to be listening, but he knew talking was simply a way of covering his own anxieties. He hoped he would be able to stop and let her speak.

They crossed the Arno at the Ponte alla Carraia, watching the May sun set over the city as the sky became increasingly red, causing the buildings to turn into black silhouettes. Diego had stopped talking. They smiled at each other, then moved on towards Il Santo Bevitore and their dinner. Lesley hadn't been out for an evening meal since arriving in Florence and was much looking forward to the experience. And it didn't disappoint. The food was excellent and the atmosphere relaxed, and she was relieved to find they had plenty to speak about. Books, films, Florence museums, the Tuscan countryside and food. They had steered away from anything too personal, both feeling but not acknowledging that it could wait for a future date, if there was to be a future date. Age had made them both more protective of their pasts.

Without prompting, Lesley took Diego's arm as they said their goodbyes to the staff and left the restaurant, heading into the cool air of the night. Lesley had donned her shawl and was glad of the additional warmth from

Diego's arm as they walked back to the Via Porta Rossa. They said little on their return journey, simply enjoying each other's presence and both reflecting on how much they had enjoyed the evening. They reached Lesley's building and looked at each other. Lesley spoke first.

*I'm not quite sure what to do now. It's been a long time since I went out for an evening with anyone. I've had a really lovely time, really enjoyed it. Thank you so much.* She stepped towards him, and without another word, he wrapped his arms around her and kissed her gently on the lips. She responded in kind, then they separated. The ice had been broken, but neither was sure yet whether they wanted to go further.

*How would you like to go to Lucca at the weekend? We could drive up, have a look around and maybe take a picnic? The Serchio River is really lovely, perfect for a picnic and a walk.*

Lesley smiled her agreement and arrangements were made. They kissed for a second time, slowly and gently. Diego started to walk away, continuing to touch her arm until he could reach it no longer. It had been an evening he hadn't imagined could go so well, and he felt suddenly quite different about his move to Florence.

Two men stepped out from the alley next to the Hotel Davanzati, one of them lighting a cigarette as they walked along the Via Porta Rossa, following Diego on his journey home. Neither of them spoke, and although it was clear they were following him, they ensured they kept a good distance, appearing to be simply two of the few people still out in the city. Diego was oblivious to their presence, too busy thinking about the trip to Lucca.

Diego headed back towards the Arno and walked briskly towards his rented flat close to the Florence

University of the Arts. Its small roof terrace gave him a lovely view of the city with its many buildings illuminated at night to meet the demands of tourists. It was smaller than his flat in Milan, but the outside space gave it a dimension he didn't have in his own home. Maybe he would sell the Milan flat. Maybe he would buy in Florence now. Maybe he was jumping the gun. He smiled to himself, turned the key in the lock, checked for mail and began to climb the stairs.

Luca and Lorenzo Poccini continued their evening walk, passing Diego as he turned the key in the lock and entered the building. They wanted to confirm the address given to them by Detective Francesco before making any decisions. Now they were certain Detective Francesco could be trusted, they would ensure two of their men followed Diego day and night. His presence in the city made them suspicious — made them wonder if he was involved in their brother's disappearance.

*

Detective Alessandro Francesco had worked in Florence for many years and was nearing his longed-for retirement. He had had an unblemished career and was highly respected within his division. He had solved many cases where people had suddenly and abruptly disappeared as well as having some cases that remained open since he knew about and had been instrumental in the disappearance of those individuals. He had always been careful to reject any contact with organised crime in the city and the surrounding area but had been happy to make links with those who clung to the edges of organised crime across the north of Italy, and he made good money from it. The man he knew as Franco had ensured that Detective Francesco could influence events to benefit others and then be handsomely paid for his silence. He could make evidence disappear, he could ensure crime scenes were tidied up, and he could ensure assassins were never found.

Alessandro made sure he lived a quiet life, the best way to stay anonymous and unnoticed. He and his wife had a small house in the northern suburb of Novoli. They had bought it twenty years earlier when they moved to Florence from Rome and had always been happy there. They didn't need more room than they had, but Detective Francesco often imagined life elsewhere once he retired. The money he had made and kept secret for so many years needed to be used, and he was sure it would cover the cost of a modest villa on the coast. He would just need to persuade his wife it would be a good idea. This would be less easy since she had always enjoyed life in Florence, and although the sale of her art depended on a large tourist body, he hoped she would be able to give up this aspect of her life and move elsewhere. He had started mentioning the benefits of life by the sea, but she had just smiled, making no comment when he said a villa would be possible since he would have a good pension and his savings. He wasn't sure whether the smile was one of agreement or simply her way of saying nothing. It had been this way for many years.

When Franco contacted him regarding the disappearance of Pepe Poccini, he felt something was different about Franco's manner and conversation. Franco explained that the Poccini family had been in touch with him and were concerned about Detective Borroni's presence in the city and any involvement he might have in the case. Although Alessandro knew Diego had been transferred to Florence under a cloud, he had no details of why. Franco was able to fill in those details, but when asked if he had any knowledge of or involvement in Pepe's disappearance, Franco was evasive. Although he often gave only limited information to Alessandro, he had never avoided answering a question but had given definite answers, whether true or not.

His stumbling responses made Alessandro certain he must know more than he was saying. And if he did, Pepe hadn't disappeared. He'd been murdered.

# Sixteen

Franco was unhappy with and worried about the current situation and his involvement in it. Over the years, he had always maintained a healthy distance from the work carried out on behalf of his clients. He had five assassins on his books and had made sure each never knew about the others. He gave out instructions and all necessary details, and then it was up to the chosen assassin to ensure the job was carried out. Once complete, money would be quietly transferred to ensure everyone was kept happy.

Up until now, Paolo had been Franco's preferred man for most jobs. He planned meticulously and carried out the appointed job without any questions. This was what he'd expected this time as well. And had that happened, he would not now be facing the need to lie about his involvement in or knowledge of Pepe's murder to both the Poccini family and his reliable agent in Florence, Alessandro Francesco. He would not now be working for both the instigators of the assassination and those whose son had been the victim. Alessandro Francesco had helped Franco with numerous hits in Florence over the years by 'losing' evidence, ensuring things were cleared up, or assisting one of his operatives when things hadn't quite gone to plan. Thankfully, Paolo had never needed assistance until now, and although Franco had often told Alessandro stories of Paolo's expert work, he did not use his name, nor had they ever met. He needed it to remain that way.

For many years, Franco had worked on the periphery of organised crime in the north of Italy but was now feeling it needed to come to an end. In the same way the sons of doctors became doctors themselves, the sons of criminals often found themselves involved in the criminal world as adults. His father had done this job before him, and after his suicide, Franco had taken over the role more than happily. It paid well, it didn't involve any direct action, and it allowed him to maintain a lifestyle he rather enjoyed. Like Paolo, he still lived in the family villa. Built on the coast of Tuscany some miles south of the bustling city of Livorno, his father had wanted a quick exit by sea if there was ever a need for it, and so the view across the Ligurian Sea towards Corsica and the coast of France had become a reassuringly daily part of his life. The infinity swimming pool which now filled a large part of the garden, along with the new garage housing two vintage cars, were evidence of his wealth and things he wanted to enjoy.

Although the job wasn't stressful on a day-to-day basis, Franco now found himself waking in the night gasping for breath and sweating. His dreams would be vivid and always involved his own death — either murder or suicide. People would be weeping by his grave, chanting his name and the names of all those whose deaths he had arranged but never carried out himself. As a young man, he had often heard his father screaming in the night as he too dreamt of the many murders he had sanctioned, and Franco knew he didn't want to be the next suicide in the family. He wanted to enjoy the money he'd accumulated and build relationships with others that didn't involve silence and secrets. It was a lonely life that he wanted to escape from.

And, like Paolo, something had changed. His situation seemed complicated and unresolvable. He knew that he was the only person who knew the whole story and could answer the endless questions that appeared daily in the newspapers as the Poccinis sought to know what happened to their son. The Poccinis had been good customers over the years and deceiving them now seemed wrong. He was surprised he still had a conscience.

*

Diego's week seemed to pass slowly as he waited for Saturday to arrive. He thought about phoning Lesley, but he had made that mistake before — too keen. He needed to take it slowly; he needed to be certain before committing. Police work in Florence seemed to come in cycles. Days of paperwork would seem interminable, then a case would land on his desk and need his full attention. Robberies, assaults, but rarely murder. He had grown to accept that his work life would never be as fulfilling as it was in Milan, but there were other benefits. He had time to read, walk, go to the cinema, visit galleries and tend to the small array of plants on his terrace, and now he had time to get to know Lesley. His weekends and his evenings were now his own.

And Saturday was one of those days. As he drove slowly up the ramp from the darkness of the underground garage into the bright May sunshine, he could feel the excitement and apprehension of seeing Lesley again. The weather was set to be warm, and he knew the drive to Lucca would be beautiful once they left the motorway and headed towards the ancient city with its Roman remnants, beautiful squares and ancient monuments. A walk by the river and the picnic lunch he'd prepared would make it a perfect day.

He could see Lesley standing by the front door of the

flats as he drove along the Via Porta Rossa. Her head was turned up to the sun, with her blonde hair hanging its full length down her back. Diego thought she looked beautiful and remembered her text from yesterday: *Really looking forward to tomorrow and seeing you. Do I need to bring anything? L.*

He brought the car slowly to a stop right next to her, and she laughed. A nervous laugh, she thought. Diego got out of the driving seat, kissed her gently just as she remembered it from the other night and held open the passenger door, and she climbed in. Her opinion on whether they should travel with the roof down or not was sought, and the decision wasn't difficult. Of course they should. She found a scrunchy in the bottom of her bag, tied her hair loosely in it and donned her sunglasses. She hoped the rest of the day would be as much fun as the road trip was about to be.

And she wasn't disappointed. Lesley hadn't been out of Florence since her arrival in January, and although she had planned to see the area around the city by train or bus, she had felt an urgency to keep writing. It was the reason she was there. She had to make it work if she was going to change her life. And that was something she was determined to do.

Conversation came easily during the journey. There was lots to comment on, particularly when they left the A11 at Pistoia and meandered their way through the Tuscan countryside, which looked green and fresh in the May sunshine. Diego enjoyed telling her about his childhood in Cesate and the many adventures, both good and bad, he had had. He spoke fondly of his parents and his sister. As he spoke, he knew he should make more of an effort to visit them. He knew they would like that. He knew they would like Lesley. Maybe that could be his reason.

Diego's voice was always soft and gentle, even when he was telling a story that involved much animation on his part and much laughter on hers. Lesley liked that. She wouldn't go back to barbs and jibes; she wouldn't go back to being quiet so that everything would go along smoothly. She would learn to be herself at all times, and if it wasn't what he was looking for, she would stop seeing Diego. But she couldn't imagine that now. It felt comfortable and easy in a way she knew now she had never been with her husband. Why couldn't she see it then? A question she asked herself often but never had an answer to. A question she had to let go. Maybe she could now.

Lesley spoke about her childhood, telling stories of family holidays, school, dancing, football and friends. Friends who had felt it keenly when she left Scotland for Italy, friends who agreed with her family that it was a risk she maybe shouldn't take. She hoped they would see it differently now, and she knew they would if she could get her novel published. That was her drive: she had to prove them wrong. She wondered if changing the assumptions of others was what always drove her.

Diego listened attentively to the stories, making pertinent comments as needed, and he enjoyed seeing Lesley smile at him every time he did this. She seemed eager to talk and eager to help him see who she was then and who she was now. Previous relationships would be avoided for now, but he knew it would have to be a topic for discussion at some point. Their pasts included people that couldn't be ignored, people who had shaped who they were now.

As they drove round the city walls of Lucca, all conversation stopped. The ochre stone of the walls shone brightly, and Lesley was mesmerised by both their beauty and permanence. They stood tall and thick, protecting the city from enemies who no longer existed. Diego found a parking space, and soon they were walking on the city walls, viewing the buildings from a different perspective, looking down on clay tiles from various centuries and looking up at towers and domes adorning Lucca's many relics. Conversation became less personal and focused on the city. Diego, just as he had done in Florence, was able to fill in some of the gaps in her knowledge. He was able to give historical context to the buildings, and Lesley enjoyed listening to this walking encyclopaedia. They held hands as they walked, and every now and then, Diego would put his arm around her waist, pull her close, kiss her gently on the lips and smile at her. Lesley liked that and hung on to his hand even when it would have been easier to let it go and walk in single file.

After the walk around the walls, they meandered through the narrow streets, emerging every now and then into large sunlit squares. Cafes were dotted throughout the city, and they enjoyed a break for coffee at one hidden in the corner of the Piazza dell'Anfiteatro. Lucca's beauty seemed to be encapsulated in the buildings found in this square, their ancient stone and tiles reflecting the heat of the sun. They walked slowly back to the car and drove away from the city walls towards the River Serchio. Diego had clearly picnicked by the river before. He parked in a quiet spot on the opposite bank which afforded beautiful views of the city, collected the picnic from the boot and led the way down to the riverbank. Lesley followed silently and without question, taking in the tranquillity and silence of the place. She felt suddenly frightened. Not a physical fear that something terrible was going to happen but a fear of being happy again. Ten years of a difficult marriage had blunted her confidence in being able to build a positive, fulfilling relationship, but she knew she wanted to try to do that very thing with this man, who was spreading a bright red rug on the grass and laying out a picnic that looked like it held enough for ten. She watched him from a distance and tried to find that optimism which she knew she had hidden deep in her. The optimism that made her believe she could finish her novel, the optimism she had that she could live in another country alone, and the optimism she knew she'd had as a child, enjoying every experience life could throw at her.

*Lunch!* He smiled directly at her and she thought she might cry, she felt so happy. Instead, she smiled and sat down amongst the mountains of food and laughed.

*Did you think you were feeding the five thousand?* She leant across, placing her hand on his cheek before kissing him. *It's perfect. Thank you.*

The day meandered on in the way only Italians know how. Nothing else seemed to matter; it was as if only the two of them and this place existed. Time was of no importance. Once sated with food, they walked along the river enjoying the lush greenness that would change to brown once the summer heat took hold. They both enjoyed being out of the bustle of Florence, and without saying anything, they knew their lives had changed. They knew they wanted this, whatever it was, to continue.

The drive back was quicker as they raced along the motorway, heading back to the reality of their lives. As they neared Florence and the light was fading, Diego asked, *would you like to come back to my flat? It has lovely views over the city. We could have dinner and ...* They looked at each other and laughed. Lesley squeezed his hand on the steering wheel and kissed him gently on the cheek.

*Sounds a perfect end to a perfect day.* And it was.

## Seventeen

Lesley and Diego's lives found a different routine, but a routine, nevertheless. Diego would leave for work at eight every morning when she stayed over, and Lesley would take her time over breakfast and her shower before returning to her own flat to write. She would pick up lunch en route and spend her days filling the pages of her novel with more words than she thought possible. Her happiness appeared to have given her more focus, and she felt confident now that she would finish the novel in the next two months, giving her plenty of time to work on getting it published. It all seemed too perfect, but she had decided to enjoy every moment of it, intending to make it last.

Diego's flat was very comfortable, more comfortable than her own but lacking in personal touches. She realised her own flat, although she thought of it as homely, really wasn't, given there was very little of her in it. And Diego's flat was the same. But she liked being there, being near Diego and sharing her past and present with him. It felt very comfortable, and she found herself staying there more often than at her own flat. They had started discussing her moving in, and although she wanted this, she still felt concerned that it was too soon. This routine suited her very well at the moment. And she thought it suited him.

Diego leaned across the bed to kiss her and say goodbye. She was shocked that she was still asleep and hadn't heard him getting up. But the storm had made it very hard to sleep — lightning every few minutes and rolling thunder that echoed around the streets of Florence almost all night. *Don't rush to get up. You didn't get much sleep. I'll pick up dinner and see you tonight.* His lingering kiss made her want to pull him back into the bed, but she didn't. They both had work to do. She smiled. He left.

It was nearer ten before Lesley was ready to leave. When she reached the street, she realised it was still raining and she had no umbrella with her. She returned to the flat, grabbed the black umbrella that stood to attention at the front door and headed back out. As she stood under the portico grappling with the umbrella, she noticed a young man on the other side of the road looking straight at her as she raised the umbrella above her head. He was also standing under a black umbrella although he was wearing a black raincoat that reached his knees and gave him plenty of protection from the heavy rain that was bouncing on the concrete pavements and making everyone's feet wet. He carried his tall, heavy frame well, and his blonde hair was neatly clipped, giving him a severe expression. He maintained his gaze on Lesley and nodded. She looked around, hoping there was someone else standing behind her. There wasn't. He was nodding at her, but she didn't know him. She lowered her umbrella and headed out into the rain.

The walk to her flat took only 20 minutes normally, but it took longer today as she tried to avoid the puddles and the umbrellas being carried by everyone as they wandered round the city. She hurried as much as she could, desperate to check she wasn't being followed. She knew he was behind her when she reached the Ponte Vecchio and turned to cross the road. But when she reached her flat, he was nowhere to be seen. She turned the key as quickly as she could, pushing the heavy door and stumbling into the entrance.

*How nice to see you, Lesley.* Signora Conti was sweeping the entrance just as she did every day. *Don't see you as often now. How are things going with Detective Borroni?* Lesley was unsure how Signora Conti knew about Diego, but she guessed she was good at putting two and two together. There was very little that got past Signora Conti. She realised Lesley was surprised at the question. *Detective Francesco told me.*

Lesley knew she was expected to speak, but she really wasn't sure what to say. *Yes, things are going fine. We're very happy.* It sounded like the kind of answer you would give in a court room or when being questioned. Was she being questioned? Lesley hadn't thought about Pepe for several weeks and she didn't want to think about it again. It was enough that it was still in the newspapers on a daily basis, but now she wondered why Detective Francesco would have been back speaking to Signora Conti. She decided to change the subject and moved towards the stairs as she spoke. *It's a terrible day. I'll be glad to get in my flat and get writing. No sunshine to miss today.*

As Lesley placed her foot on the bottom step, Signora Conti continued speaking. *Detective Francesco was here on behalf of the Poccini family, who want to speak to all the residents about Pepe's disappearance. They hope there might be something that has been missed by the police that will help in finding him. I think Detective Francesco was a bit insulted by the implication, but I said I would be willing to meet them. I suggested you and I meet them together. I can help with any translation issues, and it would give each of us some moral support. I hope you're happy with that. He's going to let me know when they can come, and I'll let you know. I'll pop a note through your door if I don't see you.*

Lesley felt sick and was certain her colour had changed. She couldn't refuse the request without arousing suspicion, but every thought in her head was rejecting the idea. She turned back and smiled. *That would be fine, Signora Conti. How kind of you to organise it for me.*

*It's nothing, nothing at all. I'll let you know as soon as I hear.* She turned back to her sweeping and Lesley began walking up the stairs, passing the spot where she had found Pepe, and once again, his face was in her head. His face and the halo of blood. It wasn't a good day. Few words were added to the novel as Lesley debated how she would tell Diego about the day's events.

The sun finally emerged late in the afternoon, and after such a fruitless day, Lesley decided she would try to clear her head by taking a walk to the Boboli Gardens. Their hidden sculptures lurking behind plants and bushes always surprised Lesley, and the view of Florence was always one to enjoy. It would give her something else to think about. She exited the flats quietly without meeting any of her neighbours. The door felt heavy as she closed it, heavier than usual, but she was glad to have avoided Signora Conti. The sun was warm now and the steam was rising from the water-drenched streets. Soon, all evidence of the storms would be gone.

The sun was in her eyes as she turned, and at first, she didn't notice him. It was only when she turned back, alerted by the sound of a bicycle bell, that she saw him standing in the middle of the Via Porta Rossa watching her. She knew she shouldn't have, but she stopped. She stopped and stared right back at him. Although she could feel fear pounding in her chest, Lesley didn't know what else to do. She knew that facing fear was better than running from it. She should have done that more often in her life and maybe she could have changed the narrative sooner. But then she thought of Diego, his smiling face, his soft touch and his generosity of spirit, and she knew the events of her life had brought her to this moment. She couldn't regret them now.

Now holding the black umbrella tightly in his right hand and with his raincoat draped over his other arm, he smiled directly at Lesley, turned around and walked away from her. Although relieved he had gone, she wanted to run after him, confront him, find out who he was. Diego would know what to do. He would help her.

The gardens had their desired effect. Lesley felt much better, and this being late in the afternoon, most tourists were leaving the city, and she was able to enjoy the vastness of the gardens without meeting too many people. As she stood admiring Neptune's Fountain, her phone rang loudly, breaking the spell and the quiet all around her. It was Diego.

*Lesley? Are you okay? I was getting worried. You're usually here before I get back. Has something happened?* Lesley looked at her watch and realised she had been in the gardens longer than she intended. She felt sorry for worrying Diego.

*Not a very good day on the writing front, I'm afraid, so I decided to go for a walk when the sun came out. I'm in the Boboli Gardens. I'll leave now and be with you in 15 minutes. Sorry, Diego, I just forgot the time.* She would tell him the rest when she saw him. He told her he loved her, and she smiled.

*Ciao.*

Dinner was ready when she arrived. She returned the umbrella to its lonely sentry duty at the front door, found

Diego in the kitchen and hugged him tightly from behind as he stirred a bubbling tomato sauce and supervised a mountain of spaghetti. He turned slowly, careful not to spill anything, and reciprocated. *Dinner is ready. Thought we could eat on the terrace? Then you can tell me all about your day.*

Lesley carried out plates and wine as directed, and soon Diego was ready to hear the story of her day. Diego listened intently to the story of the man following Lesley and realised his brain was once again in police mode. He wanted to ask her questions, get a description, get as many details as possible that might let him find out who this man was. He knew Lesley was giving him only facts, and he knew, now that she felt safe, the strangeness of the experience would be diluted. Although glad that would be the case, he was sorry she had had a day full of anxiety. He didn't want that for her.

As he processed the story of the man, he was suddenly conscious that another story was now being told ... *the Poccinis want to meet all the neighbours to see if there is anything that has been missed by the police that could lead to them finding Pepe.* She maintained her eye contact with Diego, terrified if she didn't, he would see her guilt. *Signora Conti is going to let me know when a time is arranged and we're going to meet them together for moral support. She can also help with translation issues. Detective Francesco is going to get back to Signora Conti once he's spoken to the family.*

Diego had put down his cutlery and was looking at her in a way she hadn't seen before. Neither of them spoke. Finally Diego broke the silence. *I need to tell you something, Lesley.* A new fear had taken over now. She didn't want anything to change, but she felt it was about to.

Diego told Lesley about his work in Milan and what he had been involved in. He gave her details of how organised crime is run in Italy and the way in which his team worked to counteract its effects and arrest those at the heart of it. He explained the complexities of the Poccini case for his team and that although they were certain the family were involved in organised crime, they had no way to prove it. He explained it had then become his obsession and he had taken matters into his own hands. He related the story of his encounter with the Poccinis at Lake Como and the consequences of that. He explained he had been demoted and moved to Florence after pressure from the Poccini family and was then taken off Pepe's case once his identity as a missing person was established.

Lesley was silent. Her food suddenly felt heavy on her stomach, and she could feel a slight perspiration on her forehead. 'Organised Crime'. These were the only words she could register. She could hear Diego's voice, but no words were penetrating the panic that had now taken hold of her brain. *I don't think it's wise to meet with the Poccinis. Let me think about how we can get round that. I would come with you, but that would just antagonise the situation. It is voluntary, after all. But if everyone else has spoken to them, then it will seem strange if you don't. I'm not sure what to do.* Diego was on his feet now, pacing to and fro across the narrow terrace. Lesley could see and feel his worry. She didn't want him to worry. As far as Diego was aware, she had nothing to hide and there was nothing to worry about in speaking to the Poccinis. She had a solid story that she would not deviate from. They wouldn't know about her connection with Diego.

She would speak to them. And she said so. He agreed.

# Eighteen

Diego knew it wasn't usual for a member of the Carabinieri to organise meetings for a family who had a missing child. They would pass on all the information they felt was pertinent and they would maintain very close links with the family through a liaison officer, but they wouldn't involve themselves in blurring the lines. It was easy to blur the lines in police work. But the Poccinis, as he knew, had influential friends and they never hesitated to call on them when the family was under threat. And he knew they would be feeling under threat now. Pepe was his father's pride and joy: articulate, intellectual and untouched by the family business.

Diego wanted to find out whether Francesco had been ordered to organise these meetings or whether he was doing this under coercion from the family. But his interest had to appear casual and without the intensity he felt every time he thought about the Poccinis and the influence they had had on his life. Diego's life with Lesley gave him a joy he hadn't felt for a long time, and he didn't want that to change. He wanted to keep her safe from the world he had once worked in, but it seemed to be creeping into the world he had now created, and he knew he would do whatever it took to prevent that from happening.

Francesco's team were housed on the floor above Diego, making it difficult to casually bump into Francesco and ask him how things were going. Although he found it hard, Diego resisted the temptation to speak to Francesco in his office and waited patiently for his opportunity to speak to him in a communal part of the building — the lift, the canteen, the large foyer that led you in from the hustle of Florence to the quiet of the Carabinieri.

Much to his surprise, Lesley didn't seem to be dwelling on the upcoming meeting, nor did she report any further incidents of being followed. But she was spending every night at his flat. He liked that, and although she denied it was related to the Poccini meeting and the strange blonde man who had followed her home, he was pleased to see her back to the Lesley he loved — smiling, chatty, laughing. Her writing was going well, the novel was nearing its end, and he was to be the first to read it.

As she had with the sight of Pepe's body and her error of judgement in taking the phone, Lesley had put the prospect of the meeting far back in her mind, concentrating instead on her writing and her life with Diego. She knew staying with Diego every night was partly linked to a fear of being alone in her flat when the police or the Poccinis might call, but it was also due to a confidence in the depth of the relationship and a certainty that she wanted it to continue. Forever wasn't something she had considered a possibility since her divorce, but Diego seemed as near to forever as she could think of. Talking was easy, silence was calming rather than threatening, laughing came easily, and the tenderness of his love was evident in all his actions. He was interested in every aspect of her life and made her feel like the most important person in the world.

She knew Diego was worried about her meeting with the Poccinis, but as the days passed, he asked her about it less frequently and she began to feel it might not happen at all. She thought she might have convinced Diego to think about it in the same way. Two weeks had passed since Signora Conti had spoken to her, and now there was more to be excited about. Diego wanted to take her to Cesate to meet his parents. He wanted them to see how happy she had made him and how his life had changed. He wanted them to know he had moved on and that he had found a meaning to life outwith his work. His father knew that was important and had worried that Diego might never find it.

May was passing and the heat in Florence was increasing. It would be nice to go north, to see something different and to become part of a new life beyond the small world she and Diego had created. Lesley wanted to be able to speak in Italian when she met his parents and was glad they had agreed to speak Italian at home every second day, with English being the language of choice in between. She knew her Italian was improving, and Diego was enjoying rediscovering his excellent English. Everything was arranged. They would spend a long weekend with his parents starting next Friday.

They left Florence early on the Friday morning, planning to stop in Milan for lunch at one of Diego's favourite restaurants — Al Cantinone, an old-fashioned trattoria specialising in traditional Italian cuisine, Lesley's favourite dining experience. Diego chose the direct route via the A1, taking them from the Tuscan hills to the flatness of Milan and its surrounding area, with the mountains surrounding the lakes in the north a tantalising view in the distance. Lesley had visited Milan when she was a student, but she had forgotten how beautiful it was. Not beautiful in the way Florence is with tiny alleys, low buildings, intimate squares and cobbled streets. But grand and expansive with tall buildings, boulevards and grand squares. It was exciting to be somewhere different, and once again, Diego was an excellent guide. Although they couldn't visit Diego's flat, which he was now renting out, they walked past the building, and Diego entertained her with a graphic description of its interior. Lunch was excellent as she'd expected, then they headed north once again to Cesate and his parents' home. Lesley could feel both her anxiety and excitement mount as they drew nearer. She sat silently in the car, admiring the scenery and rehearsing her Italian greetings. Diego was also silent. It had been many months since he last visited his parents. He felt guilty about that, but he found his father's stroke very hard to deal with. The man he had played football with, gone fishing with, cycled through the countryside with, was now unable to do any of these things. His speech had been affected, and often he used words he would never have used before — often racist and blasphemous. His mother explained these were probably easier to get out and not always what his father meant, but Diego found it hard to see how the man whose ability to use the most appropriate language for every situation had disappeared. Although his father took a walk every day to maintain his mobility, Diego knew this was done mainly at his mother's behest, and the pain etched on his father's face as he did what was asked of him made Diego feel a depth of sadness he found hard to cope with. His father's love for his mother was evident in every slow step.

They drew up outside the house in Via Isonzo: a two-storey building with the garage tucked underneath the main living area, keeping the car cool in summer and warm in winter when the snow arrived. A typical Italian house design. Diego told Lesley to stay in the car while he opened the tall metal gates and drove into the short driveway, parking directly in front of the garage door. She thought Diego looked a little anxious. Before leaving the car, she took his hand and squeezed it hard before kissing him lightly on the lips. She smiled a certainty she wasn't feeling at that moment. She wanted to get it right.

As they got their bags from the boot, a cheerful voice called out to them. *Welcome, welcome. How nice to meet you, Lesley.* Before she had time to reply, a small lady with grey hair was holding her by the top of her arms and kissing her on both cheeks. She looked carefully at Lesley, smiling broadly as she took in her age, her soft face, her smile and her relaxed style. She seemed perfect, different to Tanya — no fixed smile, no makeup and no need to show her success through her clothes. Perfect. Without a second glance at Diego, who was closing the boot and picking up the bags, she took Lesley by the arm and walked with her towards the stairs, taking them up to the front door of the house. *It's such a lovely day, we've been sitting on the veranda enjoying the garden. I'll take you round to meet Diego's father while Diego takes the bags inside.* With a wave of her hand, she directed Diego into the house while she led Lesley round the veranda which covered three sides of the house to meet Signor Borroni. Lesley wasn't sure whether all the rushing was simply Signora Borroni's anxiety or whether her years of teaching meant that once she had decided on a plan, she wanted to put it into action. Either way, Lesley felt welcome.

*Here we are, Piero. This is Lesley.* Standing in front of his seat, leaning heavily on his stick, was Diego's father, pulling himself up to his full height and smiling directly at her with those same clear grey eyes she loved on Diego's face. He reached out towards her with his left hand, and without a second thought, Lesley took his hand and continued to hold it as he said hello.

*Why don't we sit down?* Piero smiled at her and slowly lowered himself to his seat, still holding on to Lesley's hand, using her strength to prevent his frailty from causing him to fall over. Lesley sat next to him, close enough that he could continue holding her hand. *What a lovely view of the garden you have from here. It's a lovely garden; you must spend a lot of time in it to get so many beautiful flowers, Signora Borroni.*

*Call me Lucia. Signora Borroni reminds me of being a teacher. Far too formal.* Lucia sat down next to Lesley on the small cane sofa that faced directly on to the garden. *Yes, I enjoy the garden very much. It's always nice to have fresh flowers for the house. And it keeps me fit.* She squeezed the muscles at the top of her arms and laughed. They all laughed.

*I had a garden when I lived in Scotland, and sometimes I miss it. But Florence has some beautiful parks, and there are always the few plants on Diego's terrace to attend to. And attention is something they really need.*

Diego stood quietly at the corner of the veranda, watching the three of them as they chatted about the garden, the house, Cesate. Lesley continued to hold his father's hand until he let it go, and she slowly slid her hand back on her lap. Although she had to pause now and again to formulate her sentences, Lesley was holding her own without any help from him, and for the first time, he realised that her ability to make you feel at ease wasn't exclusive to him. Lesley turned to look at a plant Lucia was pointing out in the garden and noticed Diego lurking at the corner to the terrace. She smiled at him and carried on with her conversation. They stood up to see the plant more clearly, leaning over the edge of the terrace, the sun highlighting Lesley's blonde hair. Lucia took her son's hand, pulling him down so she could kiss him on the cheek before taking Lesley's arm and heading to the garden for a tour. Diego sat down next to his father, took his hand, squeezed it gently and smiled. They sat in silence, content that the weekend was going to work out well and that Diego had made a good choice in Lesley.

# Nineteen

Lesley discovered the life Diego had enjoyed as a child, the places he played, the schools where he was educated, the outings he'd enjoyed with his family and the certainty his childhood had given him so that he could cope with life as an adult. They took Diego's parents out for lunch, an experience neither of them had had in a long time. Diego's sister and her family joined them: two boisterous boys and her serious looking lawyer husband, a man Lesley was certain she couldn't live with. The family were together, and despite his lack of contact, she could see how much Diego was loved and how easily he was forgiven for not being as dutiful as he could be. He seemed more at ease with his father's frailty and less awkward about helping him than she had expected. Lesley's easy way of including his father, helping him without making it obvious and remembering to look at him as often as she did at everyone else helped Diego without her saying anything directly. This was just how she was. He wanted to be like that.

Monday came round quickly, and it was nearly time to return to Florence and their life there. Lesley had volunteered to do some shopping for Lucia before she left, so directly after breakfast, she and Diego headed off toward the centre of Cesate and his mother's preferred supermarket. Although they would have to carry the shopping, they decided to walk so that Lesley could see more of the town. Diego carried the bags, leading Lesley around the maze of streets and finally taking the lane behind the Parrochia San Alessandro e San Martino as a shortcut to the supermarket. As always, Diego was able to give Lesley the history of the church, and more than that, he enjoyed relating the story of Father Rossi's murder all those years ago. He explained his father's involvement in the case and its notoriety given the fact it had never been solved. Lesley asked a few pertinent questions but soon got him back to talking about the church and its history. The murder didn't interest her. Not yet.

The supermarket was much larger than any they used in Florence, and Lesley enjoyed looking at the variety of items on sale. She could see why Lucia enjoyed going there. There would always be something new to look at as the seasons passed, with the non-food items reflecting the time of year. They adhered strictly to Lucia's list, and with Diego pushing the trolley and Lesley scouring the shelves for the appropriate items, the shopping was soon complete and they were heading back to Via Isonzo.

As they walked silently along the lane behind the church, Lesley thought of a future with Diego and what that might mean. She thought about ending the lease on her flat and moving in with Diego. She knew now she would have to tell her family about him. She had mentioned his name a few times in phone calls, but she had kept her feelings about Diego to herself. She didn't think she could do that much longer. Happiness wasn't something to fear anymore.

*Paolo, is that you?* Lesley looked up from her thoughts and saw a small middle-aged man coming towards them. He was wearing a pair of black trousers, a white shirt, black socks and shoes, and was carrying a small bag for his shopping. *Diego, Diego Borroni. You must remember me.* Diego put his bags on the ground and extended his hand towards the man, who was now right next to them, standing straight and still. Lesley stood silent as she realised who this man was. The man briefly took Diego's hand, then let it go as if an electric shock had struck him on contact. Lesley was surprised at his willingness to touch another person. *Lesley, this is Paolo Bianchi. We went to school together. How nice to see you. Mum said she met you at the supermarket and that you are still living in Cesate. I'm in Florence now working for the Carabinieri. How are you?*

Neither Paolo or Lesley spoke; they both simply stared. Diego, certain in the knowledge that Paolo would need time to process the situation, was therefore unconcerned by his silence. Lesley remembered this strange man with strange gestures, limited topics of conversation and black leather gloves poking out of his pocket. She remembered the story he had told her about his business at Lake Como, not Cesate. She remembered she had met him the same day as she had discovered Pepe's body. She remembered she didn't believe in coincidences. Paolo stepped back from the two of them and turned all his attention to Lesley, who was returning his stare with the same astonishment as he was feeling. *Oh, how rude of me. This is Lesley Hamilton, my girlfriend. She's from Scotland. We've been visiting my parents for the weekend.* Lesley extended her hand towards Paolo, whose eyes still hadn't left her face. He briefly shook her hand, wanting to understand why it was less concerning to him than touching Diego's hand, and then she spoke, smiling at him with the smile he had found so reassuring when they first met.

*I think we've met before in Florence. A few weeks ago. You were there on business, I can't remember exactly what. You were in the park when I woke up. I'd fallen asleep on the bench and then the next day you saw me by chance in a cafe. How strange we would meet again.* Lesley let go of his hand but continued to look straight at Paolo. She could feel Diego's discomfort at the exchange. Her voice had lost its usual lilt.

Paolo's expression didn't change as he spoke. *I'm afraid it can't have been me you met. I don't have a business, and it's a very long time since I've been in Florence. I spend all my time in Cesate now.* He turned towards Diego. *How nice to see you, Diego, but I must get into town for my shopping.* And he walked off in the direction of the supermarket at a faster pace than he normally would. He wanted to turn around and look once again at Lesley, to see what they were doing, to try to read their faces and their thoughts, but he resisted the temptation and continued to walk away from a complication he didn't want to have.

At the supermarket, he took one of the small blue wheeled baskets and started walking round the shop, up and down the aisles, working from right to left along the back row and then left to right along the row of aisles nearest the tills. He had nothing in his basket when he got to the end and had to start the process again. He knew he had to stop thinking about what had just happened; he could think about it later. If he didn't stop thinking about it, he would be unable to shop and would have to keep going round the shop until his anxieties subsided and he could complete the task he had come to perform. He turned to face the shelf nearest to him — sun creams. He stared at the price tickets, memorising the prices to divert his brain from the anxiety gripping every part of him and obscuring logical thought. It worked. Soon he was able to look only at the products and silently say their price in his head. His shopping could be completed now.

*It can't have been Paolo you met, Lesley. He may be a bit odd, but he remembers everything. He wouldn't forget meeting you.* Diego put his arm around her shoulder, kissing the top of her head before moving the shopping bags between his hands until he found a balance of weight that would make the walk back easier. She smiled at him, but he knew she wasn't convinced. *It's strange you would remember those events and that day so clearly.*

She knew it was her opportunity to tell Diego about Pepe and her memories of that day, but she still wasn't sure whether she was ready to do that. She knew it would change everything, and she didn't want to do that. But increasingly, she felt it would have to be told; it was just a matter of when. *It was before I met you, Diego. He was very memorable — rigid body language, fixed eye contact, limited conversation, unsure how to end a conversation, dressed exactly as he was today apart from a pair of black gloves which seemed quite inappropriate for the day. I remember the unusual, Diego, rather than the usual. I'm sure it was him. I'd like to be wrong.*

Black gloves. Someone had mentioned black gloves when he interviewed the neighbours. He couldn't remember who it was, but he knew he would check it when he got back to his office and his notebook.

*Tell me, what he was like at school?* Diego remembered his strange habits, the different routines put in place just for him, the murder of the cat and the afternoons trying to play with him when he lacked the skills to do just that. Diego knew she was right: once met, you wouldn't forget Paolo. And as he related all these details out loud, he became more convinced that Lesley had met him. But why would Paolo lie about being in Florence? And what were the chances Lesley would meet him twice in two days? He didn't believe in coincidences either; his work had taught him that. Things generally happened for a reason.

# Twenty

For Lesley, life returned to its usual routine once they were back in Florence. Her writing continued in her flat, which had now become simply a place to work. All personal items had made the short journey to Diego's flat and plans to buy her a writing desk to be housed in the small alcove in the corner of the living room were well underway. One more month of working in the Via Porta Rossa before her lease on the flat would terminate and her life with Diego would be a reality. She thought the novel would be finished in its first draft by that point, and then she could spend her time getting it ready for a publisher's eye. Although she was happy with it so far, she knew preparing it for publishers to look at would be the most complicated part. Writing from the story in her head as it flowed easily on to the white pages of the computer was the most exciting part of the process, but reviewing and altering the text meant criticising what had been written, thinking about other people reading it and letting it belong to the world rather than just you.

Although she wondered each day whether there would be a note behind her door indicating a date and time of a meeting with the Poccinis, as each day passed, she thought about it less and wondered if it would ever happen. She hoped it wouldn't. Pepe's face was no longer seen in the newspaper. He was no longer a news story. Then three weeks after their return from Cesate, a sheet of folded white paper was dragged across the doormat as she pushed open the solid wooden door into her flat. The meeting was arranged for the next day at 2.00 pm in Signora Conti's flat. She had no reason not to go. She would tell her story just as she had told it to Diego and

Detective Francesco. She was certain she would be able to do that.

*

Diego was surprised not to have seen Detective Francesco since his return to work. His plan to meet him casually as they went about their business in the large Carabinieri building wasn't happening, and he knew he would have to visit him in his office if he wanted to speak to him. Although he was confident that Lesley could manage the meeting with the Poccinis and tell her story clearly, just as she had done with both him and Detective Francesco, he wanted to know what their motivation was for meeting all the neighbours. And the only person who could tell him that was Detective Francesco.

But he didn't have to wait long to find out. As he filed another piece of paper into the green filing cabinet located in the corner of his office, there was a quiet knock on the glass door that gave him a view of his colleagues and the work being done by them. As he turned, expecting to see one of his team waiting to enter, Alessandro Francesco was pushing the door open and smiling directly at Diego. *How are you, Diego? Is it okay if I come in?* Diego realised as Alessandro sat down on the small black couch next to Diego's desk that the question didn't require an answer, nor was it expected to be given an answer. He felt instantly at a disadvantage and chose to sit in the office chair positioned behind his desk, a place where he felt at home and in control. But he realised quickly that he wasn't.

*I don't know if Lesley will have told you, but the Poccinis are speaking to all the neighbours to see if they remember anything about the day Pepe disappeared. I'm attending all the meetings, and I just wanted to let you know that Lesley's meeting is tomorrow.* Diego said nothing. Lesley hadn't told him. He didn't know about the meeting. He didn't know what to say, but he didn't need to say anything. Detective Francesco recognised his puzzled expression. *She probably only got the information today. I told Signora Conti yesterday evening. It was a bit of a last-minute decision by Signor Poccini. He wasn't sure he would still be in Florence tomorrow. Anyway, I just wanted to let you know that I haven't told the Poccinis about Lesley's connection with you. Don't want to be stirring up any old animosity. No point in that.* For the first time since starting to speak, he turned his head and looked directly at Diego. Diego didn't believe him. He had no concrete reason not to believe him and knew Detective Francesco was highly respected by his colleagues throughout the Carabinieri, but Diego had met more liars than most and felt he could detect a lie with ease. And he felt Alessandro was lying now. His visit to Diego's office was staged, the words rehearsed, and the lack of eye contact made it seem less than genuine. He wouldn't fall into the trap. Then Detective Francesco continued. *Just thought it was a courtesy to let you know.*

As Detective Francesco stood up from the couch, Diego remained in his chair, watching this man navigate the office furniture and place his hand on the handle of the door. Diego decided he would speak now. *Thanks for letting me know, Alessandro. I was aware from Lesley that meetings with the Poccinis were being arranged, and no doubt she'll let me know this evening about her meeting tomorrow.* He paused deliberately, and Detective

Francesco turned to look at him. He was about to speak, but Diego knew he had his attention now and continued speaking. *I was surprised when Lesley told me about the meetings. I wasn't sure why the family would be given such an opportunity. I didn't think it was usual practice.*

Alessandro maintained eye contact with Diego, silent. Then he spoke, dropping a bombshell Diego wasn't expecting. *Forensics found the tiniest trace of Pepe's blood on the stairwell. It could be a murder case now, so I want every opportunity to speak to the neighbours even if I'm not the one directing the questions. The family don't know about the blood yet; it's my opportunity to catch people off-guard. I trust this information won't leave this room.* Detective Francesco pulled the door towards him and walked slowly through the maze of desks, happy in the knowledge that he had had the final word. He hoped Diego believed the Poccinis knew nothing of the blood.

*

Lesley was singing along with the radio while putting a large vegetable lasagne into the oven when Diego stuck his head round the corner of the kitchen. He waited until the oven door was safely closed before he spoke. *Good evening, my little diva.* Lesley laughed as he took her hand, pulled her close and kissed her. She reached out towards the radio and turned down the sound, no longer needing the noise of the music to prevent her from thinking about the meeting tomorrow. Diego's presence would be enough. She would tell him about it and he would reassure her that everything would be okay. They held on to each other longer than they would usually, both worried that events outside their newly made world would destroy the happiness they had found with one another. They both knew how easily that could happen.

*You get changed and I'll finish getting dinner ready. I thought we could have it on the terrace?* She paused, then added, *I've got lots to tell you.* He immediately felt better and began to relax. He knew she would tell him everything and wasn't sure where his doubts had come from.

It was a beautiful late May evening in Florence. Although the sun was beginning to set, the air was warm, and the buildings were coming to life as the lights designed to show off their beauty to the many tourists visiting the city were gradually coming on. As instructed, Diego changed from his suit into casual clothes that helped him make the distinction between the formality of his day and the calm of his evening. It was something he had only started doing since coming to Florence and meeting Lesley, and it always had the desired effect. As Diego looked over the glass and iron balustrade of the terrace at the Arno flowing steadily towards the Ligurian Sea, Lesley brought through the salad, lasagne and plates, ready to start dinner. Diego poured two glasses of red wine, took his seat and enjoyed watching Lesley struggle with the lasagne, which appeared to have developed a life of its own as she scooped it from the deep dish.

*I got a note today from Signora Conti about our meeting with the Poccinis. It's tomorrow at two pm. I'm glad I only found out about it today since it's less time to worry about it. And I'm sure it'll be fine. I'll just tell my story; I really have nothing else to say. No doubt Signora Conti will have lots to say. That will make it easier for me.* Diego thought Lesley looked genuinely relaxed about it, although her eagerness to get the whole story of the meeting out did indicate some anxiety. He reassured her she had nothing to worry about and that she should, as she said, simply stick to the details of her own story and not be drawn into anything else. He had already decided not to tell her about the discovery of blood in the stairwell; she didn't need to know. And so they enjoyed their dinner, discussing what they might do at the weekend, what had happened in Diego's day and when would be the best time for Lesley's mother to visit from Scotland. Late June seemed the best time, before the enervating heat of the summer made it difficult to enjoy sightseeing.

Lesley's family knew about Diego now. Although her sister still felt she should never have left Scotland and that in some way she was abandoning their mother, her mother could tell from the tone of letters and the lilt in Lesley's voice when they spoke on the phone that Lesley had found happiness with Diego, and she was glad about that. Happiness was all she had ever wanted for her daughters. One of them had found it, and she felt that was an achievement. The novel was almost finished. Lesley's determination was always something to be admired. Lesley would call her mother tomorrow and suggest the last week in June for a visit. Diego would take a few days off and they would be able to show her the beautiful Tuscan scenery together, while the days with only Lesley could be spent exploring the many sights of Florence. A perfect combination.

As they lay quietly in the darkness of their bedroom, Lesley went silently over and over the details of her story in her head. Diego's arm lay across her stomach, holding her gently by the waist as he slept soundly, content that things would be okay. And she was sure they would be.

## Twenty-one

Lesley had slept sporadically, so was glad when the alarm rang and it was time to get on with her day. She would stick to her routine and the day would pass as everything always did. She lay quietly with her head in the crook of Diego's shoulder and her arm spread across his chest, enjoying their closeness and the softness of his skin against hers

She left for the Via Porta Rossa at the same time as Diego. They parted company in the foyer of their apartment building, Diego heading for the underground car park and Lesley walking out into the warmth of the morning and the distinctive smells of summer. Diego reassured her everything would be fine and said he would book a restaurant for dinner at 8.00 pm. Always thoughtful. It surprised Lesley every time and never failed to make her realise how much unhappiness she had endured. She wouldn't let that happen again. They kissed goodbye and headed off to fulfil the demands of their day.

Lesley enjoyed the walk to her flat and was pleased to meet no one when she arrived. Signora Conti's window was closed, unusual but not unheard of. She suspected Signora Conti hadn't slept well either and was off out for her shopping early since she wouldn't be able to carry out that task this afternoon as she usually did. Lesley's flat felt very bare now since removing the few things that made it her flat and not just anyone's flat. But once her computer was placed on the table, the window opened and her juice and food supplies laid out before her, she knew she was ready to power on and get to the end of the novel. She had known the ending from the start; it had always been certain, unlike the rest of the novel, which regularly took an unexpected turn away from the plan which she had loosely laid out in her notebook.

The morning passed quickly, with hundreds of words appearing on the white screen as she typed furiously, wondering how it would read when editing began in a few days' time. She would do that in her new home. Lesley knew she wouldn't want to write after lunch. She would want to think about what she would say and be well prepared for the meeting, so she closed the laptop just after midday and ate her lunch. She was ready.

Signora Conti greeted Lesley like a long-lost friend when she knocked on her door at 1.50 pm exactly. *How nice to see you, Lesley. In you come.* And she led the way through to a small living room furnished just as it was when Signora Conti moved into the flats with her husband 40 years earlier. The sofa Lesley sat on wasn't comfortable with its hard mauve cushions and wooden arms that were ornately carved with the intention of prodding you as you tried to relax. She hoped this wasn't where Signora Conti usually sat. It felt like a museum, a tribute to an earlier and probably happier time. Although there were three other chairs in the room, Signora Conti sat down next to Lesley on the sofa, forcing her further towards the wooden arms. *I thought we could sit here together, Lesley. Does that suit you?* Lesley nodded her agreement.

The doorbell rang. Signora Conti smiled briefly at Lesley, then went off to answer the door.

Detective Francesco was first to enter the room, smiling directly at Lesley, who stood up to shake his outstretched hand. *How nice to see you, Miss Hamilton. How kind of you to agree to come to the meeting. It won't take long, I'm sure. Let me introduce Signor Marco Poccini, Pepe's father.* And from behind Detective Francesco, a man no taller than Lesley but with a slight stoop stepped forward to shake her hand. Although his body appeared frail, his face looked strong and certain. His grey hair, although receding, was plentiful and combed in order that it would flow towards the back of his head. He smiled briefly while his eyes fixed themselves on the face of this young woman standing in front of him. Then he spoke.

*How nice to meet you, Miss Hamilton. Thank you for agreeing to meet me. My apologies for giving you such short notice of the meeting. I just wasn't sure if I would still be in Florence today. I have left my sons in charge of our businesses for a few days. Do sit — everyone else seems to have.* It was only then that Lesley noticed both Signora Conti and Detective Francesco were sitting behind her, Signora Conti ready to answer the questions Marco Poccini would have for them. As she sat down on the small sofa, a noise behind her made Lesley turn towards the doorway. And there standing in the door frame was a young man with a tall, heavy frame and neatly clipped blonde hair. He smiled at her, the same smile he'd given her the day he followed her. *This is my assistant, Leonardo.* Signor Poccini's voice sounded far away as Lesley processed this information and what it might mean.

Her link to Diego wasn't a secret; it never had been. Leonardo knew exactly who she was, which meant Signor Poccini knew exactly who she was. Lesley turned back to look at Signor Poccini, scrambling around in her brain to process the implications of this and whether it changed what she should say. She could feel her face redden with anxiety and was pleased that in the dullness of her brain she could hear Signora Conti answering questions being put to her by Signor Poccini. She would stick to her story and focus her eyes on those sitting down.

It was soon her turn. Signor Poccini asked his questions slowly and deliberately, a routine she felt was both practised and menacing. It wasn't hard to give her story; there wasn't really much to it if you took out the part when she found Pepe's body on the stairs. She gave some background to her arrival in Florence and how long she had been there. Her answers seemed quite stilted compared to Signora Conti's and she found herself apologising for her limited Italian and necessary thinking time. Signor Poccini smiled and thanked her for agreeing to speak in Italian. It was much easier for him. And she felt it gave him the pleasure of watching her squirm as she tried to dredge up the appropriate words for her answers. Diego had said detail was important, so she gave authenticity to her story by commenting on her breakfast order, the size of the supermarket, the number of people there and her pleasure in the Santa Croce at seeing, once again, the wonderful frescoes done by Giotto so long ago. Signor Poccini maintained an unhealthy amount of eye contact with Lesley as she was telling her story. He nodded as she responded and finally asked the question she'd hoped wouldn't be asked: *You definitely didn't see Pepe on the day we believe he disappeared?*

*No, I'm afraid I didn't, Signor Poccini.* Then there was silence. Signor Poccini was now looking at the floor and it was Detective Francesco's turn to speak.

*Thank you for agreeing to speak to us again, ladies. We really wanted to make sure we hadn't missed anything.* He paused. *Forensics found a small trace of Pepe's blood further down the stairwell, so we felt we had to go back to everyone and double-check no one had seen or heard anything.* Lesley felt sick. *So thank you once again. If there is anything else you remember, you have my card.* He stood up. Signor Poccini pulled himself slowly out of his chair, shook Signora Conti's hand then turned towards Lesley, taking her hand tightly in his and shaking it.

*I loved my son very much, Miss Hamilton. I will find out what happened to him. Thank you for your help.* He, like Diego, had met many liars in the course of his business dealings, and he wondered if Miss Hamilton, with her imperfect Italian and perfect manners, was lying now.

He let go of her hand and turned to leave. Lesley's guilt almost overwhelmed her at that point, almost made her speak, until she realised that Signora Conti had started speaking … *hiding in the alley next to the Hotel Davanzati. I couldn't see his face but thought his black gloves seemed very strange. I saw him for only a couple of days. I mentioned it to both Detective Borroni and Detective Francesco. I don't know if it's important. It just seemed strange and a bit of a coincidence it was around the time Pepe disappeared. I guess there could have been all sorts of reasons for him being there. I should have mentioned it again when we were sitting down. My apologies, Signor Poccini.*

Signor Poccini pulled himself up to his full height and turned. *Yes, we were aware of that, Signora Conti, and I know Detective Francesco is making enquiries about who that person might have been. Thank you once again for mentioning it. You have both been most helpful.* And the three of them left. Leonardo was last to exit, staring and smiling directly at Lesley as he pulled the door behind them.

Lesley had coffee with Signora Conti without hearing a word that was said. She kept a smile on her face, maintained eye contact with Signora Conti and drank her coffee slowly. But all the time, she was certain the man with the black gloves had been Paolo Bianchi, the man she met in both Florence and Cesate. The man who lied to her about their meeting. The man Diego had told her so much about.

Detective Francesco spoke briefly to Marco Poccini before he was driven off to Milan by Leonardo. He assured Signor Poccini he would be in touch as soon as he had any information for him.

And he knew that would be soon. The man with the black gloves was, he was certain, an assassin on Franco's books. Although he didn't know the man's name, he had heard much about him and his ability to kill without being seen. He could speak to Franco himself to get the information, or he could hand Franco over to the Poccinis. The latter would mean less involvement for him and none of the mess to clear up. He would do that tomorrow.

## Twenty-two

Once Lesley had finished with Signora Conti, she retrieved her computer from her flat and walked back to her new home. The Arno looked flat and calm as she walked along the pavement next to it. Although it wasn't yet the height of the tourist season, Florence was still busy, and walking along the pavement required numerous sidesteps onto the road to avoid people with cameras and groups who had stopped to study maps. She didn't think she would return to her flat in the Via Porta Rossa. She would write at her new desk and only return to the flat for a final check before handing in the keys. She wanted no further involvement in the outcome of Pepe's disappearance. She needed some distance from it. Physical distance.

As she prepared dinner and waited for Diego to come home, she made decisions around what she would tell Diego and what she would keep to herself. After much deliberation, she decided that although her discovery of Pepe would have to remain a secret, she would tell Diego everything else. She knew secrets could destroy relationships, but Pepe's death was a secret she thought she could never divulge. Not to Diego, not to anyone. Diego was her future and she didn't want to jeopardise that.

Although the evening was warm, Lesley decided dinner would be eaten indoors. All over Florence, those with a terrace were making good use of them as summer arrived, but that meant hearing others' conversations. Lesley liked the openness of the Italians, the public displays of emotion and the need to be noticed, but she didn't want their conversation to be overheard this evening. Diego made no objection to dinner indoors and carefully ensured the doors out to the terrace were closed tightly as they sat down to eat. Lesley began her story and asked Diego not to ask any questions until she had given him all the information. She felt very tired now and hoped she would be able to answer the questions Diego would inevitably ask. In some ways, she would rather have waited until tomorrow to tell him. Her head would be clearer and she would feel less emotional than she did at that moment.

She told him about the identity of Leonardo, and she related her story just as she had told it to Signor Poccini and Detective Francesco, even including the helpful remarks Signora Conti had added to confirm her story — *Lesley always shops in the morning. She writes all day. I usually hear or see her go out later in the afternoon.* Finally, she gave him the details about the man with the black gloves. Momentarily, he stopped eating. Then she waited. While Diego was processing the information she had given him so far, she told him they had found a trace of Pepe's blood in the stairwell. Diego unexpectedly looked up from his meal, feeling the guilt of not having forewarned her that that might come up while at the same time feeling reassured that he had done the right thing. She said she had made no comment about the blood since she knew nothing about it. As she felt her heart rate increase, she hoped her face wasn't reddening.

They finished dinner in silence. Lesley knew Diego was processing the information just as she had done during her walk home and while making dinner. He just needed time. Diego filled the dishwasher while Lesley sat on the terrace enjoying the evening view over Florence, waiting for him to be ready to speak. Although she still had her secret, she felt better for having been able to tell him everything that had happened in the meeting. He would know if there was anything else that needed to be done. And she thought something would have to be done.

*

Alessandro Francesco was also eating his dinner in silence. Unlike Lesley and Diego, this wasn't unusual. He had little to say since his work was something he had always kept to himself, and his wife had long ago run out of enthusiasm to keep any conversation going. Tonight the silence allowed him to consider how he would tell Signor Poccini about Franco and the possible connection to the man in the black gloves.

If they hadn't found the traces of blood, he would have assumed Pepe had disappeared, leaving a life he didn't want to belong to. It seemed a logical conclusion for a young man who had been kept apart from his father's business dealings and who never sought any involvement in them. A young man who had taken himself away from the heart of the business to a city where culture could seep into his bones and he could build a life of his own. But the traces of blood changed everything. A revenge killing neatly tidied up but not quite neatly enough. A contract killing. Probably. He knew this was exactly what the Poccinis were thinking. It would be no surprise to them when he spoke to them the next day.

*

Since meeting Diego and Lesley, Paolo found it hard to fill his days without thinking about the two of them, the meeting in Cesate and the knowledge Lesley Hamilton now had. He ate every meal in silence, always laying an extra place at the table for his mother, imagining times when his mother was there and they had sat in companionable silence, knowing they would support each other whatever happened. But now he found himself more often imagining Lesley sitting there with her fixed smile and beautiful blonde hair. He knew he shouldn't. Obsessions didn't generally work out well for him, but the pulsing noise in his head kept her alive for him.

*

*Do you think Paolo Bianchi was the man in the alley with the black gloves?* This wasn't the first question she was expecting Diego to ask. She looked up at him, surprised, but nodded, not knowing the direction this conversation would now go in. *You think he killed Pepe?* This seemed a big leap for Diego to have made given he had no knowledge of Pepe's death. She looked puzzled. *If they hadn't found the traces of blood, like you I wouldn't know whether or not Pepe was dead. But given the way families like the Poccinis operate, I can only assume he is dead. Probably a contract killing to mete out revenge for some error of judgement that we would find hard to understand. An effective way to strike at the heart of the family. Pepe was much loved by his father. I always felt Marco Poccini sought his own redemption through Pepe's life, so different to his own.* Then there was a pause. *But why would Paolo be following you if he was the killer? Why would he take such a risk? And what makes me think he might be the killer?*

Lesley found it hard to answer any of these questions.

She found it hard even to look at Diego. She had the bit of the jigsaw that made it all fit. The bit of the jigsaw she couldn't reveal, wouldn't reveal. If Paolo was the killer, then he was the only person who knew she had seen the body and taken the phone. She assumed he wouldn't be divulging that to anyone. Now, as she looked at her hands, she hoped Diego would leave it there. There was no concrete evidence that either Paolo had killed Pepe, or that in fact, Pepe was dead. There was nothing for him to go on. Or so she thought. Circumstantial evidence at best, she thought. But for Diego, that was enough to get the ball rolling.

*I need to speak to my father.* He paused, thinking. *He always thought Paolo killed Father Rossi all those years ago but couldn't prove it. I guess it was a hunch. A feeling in his gut that he was being lied to. I never saw Paolo like that. I saw him as pathetic and needy, alone in the world through parental pressure and a lack of understanding of how the world operated. But I watched from the dining room the day he killed the cat. It was terrifying and accomplished. He just kept eating as if nothing had happened. He didn't understand our distress. I'll call Mama and see if we can go up to Cesate for a couple of days this weekend.* Diego sat clasping his hands as he thought some more. *You definitely didn't see anything else that day, Lesley?* He looked straight at her.

*No.*

## Twenty-three

Alessandro Francesco woke early. He had no need of an alarm clock, as he always woke at the same time. Sleep hadn't come easily to him for many years, and he learnt that once he was awake, there was no point in remaining in bed. Sleep wouldn't return. He always enjoyed the few hours he had to himself before both his wife and the world would wake. He imagined it was what limbo would be like. A place of peace and quiet where none of the troubles that filled your head during the noise of the day would matter. They couldn't be acted on; they couldn't consume you. Nothing like the limbo portrayed by the church.

It was a warm morning, so he sat on the terrace of their house reading his latest novel and enjoying his first coffee of the day. He knew how he would move things forward; he just had to start the ball rolling. But not until the rest of the world was awake, a couple of hours yet. Showering, dressing and breakfast filled the next hours until it was time to head for his office and his phone call to Marco Poccini. His wife appeared just as he was leaving, a routine she had perfected over the years which suited them both. *Ciao.* He kissed her cheek briefly, one of the few moments of human contact they shared in their routine life. He wondered, as he often did, where she had her physical needs met. He knew where he went, but he guessed it was best they both kept those secrets securely to themselves.

The office was quiet when he arrived at 8.00 am. A few of the foot soldiers were at their desks trying to impress, looking for a way to climb the Carabinieri ladder. Alessandro ignored them all, entered his glass-windowed office and closed his door. He was often in early making phone calls, so no one would think his behaviour unusual. He had no appointments organised for the day, so arranging to meet the Poccinis wouldn't be difficult. He assumed they would want to meet in person, and he wasn't wrong.

*Marco Poccini, please. It's Detective Alessandro Francesco from Florence.* He used his work mobile, knowing that although the call would be traceable, there was no danger that anyone else was listening in. He had no evidence that his private calls had ever been tapped, but taking risks wasn't something he was inclined to do. His systems had worked well up to that point. Why would he change them?

*Alessandro, I didn't expect to hear from you so soon. Have you got any news for me?* Marco Poccini's voice always sounded the same, slightly upbeat and cheerful. Alessandro knew it didn't always reflect what was going on in his head.

*Yes, I need to see you. I have some information I think you'll be interested in and that you may want to act on. I can't. Probably best we meet in person. I'm free all day, a paperwork day.* He waited while Marco Poccini decided on what should happen.

*Let's meet near Parma for lunch. Would that suit you okay? Midday?* Alessandro Francesco had been useful to Marco's family on many occasions. He didn't want to make things difficult for him. He knew he might need him again if he was going to find and punish his son's killer.

Alessandro was more than happy with the arrangement. It would get him out of Florence, where he might be seen with the Poccinis, and it would fill his day since paperwork was something he rarely actually did these days; he just checked the work of others. They arranged to meet in Coloreto, a village twenty minutes outside Parma at the Trattoria Ai Due Platani. A private venue, somewhere the Poccinis regularly used. A trusted family. No doubt a family on their books.

By the A1, the drive to Coloreto would take about 2 hours, but he had plenty of time and it had been a while since he had last driven through the Tuscan countryside, with its grand vistas and rural villages. He would take the alternative route and leave now.

It wasn't yet 9.00 am, so although the underground car park was beginning to fill up, he was able to make his escape without speaking to anyone. No one would wonder where he was: he had put appointments in his online diary that couldn't be traced but would explain his absence.

The car journey was magnificent. The days were now warm and bright, highlighting the variety of greens that had erupted in the spring after the relative cool of winter. Spring was short in Tuscany, and there were only a few weeks when a palette of greens could be seen across the hills and villages before the sun's heat made everything start to fade from green to a range of browns.

Coloreto proved to be a small town with limited facilities but a very nice restaurant — a satellite town for those working in Parma who could afford the prices the houses in the town fetched. Good schools, open spaces: a rural idyll for families seeking a different lifestyle. Alessandro was first to arrive and explained to the owners that he was there to meet Marco Poccini. He was escorted through the main part of the restaurant, across a small courtyard at the back of the building and then through a gate to a terrace that covered one third of a walled garden. Only one table with four chairs was set on the terrace. Marco Poccini must be bringing his sons.

Alessandro made himself comfortable and waited. There were worse things he could be doing.

*

*Yes, next weekend would suit us just as well as this weekend. We can come up on Friday evening and head back on the Sunday.* Diego was silent, listening. *No, it's not urgent. I just wanted to speak to Papa about a case that's come up here in Florence. I think there might be a link back to Cesate.* Once again, Diego was silent, listening. *Yes, I think you're right. He'll like that I want to discuss a case with him. Maybe I should have done that more often.* His mother reassured him on that score, but he knew that the distance he had maintained from his family hadn't been good for those relationships. He was lucky they never held it against him.

*

Marco, Luca and Lorenzo Poccini arrived exactly on time. Alessandro stood up as he watched them approach. Leonardo, their trusted bodyguard, nodded in his direction, then turned to face the gate leading to the terrace, the only vulnerable point in the walled garden. Although Alessandro had carried out work for the Poccinis on a number of occasions, he had rarely met the sons and had never spoken to them about a job. But he guessed this was quite a different matter given that it involved a family member. A family member they had worked hard to protect from the rigours of their second life — the life that stayed behind closed doors but funded their lifestyles as well as the life Pepe enjoyed in Florence. They ordered their food and commented on the weather and each of their journeys to Coloreto before getting down to the business of the meeting. Alessandro did all the talking. The Poccinis listened intently.

*There's a man I've done some work for over the years who has five or six assassins on his books. He contracts them to carry out jobs across the north of Italy for families and businessmen who need something ...* he paused ... *tidied up. One of those men is known by his black leather gloves, which he wears when carrying out a job. It is his trademark.* He let them think about that before he continued. *It seems unlikely to me that Pepe is still alive. If he were, there would have been a ransom, I expect, and if he had simply taken himself off somewhere, I can't imagine he wouldn't have been in touch with you at some point in the last couple of months. He hasn't used his bank cards anywhere, nor have there been any sightings of him as a result of our national campaign.*

The Poccinis stopped eating and looked at each other, digesting the information. No one spoke for several minutes. *Yes, like you, we think Pepe is dead, murdered. Revenge. Although we have no idea who would have put out the contract or why. None of our usual contacts know anything.* Luca Poccini, as eldest son, did the talking, Marco's sadness at the loss of his youngest son evident in his silence and rigid body, Lorenzo looking straight ahead across the garden. *We want to find the man with the black gloves, so we would want to meet this man who contracts him out. You don't need to worry. You won't need to be involved. No one will ever know you gave us his name.* All three looked at him, waiting for the details.

*You already know the man.* The tension was now palpable. Marco's chair scraped on the stone slabs of the terrace as he pulled himself up and out of his chair and turned to look across the walled garden with its lavender borders and rows of home-grown vegetables that enhanced every dish on the restaurant menu. The sunlight made everything seem clearer and brighter. Luca and Lorenzo had fixed their gaze on Alessandro, waiting for him to speak. *It's Franco.* He paused again, aware that they needed time to process what he was telling them. Time to realise that the man who had promised to help them in their search for Pepe most likely knew what had happened to him and who had killed him.

Marco turned around slowly, placing his hands on the back of his chair for support. He looked straight into the face of Alessandro. *Give us his details. We will take it from here. Thank you for your help, Alessandro. Your payment will be transferred tomorrow to the usual account.* Alessandro realised his job was done and that finishing his meal wasn't an option. He placed a pre-prepared envelope containing Franco's details on the table, nodded his understanding of what he should now do and headed towards the gate. Leonardo let him out. It was time for him to make his way back to Florence and file Pepe's case in the unsolved drawer of his filing cabinet.

## Twenty-four

Franco never tired of the view from his home. It was particularly beautiful early in the morning when the low sun caught the headland and reflected into the blue sea, whose colours changed hourly as the sun moved across the clear blue sky. The edge of the garden appeared to merge with the sea although there was a significant drop from which there was no protection other than your own desire not to fall. Each morning, Franco would pull open the large patio door that slid silently along its runner, revealing the morning light, the sounds of the sea and the cool air that would seem imagined later in the day when the world became enveloped by heat. Twenty lengths in the pool followed by a shower brought him quickly out of his slumbers and cleared the nightmares that haunted him. Breakfast on the terrace and then he was ready for the day, the isolation of his home both his protection and his vulnerability.

His routine was no different the day the Poccinis came to call. As he sat pondering how he could solve his current problems and ultimately disappear from the world he had created, he heard the gate at the bottom of the garden click shut. Metal on metal. He was immediately alert.

No one used that gate. It provided him with a narrow path down the cliffs to the white sand below and the turquoise blue beauty of the Tyrrhenian Sea. His private beach, his personal escape route. Someone had done their homework.

His first instinct was to go inside for his gun, but he knew it would take him longer to do that than it would for the person to walk across the garden to the house. Would he be at a disadvantage if he didn't retrieve his gun? His first mistake. As he pondered this question, a young man of considerable height with blonde hair shining brightly in the sunshine was striding across the lawn, past the infinity pool and straight towards the terrace. He was smiling and speaking as he moved. Franco couldn't hear what he was saying but was pleased to see he was alone and apparently unarmed. The young man's shorts and t-shirt made him confident there was nowhere to hide a gun. *What can I do for you? You shouldn't really be here; this is private property. Have you lost your way?*

The young man was nodding his head and Franco was moving towards him, the better to hear what he was saying. His second mistake. As soon as he was within striking distance, the young man with the smiling face threw a punch straight into the centre of Franco's face that caused him to lose his balance and fall backwards onto the grass, hitting his head sharply. Franco knew then that he should have gone for his gun; it was his only means of defence. He hadn't fought another human being since he was a teenager, and he knew that he had no chance of hurting this man whose size and power would overwhelm him quite easily. He could taste blood in his mouth as it trickled down from his burst nose. He tried to sit up, but the pain spreading across his face and around the back of his head made this very difficult.

He was still trying to work out how he would get up when the young man took hold of his left arm and pulled him upwards to his feet. The world was turning now, and he could no longer see clearly. His home appeared to be moving as they moved towards it, the young man dragging Franco when he could no longer move his legs as he usually would. Unceremoniously, the young man dropped Franco into a chair on the terrace next to the breakfast table laid out with fruit, bread, orange juice, coffee and yogurt.

As Franco tried to compose himself and regain some of his equilibrium, the young man pulled three nylon ties from his pocket and immediately tied Franco's ankles to the chair, then tied his hands together behind the chair. This made it more difficult for Franco to breathe. He could no longer wipe his bloodied nose or make an attempt to stem the flow of blood. He was relying on breathing through his mouth now, a feeling that induced fear whether it was legitimate or not. The young man knew now that he was in complete control. He turned his back on Franco, pulled out his phone and made a call. *All is well, Signor Poccini, I'll open the gates now. We're on the terrace as agreed.* And he disappeared into the house in search of the mechanism that would allow him to open the gates and unleash the fury of the Poccinis. It wasn't hard to find, and soon he was back standing in front of Franco, listening to the crunch of tires on pebbles, knowing that the plot hatched only two days ago was going to plan.

It seemed a long time to Franco before Marco Poccini and his two sons appeared around the side of the house, but he knew that couldn't be the case. It was a very short walk. Everything seemed to be happening in slow motion as his brain tried to understand the situation he now found himself in. He knew they must have information linking him to Pepe's disappearance and they would be determined to get that information no matter what was needed to do that.

*Well done, Leonardo, a good job.* Marco Poccini patted the young man of few words on the back. It was clear that Marco Poccini was becoming increasingly frail, as Leonardo swiftly took a chair from the other end of the table, placed it at the edge of the terrace and ushered the old man to sit in it. Marco's two sons stood behind him awaiting their instructions, although it was clear that Leonardo would be in charge of the punishment that was about to be meted out. Luca handed Leonardo a small bag which he put on the table next to the strawberries that now looked so out of place as bright red blood continued to flow from Franco's nose.

*Now, Franco. I'm sure you can guess why we're here. You haven't been quite truthful with us. You have such a reputation for honesty. Very disappointing.* Marco paused, hoping for an early response from Franco. In his experience, he found that those who had never had blood on their own hands generally were willing at an early stage to pass on the necessary information. They didn't want to see more of their own blood. But he didn't know Franco and he didn't know that Franco felt the blood was on his hands even though he had never carried out or witnessed a murder. His guilt had become increasingly overwhelming. *It would be best you tell us everything you know about Pepe's disappearance now. Best for you, I mean.* But Franco knew that even if he gave them all the details, they would kill him anyway. Collateral damage in their world. He had seen it as a child, and he understood the importance of loyalty in this situation. His assassins had always been loyal to him, and he had no intention of giving their names to anyone. A few minutes passed as they waited for the hoped-for response. Marco nodded at Leonardo, then turned to admire the stunning view.

Slowly, from the small black bag, Leonardo removed a brass knuckleduster and forced it onto his right hand, ensuring it was firmly in place before he swung at Franco's face. It caught his face just beside his left ear. Hard and painful, far away from his nose, which he could no longer feel. He made no effort to move or avoid the punch. He was aware the Poccinis were discussing the view and the beauty of the sea as he tried to right himself from the blow. More blood.

*Now, Franco. I'll give you some information to help you remember. It's probably hard to remember now. It will become harder for you to remember if you don't tell us everything you know now. Leonardo is very strong and very efficient.* The young man smiled directly at the old man, hoping his loyalty would be adequately rewarded and foolishly assuming his strength would always protect him. Franco knew that was a false hope. *You don't look so good.* Marco Poccini coughed into his pristine white handkerchief before continuing. *We are certain Pepe is dead. We are also certain one of your assassins killed him. Detective Francesco knows one of your assassins is known for his wearing of black leather gloves, and we know he was in the area when Pepe disappeared. We have a witness.* Paolo had got this more wrong than Franco knew. *Seems quite a coincidence. We don't know who wanted Pepe killed or why. We can only assume revenge.* He coughed again. *So, what we need to know from you is who put out the contract and who is this assassin? Not a great deal to ask. Give us the answers and we'll be on our way.* Marco looked at the ground when he said this. Franco knew it was a lie. He had known from the minute Leonardo hit him the first time that this was the end of the road for his work and his life.

No one did or said anything for several minutes. Franco decided that, like Paolo, it was best to say nothing and keep your secrets to yourself. He had promised Paolo's mother he would always look out for him, and he had no intention of deviating from that plan. He would not betray him now. Would that one good deed provide him with forgiveness for all the deaths and all the blood? He hoped it would. A loose family connection the only thing between his own death and Paolo's death. Paolo's mother had been glad to free herself from her family when she married Paolo's father. She thought then she would be able to put the brutality behind her, but once Father Rossi was murdered, murdered by her own son, she knew she needed their help. Paolo's father had washed his hands of them and Franco's parents were the only family she had. And so she had tracked down and contacted Franco's father. His protection was given freely and the plan for Paolo's life was hatched in the knowledge he would do whatever his mother asked of him. And he had. Franco knew all eyes were on him waiting for an answer to the questions, but he kept his eyes fixed on the ground. *The house, boys. See what you can find.*

Luca and Lorenzo took gloves from their pockets and donned them before entering the house and starting their search. Marco had suspected Franco would be reluctant to give them information. He knew he had a reputation for loyalty, and he knew that his simple life with no attachments meant there were no emotional ties that could be used to open him up. They would have to try to find the information in the house. He would have to keep all those details somewhere.

Leonardo moved to stand behind Marco, continuing the discussion he had been having with his sons about the view. Franco sat quietly, wishing the punch had been higher, on his temple, enough to kill him outright. Enough to cause blackness.

Luca and Lorenzo had carried out a number of searches over the years and methodically began to go through every room in the house looking for secret hiding places, phones, computers, safes — anywhere that Franco might have put the information. But they were looking in the wrong place, which pleased Franco. He kept nothing in the house. No connections to the life that now haunted him when sleeping and waking. A small flat in Livorno under a different name was his place of work, his place of hiding and the place where all his secrets lived. It had been this way for a number of years. He knew they would find nothing.

As he waited, Franco drifted in and out of consciousness. A consciousness unhampered by nightmares. Luca and Lorenzo returned, shaking their heads. They had searched everywhere. They had found nothing. Franco would have to give them the information. But his silence did not make it seem likely that he would, no matter how much pain they inflicted. Marco Poccini got up slowly from his chair and walked out onto the grass in front of the house, taking Leonardo with him. Giving him instructions. Leonardo listened attentively, then returned to stand in front of Franco.

As he raised his head, Franco saw Leonardo's right arm move once again, but instead of moving his head away from the incoming punch, he moved his head towards the brass knuckleduster and the incoming force. It worked. Blackness. Silence. Peace. The chair rocked from the power of the punch and toppled sideways to the ground. It was over.

This wasn't the plan. These weren't the instructions.

Marco Poccini walked quietly over to the bloody scene, placed his hand on Leonardo's back and waited for him to speak. *I didn't mean to hit him that hard.* Leonardo looked genuinely stunned. Marco was angry and upset. Finding his son's killer had just got a lot more difficult, but he treasured Leonardo's loyalty and would do nothing to spoil that. Not now anyway. It wasn't the first time he had found himself in this situation. Things didn't always go according to plan.

*We need to get things tidied up here, Leonardo. Move the body inside. Take him out of the chair but leave it in the house somewhere. Get the fire accelerant, Luca. We'll burn the place to the ground, no trace we were ever here. Once it's well alight, you will leave the same way you came, Leonardo, and make your way back to Florence just as we discussed. We'll meet you there, then head back to Milan. We'll have changed the number plates by the time you get there and be ready to go.*

Once the body was in place and piles of strewn belongings had been grouped together to ensure the fire would take hold, Marco and his sons took their leave. Leonardo waited until they were safely out the gates and heading along the coast road before lighting the four fires placed strategically around the house. It didn't take long until the fire took hold and he could leave the scene — leave exactly the same way as he'd arrived.

He strode across the lawn towards the small wooden gate, which clicked quietly shut behind him. The narrow path led him along the headland to the stolen motorbike hidden behind bushes out of sight of the beach and the rest of the headland. Quiet and peaceful. Once back at the bike, he turned to look at the house, which was now well alight. Its isolation would ensure he had plenty of time to make good his escape before the alarm was raised. He knew he needed to ensure he never made this mistake again. Marco Poccini would only forgive him once.

Marco and his sons drove in silence towards Livorno and the road back to Florence. As he wondered how he could now discover the identity of the assassin and the location of his son's body, he considered all the witnesses he had spoken to with Alessandro Francesco. And then he remembered Lesley Hamilton. The excellent eye contact and very clear answers. Rehearsed answers. He was sure she knew more than she was saying. And he wondered if she was protecting Diego Borroni.

## Twenty-five

*Yes, next weekend would suit us just as well as this weekend. We can come up on Friday evening and head back on the Sunday ... No, it's not urgent. I just wanted to speak to Papa about a case that's come up here in Florence. I think there might be a link back to Cesate ... Yes, I think you're right. He'll like that I want to discuss a case with him. Maybe I should have done that more often.*

Lesley listened carefully to the conversation, relieved that Diego wasn't going to act immediately. There would be time to consider all the possibilities. More than anything, Lesley wanted life to return to what it had been before: quiet days filled with the joy of being with Diego. And so they did. Although the upcoming visit to Diego's parents and the possibility that she knew Pepe's killer continued to flit in and out of her mind from time to time, she immersed herself in writing the final chapters of the novel and walking the streets of Florence in the afternoon sunshine. Her evenings with Diego always involved a meal, either at home or at favourite restaurants. Walking with him around Florence, she got to know both Diego and the magic of Florence better. Neither ever disappointed. Life was good. Diego appeared to be satisfied to wait.

But Diego was struggling with his newfound knowledge. Unknown to Lesley or his Carabinieri colleagues, he had begun researching Paolo Bianchi and his family. He had always assumed that like his own family, they had no secrets to hide and lived a mundane middle-class life, as did most people who lived in Cesate. But he soon found out how wrong he was. Unlike her husband, who had nothing to hide and whose escape from the house of silence to a new life with a second wife now seemed less surprising, Paolo's mother had much to hide. Silence helped with that. She had done much to hide her numerous family links to organised crime in Corsica, but once Diego started digging, skeletons began tumbling out of the cupboard one after another. Diego still had loyal colleagues working in Milan who were more than willing to help him once he explained the Poccini link. They always felt Diego had been the scapegoat, and although there was no active surveillance on the Poccinis, they were happy to help with anything that might result in them being linked with any current or unsolved crimes. They asked Diego for no details, they just located and passed on information, helpful information that made it possible for Diego to form a picture of the Bianchi family and the strangeness of their lives. Not so strange if one of you wanted no one to know the complexities of your life.

Next, Diego wanted to see the file on Paolo held by the police in Cesate. Part of it would have been written by his father. He wanted to see it before he met with his father. He was certain there would be clues in there to his father's suspicions. He might need those suspicions to jog his father's memory, which wasn't as good as it once was. But, as he feared, the file was too old to have been transferred to a computer, and he would need to make the trip to Cesate to see it. And he did. Quietly, without telling either his colleagues or Lesley. He convinced himself he was doing it because he didn't want her to worry, but he knew his need to do it in secret was a worry in itself.

There was little content in the file other than the statements given by staff and pupils who had witnessed the killing of the cat all those years ago. Facts that he could himself bear testament to, although his view of the murder was from the noisy dining hall — far enough away not to hear the cat's struggle for breath but close enough to be horrified that this small boy had such strength and wouldn't stop even when adults tried to intervene. And a statement from Paolo, who murdered the cat: *because he scratched me. I don't like being scratched. I don't like being touched.* And then he found his father's notes following his visit to the Bianchi house after the murder of Father Rossi. A brief statement of facts from Paolo followed by a series of comments from his father:

*Poor eye contact*

*Looking at the floor*

*Single syllable answers*

*No explanations*

*Mother silent on their movements in the evening*

*Could he have done it? Possibly.*

But when he went looking for information on Paolo Bianchi after university, none could be found. He didn't appear to have worked in all those years, yet he managed to live comfortably in his home in Cesate. His bank account revealed nothing irregular. There was enough money going into it every month for him to live a simple life, but it was unclear where that money came from. And finding that out would be far more difficult. He wouldn't be able to do that alone; he would have to wait until he was more certain that Paolo could be Pepe's killer, could be an assassin. It still seemed ridiculous to him when he said it in his head.

Diego knew assassins usually had a middleman who directed operations and protected the assassin from those who might want to locate and kill him. He thought Paolo would be no different. Human contact was something he knew Paolo always wanted to avoid. Diego decided this would be his next line of enquiry and that he would start with Paolo's family connections. But he would wait until he'd spoken to his father. Life with Lesley was too good to be spoiled by immersing himself in his work. This was what he had done with Tanya, and he'd lost her. However, he was also well aware that his work had also been a means of avoiding her demands. Lesley made few demands, happy to be with him, whether in a busy restaurant surrounded by noisy city dwellers and tourists or silently sitting in the Tuscan countryside, eating a picnic prepared with much laughter by the two of them. He didn't regret losing Tanya because it had brought him to a better, happier place, but he regretted he had been instrumental in both of them wasting five years of their lives.

*

Although Paolo was forcing himself to follow the routines that had always ruled his life, Lesley remained a dominant image in his head. Pounding in his head day and night. A noise he couldn't be rid of no matter how hard he worked or how busy he kept himself. His morning shop was now earlier; he didn't want to risk seeing Mrs Borroni again. Jobs in the garden and cleaning in the house filled the rest of his day, then dinner, reading and bed. But bed brought him no relief from his thoughts. He had tried sitting in his mother's room before going to bed since that had always worked in the past, but now it had no effect. It made him angry. Angry she had left him to cope on his own, angry she had never taught him to cope with the world as others coped with it, and angry that he had wasted all those years doing what she wanted only for her to leave him to cope with the aftermath by himself. He knew this anger was anxiety he couldn't cope with. Anxiety he needed to escape from. The same anxiety he had felt all those years ago when he left the church with his mother in tears and his only solution to be rid of it was to kill Father Rossi. He considered whether that was the solution now.

Lesley's death would rid him of these feelings, would stop the pounding in his head. It would also rid him of the one witness to the killing of Pepe. It would solve so many problems and he could go back to living his routine life. He could close that box and live back in the world he had enjoyed before Lesley. Before her smile. He started to plan.

*

After the murder of Franco, Marco Poccini left his sons to deal with the factories in Milan and retreated to his home on the edge of Lake Como. He hoped the vastness and beauty of the view, his proximity to the calming effects of the lake and the freedom life at the lake gave him compared to the pressures of life in the city would help him deal with his grief and ponder whether happiness would again be possible. His wife had been staying there since Pepe's disappearance, struggling to come to terms with the loss of her innocent son and whether she had played a part in his death through her work with and for Marco. She had married him to escape a chaotic life and find security where no one could threaten or harm her or her family. But they had. And now she had to deal with her part in that. A guilt that would not go away.

Now that Marco was sure Pepe was dead, he needed space to plan what he would do next. Lesley Hamilton's face and rehearsed answers were a constant theme in his head, and she was the one witness he kept returning to. He knew her connection with Diego Borroni was also influencing him, and he knew this appeared to be without any justification. Alessandro Francesco had assured him that Diego was carrying out routine police enquiries and had shown no interest in Pepe's disappearance. And so Marco Poccini set his men to follow Lesley. The routine she had described to him was exactly what was reported to him daily — out shopping early in the day, sometimes with a visit to the Santa Croce or breakfast in one of her two favourite cafes, time in the flat, then a walk late afternoon before returning to the flat. She spent her evenings with Diego, either dining in the flat or at a restaurant, attending a theatre, seeing a film at the cinema or simply walking through the streets, enjoying each other's company. Often walking by the Arno, listening to its noise as it moved through Florence towards the coast and the Tyrrhenian Sea. Often admiring its changing colour as the light of the evening changed. But her clear blue eyes and fixed eye contact continued to replay in

Marco's head. He wanted to speak to her again, to put pressure on her, to break her story if he could. He had to decide how he could best do that without arousing too much suspicion. Signora Conti might be his way in once again.

*

Signora Conti found herself thinking of Pepe and what might have happened to him more often than she wanted. The discovery of his blood on the stairs, she knew probably meant only one thing. He was dead. It hadn't been said overtly, but she knew that was the implication. And that was the reason they were told this vital piece of police information — in the hope that it would scare them into remembering something they hadn't already said. Although the thought of the young man being murdered while she slept disturbed her, she felt safe in the routine of her life and her certainty that no one else was in danger. She remembered the stories in the newspapers about the Poccinis, and although she couldn't remember his name, she knew there had been a detective inspector from the organised crime squad in Milan accused of harassing them. She knew from her working life that links to organised crime could be found in almost every violent offence, and she knew she wanted nothing to do with it. She knew she had given them all the information she had, and she now had no intention of having anything more to do with the case.

*

Planning Lesley's murder was more complex than Paolo felt it should be. He couldn't carry out his usual surveillance, couldn't do his usual planning. Like the murder of Father Rossi, it would have to be more spontaneous, less planned. He didn't like that since it meant more opportunities for mistakes that could later be his downfall. He spent days trawling the internet, trying to find out where Diego lived in Florence since he knew if he could find him, he could find Lesley. But with no success. Just as he thought his only other option would be to go to Florence and search them out, he once again ran into Mrs Borroni during his morning shop.

*Hello, Paolo. Another lovely warm day. I'm doing an extra shop this week. Diego and his girlfriend are coming up on Friday for the weekend. It will be lovely to see them, but I'll need more food in the house than I normally have. Diego has a very healthy appetite.* She smiled. Paolo knew this was his opportunity. He would have to carry on the conversation, and he would try to make it sound natural although he knew it wouldn't. And it didn't.

*How lovely. You'll be looking forward to that.* She smiled. *Do you ever visit them in Florence? I haven't been there for many years.* He stopped. She knew it was her turn to speak.

*No, we can't really go anywhere since Mr Borroni's stroke. It's a pity, really. Diego has a lovely flat overlooking the Arno, just behind the University of the Arts and a very short walk to his work. Couldn't be better for him. And Lesley, his girlfriend, seems to really like it. I'm sure she'll have made it more homely. She's a lovely person. We all like her a lot. Well, nice to see you, Paolo. I must get back home. Maybe we'll bump into each other again.* And she wandered off through the car park with her three bags of shopping, wondering why she had said so much. Paolo's awkwardness always made her feel she had to say more. It always had, even when he was a very young boy.

Paolo, for the first time in days, felt an inner contentment. It wouldn't be perfect, but he knew he could now formulate a plan. He was glad he'd kept the silencer for the one gun he still retained in case it was ever needed. It was needed now.

## Twenty-six

On Thursday afternoon, just after lunch, Paolo donned his white shirt, black trousers, black socks, black shoes and black leather jacket. His black leather gloves, along with the gun and the silencer, were now in the small leather bag he was planning to take with him. One thousand euros were tucked in the back pocket of the bag, and he was ready to go. He made sure the house was securely locked up before taking the internal stairs down to the garage and his car, which was now sporting new number plates. Number plates that would conceal the car's home in Cesate, instead making it appear to be from the Naples area. CCTV cameras had made the life of an assassin more difficult, but Paolo had always enjoyed the challenge each new piece of technology afforded him. He drove quietly out of the driveway, making sure the gates closed completely before he headed into Cesate and on to Florence. The forecast was for sun. He knew it would be a lovely drive.

*

Lesley had finished her novel now and spent some time each day reading and rereading it, hoping to improve the parts she didn't like so much and trying to look at it with a publisher's eye. Although she had enjoyed the process of creating it, preparing it for someone else to look at was far more stressful and much less satisfying. So, given they were going away to Cesate tomorrow, she decided to leave it lying on her little desk and prepare their suitcase for the trip instead. It would also mean she would have time for a walk, a pattern to her life in Italy which she really enjoyed. As she placed the items in the suitcase, she hoped that Diego's father would have no answers to the questions Diego was undoubtedly formulating and that they could put it all behind them. Lesley liked to put things behind her. The future was always more interesting than the past.

\*

Diego wanted to get all his paperwork done before the weekend, so he spent most of Thursday at his desk. He enjoyed the finality of paperwork and the knowledge that everything he had in his head and his notebook could be safely stored for future reference on the police computer files. He liked the certainty that his findings and thoughts might be used to solve future crimes long after he'd retired. But he also knew that he often kept information in his head until he was certain of his facts. Then he would commit it to the files. This was exactly what he was doing in relation to Paolo. No trail of paper, just a trail of thoughts. He would add them to the files next week or the week after, once he'd decided what to do.

\*

Paolo arrived on the outskirts of Florence just before 4.00 pm. He parked in suburbia, where cars on the street were rarely noticed and CCTV cameras didn't carry out their monitoring duties. He knew it would take him about an hour to walk into the centre of Florence, where he would take up position on the Lungarno delle Grazie, probably at a cafe, and watch for Diego or Lesley returning to their flat. It was a lovely walk, looking at the beautiful buildings, feeling the warmth of the sun on his face and navigating his way through the crowds of tourists eager to see the next beautiful building and oblivious to those walking past them. Paolo knew he should eat now because he would not be eating again for some time, so he parked himself in the window of a cafe on the Lungarno delle Grazie where he could watch those passing by and eat some pasta. The Bolognese sauce wasn't as good as the one made by his mother, but he enjoyed it and felt satisfied. It was nearly 6.00 pm when he spotted him. Diego was carrying his jacket over his arm, his tie had been loosened at the neck, and he looked like a man who had finished with his work and the stresses it imposed. A man who didn't know the calamity that was about to befall him. Paolo saw him go into a block of flats about 200 yards from the cafe. Home.

Paolo knew that he should wait some time before leaving the café, so he did. He enjoyed a cup of very strong coffee before paying his bill and wandering out into the street, which still seemed to be busy. He walked past the flats, looking carefully at the entrance, its neatly mounted cameras ensuring security for all those living there. He couldn't use that entrance, so he spent the next hour walking the streets and winding his way through numerous alleys until he found the back of the building and the underground car park.

Although the main entrance had been carefully thought about, the underground car park was not entirely walled in. There were two gaps in the walls, he assumed for ventilation, which were just wide enough for him to squeeze through. And he did, having checked for people and cameras. Paolo knew he would have to wait for many hours before climbing the stairs and breaking into

Diego's flat, but he didn't mind that. He had often had to hide in strange places when doing his job, and this was no different. He looked carefully at the cars, assessing which ones looked like they hadn't left the car park for some time. The blue Mercedes in the corner. Perfect. He could sit behind it, secure in the knowledge that unseen, he would be able to see anyone entering or leaving the car park. He took the gun and silencer from his bag, fitting them together in case they were needed, then he placed the bag on the ground as his cushion and sat down. And waited.

Lesley and Diego had a lovely evening. Dinner on the terrace, tidying up, reading, listening to music and then the pleasure and security of going to sleep in the same bed. Curled up together. Content.

It was 2.00 am when Paolo broke into their flat. Silently and without any fuss, he navigated the lock and opened the front door. He knew this was the dangerous moment in his plan. He had no idea of the layout of the flat and knew that he might have to shoot them both immediately if he was heard, but that didn't worry him; it would simply spoil his plan. Once he had closed the door behind him, he stood very still with his back against the door, assessing the situation and his options. The front door led immediately into a large living area including the kitchen. A door in the opposite wall was the only other door in the room. That, he guessed, was where the bedrooms would be. There was a chair positioned quite close to the front door where, if he were to sit, he would have a 360-degree view of the flat. A perfect spot. He sat down and waited, his gun in his hand.

Windows covered by an electrically operated shutter filled one wall of the room. Paolo imagined the light that would afford them and the beautiful view they would have of the Arno and across Florence. He imagined the terrace hiding behind the shutter and thought about the meals that would be enjoyed there throughout the year. Although it was a large living area, he noted that everything seemed to have its place, and he liked that. The sofas faced each other in a sociable and intimate way, and a small desk sat in the alcove in the corner with a laptop sitting open, ready for use. Apart from a sound system and a television, there was very little else that enlightened you about its occupants. A pale pink jumper neatly folded and laid over the arm of one of the sofas was the only link to Lesley. All he had to do was wait.

He heard an alarm go off around 7.00 am and readied himself for what would have to happen next. He hoped Diego and Lesley would appear one at a time, making things easier for him, but he knew he had to be prepared for whatever might happen. He could hear a shower running, muffled voices, and he thought, a radio. And he waited. Then he saw the handle turn on the door he had been facing for hours. Diego Borroni walked through it and turned to walk towards the windows. His morning routine. Shutters first, then breakfast. He hadn't noticed Paolo sitting in the semi-darkness, silently, menacingly. Then he heard his voice. *Leave the shutters, Diego. Just put on the light on the small table next to the sofa, then sit down. Thank you.* Diego turned to face the intruder, surprised at how calm he felt but recognising the droning monotone of the voice and the clarity of its diction. He stared at Paolo for a few moments, then did as he was asked. Paolo was on his feet, pointing the gun directly at

Diego. Diego was waiting for the shot. He knew how assassins worked: no questions and no concerns about pulling that trigger. But he didn't pull it. Paolo remained stationary but alert.

*I'm sorry about this, Diego. It isn't something I really wanted to do, but once Lesley recognised me, I knew I had no choice. I knew you would join the dots and you would track me down, looking carefully for evidence, ensuring I would be found guilty of all the crimes I've committed. You always had a forensic mind, enjoying the mathematical challenges set at school. You were the only person who could compete with me and who tolerated me; I always appreciated that. And your mother ... always so kind.* Paolo realised in these situations that he sounded rehearsed and unfeeling. Both were true.

*I don't understand what this is all about, Paolo. I don't really know why you were so worried about Lesley.* Just as Diego finished this sentence, Lesley came through the door from the bedroom, looking puzzled, initially, by the artificial light. Then she saw him. And she saw the gun. She followed the gun and realised it was pointing straight at Diego. She felt a rising sense of panic. She wondered what had been said; she wondered whether Diego now knew her secret. She kept her eyes firmly fixed on Diego, who tried hard to smile at her reassuringly, knowing all the time that there could never be a positive outcome in this situation. Paolo held all the cards.

*How nice to see you, Lesley. Please sit down on the chair at the desk.* The drone of his voice reverberated around her head. She kept hearing the words but couldn't move her feet. She turned to look straight at Paolo, staring at him in the unnerving way he stared at them. He didn't like it. *Do it or I'll shoot him now.* Silence.

Lesley moved towards the chair and sat down, unable now to see Diego's face. The back of his head would be her last view of him. No kind grey eyes. No smiling face. Just this. This.

Without saying another word, Paolo pulled the trigger. Lesley was aware of a very quiet popping sound, then Diego's head exploding, causing blood to seep its way through, round and down the sofa. Blood and brains stuck to the shuttered windows, with the early morning light accentuating their shape and redness. She knew this was her fault. Her decision to pick up the phone, Paolo's phone, on the stairs when she found Pepe had brought her to this moment and ended her happiness, her future. She thought once again how your life could be altered for better or worse on the basis of one decision, one moment. Unable to move, she continued to stare at the sofa, waiting for the popping sound of the second bullet and the end of her life. Then she became aware of his voice. *Can you drive, Lesley? I assume you can.* She didn't respond, but he needed her to respond, so he stepped towards her, raising his voice and changing its tone. Now she was alert and aware of her own situation. He repeated the question. *Can you drive, Lesley?* She nodded. *Get the keys and a coat; you won't need anything else.* He needed to leave the police a puzzle that would take time to solve or that might never be solved.

Lesley stood up slowly, unable now to look at Diego. She walked towards the front door, where the car keys rested in a small red bowl on a console table and her coat hung on a peg just above. Paolo followed her, ensuring that he was close enough to see every move she made.

They exited the building via the service stairs, arriving

in the underground garage unseen. It felt cold and damp in the garage. Lesley shivered, unsure whether it was the garage or shock causing it. She led Paolo towards the car, pressing the keys to open the doors as they got near. He asked for the keys, and she handed them to him before getting into the car as instructed. Once Paolo was safely in the car and the gun concealed inside his coat, he gave Lesley the keys and told her to start driving. He lowered the sun shield at his side of the car to make sure he wouldn't be detected on the CCTV as they drove out, unconcerned that Lesley would be seen as the driver.

As she drove, Lesley wondered why she hadn't refused to drive, hadn't refused to leave the flat. She could have forced his hand. She could have died beside Diego. But she didn't. They crossed the Arno and began driving east. Just where the Arno began to meander towards Le Sieci, Paolo told Lesley to turn left, and they drove towards the river, parking under a tree about 20 metres from the river itself. Today the Arno, no longer beautiful to Lesley, seemed dark and menacing. She knew this was where she would die. After a few minutes of sitting silently in the car, Paolo asked her for the keys and she gave them to him, his black gloves holding them tightly as they got out of the car and walked towards the river, which could be glimpsed through the trees growing at the side of it, thick and dense.

Paolo told Lesley to get into the shallow part of the river next to the trees and kneel down. He checked they couldn't be seen from the other bank and was satisfied that he could finish the job here. Neither of them spoke. He realised then it would have been simpler to kill her in the flat with a single, silent shot and leave all the mess there, but he looked again at her soft white face and long blonde hair and knew he couldn't have spoilt that image, the image he would always have of her. Paolo lay the gun on the grass next to him and leant over towards Lesley's head, which he grabbed with one hand, placing his other hand on the solid ground so that he would have sufficient purchase to push her under the water and hold her there.

*You should have called the police, Lesley. You should never have taken my phone.* She knew he was right. As he finished the sentence, she felt the pressure of his hand pushing her head down into the shallow water. Paolo expected some resistance but there was none. She allowed him to hold her there until there was simply darkness and silence.

He tucked her limp body under the bank, knowing it would be found, as bodies often are, by a dog out for its usually uneventful afternoon walk. It was hard to leave her since he knew he was leaving her forever, but he had done that with his mother and survived. He was certain he would survive again. And the noise in his head was silent; he had made the right decision. He drove back to the outskirts of Florence, parked the car, lost the keys in a drain and walked back to the northern suburbs and his own car.

Paolo felt quite hungry now so stopped for a bite to eat before locating his car and driving back to his routine life in Cesate.

*

Marco Poccini sat quietly on the terrace eating his breakfast, looking out over Lake Como, pleased to be there away from the pressures of life in Milan. Able to think. He would arrange to see Lesley Hamilton again.

Tomorrow would be good.

## Twenty-seven

Detective Alessandro Francesco was first on the scene. He shouldn't have been the first person to see the body, but the telephone call from Lucia Borroni had been put through to him late in the day and the note of determination in her voice along with the clarity of her story and his knowledge of the victim meant he had to act.

*Detective Francesco, my name is Lucia Borroni. I am Detective Diego Borroni's mother. I understand from the receptionist that you deal with missing people, and I believe my son is missing.* There was a brief silence, allowing Lucia Borroni to gather her thoughts and stem any tears she might be in danger of shedding. Detective Francesco had experienced similar calls on many occasions and was used to the silences that would punctuate the conversations. *Diego and his girlfriend Lesley were due here for lunch at twelve-thirty today. They were visiting us for the weekend. I spoke to Lesley only yesterday and they were all set for their visit. We even discussed where we would have lunch tomorrow.* A second silence. *I have been trying to contact them on their phones, but I just keep getting the voicemail. It isn't like them. They are very good at calling, and Diego would never want us to worry, so I know he would have found some way of contacting us if they had broken down or ... had an accident.* A third silence. *I've even contacted the hospitals between here and Florence to check they haven't had an accident. I probably shouldn't have.* Alessandro knew she was right. Hospitals never give out information regarding patients who have been admitted following an accident. There are procedures in such situations. Procedures which involved the police in telling relatives the news, good or bad. He didn't give the usual answer that the subject hadn't been missing long enough; this was the mother of a detective. *I hope you can help me.*

Alessandro looked out from his glass-fronted office to see who was still on duty. He would send one of the team. But the team was leaving. It was Friday, and most of the officers had left for the day. Those remaining at their desks were tidying away papers and gathering together their possessions before heading out into the Florence sunshine and their lives beyond the job. Alessandro had nothing to return home for and was often the last person in the office. His colleagues saw this as dedication, but he knew it to be otherwise. Friday nights were his evenings for seeing Carla, to have his most basic need met, before returning to his home where the reality of his long-dead marriage was all too much in evidence. But he knew now he would have to cancel Carla and go to Detective Borroni's house to check on his whereabouts. Although he knew where Detective Borroni lived, he asked Lucia for the address and assured her someone would be in touch with them over the course of the evening.

*Thank you, Detective Francesco. We shall await news.* The phone went dead.

As he turned to lift his jacket off the back of his chair, he realised everyone had now gone and the cleaners were busying themselves with dusters and mechanical sweepers. He would have to go to the flat alone. As he descended the stairs, his token gesture at any form of exercise, he decided to stop at Borroni's office and check whether he was there or whether there was evidence of him having been there. As with Alessandro's team, the officers managed by Borroni had also left the building, ready to enjoy their weekend. And, as he suspected, Borroni's office was empty and his desk neatly organised. He was sure he hadn't been there at all today.

It was only a ten-minute walk to Diego's flat, giving Alessandro time to call Carla and cancel their evening plans. He assured her he would be in attendance as usual next Friday. She sounded disappointed, but he wasn't sure whether she was or whether she was worried she wouldn't be paid. Once he explained he would transfer the money tomorrow, her mood seemed to lift, and the reminder that their ten-year relationship was no more than a contractual agreement hit him hard. He said his farewells and continued his walk to Diego's flat, watching the Arno flow steadily and relentlessly through the heart of Florence. A constant in an ever-changing city. He thought about calling Marco Poccini to make him aware of this latest development but decided against it until he had more information and knew exactly what had happened to Diego.

Standing under the small portico which gave those entering the block of flats some shelter from rain, or more often, sunshine, Alessandro rang the bell marked concierge. A man in his fifties with a slight stoop, dressed in a dark blue boiler suit and seemingly unused to answering the door, appeared after a few minutes and let him in. Alessandro showed his Carabinieri badge, explained his presence and entered. The beige marble walls and flooring were clean and shining. The lift to the upper floors was situated directly ahead of them, and a door on the right was clearly labelled as the service stairs. As he passed a door on the left, he noticed this was a small office, the working domain of the concierge now standing in front of him.

*Have you seen Diego Borroni or Lesley Hamilton today?*

*No, I rarely see the people who live here unless something goes wrong in their flats. Then they want to speak to me. I do a lot of cleaning and make sure the underground car park is always in operation. We've had a lot of trouble with the electronic door.*

*But you know who they are?*

*Yes, Lesley always speaks to me when she sees me, she isn't like the others. She speaks to everyone. I like her.* Although Alessandro had only met Lesley on a couple of occasions, he understood this man's sympathy towards her. Her smiling face and apparent openness were attractive to everyone, particularly those whose social skills were less well mastered.

*Could you let me into their flat? Diego's mother was expecting them at lunchtime today and they haven't arrived. She's worried something's happened.* The man seemed unsure. *You can come with me. It won't take a minute, I'm sure.*

Silently, the man went back into his office, returning with a large bunch of keys before leading the way to the service stairs and beginning the climb to the fourth floor, the top floor. Alessandro would rather have taken the lift, but he guessed this was the man's usual route to the upper floors, so he followed him without question. As they came out onto the fourth-floor landing, the man spoke. *I certainly haven't seen Diego's car in the car park today, so maybe they are away.* The man knocked loudly on the door. They waited for a response. None came. *Will I open it?* Alessandro nodded.

Once the key had turned in the lock, the man stood back, leaving Alessandro to push the door firmly to one side and enter. The smell of blood, metallic and heavy in the air, hit him instantly. It was semi-dark, shutters down. He looked for a light switch and flicked it. His eyes were drawn first to the kitchen area, neat and tidy. Unused. Then he saw it. A body resting on the sofa, surrounded by blood and missing half its head. Diego Borroni's body. It had been a long time since Alessandro had seen the consequences of an act of violence, although he had been involved at a safe distance in the murders of many through his involvement with Franco, the Poccinis and others like them. He felt suddenly sick and placed his hand on the console table next to the door to steady himself. He wondered where Lesley was. He could see no other body in the room. Should he check the rest of the flat for her body? He couldn't think straight, and he couldn't decide what to do. He could hear Lucia Borroni's steady voice in his head and imagined her shock when her son's fate was revealed to her later in the day. A day she would never forget. A noise behind him brought him back to reality.

The concierge took a step towards him. He told him to stop, aware now that this was a crime scene. Aware it would be cruel to reveal the brutal act to this man. Alessandro stepped back into the corridor and asked the concierge if he had any plastic gloves that had not been used. He said yes. He told him to go and get them. Once the concierge disappeared into the lift, aware now of the urgency of the situation, Alessandro called for assistance and waited. The concierge was back in a few minutes. Alessandro donned the gloves and went back into the flat in search of Lesley after sending the concierge to the building's front entrance to bring the teams who would soon be arriving directly to the flat.

Now that he was in the living area alone with the body, he could clearly see that it was Diego Borroni. If looked at from one side, his profile appeared intact, so Alessandro focused on that. He moved towards the door at the opposite side of the room, assuming the bedrooms would be there. And he wasn't wrong. Two bedrooms. One facing the terrace and the view of the Arno, the one where they slept. The other, a place for storing things that couldn't be stored elsewhere, including a recently packed suitcase just waiting for its final items before heading off to Cesate for a weekend with the family. But no Lesley.

*

It was just after lunch when Paolo Bianchi arrived back at his home in Cesate. The street was quiet as he drove towards his house, maintaining the twenty kilometres per hour speed limit. Ensuring, as always, that he drew no attention to himself. Once in the driveway, he opened the garage door, drove the car into its central position, then closed the gates before shutting and locking the garage doors. The number plates would need to be changed and the car cleaned, but he was hungry, so decided he would have lunch first. He always felt better after eating.

As he climbed the internal stairs from the garage to his home, he realised that his black trousers still had a faint line of mud just above the hems, and the knee area of one trouser leg, although dry, appeared a little stained. A grass stain. Everything would need to be washed.

As a small boy, Paolo had often taken all his clothes off no matter where he was when one item got dirty, but over the years, and with a lot of training by his mother, he had learned to wait until he was alone at home before taking off his clothes and replacing them with clean ones from his wardrobe. It was something he still found quite difficult since spillages and stains always changed the smell of his clothes, provoking in him an almost reflex reaction to remove them. He turned back down the stairs to the garage, where he happily removed all his clothes, placing them in the washing machine, ready for a high-temperature wash. His shoes, he placed in the sink for cleaning after lunch. There was no one to upset: one advantage of living alone.

Quietly and calmly, he ate his lunch, the noise in his head that had been upsetting him for weeks now gone. Although he had found drowning Lesley a difficult task, her death meant he no longer had to worry about her knowing too much. And he could focus on remembering the two occasions when they had met and spoken in Florence. He pretended now that they had been arranged meetings, both of them wanting the meetings to take place rather than them being the consequence of his manipulations to ensure that they met. Her smiling eyes, her long blond hair, her soft voice were his most lucid memories. Then he remembered the unexpected lack of resistance when drowning her. She'd wanted to die. Without Diego, there was nothing else left for her.

The afternoon passed in a list of jobs:

change the number plates
wash the car
clean the interior of the car
clean his shoes and disinfect the soles
wash and dry his clothes.

Order restored, he ate his evening meal, then picked up La Nazione from the selection of newspapers neatly stacked on the table to catch up on that day's news. As he turned it over to look at the front page, a familiar face was staring straight back at him beside a photograph of a burnt-out house. Franco was dead.

\*

Four men and women wearing blue plastic slippers, white paper boiler suits and white face masks were busying themselves collecting evidence from and around Diego Borroni's body. Silently, they each carried out their tasks without acknowledging each other, a well-practised routine. A routine particularly helpful when dealing with a colleague's body.

Next to the console table, Alessandro stood quietly beside Detective Chief Inspector Gianfranco Valdi, head of homicide, a small, round man with steely blue eyes and an unchanging face. A man who had seen many dead bodies and whose reputation for catching murderers had brought him from Rome to Florence ten years earlier in an effort to end the power of organised crime in the city. It had worked to a certain extent. And his reputation had only grown. But for Alessandro, he was a man to watch, a man to be careful of, a man who could discover his own links to organised crime if a mistake were made. He hoped he hadn't made a mistake by being first at the scene.

Gianfranco Valdi's phone vibrated in the inside pocket of his blue serge jacket, breaking the silence they had stood in for over half an hour. He moved quickly to answer it. Momentarily, the white-bodied workers stopped to look across at the two men standing so close to the door, waiting for the work to be completed so that they could explore the rooms for clues. Once outside the flat, Gianfranco began to speak. ... *A body?... In the Arno near Le Sieci ... Drowned? ... Send me the exact location ... You think it's her? ... Okay, get all the necessary equipment down there and the other forensics team ... I'll bring Detective Alessandro Francesco as well - he's met her ... Ciao.* He waited for the location details to arrive before sending two of his officers to the scene with instructions to get a statement from the person who had found the body. A dog walker, he imagined.

*Looks like planned murders to me, Alessandro. Who would want to kill them, and why not kill them both here? Why take additional risks?* Alessandro didn't respond; he knew he wasn't expected to. Over the years, Gianfranco had many times worried for the safety of his own family, and watching the forensics team finish their work, he knew he would be checking his home security once again.

## Twenty-eight

The house was in darkness when the front doorbell chimed. Lucia and Piero Borroni were still sitting in their usual chairs, Piero's chair high-backed with long arm rests and firm cushions assisting his weakened body in staying upright, Lucia's chair smaller and heavily padded with purple cushions, ensuring she could touch the ground with her short legs. She placed her rosary beads on the small table next to her chair and switched on the lamp. She smiled at Piero as she stood up, but he didn't smile back. All the way to the front door, she imagined Diego and Lesley on the other side with some extraordinary story to explain their lateness. She thought if she imagined it hard enough, it might actually happen. But it didn't.

Standing in front of her was Davide Ruci, station sergeant in Cesate, a friend of Piero's and a well-known face in the town. *Lucia* ... He took both her hands in his and kissed her on both cheeks just as he would normally. But nothing felt normal. Without speaking, she turned to walk back towards the living room and Piero. Davide quietly closed the door and followed her. Piero was on his feet now at his chair, tears running silently down his cheeks. Lucia wanted him to sit down, but he was reluctant to. She didn't want him standing, vulnerable, when he got the news. Davide could barely watch as Lucia persuaded his friend to sit down, knowing the news they were about to hear would alter their lives forever. His old friend, who would have been Lucia's protector before his stroke. But not now. Finally, Piero sat.

Lucia sat on the arm of her husband's chair, holding his hand as tightly as she ever remembered having done.

Davide sat down slowly on the chair Lucia had vacated, filling it with his large body. After many years of experience in telling families bad news, he knew it was always best to give people the news directly, without embellishment. Usually, they knew already the news would be bad.

*Diego has been found murdered in his flat. Shot.*

Lucia's hand went directly to her mouth to stifle the screams she wanted to come out. Piero continued to cry silently, staring at his friend, who also looked on the verge of tears. Nothing was said. Lucia felt she was falling, falling silently into a deep, dark hole she may never get out of. Worried she might fall off the arm of the chair, she knelt next to her husband's chair, her face on top of their tightly clasped hands, hoping the pain she felt might go away. But knowing it never would.

\*

Gianfranco and Alessandro saw the crime scene before they reached it. Lights stood tall and erect, illuminating the riverbank and the surrounding area with the help of a small generator that hummed monotonously. Gianfranco parked the car in the small area cordoned off by his colleagues before they walked towards the riverbank and another body. The team, dressed in the same white boiler suits and masks the two men had just left, were standing a short distance from the riverbank, having left the body in situ until Gianfranco saw it. They stopped talking when they saw Gianfranco, and Doctor Brio Ricci, forensic pathologist, moved towards them, directing both men to the riverbank where Lesley's body still lay tucked, dead and cold.

*We're pretty certain it's Lesley Hamilton. But we will need to have her formally identified. I believe you've met her, Detective Francesco?* Alessandro nodded. *Your help will mean we can move things along more quickly.*

*Was she murdered, Brio? Can you tell yet?* Gianfranco always wanted answers quickly; it generally resulted in a greater chance of catching the offender, but he knew in this case that if Lesley didn't kill Diego Borroni — and why would she? — then this was most certainly a planned hit. Finding the killer would be much more difficult. The world of organised crime was very good at covering its tracks.

*I can't tell for certain until I get her back to the lab. There is some bruising on the back of her neck consistent with being held down, but I can't see any defensive wounds. It would mean she put up no fight.*

Silence.

*Her hands weren't tied together?* Gianfranco knew he didn't really need an answer to the question since he could see one of her arms floating in the water, untethered.

*No.*

*Has the surrounding area been examined for clues?*

*The team have done as much as they can today, but a further search can be carried out in the morning.* Brio knew Gianfranco wouldn't be happy with that answer, but there was little they could do, as darkness had fallen. He would have to wait for more information tomorrow.

*Okay, she can be taken out of the water.* As the three men moved back from the riverbank to a brightly lit area where plastic sheeting had been laid out, those working with Doctor Ricci, gently and with a level of care that always surprised Gianfranco, removed Lesley's body from the water and placed her on the ground in front of them. The black plastic sheeting accentuated the blondness of her hair and the fairness of her skin. He thought she looked at peace, unlike Diego, whose shattered head screamed violence. If she had witnessed Diego's death, Gianfranco wondered if the possibility of her own death held no fear for her, no need to fight. A voice brought him back to reality.

*That is definitely Lesley Hamilton.* Alessandro turned away from the body and began walking back to Gianfranco's car. There was nothing else for him to say.

*I'll be able to give you more answers tomorrow, Gianfranco. I'll get back to the lab and start the process. Detective Borroni's body will be there by now. Did you know him, Gianfranco?*

*I met him a couple of times. He seemed very straightforward and honest. He was well liked and respected, I know that. Seems an unlikely end, but ...* His voice trailed off. He smiled at Brio before confirming with his officers that the crime scene would be lit and guarded all night. He would return tomorrow.

\*

*What about Lesley? Is she also dead? Was she in the flat?*

Davide had no answers for Lucia. He was waiting for further information, hoping his phone would ring and give him the answers to the questions Lucia wanted answered.

*She needs to be found.*

\*

Gianfranco and Alessandro returned to the Carabinieri building in Florence in silence. Gianfranco was surprised at Alessandro's reaction after so many years in the police force, but he knew that the death of someone you'd spoken to only recently was always more shocking. As they parted, Alessandro for home and Gianfranco for his office, they agreed to meet tomorrow afternoon. Gianfranco could ask all his questions then.

Lesley's family would need to know what had happened to her. As he settled himself in his chair at his all-too-familiar desk, Violetta Morelli, the youngest detective on the team, knocked gently on the glass of his open door. *I have the contact details for Lesley Hamilton's family in Scotland. I thought you would need them tonight.* Violetta was an officer who would go far. She completed tasks thoroughly and often pre-empted requests he was about to make. He liked that. She laid the paper on his desk and turned to leave.

*Thank you, Detective Morelli. A good job.* She smiled to herself as she left his office, noticing he had already begun reading the details, no doubt making decisions about which police force to call. He would speak to Lesley's family once they had been told. That needed to be done in person. That was the procedure he always liked to follow, no matter whose toes he might step on.

\*

Helen Hamilton was switching off the lights in the living room before heading to bed when she heard a car in the driveway. She expected Lesley's sister to be the visitor; anxious or angry, she always sought her mother's support. But when she opened the front door, it wasn't Kate standing in front of her. Instead, a uniformed police officer and a man in plain clothes were filling the doorway. *Mrs Hamilton, we need to speak to you. Can we come in?*

Lesley. She knew the news would be about Lesley. And she knew it would be bad.

*

Just as he picked up the cup of coffee Lucia had insisted he have, his phone rang. Davide stood up and moved into the hall to speak to his colleague. He listened carefully, his sadness almost overwhelming him. He replaced his phone in his pocket before turning back to look directly at Lucia and Piero.

*They found Lesley. I'm so sorry.*

The silence was broken as Lucia's half-drunk cup of coffee dropped to the floor, and out came the screams she had fought so hard to contain.

# Twenty-nine

Signora Conti pressed the play button on her answering machine for the third time and listened once again to the gravelly voice of Marco Poccini speaking directly to her. *I hope you are well, Signora Conti. I was wondering if you and Lesley would meet with me again. I just have a few more questions for you, particularly about the man with the black gloves. It has been a very difficult time for me and my wife, and any help you can give us would be most welcome. You can call me on ...*

She stopped listening and sat down at the table, wondering what to do next. She wanted nothing more to do with the Poccinis, and she was certain neither she nor Lesley had any more to add to their previous statements. And so she called Lesley. She called three times, leaving a short message on the final call asking Lesley to call back. Then she waited. But waiting was unbearable, so she decided to call Detective Alessandro Francesco, who had facilitated the last meeting with the Poccinis. She needed to speak to someone. Living alone meant she needed answers more quickly than someone who had the knowledge that a spouse or partner would be home at some point in the day, able to dissipate any anxieties by bringing perspective to a problem. She missed that. Maybe Detective Francesco could speak to Marco Poccini on her behalf. It seemed like the only way forward. And so she phoned.

*Are you okay, Signora Conti?* Detective Francesco could hear nothing at the other end of the phone. No tears. Silence. *I'm sorry to be the one to break the news about Lesley and Detective Borroni. Don't worry about Signor Poccini. I'll call him and sort everything out.*

*There won't be a problem.* Silence.

*Thank you, Detective Francesco.* She ended the call. Lesley and Detective Borroni dead. Murdered. Signora Conti continued to sit at the small table tucked in the corner of her kitchen, shocked by the news, unable to cry and unsure why she felt their murders were linked to the man in the black gloves. Unsure why Detective Francesco would have given her so much information but certain the murders were in some way linked to the Poccinis.

*

Alessandro wondered if Diego and Lesley had been murdered by Marco Poccini's men. He knew Marco would have been happy to see Diego dead, revenge the motive for most of his actions, but he was certain that they would have both been killed in the flat if that was the case. Although the methods of Marco Poccini's men were effective, they weren't sophisticated. Get the job done and get out.

Just as he ended the call with Signora Conti, Alessandro's wife appeared on the terrace carrying a small tray with her meagre breakfast: coffee, banana, a sweet pastry. She placed it on the table and sat down at the other end from Alessandro. No words were exchanged. *I have to go into work today. I'm needed to help with a new case.* She nodded her acknowledgement, then sat back in her chair looking out at the garden bathed in warm morning sunshine. She would have the day to herself, just the way she liked it. Gardening and painting without interruption. She didn't notice him stand up, and neither made any effort to say farewell.

Alessandro had agreed to meet with Gianfranco Valdi in the office later in the afternoon to pass on any information he had regarding Diego and Lesley, so he had the morning to make contact with Marco Poccini and meet him if necessary. He would call him as soon as he could locate a public telephone. Meticulous in his thinking, Alessandro didn't want a call to Marco Poccini logged on either his work or personal mobile now that Pepe Poccini's disappearance had been filed in the unsolved crimes drawer of his filing cabinet. Questions he wouldn't want to answer could be asked.

Alessandro drove into central Florence, parking a short distance from the Santa Maria Novella railway station. Florence was busy already with tourists arriving by train and bus to spend the day visiting as many attractions as they could fit into their eight-hour sprint, returning exhausted to their cruise liner or holiday accommodation far from the bustling city. He always felt Florence deserved better from its tourists. It was a city where you could immerse yourself in history, eat fine foods and spend many happy hours watching the world go by from the terraces of the many cafes dotted across the city.

Alessandro walked in the direction of the Duomo and the nearby public telephone which he had used on so many occasions. No CCTV to worry about and enough noise that he wouldn't be overheard. He got through first time. *Marco Poccini*, the voice on the other end said.

*Alessandro Francesco, Signor Poccini.* Calling this man Marco was something Alessandro had never been able to do despite the many years he had helped the Poccinis hide their criminal activities. *I have some news for you that won't have hit the press yet. Diego Borroni and his girlfriend Lesley Hamilton have been murdered. Their bodies were found yesterday. Diego was killed in his flat; Lesley was drowned in the Arno near Le Sieci. Gianfranco Valdi is leading the case. I'm meeting with him this afternoon. I'll have more information after that.*

*Murdered?* A pause. *Who would want to kill the girl? Borroni, I understand.*

*She may just have been collateral damage.* Alessandro knew he couldn't ask him directly if his men had been involved, but he felt the shock in Signor Poccini's voice was genuine. There was a further silence as Marco Poccini digested the news.

*I left a message on Signora Conti's phone asking to meet her and Lesley. I won't need to now. Lesley was the one I wanted to speak to. I don't think Signora Conti had anything further to add to what she'd already said. If Lesley did, as I suspect, know more about Pepe's disappearance, maybe that was the reason for her murder, and Diego Borroni was the collateral damage.* Alessandro couldn't agree with this deduction and made it clear that he felt Lesley had nothing more to add to the story of Pepe's disappearance. He thought her poor Italian had made Marco Poccini suspicious rather than there being any concrete reason not to trust her.

*Yes, Signora Conti called me about your message. I told her I would speak to you. She's not expecting me or you to call back. I should have more information on the murders tomorrow. My knowledge of Diego and Lesley means I can make myself valuable to the investigation. Do you want me to call tomorrow with an update?* A brief silence.

*No, let's meet in Coloreto at the Trattoria Ai Due Platani at midday. They'll be expecting you just as they were the last time.* The phone went dead.

Alessandro had the rest of the morning to himself. He tried calling Carla to see if she would be free but got no reply. Instead, he decided to visit the Boboli Gardens before having lunch at Trattoria Giovanni. They would squeeze him in no matter how busy they were. They always did.

*

Gianfranco Valdi usually enjoyed Saturday breakfasts. It was one of only two days in the week when they had breakfast as a family. Concetta, his wife, would buy in all their favourite pastries, hams, breads and cheeses, and breakfast could last for more than an hour as the family caught up with all the week's news, feeling that unlike most days, Gianfranco was part of the routine of their lives. As he watched his two daughters, Gianna and Anna, devour their favourite pastries, he wondered again how much danger his family were in as a consequence of his work.

He had arrived home late the previous evening, tired and emotionally exhausted. Once in bed, his arm had pulled Concetta close to him as she said a feeble hello before falling back to sleep. He kissed her forehead, stroking her soft black hair as it lay on the pillow next to him. But he hadn't slept well, repeatedly seeing Diego's fractured head when he closed his eyes. He knew Diego had solved many cases against those in the world of organised crime, and his murder certainly had the hallmarks of a paid job. But the murder of the girl, whose soft white face and long blonde hair also filled his head, was quite different. A quiet and gentle murder, if such a thing existed.

*You're not listening, Papa. I'm certain you aren't.* And she was right. He reached across the table and took Anna's small hand in his own, wondering how he could keep them safe from the world he frequented outwith his home.

*My apologies, Anna. You are quite right. I have to go into work today and I don't want to. I would rather spend the day with my three girls, but ...* For a moment, he thought he might cry, but he managed to smile at the three of them and make light of the situation. *But I will be home tonight, and we can watch a film. It's your turn to choose, Gianna. I don't mind what it is.*

*I know why you never mind what it is. You never stay awake.* The girls laughed. Concetta knew why he had to go into work, and although she had never met Diego, she understood that the murder of a colleague always reminded her husband of the dangers of his job and how easily his life and the lives of those he most loved could be wiped out. She never went there in her head. They had excellent security on the house, and a walled garden and living on the outskirts of Florence made her feel safe. It seemed far away from the crime her husband experienced every day.

*I'd better get going.* Gianfranco knew that Doctor Ricci and his team would have been working on the bodies through the night, waiting to give him their initial findings before going to their own homes and a slice of normality. He didn't want to keep them waiting. The girls continued with their breakfast, discussing their plans for the day. He kissed Concetta firmly on the lips as if it might be the last time he felt their softness and smelt the coconut perfume of her shampoo. They smiled at each other; nothing needed to be said. He would be home in a few hours. He was certain he would be.

Gianfranco parked his car close to the lift in the underground car park of the Carabinieri building. It was only at weekends that he managed to get that close. He pressed the button for the sixth floor. When the doors opened, he could see Doctor Ricci and his team of two sitting in soft chairs around a small brown coffee table covered in coffee cups and pastries. A diet to keep you awake for as long as was necessary. As he walked towards them, Doctor Ricci rose from his chair, while his team went to the lab to gather the information they had put together as they worked through the night. *Good morning, Brio.* They shook hands. *Thank you for waiting for me. I appreciate it, and it will help get the investigation off to a quicker start than it might have.*

Gianfranco and Brio had worked together for a number of years, and although there was no need to thank Brio for his work, he always appreciated Gianfranco's thanks and his kind words. Gianfranco followed him through to the office where the findings of the night were laid out on a long table bathed in Florence sunshine. Brio nodded to the young man sitting at the far end of the table. Then he began to speak.

*We'll start with Diego Borroni.* He gave the usual information regarding his age, height and weight before giving any details relating to the murder. *As you are aware, he was shot at close range, directly into his skull. One bullet killed him. The details of the bullet and the gun are in the report.* They knew Gianfranco liked their thoughts and opinions during this initial discussion, preferring to read the finer details in the privacy of his own office, where he could digest their meaning without interruption. *He died between oh-five hundred and oh-eight hundred. We think he must have just come through from the bedroom since the blinds were still closed and no food had yet been prepared for breakfast. This might suggest the gunman was already in the flat, waiting. The catastrophic injuries would suggest the gunman was no more than a few feet away when he shot him. Possibly the other side of the coffee table.* Gianfranco would revisit the crime scene. *Detective Borroni would have died instantly, but it would have been a shocking experience for whoever was there. We are sure Lesley Hamilton would have been there; evidence of her presence was everywhere. It might explain some of our findings relating to Lesley's murder which seem surprising.* He looked towards his colleague, who seamlessly began speaking about the second murder.

*Lesley Hamilton was drowned, which I think we all felt would be the case. Although some bruising was evident on the back of her neck, no other injuries, either inflicted or defensive, were found on her body. She had a few small bruises on her knees from the pebbles she was kneeling on, but nothing else. She did not resist the murderer in any way.* There was a brief silence. *If she witnessed Diego's murder, she could still have been in shock, unable to react to what was happening to her, or she may have been too frightened to react, or she had felt that death would be better than living now that Diego was dead. We know she died a short time after Diego, almost in the same time frame, which means she and the murderer would have had to leave the flat very quickly after Diego's murder. CCTV from the entrance to the underground car park confirms this. Although we can see Lesley driving the car, the murderer is shielded by the sun visor, which has been put down to ensure we can only see his black gloved hands. The car is picked up at different points on its journey, but there is no CCTV coverage at the murder site.*

Gianfranco was surprised so much evidence had been gathered in such a short time, but he knew the murder of a colleague motivated everyone to do their job more quickly and possibly more thoroughly than they would normally. It made everyone consider their own mortality in a way they didn't do when the victim wasn't known to them. *Any DNA relating to the murderer?* Silence. Doctor Ricci spoke.

*We have one or two strands of very short black hair which we found on the chair just inside the door and on the headrest in the car. They don't belong to the victims, so they have been sent to the lab for DNA analysis. They may not even belong to the murderer, of course, but they are the only clue we have which doesn't contain Diego or Lesley's DNA.* He paused. *Whoever carried out this murder was very thorough and knew exactly what they were doing. They were confident they could get in and out without being seen or leaving any evidence, and for some reason, chose different murders for each of the victims. I would feel certain they have murdered before.* He turned to look out of the window at the Arno flowing gently through the city he had lived in his entire life. *He or she may have been paid to do so. We'll let you know what the DNA results throw up. We suspect from the scant evidence in the car that the murderer was male.*

Gianfranco picked up the folder of evidence that had been put together for him, thanked them once again and began walking back to the lift. As he waited for the lift to arrive, he heard footsteps behind him. Doctor Ricci was walking towards him. *It is a puzzling case, Gianfranco. I'm sorry we don't have more information or evidence for you. If only Detective Borroni had been killed, I would have said this was a pre-ordered assassination, bought and paid for by someone seeking revenge without getting their own hands dirty, but the girl's murder has none of those hallmarks. Some of the team are back at the flat today to see if there is any further evidence to help us. We'll do the best we can.*

*I know you will, Brio, you always do. It's a difficult one for us all. Reminds us all of the dangers of the job.* The lift doors opened. He shook Doctor Ricci's hand and patted him on the back before taking the lift back to his own office to read the report. He would visit the crime scenes once again before meeting Detective Francesco this afternoon. He hoped Francesco would have information that could help him.

# Thirty

The items contained in the small wooden box now lay on the mahogany dining-room table in front of Paolo, who was digesting what he had found. The article from La Nazione detailing Franco's death lay neatly cut out at one end of the table next to the four items that answered some of the questions he had asked himself many times over many years but had always been too frightened to ask his mother. He thought of her now and her instructions to him as she had lain quietly in her bed, waiting to die.

*Paolo, this box must never be opened by you until Franco is dead. If he's dead, you won't be working, and the contents of this box will help you understand your life as well as giving you a means of erasing your links with Franco. Do you understand?* He had nodded obediently as he always did. *Only open it once he's dead.* She had handed Paolo the box, tired from the exertion of holding the box and speaking but confident that Paolo would do as she asked and confident that his ability to follow rules meant it would never be opened until Franco was dead. And she had been right. Paolo had placed it back on the third shelf of his mother's wardrobe and hadn't thought about it again until today, when the article detailing Franco's death made him realise he could now open it.

Before opening the box, Paolo had sat anxiously looking at it, wondering what secrets it held and whether his mother was right in thinking explanations would help him. He knew explanations often confused him unless they resulted in solutions. He liked solutions. They stopped the pounding noise in his head when anxiety would grip him and he could only see one way out. That was the case with Lesley. He could enjoy the memory of her now in a way he couldn't enjoy the reality of her. He thought he felt sorry about Diego, but he knew his choices had been limited. And so he had had to die too.

Paolo's mother had numbered and labelled the items, helping him make sense of it all. The first item was a birth certificate, his mother's birth certificate. Her name and date of birth were on it, but he recognised none of the other names. It wasn't the birth certificate he had used when registering her death; that contained different names and looked entirely different from this one. He took the sheet of paper that had been clipped to it and began reading.

*I was born in Sicily, Paolo, into a family whose business was organised crime — murder, drugs, money laundering and many more unscrupulous activities. I saw my father murder a man in the yard of our farm when I was six. I don't know who the man was or what crime he might have committed, but I knew then that my father, the man who sang songs to me and sat me on his knee, was not the man I thought he was. I think I knew then that I wanted to leave as soon as possible. And so I did. I bought myself a forged birth certificate when I was 18 and left Sicily for good. I came to Milan, where I found work and eventually met your father. We moved here to Cesate after our marriage, and you were born two years later. I was so happy. Life was good for a few years. Then your father discovered my deception and things changed. He couldn't forgive me. And, as you know, he eventually left us. I was always scared others might find out about my past, hence the quiet and isolated life you experienced. Your father didn't want that life. He wanted to be able to live in the world, not apart from it. I understand that now.*

It was strange for Paolo to hear his mother's voice once again, speaking so directly to him as she always did. He read on.

*Now you need to look at item number two and read the accompanying note.*

Paolo picked up a grainy black and white photograph, torn slightly in one corner, containing an image of a young man holding a small boy. They looked like they were on a beach. They looked happy, he thought, or at least they were smiling. Once again, he removed the paper clip so neatly in place and began to read his mother's words, hearing her voice so clearly in his head.

*This is a photograph of Franco in the arms of his father many years ago. The man holding Franco is my second cousin, Luigi, a man I remember little about but whose son helped me when I needed it most. Luigi left Sicily in his late teens, moving to Livorno, where some of the family businesses operated. He, like Franco, organised assassinations for various families in the north of Italy and sometimes carried these out himself. They lived well, building the house on the Gulf of Baratti for the family to live in. But Franco's father found it hard to cope with the things he had done and eventually committed suicide, leaving Franco to carry on the family business. I tracked Franco down and contacted him when you were nearing the end of your time at university and told him about Father Rossi. He was impressed that you could have committed such a murder at such a young age and never be identified as the murderer. But, for me, I needed to know you would have secure employment in the event of my death, and I knew better than most that blood is thicker than water, and so I arranged for Franco to meet you at the university and explain to you the job he was able to offer. I knew he would always look out for you; that's what families do.*

Paolo looked carefully at the photograph, studying the features of this man whose connection to his life seemed so tenuous. He looked carefully at his face, wondering if he could find any resemblance to his own features, surprised to find there was a bigger family beyond his mother and father. But the photograph was too small for Paolo to see the man clearly. Franco could have only been about three in the photo, his innocent face and dark eyes staring out at Paolo, moving him to ponder how different life could have been for Franco if, like his mother, he had been able to escape the world of his family, a world of crime.

As he laid the photograph back down on the table, his attention turned to the next item so carefully laid out on the table. A folded white shirt. As he lifted it up from the table and shook it out to its full size, he noticed stains on the sleeves. Old stains, small and brown. Then he saw his name on the label, clearly written in permanent marker by his mother. It was his shirt. And he knew which shirt it was. A sheet of paper written in his mother's neat hand lay underneath the shirt, but he was reluctant to read it. Reluctant to revisit that night. So he placed the shirt over the back of the chair next to him before venturing out of the house and into the garden. The pulsing in his head was getting louder again; he needed to do something routine, something that would lessen the noise and help him to think. Something that would rid him of the panic he was now feeling. He moved towards the hedge which surrounded all four sides of the garden and began walking as close as he could to it in a clockwise direction. The movement of his feet on the camomile lawn released the calming smell of the plant, and after ten minutes of pacing, he felt calm enough to think about the night he killed Father Rossi.

Although he had committed many murders over the years, he rarely thought about them and never thought about them in the way he thought about Father Rossi. There had been no distance between him and Father Rossi as he smothered the life out of him, listening to his choking and spluttering under the pillow, watching his hands trying to grab his assailant or the bed clothes, something that might give him purchase to fight back. But he hadn't managed to do that. And so he had died, releasing the noise in Paolo's head, the pulsing of his mother's cries gone. He was ready now to read his mother's words.

*I want to start by saying how sorry I am that I was the cause of you murdering Father Rossi. I knew that crying was something you found very hard to cope with — the noise drumming so loudly in your head and your inability to understand why someone cries. I should have remembered that. I should have had more control when I came out of the confessional. But Father Rossi's disregard for my feelings reflected the disregard your father had for my feelings, and the pain I was feeling as my marriage fell apart seemed to be all my fault. Father*

Rossi laid the blame squarely at my door as I bared my innermost thoughts to him. I regretted unburdening myself to him as soon as I did it. After we returned home from the church and you went to bed, I also went to my room but was unable to sleep. I lay for hours thinking about my problems with your father and how I could resolve them, knowing that was most likely impossible. And while lying there, I heard you go out. I'm unsure why I didn't go after you, why I didn't stop you, but I didn't. I saw you leave the garden and assumed that you needed the night's silence to recover from the upset I had caused you. The next morning, I was up first, and as was my routine, I went to the utility area to put a load in the washing machine. And there I found this shirt. The brown marks you can see on the sleeves looked like you'd been sick. I was going to put it in the sink to soak, but I heard you moving about upstairs and decided to leave the washing and see if you were okay. And you were. You had had your shower and were setting the breakfast table just as you always did. You smiled when you saw me, and we ate breakfast discussing the weather and what would be happening at school that day. Then you left. It reminded me of the morning after you killed the cat. No remorse, just relief. A clean slate. A short time later, news of Father Rossi's murder was announced on the radio. Smothered. I imagined him choking and spluttering. I imagined the debris from his mouth getting on your shirt as he gasped for breath. I imagined you killing him. I guess I should have destroyed the shirt, and I considered doing it many times over the years, but I needed you to know how I came to the conclusion that you were Father Rossi's murderer. And why I sought out family support for your future. You should destroy the *shirt now.*

Paolo knew for certain he would destroy the shirt, burn it. And he would do it today. He hated loose ends and was angry that his mother had kept this shirt for all these years. A shirt that, had it been found, would have identified him as the killer. These were risks he would never take. Evidence always had to be destroyed, or better than that, you made sure you left no evidence in the first place. His eyes wandered towards the fourth and last item laid out on the table: a set of keys attached to a keyring showing a limited view of the city whose name adorned it, Livorno. He wanted to discover the significance of the keys, but the need to destroy the shirt overwhelmed him. He wanted it burnt completely and quickly. He retrieved a firelighter from the box in the garage, opened the glass-fronted door of the wood-burning stove in the living room and placed the shirt inside with the firelighter and some kindling on top. Then he lit it. He watched and waited until every last part of it had burned, adding more wood as the fire developed, ensuring it would never be found. Once he was satisfied the job had been done, he left the fire to continue burning and returned to the dining room to find out why he now had a set of keys.

As he sat down once again at the table, he noticed there were only two keys on the keyring, both for deadlocks. Unusual, he thought, unless you were worried about security and the possibility of a break-in. A sealed envelope marked 'Keys' sat next to them. Paolo was concerned by the sealed envelope and for a few minutes considered not opening it. He knew it must contain details his mother had felt had to be hidden, and he feared they were details he may have to act on. He knew he didn't want to return to the life he hoped to turn his back on. But his mother's voice was strong in his head, humming gently every time he moved. He would have to open the envelope.

*Franco wasn't unlike you, Paolo: meticulous. He found himself in a world of crime inherited from his father and he didn't want to be a victim of that world, nor did he want the assassins he employed to be a victim of that world. His family home was his place away from the world he worked in, with no information relating to his work or the work done by you and others contaminating it. Instead, he kept a small flat in Livorno for his work, and these are the keys to that flat. In it he kept his files, his phones. In essence, all the things that could link you and others to many murders committed across northern Italy in the past twenty to twenty-five years. Evidence that now needs to be destroyed before someone wonders why he hasn't been at the flat for a number of days. And you have to do that, Paolo. You have to go there and destroy all the evidence. It is the only way you can protect yourself. You wouldn't survive prison.* She was right.

Although he lived a life of routine, it was one he created for himself which allowed him to meet his needs, not one dictated by others. He turned to look at the pile of newspapers in the corner, knowing that no one else bought six daily newspapers in order to compare and contrast the weather forecasts detailed in each of them. He always looked forward to that part of his day, rewarding himself with an hour of weather forecasts when he had completed the other tasks he had scheduled. His mother understood, but few others did.

*You need to destroy it soon, Paolo, very soon.*

At the bottom of the page was the address for the flat in Livorno. He placed the sheet of paper back on the table, sat back and considered his options, soon realising there weren't really any options. He didn't want to be found. He would destroy the evidence; he would go tomorrow. But first, he would destroy the evidence lying in front of him. He tore off the address from the bottom of the sheet of paper, folded it in half and placed it in his wallet. The keys, he placed in the bowl by the door, and everything else, he took to the wood-burning stove and threw in. He sat back in the brown velvet chair directly in front of the fire and watched them burn until he was sure they had gone completely.

## Thirty-one

Helen Hamilton had had a very difficult night. The news about Lesley's murder was so final, so shocking. Then having to tell Lesley's sister Kate the news. Kate found life difficult and coped in the main by thinking only of herself. Her mother and sister only mattered to her in terms of how they could support her, and Helen had wondered how Kate would take the news. But she needn't have. Kate looked inward as usual and picked fault with the decisions her sister had made. *I knew she shouldn't have gone. She should have stayed here with us. And getting in tow with another man when she hadn't been able to keep her first marriage on track. Insanity. And what will we do now?* Helen heard the continuing noise of her now only daughter's voice, but she'd stopped listening.

Often, and again on this occasion, she would watch and listen to Kate, wondering how Lesley had turned out so differently. Thoughtful, kind, uncomplaining, loving, selfless. She wished her husband was still alive. He would know what to do; he would know what to say to Kate; he would tell her what's what. Helen wouldn't. She found it impossible to be the one to damage her daughter even more than she already had been. But maybe that was the problem. Kate's voice became part of her consciousness ... *and she never thought of us. Never.*

*She always thought of us.* Silence.

*I'd better go now. Sam and the kids will be wondering what's happened. I'll call round tomorrow.* She kissed her mother lightly on the cheek and left. No tears, no expressed sorrow. Helen's sorrow felt so great, she wondered if she would be able to stand up, but she did.

She went to bed, lying awake for hours, rerunning her last telephone conversation with Lesley over and over in her head. Lesley's voice, happy and cheerful. So happy, so content with Diego and her new life. A completed novel as well, everything on track. Her mother's visit to Florence all planned out to make sure she had a lovely time. And now this. Why?

The police had been as helpful and as sympathetic as they could be when they came to give her the news, but she knew that at such a distance, details could be lost and her ability to understand what had happened would be limited. She would have to go to Florence, and soon. It was her only hope of resolution. She picked up the card the police had given her with the name of the detective leading the investigation, Gianfranco Valdi. She would call him on Monday once she'd arranged her flight. Kate wouldn't be happy, but at least she felt confident Kate wouldn't want to go with her. Finally, she fell asleep.

*

Alessandro was finishing his lunch at Trattoria Giovanni — prawns with chickpea purée and rosemary to start, followed by a veal chop with roasted cherry tomatoes and an assortment of roasted potatoes. A perfect end to a lovely morning. The Boboli Gardens had been looking resplendent as they slowly reached their summer majesty, and lunch, as always, was perfectly cooked. The single glass of red wine lifted his mood. He was ready to meet Gianfranco Valdi and acquire as much information as he could.

He walked the short distance back to the Carabinieri building and took the lift to Gianfranco's office. As he made his way through the empty desks, he noticed, sitting quietly at a desk in the corner inputting information into the computer, a young woman with striking eyes and shining dark hair. She smiled at him but said nothing. Alessandro wondered why she was there and hoped she wouldn't be joining the meeting. He wanted no witnesses, no one who might pick up on his hesitancy to give answers or impart information. It would be hard enough maintaining a relaxed pose with Gianfranco, whose ability to detect false information was well known.

Gianfranco Valdi got up from his chair when he saw Alessandro, coming round the side of his desk to shake his hand and offer him a seat on a small leather sofa tucked in the corner. Gianfranco stuck his head out the door and called, *Detective Morelli.* She got up instantly from her desk, bringing a notebook and pen with her. Gianfranco sat in the chair next to the sofa while Detective Morelli sat on a wooden chair next to the desk, the only other chair in the office apart from Gianfranco's desk chair. She knew she shouldn't sit there. *This is Violetta Morelli, Alessandro. She is going to take some notes for me if that's okay, not a statement or anything. Just an exchange of information.* Alessandro nodded his reluctant agreement. *Good, let's get started. I thought you would want to know what we've found out so far in terms of forensics.* And so Gianfranco went over the information he had received that morning from Doctor Ricci.

Most of it wasn't a surprise to Alessandro. He had seen the bodies, seen the injuries. But three things stood out for him — Diego had been killed before Lesley, she had not resisted her murder, and the man in the car with Lesley was wearing black gloves. He knew that was significant. Was that the same man who had been seen in the Via Porta Rossa around the time of Pepe Poccini's disappearance? Gianfranco stopped speaking. Alessandro thanked him for sharing the information and asked if he could see the CCTV footage of the car. He wanted to have as much detail as possible for Marco Poccini.

Without hesitating, Gianfranco turned his computer screen to face Alessandro, and he clicked on the screen. It was a very short piece of footage. He could see Lesley quite clearly, but as described, only the hands and legs of the man next to her could be seen. Black gloves, black trousers. He thanked Gianfranco for letting him see it, then asked if any fibres or hairs belonging to this man had been found in the flat or the car. *We have some hairs; they're at the lab. But nothing else. He had either planned very carefully or had murdered before. No fingerprints, no careless leaving of evidence. We think he was in the flat during the night waiting for them to get up. Probably a professional.*

Alessandro looked down at the floor and began speaking. He had had all morning to plan what he would say, and so he started. Violetta began taking notes, thinking all the time that Detective Francesco sounded like he was reading from a script. A strange way to pass on information unless you were being careful to pass on only what you wanted others to hear. Detective Gianfranco Valdi appeared oblivious to this, but it was always hard to tell what he was thinking. She returned to her note-taking.

*I didn't know Detective Borroni particularly well given we worked in different areas. Our paths crossed recently with the disappearance of Pepe Poccini. His apparent disappearance was reported by a neighbour,* and Diego was first to make enquiries at the building where the young man lived. Once they discovered the missing boy was a Poccini, I was drafted in. He looked at Gianfranco, wondering what he knew already about Diego Borroni. He continued. Diego had worked on a case relating to the Poccinis when he was in Milan and had gone a bit far with his investigations. The Poccinis complained and Diego was transferred. All those years in organised crime gone in an instant, a poor decision, I think. Gianfranco's face didn't change, but he nodded his agreement. Alessandro felt his heart beating more loudly than usual in his chest, anxious not to say too much but eager to ensure he said enough. I carried out my usual investigations, and although it was clear the boy had disappeared, there were no leads as to where he might have gone. I'm afraid he's now in the drawer with my other unsolved crime cases. Never a satisfactory outcome. Diego met Lesley when he interviewed her before I took over the case, and they got together after that, I think.

Gianfranco stood up from his chair and walked towards the window behind his desk. Violetta said nothing, sitting with her pen poised close to the page of her notebook, comfortable with the silence. Yes, I've read Detective Borroni's file, and you're right. He was transferred following his over-involvement with the Poccini case. Calling it a case would be inaccurate, I guess, since most of his suspicions were just hunches. They must be powerful people if they can get a senior police officer demoted and transferred. I think I need to know more about them. Detective Morelli will go to Milan on Monday to look at the files. She looked momentarily surprised, then pleased. She smiled directly at her boss as he continued talking. *I know the connection to the Poccinis may not be relevant, but I wouldn't want to leave any stone unturned. Would you be good enough to bring your file on Pepe Poccini to my office before you leave the building, Alessandro?* He nodded his assent. *What do you think happened to the Poccini boy? What was your conclusion?*

*It could be that he simply left Florence to start a new life somewhere else, but we found no evidence of him travelling anywhere, and his bank accounts were never touched. He would have to have been very organised to do that.* He paused, knowing he would have to mention the blood. *Some of his blood, a very small trace, was found on the stairwell, meaning he could have had an accident or ... been murdered and the body taken away.*

Gianfranco turned quickly. *And that information was never passed on to my team? The homicide team? The people with the expertise in this area?* He fixed his eyes firmly on Alessandro. It was the question Alessandro didn't want to answer.

*The Poccinis thought it most likely Pepe had simply taken himself away from his life in Florence. The blood could have been there for months. There was no other evidence pointing to murder. I guess it was only a thought in my head.* It sounded pathetic, and he knew Gianfranco Valdi, the man brought to Florence to clean up the city, would know it was pathetic and most likely untrue.

*Thank you for your time, Alessandro. If you could bring the Poccini file to my office before you leave the building, that would be very helpful. I'll be in touch if we need any further information.* Alessandro stood up from the sofa and put out his hand to Detective Morelli. She shook it and smiled. Gianfranco had turned back to the window, unable to hide his anger and unable, therefore, to shake Alessandro's hand. He waited until Alessandro was safely in the lift before he spoke to Violetta. *I want those notes formally typed up, Violetta, and kept securely in our data files. Then I want you to go to Milan on Monday, meet Diego's old team, and find out everything you can about his work in relation to the Poccinis and anything else that might lead us to the person who would want to murder him. If you have to stay a couple of nights, just do that. We need to find out what else is being hidden from us.*

Alessandro Francesco would need to be watched. He would organise that on Monday.

*

Alessandro retrieved Pepe's file from its drawer in the cabinet next to his desk, hoping Gianfranco Valdi would simply consider him incompetent in this instance rather than deciding that all his unsolved cases would need to be reviewed. That was a can of worms Alessandro hoped would never be opened. As he came out of the lift and walked towards Gianfranco's office, he saw Violetta Morelli get up from her chair and come towards him. *I'll give him the file, Detective Francesco. He's busy reading the other files. Probably best he's not disturbed.* Happy not to have to speak to Gianfranco again, he handed her the file and watched as she went into the office and laid it in front of Gianfranco without saying a word. He turned and left, keen to see the Poccinis tomorrow and plan how to move things forward.

Gianfranco stared at the file lying on his desk and knew he would have to stay in the office reading all day. He wanted to have more to think about tomorrow, when he would spend the day with his girls rather than frequenting the silent corridors of the Carabinieri building. He would at least be with them in body even if his mind was elsewhere.

\*

Time seemed to pass very slowly for Lucia and Piero Borroni as they tried to come to terms with Diego's murder and the murder of Lesley, the girl who had made their son so happy. Piero found it hard to stop crying. Silent tears would run down his cheeks as he sat quietly, finding it harder than usual to string any words together. He wanted to be strong for Lucia, but once again she would be the strong one, keeping the routine of their lives on track and comforting him in his despair.

Lucia's grasp of English was rudimentary, but she was eager to speak to Lesley's mother. She felt keenly that this woman she had never met would be the only person feeling exactly as she was feeling: the physical pain that seemed to envelop her limbs as she struggled to keep some of the daily routines going, the continuous images of her son flitting through her head, and the knowledge that the pain would be there until death took her as well. And so she sat down in her favourite chair and dialled the number that would give her the opportunity she so craved. It rang three times before it was picked up and a quiet voice said, *Hello?*

*Hello, Mrs Hamilton. This is Lucia Borroni, mother of*

*Diego Borroni. I knew your lovely daughter Lesley. I'm so sorry ...* and then she began to cry, unable to finish the words she had rehearsed so often in the night as she lay awake wondering if she would ever sleep again. They both cried, waiting for the need to cry to pass before speaking again.

*Thank you for calling, how kind of you. Call me Helen. I'm flying to Italy on Monday evening. Would I be able to see you while I'm there?* Though surprised to hear this, Lucia was delighted. *I think Lesley would want to be buried next to Diego. He had made her very happy. But I'm not sure how you would feel about it? And I'm not sure how I go about it. Could we talk about it when I get there?*

*Of course we can. We can talk about everything.* And so arrangements were made for Helen to stay with the Borronis after she had had a couple of days in Florence. Maybe by then, the bodies would be released, and maybe then they could all begin the journey towards peace.

## Thirty-two

Livorno was a good three-and-a-half-hour drive from Cesate if there were no delays, so Paolo rose early, earlier than usual, and was driving his car out of the driveway before the church bells of the Parrochia San Alessandro e San Martino had chimed seven. It was a beautiful day of clear blue skies and bright sunshine. But despite the heat that would build and grow as the day progressed, Paolo wore his customary black shoes, black socks, black trousers, white shirt and black leather jacket. His black leather gloves were tucked inside the small bag that sat on the passenger seat next to him along with the gun that had killed Diego Borroni and many others. He hoped the gun would never be needed again, but the security he felt when he carried it meant he couldn't leave it behind, couldn't take that chance.

Paolo enjoyed driving, particularly when most of the journey could be done on motorways. He could consider his speed, his average speed, his fuel consumption, his average fuel consumption, removing himself from the world of emotions and concerns to a world with predictable and concrete answers. The world he preferred.

As he drove into Livorno, vague memories of a visit there as a small boy came back to him. He wasn't sure who else had been there, but he remembered his mother holding his hand and guiding him through the railway station. It had been full of people and noise. A tremendous echoing noise. He clung so tightly to her hand that his nail cut through her skin, causing blood to gather in the palm of her hand and consequently in his. It had felt warm and sticky in his hand, a sensation he abhorred. A painful sensation that made him cry. He had cried so loudly and for so long that once his hand was cleaned, they had simply got back on the train for Milan and home. He wondered now why they had been in Livorno and whether his mother, even all those years ago, was searching for her family. For a connection to a past that she had previously wanted to escape. For a brief moment, he wished she was still here so he could ask her.

As he entered the edges of the city, he pressed the button on his sat nav, having already put in the name of the street where Franco's flat was located. But he had used a house number from elsewhere in the street. He knew GPS could be stored and read, and he didn't want to lead anyone directly to the door of the flat. Like Florence, Livorno paraded its history around every street corner. Four-storey palazzos sat adjacent to canals peppered with small boats, giving the city a coolness in the heat of the day that many other Italian cities lacked. The buildings were in good order, with most of them now converted into flats. As he followed the clipped directions of the electronic female voice, he realised that New Venice, the location of Franco's flat, was small and heavily populated. Getting a parking space would be problematic, so he took the first available space, cleared his GPS, put on his black gloves, then got out of the car, ensuring his small bag was securely closed and draped across his body, to search for the flat on foot. Although using his phone to find the street would be easier, he had had it switched off since he left Cesate and had no intention of putting it back on until he got home.

He liked New Venice. The canals smelt of the sea, a smell he had enjoyed as a boy and which held many happy memories for him. Cafes and restaurants had prime positions next to the canals, and Via Traversa, the location he'd been looking for, ran at right angles to the main canal system, affording its residents easy access to their boats and the cool sea. Maintaining the same pace he'd been keeping since he left the car, he looked for number 140. A large wooden door several centuries old marked the entrance to the flats. It wasn't open and Paolo was worried he needed another key since the original lock was still in place. He needn't have worried. The door moved easily as he gently pushed it open, leading him into a small courtyard that allowed sunshine to fall on the small group of pot plants that sat huddled together in the centre. Stone stairs leading up to the higher floors were located in the far corner and he walked smartly towards them, hoping no one was looking out of their window, wondering who this visitor was. A visitor they had never seen before. As he climbed the stairs to the fourth floor, he removed the keys from his bag, preparing to get into the flat as quickly as possible.

Paolo climbed slowly, silently placing his feet on the stair treads, ensuring he wouldn't be heard. As he reached the fourth floor, the door to the flat was directly in front of him. Two dead locks that opened easily. He was in.

Although he wasn't sure what he'd been expecting, he knew that what was in front of him wasn't what he had envisaged. He had expected a flat furnished comfortably but not luxuriously. A flat you could actually live in. Instead, he found himself immediately in a large room, empty apart from a white table lamp sitting alone on a small wooden table in the corner and windows draped in heavy lace curtains that let in the light but prevented anyone seeing in. A timer ensuring the lamp gave a sense of occupancy was connected to the lamp. The wallpaper was old and coming off in places. Next to this room was a small kitchen with a heavy porcelain sink and a few cupboards. A kettle, two cups and a small fridge sat on the worktop. He looked in the fridge and was pleased to find it empty and clean. He returned to the larger room and went through the door in the corner — another large room hidden from the public by heavy lace drapes, with a small bathroom off it.

There in the centre of the room were the items his mother had mentioned: a long wooden desk, a small filing cabinet tucked neatly under the desk and an array of mobile phones lined up along the edge of the desk labelled with, he guessed, the names of the assassins Franco had employed. Pleased he couldn't see one with his name on it — already destroyed, he imagined — he sat down in the leather chair that had been tucked under the desk. The only concession to comfort.

As he sat looking at the items on the table and the files placed in the filing cabinet, Paolo realised that Franco had always been a man who could be trusted, a man who would protect his valued workers from the world of crime they dipped in and out of. He began thinking about how he might destroy the evidence. Ideally, he would have removed it all, taken it back to Cesate and destroyed it gradually as he felt like it. But he knew that getting it out of the building without being seen would be very difficult. He would have to make several trips to the flat, and he didn't want to do that. He had been lucky today not meeting any of the neighbours, but he knew that luck could easily run out. Alternatively, he could take with him what he could carry, then burn the building down. He thought that might be his preferred option since it would erase all traces and links to Franco, but he knew that ran other risks, mainly for its occupants, but also for him.

It was a long time since he had left Cesate that morning, and he was feeling quite hungry. He decided to get some lunch. The decision on how to proceed could be made later at home, where he could think things through clearly. There seemed little urgency to make a decision today. He took the one file in the cabinet with his name on it, folded it in four and put it in his bag.

*

Alessandro Francesco drove into the car park of the Trattoria Ai Due Platani in Coloreto fifteen minutes before the agreed time. As he emerged from the car, he checked the car park and the road for any cars that looked like they might have been following him. He didn't trust Gianfranco Valdi not to have someone following him. The cars were flowing freely on the road, and none of the cars parked in either the car park or on the road had anyone in them. He felt safe.

Alessandro gave the owners his name and explained who he was meeting, and he was taken once again to the terrace of the walled garden at the back of the restaurant, where a lunch table was set for four. And he waited, passing the time admiring the kitchen garden with its rows of neatly grown vegetables and clipped hedges of lavender buzzing with insects. After about twenty minutes, the wooden door to the garden opened, allowing the Poccinis to enter. Marco Poccini, slightly stooped, walked slowly towards Alessandro, smiling at him as they shook hands. Luca and Lorenzo, his sons, walked straight to the table and sat down without looking at Alessandro, while Leonardo, their trusted bodyguard, took up position at the gate to the garden, ensuring no one would disturb them. They were ready for business.

Lunch was brought to the table promptly, and soon they were alone again in the garden, ready to talk business. Alessandro began by giving them the forensic details he had regarding the murders of Diego and Lesley. He described the CCTV footage of Lesley driving the car and the black gloves worn by the murderer. He explained that DNA testing was taking place on some hairs they couldn't attribute to either Diego or Lesley. He detailed the injuries to Diego's head and the lack of injuries to Lesley. The Poccinis continued eating silently, occasionally looking up as Alessandro went through all the information. When he stopped, there was silence. The Poccinis placed their cutlery neatly on their plates before starting their questioning.

*Who do they think was the target of this attack, Alessandro?*

*They're not sure at the moment. It certainly has all the hallmarks of a hit on Diego Borroni, but why kill him in his flat and have the complication of killing his girlfriend? And why kill her elsewhere? That seems unusual.* He paused. *I think she was the target and Diego, the collateral damage, but Gianfranco Valdi seems to think otherwise.*

*Why would she be the target?*

Alessandro paused before answering because he knew this was the moment he would have to tell them that Gianfranco Valdi now knew about Pepe and the blood on the stairs. *If the man in the car is the same man seen in the Via Porta Rosa when Pepe disappeared, then it is likely the killer on both occasions was the same person. And it is possible that Lesley Hamilton witnessed or saw* something to do with Pepe's disappearance, making her murder a way of tidying things up. He looked directly at Marco Poccini before continuing. *You thought she was hiding something, Marco, didn't you?* Marco nodded and waited for Alessandro to continue. *Diego was no longer involved in investigating organised crime, and unless someone had a long-held grudge, it seems unlikely that he would have been the target at this precise moment. His work in Florence didn't ruffle many feathers.* Alessandro paused again, knowing that the Poccinis' long-held grudge against Diego Borroni made them suspects in his killing, and he wondered if he would see any signs in their faces that they had been involved. But there were none. *These are only my thoughts. I may have more information in a few days. Gianfranco Valdi is a very good investigator; I'm sure now that he has Pepe's file and the knowledge Pepe may have been murdered, he will make every effort to find the man responsible for all three murders.* They seemed unsurprised at this turn of events, and Alessandro wondered, not for the first time, if he wasn't the only Carabinieri insider to be working for the Poccinis.

Luca spoke. *And if you're right, how do we now find this man in the black gloves? Franco is dead, Lesley Hamilton is dead, Diego Borroni is dead. We have no other sources. No one else who can tell us who this man is.*

*I need more time. I need to see what happens over the next couple of weeks.* Luca shook his head, but Marco Poccini nodded his agreement. *I plan on looking at Diego's files, going to his funeral and making myself useful to Gianfranco Valdi so that I can get more information.* Although he hadn't got off to a good start with Gianfranco, he was certain he could turn that around. He waited for a response. The three men looked at each other before Marco spoke.

*We will meet here again two weeks from today at the same time. If you have any information before then that would be useful to us, I expect you to contact me as you usually do. Is that understood?* Marco continued to stare steadily at Alessandro, ensuring he understood that two weeks was all the time he had. Alessandro understood. He also knew it was time for him to leave. He shook hands once again with Marco Poccini, nodded to his sons and left the garden by the old wooden gate held open for him by Leonardo.

When he got back to his car, Alessandro could feel beads of sweat running down his back, and the palms of his hands needed wiping before he could start driving. It was the first time in a long time that he had felt worried for his own safety. He knew he had to have more information in a fortnight, no matter how scant it might be. Before driving off, he tried calling Carla once again, hoping she would answer, hoping she would be free. But the phone rang on and on with no reply and no facility to leave a message. He would have to return to his wife, to the silence of his marriage, and wait for his Friday appointment with Carla to come round again.

# Thirty-three

Gianfranco Valdi listened carefully to Helen Hamilton, who, eager to call him, had phoned first thing on Monday morning. She explained she was flying to Italy later that day and would be in Florence for three nights before going to Cesate to see Diego Borroni's parents. An appointment for the Tuesday afternoon was arranged. He understood why she needed to come and her hope that by coming to Florence, she would get some closure on the terrible death of her daughter. But he knew better than most that closure was rarely possible where murder was concerned. Imagining your relative's death being both frightening and painful would haunt those left behind for many years and often resulted in needless suicides when people could no longer live with the thoughts in their heads.

Helen's voice did not waver throughout the conversation, and he wondered if she was still in shock from the news of her daughter's death or whether her focus on getting to Italy meant that she didn't need to cry. Not yet anyway. Her voice sounded soft and kind, and he considered for a moment if Lesley's voice would have sounded the same. They said their goodbyes.

Gianfranco Valdi wasn't yet sure how to move forward with the case. He needed more information about Diego Borroni's working life before coming to Florence; Violetta would gather that. And he needed to know more about Detective Alessandro Francesco and why he wouldn't have passed on the Pepe Poccini case when he suspected he had been murdered. He needed him followed. As he looked out from his office at his team of detectives carrying out the many tasks he had given them, he considered who was the most trustworthy and who would be able to follow Alessandro without being seen. Corruption, he knew, was part and parcel of life in the Carabinieri, so he needed to be as certain as he could be that the person he chose had no links to Detective Francesco. In the far corner, sitting alone at his desk, was Rigoberto Copelli. He was the person for the job.

Rigoberto had worked in Florence for only three months, transferring from Naples when an opportunity to work in the team of Gianfranco Valdi came up. An opportunity he didn't want to miss even though it meant his young family remaining in Naples for a few months while they sold the house and bought one in Florence. He had expected to miss his family more, but the job was demanding and tiring. Going home alone meant he felt refreshed every day and able to give of his best. He would have established his routines when his family finally arrived.

Gianfranco remembered Rigoberto's interview well. Considered and confident answers, excellent eye contact, pertinent questions at the end and a sincerity that was convincingly genuine. He'd liked him from the start. And he was as certain as he could be that he had no pre-existing loyalties in the Florence Carabinieri. He would have him start today. Gianfranco worried he had already given Detective Francesco too much rein.

*

*I was so sorry to hear about Diego and his girlfriend. It must be a terrible time for you and Mr Borroni. They looked so happy when I saw them.* Paolo thought he should stop there; he had to appear as he always did.

Distant, detached, formulaic.

On his return from Livorno the previous evening, Paolo had been very tired. So tired that he had simply placed the file with his name on it in the centre of the dining-room table and gone to bed. But sleep had evaded him for a long time, and he didn't like that. He knew there was enough food in the house for his breakfast, but a trip to the supermarket would be needed that morning to ensure he was able to eat for the next few days. So he rose early, before the alarm on his phone went off, hoping if he returned to his usual routine, then he could settle his mind. The file remained untouched. He wanted no more information to digest or feel anxious about.

He took the quickest route to the supermarket, hoping he would meet no one he knew on his way. And he didn't. The car park had only a handful of cars in it, none of which he recognised. The familiar droning of the air conditioning welcomed him when he entered, and dragging the small blue trolley behind him, he began his usual route round the aisles, picking up almost automatically the items that would see him through the next few days while he decided what he was going to do about the flat in Livorno. He would return there on Friday. That would give him enough time to plan.

As he exited the cool air of the supermarket, switching his two shopping bags from one hand to the other, he saw in front of him the small figure of Mrs Borroni. He thought she seemed smaller than usual, and he hoped that given her head was bowed as she walked towards the entrance, he might be able to avoid speaking to her. But her head did not remain bowed. She looked up, and on recognising Paolo, she smiled at him and spoke. *Hello, Paolo.* He knew he had to respond.

*I was so sorry to hear about Diego and his girlfriend. It must be a terrible time for you and Mr Borroni. They looked so happy when I saw them.* He could see tears forming in Mrs Borroni's eyes as she reached out to touch his arm, suddenly withdrawing it when she remembered his hatred of touch.

*Thank you, Paolo. Thank you. It is so nice to see you, a welcome reminder of Diego and his life.* There was silence as they stood sharing the same space but not the same emotions. *I'd better get on with my shopping. Lesley's mother is coming to stay with us in a couple of days, must get myself organised.* She smiled directly at him once again before taking a trolley and heading into the supermarket. Paolo said nothing. He didn't know what to say. It was a situation he had never encountered before. He had never met the relatives of any of those he had murdered. He could feel his heart beating faster than usual, and the pulse in his head was throbbing loud and hard. He had to get home as quickly as possible and get on with his day. So he took the quickest way home once again. The file would need to be destroyed.

*

Helen had always enjoyed travelling and was more widely travelled than many women her age. Her husband had travelled extensively before they met, and that had continued throughout the years of their marriage. Australia, Canada, Africa, Europe. But Florence was somewhere she had never been, and she felt somewhat guilty for looking forward to seeing it. She wanted to see and experience the places and things Lesley had talked about so enthusiastically on the telephone. She wanted to understand the source of her happiness. And she knew that being on her own would help her cope with the grief. It always had in the past. Kate, however, was much less happy with the arrangements. She thought her mother should stay in Scotland and have the body flown home once all the necessary investigations had been carried out. She felt abandoned and saw this, in her skewed view of reality, as another example of Lesley's selfishness even in death. Helen couldn't agree and she didn't. That meant that when she locked up her house and got into the taxi for the airport, she did it alone. On one level, she was happy not having to say goodbye to Kate, but she knew things would be difficult on her return. And she knew that although she should have told Kate about her plan to have Lesley buried with Diego, another tantrum would have ensued, and she wasn't feeling strong enough for another argument. She was content in her own mind that it was what Lesley would have wanted.

The flight was quiet and uneventful. Evening flights, she remembered, often were. A taxi arranged by the hotel was waiting for her when she landed at Pisa International Airport, and soon she was speeding through the Italian countryside towards Florence. She spoke no Italian and the driver spoke no English, allowing her to sit in silence and imagine what the coming days would bring. She had always found working through possible scenarios in her head helped her cope with difficult situations that might arise. Soon they were on the outskirts of Florence, heading towards the centre, its floodlit buildings accentuating the stunning architecture in the clear night sky.

Her booking at the Hotel Porta Rossa didn't disappoint. The sympathetic restoration of the building meant the modern fittings were outclassed by the centuries-old frescoes adorning the walls of every room. She was tired now, very tired. After organising her room and bathing, she lay down on the bed, knowing she needed to sleep well if she was going to be able to face the rigours of tomorrow. The soft white cotton sheets lightly covered her, and she stared at the frescoes, trying to imagine who had painted them. They were beautiful. Lesley had spoken to her often of the beauty of Florence and of the many frescoes she had seen in the city. She was struck then by the fact that Lesley would never see another one.

Finally, Helen was able to cry.

*

Paolo's day involved gardening, eating, gardening, eating, newspapers and then dusk. And during all this activity, the cardboard file with his name on it still lay staring out at him every time he used or passed the dining-room table. He wanted to destroy it without looking in it, but the temptation to see the information Franco kept became too great. Paolo picked it up, aware that its contents could upset him, could cause him to have another restless night. But aware also that if it contained nothing he didn't already know, he would be able to burn the contents, rid his mind of its memory and sleep soundly. He hoped the latter would be the case.

Franco's scrawled handwriting covered the yellowing pages with details of every job Paolo had carried out in the last twenty years: the names of those murdered and the names of those who had paid for the murder to take place. He read the pages twice, checking each time that

Franco hadn't missed anything. And he hadn't. Facts and figures, nothing else. And so he burnt it successfully in the wood-burning stove before going to bed, where he slept soundly, feeling the benefit of such a settled sleep when he woke.

## Thirty-four

Rigoberto Copelli was pleased to have been singled out by his boss for this particular job, but tailing another officer, a potential colleague, did make him somewhat uncomfortable. After speaking to Gianfranco in the silence of his office after most of the team had gone home on the Monday evening, he guessed he had been chosen for a number of reasons: he was new to the team and had no loyalties, he was keen to impress and wanted to be seen to do a good job, and he had made few friends on the team since arriving, so neither he nor Gianfranco Valdi would have to explain his whereabouts to the others. And more than that, Gianfranco knew that he could work long hours since his family hadn't yet arrived from Naples.

He was surprised at how open Gianfranco was in explaining his reasons for having Detective Alessandro Francesco followed. He gave Rigoberto every detail of the case, Alessandro's involvement, and crucially, the fact that he hadn't alerted the homicide team to the possibility that Pepe Poccini might have been murdered. Rigoberto was aware of the Poccinis from his work in Naples. Their name had come up in some of the cases he'd worked on, but no criminal involvement had ever been proven. He knew they were slippery customers.

Once Gianfranco had finished his briefing, he set Rigoberto to reading a number of relevant files, ensuring he had all the details he would need regarding Alessandro Francesco. It seemed a long shot that Diego Borroni or Lesley Hamilton had been murdered because of Pepe Poccini's disappearance, but he knew that if Gianfranco Valdi thought it was a possibility, then he should too.

It was late when Rigoberto finally left the office for his bare, lonely apartment. He heated up and ate a tin of pasta, which simply reminded him of how much he missed his wife's cooking rather than satiating his hunger. He missed much more than just her cooking, but he was too tired to think about that. He would have to be up early to make sure he was at Alessandro Francesco's house before he left for the office. There would be no call home tonight.

*

Helen woke to a myriad of sounds from the Via Porta Rossa, surprisingly refreshed. As she lay quietly, looking once again at the impressive frescoes adorning her walls, she realised the noise from the street would be the same sounds her daughter had listened to. To Helen, it seemed noisy for 7.30 in the morning, but she remembered Lesley had said that in Florence, people generally started work early, enjoyed a long lunch and finished later than they would have in Scotland. Lesley's voice was so clear in her head now, popping up and speaking to her when she least expected it. It was comforting in a strange way, making her loss seem less real. She remembered she had felt the same after her husband died. His voice filled her head for months until eventually she could hear it no more, and if it hadn't been for some home videos they had taken when the girls were young, she knew she wouldn't be able to remember it now. And she knew it would be the same with Lesley. The sound of her voice would eventually disappear from her head, and the voicemail Lesley had left her when she first arrived in Florence would be her only means of remembering the gentleness of her voice.

Given that her meeting with Inspector Gianfranco Valdi wasn't until the afternoon, Helen decided the morning would be devoted to exploring some of the places Lesley had spoken about. It gave her a purpose, a reason to get up. So she did.

*

Rigoberto Copelli drove a Fiat 500, dark blue in colour with chrome trimmings. The family car, he had left in Naples for his wife's use, investing instead in a small city car that could be easily parked and which, thankfully, had few distinguishing features. He wouldn't be noticed. At least that was his plan. He was uncertain when Alessandro Francesco generally left his home for the Carabinieri offices, but Rigoberto was determined he wouldn't miss him and so parked up in the suburban street where Alessandro lived before 6.00 am. He had a flask of coffee and some pastries in a small brown bag nestled in the footwell of the passenger's seat. And realising that nothing was happening in the street and probably wouldn't for some time, he settled down to have this very limited breakfast.

There was nothing particularly remarkable about the street where Alessandro Francesco lived. Every house was detached with its own garden, fenced off from others and the street by high metal fences and ornate gates. There were four or five cars parked in the road, but the majority were hidden from view in the small driveways behind the metal gates, solid at the bottom, railings at the top. He was able to park between two of the cars, giving him a good view of Alessandro's house while at the same time hidden from view. He had checked the houses for CCTV when he arrived and could find none. He was as well-hidden as he could be.

The sun was up, making the world feel pleasantly warm. A tabby cat was making its way towards him, striding purposefully up the middle of the road, following the white lines that split the road down the middle. It would stop every now and again to look around and ensure it was safe before moving on. He recognised the behaviour, the need to feel safe.

Although he had tailed criminals many times, he had forgotten how dull it was most of the time, particularly when you were on your own. It was 8.00 am when the gates to Alessandro's house finally opened and he drove slowly out, stopping at the edge of the road to check for cars before turning left towards the main road into Florence. Rigoberto quickly put away his mobile phone and prepared to follow him. The road was so quiet, he gave him a one-minute start before heading out after him. Once on the main road, he kept at least one car between him and Alessandro. But he needn't have bothered. Alessandro drove straight to the Carabinieri building by the most direct route, unconcerned, it would seem, by the traffic around him.

They both drove into the underground car park, Rigoberto still a couple of cars behind, and parked in their allocated spaces. Rigoberto could only see the top of Alessandro's silver Mercedes, but he had a clear view of the entrance to the lift, ensuring he would see Alessandro when he decided to leave. As he moved position so that he could stretch his legs into the passenger seat footwell, he hoped Alessandro wasn't planning a day in the office. If he was, it would be a very long day.

*

The first thing that struck Helen when she stepped out into the Via Porta Rossa was the heat. Although the road was narrow, with old buildings on both sides of the street, the sun caught the pedestrians by surprise as they navigated their way along the road. She realised quickly that walking in a straight line was difficult, partly due to the number of people using the thoroughfare, but also because the need to crane your neck to admire the architecture meant you strayed from the walking line you had started on. But the architecture couldn't be ignored. She understood now why Lesley said it was impossible to move quickly around the city if you were going to take in all the history it had to offer.

As she made her way along the Via Porta Rossa, Helen kept checking the numbers on the doors, determined not to miss the door that led to the flats Lesley had lived in when she first came to Florence. It wasn't always easy to see the numbers since they were sometimes on the right or left of the door, on the door itself or on the lintel above the door. Finally she found it. A strong wooden door. A heavy door, a protecting door. She stood still in the middle of the road, looking at the door, trying to imagine Lesley's excitement when she first arrived and realised how old her new home was. She tried to imagine her coming in and out as she settled into her new writing routine. And she tried to imagine what the interior of the flat would be like.

*Did you know Lesley?* Standing next to her was a woman not much younger than she was who was looking straight at her. *Did you?* Helen's surprise soon turned to recognition when she saw that the woman standing anxiously next to her was wearing a clean white apron with small blue flowers all over it.

*Signora Conti? You must be Signora Conti. Lesley spoke of you often, fondly, I would have to say. You helped her so much when she arrived. Thank you for that.* She took Signora Conti's hand. *I'm Helen, Lesley's mum.* There were tears in her eyes as she said it, and she could see that Signora Conti was also on the verge of tears. Helen was pleased to know that Lesley had been loved by others, not just her.

*Let's go into my flat and I can tell you all about Lesley and her time here in Florence. You'll be needing some coffee.* They continued to hold hands, Signora Conti directing Helen through the heavy door and into her flat, where the thick stone walls caused the temperature to drop and the sunlight, which had been so dazzling, to disappear. Signora Conti continued to speak. *I thought you must be her mum; I remember her telling me about your auburn hair, and she showed me a photograph that was taken with you before she boarded the plane to Florence. She liked that photo very much; I think she showed it to anyone who would look at it.* Helen still felt like crying and she wasn't quite sure why. Sudden acts of kindness often caught her off-guard and made her want to cry. This was no different. *Now you sit in here and make yourself comfortable, and I'll be through with the coffee in a just a minute.*

Helen was sure this room hadn't changed in years. The dark brown furniture was dated but in perfect condition. Lovingly cared for, she had no doubt, not unlike many of her own pieces of furniture, which she kept as a reminder of her past and her husband, not because she particularly liked them anymore. Photos in ornate silver frames were dotted around the room. Signora Conti and her husband, she guessed, and relatives from many decades ago.

*Lesley often came in for coffee when she was living upstairs. It was always a pleasure to see her and a rare opportunity to practise my English. Her Italian had really improved before* ... Silence again as she placed the brimming tray on the small round coffee table, realising her mistake. *I didn't see her so much after she went to live with Detective Borroni, but she would pop by at least once a week. I'm afraid I have a very rigid routine, so knowing when I'll be around isn't very hard. Coffee?* Helen nodded, and Signora Conti kept speaking. *She was very happy here, Mrs Hamilton. She was very happy with Detective Borroni, I'm sure you would have liked him.* Helen nodded and drank her coffee, wanting to eat for the first time since news of Lesley's death had reached her. She had made herself eat up to this point, knowing that eating would make her feel better even if she had to force herself to do it. But the fruit cake neatly sliced and lying on its side on the plate in front of her seemed very appealing. *Cake?* Helen nodded, and a small china plate with a slice of cake on it was handed to her to enjoy.

*It has been a very strange couple of months, Mrs Hamilton. I assume Lesley told you about the disappearance of the young man who lived in the flat above me?*

*Yes, she did tell me about it but really in relation to her good fortune in meeting Diego. She didn't say much else. I was due to come out for a holiday in a couple of weeks; she would probably have told me the whole story then. Some things are easier to explain face to face, don't you think?*

*Indeed.* And Signora Conti immediately launched into

243

the retelling of Pepe Poccini's disappearance and the involvement of the police. She told the story in its entirety, something she hadn't done with any of her friends: the interviews with the police, the meeting with Marco Poccini, the blood found in the stairwell, the message left by Marco Poccini on her answering machine and the man with the black gloves. Helen listened intently, recognising in Signora Conti the need of those who live alone to tell a story when that story has been preying on their mind. As she listened, she was aware Lesley had told her only a small part of the story but was unable now to decide how significant it was in relation to Lesley's death.

*I'm meeting with Inspector Gianfranco Valdi this afternoon at two pm. Would you come with me?* Helen wasn't sure why she wanted Signora Conti there, but she knew now there were more questions to ask than she had thought of. And Signora Conti was probably the woman to ask them.

*Of course, I'd be delighted to. He's a good man, Inspector Valdi. He'll listen.*

\*

Gianfranco Valdi always found this stage of the investigation process the most frustrating and the least satisfying. Although a great deal of information had been gathered and he was able to start hypothesising, there was still much information he needed, and that meant relying on others to find that and bring it to you. He knew it was his desire to be in control of everything that made it so difficult, and although others praised him for delegating responsibilities across his team, he knew it always made him feel vulnerable, wondering if some vital piece of information that would bring an investigation to a swift conclusion would be lost or missed. As he looked out from his glass office, every member of the team was hard at work gathering the evidence they had been designated to find: some reading paper files, some reading computer files, some making phone calls, some discussing their finds with each other. As he walked towards the large white board on the opposite wall where pictures of Diego and Lesley as they looked before and after their murders stared back at him, he realised that although he worried about information being missed or lost, he had no intention of telling the team about Pepe Poccini just yet nor his suspicions regarding Alessandro Francesco. Violetta and Rigoberto would have to be his confidantes. He hoped they truly could be trusted.

*Helen Hamilton is at reception to see you, Inspector.* The room went silent. Gianfranco nodded and smiled at the officer. As he walked towards the lift, the silence in the room seemed overwhelming. Everyone had stopped working, thinking about their own families and the myriad of possible harms they could come to. A thought he knew all police officers pushed to the back of their minds in case it would suddenly jump out and prevent them from doing their job. Gianfranco knew the team would return to their work as soon as the lift doors closed. And they did.

As he emerged from the lift, he saw two women standing close together in the small seating area that afforded views of Florence and the ever-flowing River Arno. He smiled as he walked towards them. The smaller of the two women, with striking auburn hair, put out her hand to shake his, introducing herself as she did so. *How nice to meet you, Inspector Valdi. I'm Helen Hamilton. I wish I could have met you under better circumstances. This is Signora Conti, who was a neighbour of Lesley's when she lived in the Via Porta Rossa. I feel she may have some information that could be useful to you, so I brought her along. I hope that's okay. Moral support for me as well, I suppose.* Gianfranco shook Signora Conti's hand, remembering her name had been mentioned in the Pepe Poccini file.

*That's not a problem, Mrs Hamilton. I trust your trip to Florence went smoothly?* She nodded as he led the two women through the large brown door next to the lift and on through two or three corridors until they reached a small room looking out on a garden courtyard. It contained two blue sofas with a small oak coffee table sitting between them and coffee making facilities snugly located in the corner. *Would either of you like a coffee?* They both declined. He wasn't surprised; most people did. As he sat down on the sofa opposite the two ladies, both women sat forward on the edge of the sofa cushions, waiting for their opportunity to tell him the information they felt was so crucial. Learned politeness prevented them from starting the conversation, but he knew once given an opening, they would have lots to say.

*I am very sorry for your loss, Mrs Hamilton.* As always, it seemed a completely inadequate sentence when compared to the loss of her child. But the routine sentences helped him cope in these situations, and the genuine warmth with which he said them reassured those listening that he was a man who could be trusted. *Lesley's body is in this building, Mrs Hamilton, and if you would like to see her, I can call Doctor Ricci and we can go up and see her.* It was the first time this small woman in her blue trousers and turquoise top had looked like she might cry.

*I have given this much thought, Inspector Valdi, and have decided I don't want to see her.* She looked down at her clasped hands and fell silent for a few moments before speaking again. *I know they say seeing the body is important in coming to terms with the person's death, but I don't want it to be my last image of Lesley. She was a very lively, bright person who smiled a lot, and that is how I want to remember her. However, if you need me to see her for identification purposes, I will do that.* She could feel tears welling in her eyes as she said these last words and hoped Inspector Valdi would fill the void, giving her time to recover.

*No, we have identified Lesley from medical records, and Detective Alessandro Francesco, who met with Lesley, has also confirmed her identity.* The two women looked at each other. *That will be sufficient, I'm sure. Would you like me to tell you what we know so far?* Helen nodded, and Gianfranco launched into a detailed account of how Lesley's body was found, where she was found, the time of death, the injuries sustained, the forensic information they had so far, and the lines of enquiry being followed by his team.

Helen listened as carefully as she could, glad now that she had brought Signora Conti. Every word spoken by Inspector Valdi made the physical pain she felt in her heart seem more acute. Her instinct to protect her children had been strong when Lesley was a child, and she had done everything she could to keep her safe. Lesley often had accidents, and on a number of occasions, Helen and her husband had had to take her to the hospital to have her jaw, elbows, arms and legs checked out. But she'd survived it all. Helen wished she could have protected Lesley from this, this death inflicted by a stranger in a strange land, far from her family. And yet she knew Lesley was happier than she had been for many years, enjoying a happiness not everyone is lucky enough to find even if they search for it their whole life.

*Do you have any questions, Mrs Hamilton?* They were all silent for a few minutes. Gianfranco waited.

Helen found the strength to speak. *You haven't mentioned the disappearance of Pepe Poccini. That's one of the reasons why I've brought Signora Conti with me. She spoke to Detective Francesco and she spoke to Signor Poccini. So did Lesley. But then, I'm sure you know that; you won't want the facts being repeated again.*

As always at moments like this, Gianfranco hoped his face did not betray him as his brain tried to make sense of what Helen Hamilton had just said. Yes, he knew of Signora Conti; he had read her statement. Nothing much in it, very little detail. But he knew nothing of her meeting with Marco Poccini, and more importantly, he was unaware of Lesley Hamilton having met with a man whose reputation, although unsubstantiated, was one of underworld crime and brutality. *On the contrary, Mrs Hamilton, it is always good to have facts repeated. Sometimes you hear the same fact in a slightly different way and a new line of enquiry opens up.* He turned to look at Signora Conti. *Please…*

Signora Conti retold the story of Pepe Poccini's disappearance in the same detail she had told Helen earlier that day and in the same detail she had told Detective Francesco and Marco Poccini. She spoke about Lesley and her contribution to the meetings. She described Leonardo, the man who had accompanied Marco Poccini to the meeting. And then she described the man she had seen lurking in the alley for a few days either side of the young man's disappearance. *I couldn't see him clearly, I'm afraid, but he was wearing black leather gloves which seemed quite inappropriate for the day, and the rest of his clothes appeared to be black. I should have gone out and had a better look, but it seemed silly of me to be worrying about a person standing in the alley; many people do that. But several days?* She looked directly at Gianfranco Valdi and said, *I hope that was helpful.* He smiled.

He knew now for certain that Alessandro Francesco was not to be trusted. And he wondered, just wondered, if the man in the CCTV footage wearing black leather gloves was the same man who had killed Pepe Poccini. It seemed likely.

*

Rigoberto spent the whole day in his car, occasionally stepping out to stretch his legs when he was sure no one else was in the car park. On two or three occasions, he had wondered if Alessandro Francesco had left the building on foot, but he had no way of knowing, so he decided he should wait in the car park. It was a dilemma he hadn't come across before when tailing suspects since generally, you worked in teams, but Gianfranco had made it clear that that wouldn't be possible until Violetta returned from Milan tomorrow. Gianfranco had already arranged a meeting with the two of them for the Wednesday evening once everyone else had gone home. Rigoberto's only worry was that he would have nothing to report.

Alessandro Francesco rarely spent an entire day in the office, and as he came out of the lift and walked towards his car, he realised that not only had he been indoors all day but he had survived only on coffee, and his resulting headache seemed more pronounced as the stark white light of the car park strip lighting filled the darkness. Knowing his wife would be out teaching her weekly evening art class at the local secondary school when he got home made him smile. An evening to enjoy a pizza carry-out from the local restaurant and a fine bottle of wine. He never asked his wife about the class. He wasn't interested, and for a brief moment, he wondered if the art class existed or if she, as he did with Carla, was enjoying an evening of intimacy with a man he didn't know. He took his phone from his pocket, ordered his pizza to be delivered to his home in forty-five minutes and headed towards his car.

The drive home would take about twenty minutes, plenty of time to get changed, organise his eating arrangements and open a bottle of wine before the pizza arrived. Then he could relax. He would need to be up early tomorrow since he was going to Cesate, Diego's hometown, to see if any clues to his murder could be found there. He knew it was a long shot, but his day in the office delving into files and online diaries had revealed nothing other than the fact that Diego Borroni had visited Cesate a week before his murder. There was no detail of any arranged appointments, but he knew Diego wouldn't have put it in the diary if he had simply been visiting his parents. He felt sure he must have had another reason for going. He would start at the local police station and see what he could find out.

As he drove out of his parking space, checking no cars were coming from his right, he saw car lights come on several spaces further down. He knew he hadn't seen or heard anyone come out of the lift when he was ordering his pizza, and he wondered how long the person had been sitting in their car. And he wondered if they were waiting for him. He was in no doubt that Gianfranco Valdi didn't trust him, and after their meeting on Monday, he had suspected Gianfranco would have him followed without hesitation.

He drove slowly towards the exit, ensuring he could see the car that had now left its space and was following him towards the exit barrier. A dark blue Fiat 500 with no distinguishing features. He tried to get a look at the person driving the car and its number plate, but the reflection of the pure white penetrating lights prevented him from seeing either. Once the barrier lifted, Alessandro sped up, joining the rush hour traffic as quickly as he could, hoping to get away from the small car lagging behind him. But he didn't.

Although it remained two, or sometimes three, cars behind him, he knew he was being followed. And he knew he was being followed by a fellow Carabinieri officer. As he drove into his driveway, exited his car and walked back to close the high gates, he took his phone from his pocket, hoping the Fiat 500 had parked close enough that he could get a photo of it. But it hadn't. Its lights were off now, and it was parked between two cars further up the road, neatly hidden. He'd have his pizza and consider what to do next.

## Thirty-five

As Paolo sat quietly on the terrace that surrounded three sides of his home, affording him views across the garden as well as up and down the road outside his house, he realised that without really thinking about it, he had decided what he would do with Franco's flat. He would go back to Livorno on Friday evening and remove all the paper documents and phones before setting fire to the flat. He knew it would give him a certainty that everything had been destroyed as well as giving the police a possible link between the burning of the flat and Franco's burnt-out house once they realised Franco was the link between both arson attacks, thus removing any link to him. It felt satisfying to have a plan; it settled his thoughts and now he would be able to get on with his day.

He had momentarily considered the other residents of the flats, but solving his own problems always took priority and this time was no different.

Paolo thought the garden looked good in the soft morning light with the camomile lawn glistening from its overnight watering and the small border he lovingly looked after displaying the first of its flowers. He had two jobs for today: trimming the ivy clinging resolutely to the outside stairs and weeding the driveway, a job he particularly enjoyed due to its repetitive nature.

He tidied away his breakfast things and began his work.

\*

It was 7.00 am and Alessandro could see the dark blue Fiat 500 parked once again between two cars further down the street. He rarely came into this bedroom, but it afforded the best view of the street. It was a small bedroom never discussed and rarely entered by either him or his wife. The small white cot still nestled in the corner with its bird mobile dangling above it, the only furniture in the room. But the air was filled with memories of a tiny child who had come into their lives for months, not years, and then destroyed their happiness by leaving them so suddenly.

He put those memories to one side as he always did and left, the closed door a means of shutting down that pain.

He gently touched his wife, who was still asleep, knowing she wouldn't appreciate being woken so early. *I need to take your car today. I can't explain just now. I'll leave my car keys on the table for you. I'll see you this evening.* She grunted her agreement before turning over once more to enjoy some more sleep.

Alessandro climbed into his wife's red Fiat Panda, pushing the driver's seat back to its full distance in order that he could drive more comfortably. He put down the sun visor to make any view of him smaller, then he opened the gates and drove out, turning left away from the parked car, watching to see if he would be followed. The dark blue Fiat 500 remained in its space. As he turned right at the end of the road heading towards the A1 and its route north to Cesate, he was confident the driver had been fooled.

The route north was quiet so early in the day, and even though his driving position was less comfortable than in his own car, he enjoyed the drive through the rolling hills towards the flat plains around Milan. He had never been to Cesate; in fact, he was previously unaware of its existence, but the sat nav on his phone got him there without any problems, and soon he was parking outside the Carabinieri offices. He hoped Davide Ruci, the station sergeant, would be on duty since his was the only name he had, and he knew he needed to sound as if Diego might have spoken to him about his trip to Cesate if he was to sound convincing.

As he climbed the three steps to the front door of the building, he straightened his tie and buttoned his jacket, knowing the officer on the desk would more than likely instantly recognise him as a fellow officer: they usually did. And he wasn't wrong. There was no one else in the foyer or at the desk as he entered, and the young officer behind the desk, who looked up slowly from the piece of paper he was filling out, instantly stood tall and straight. Alessandro took out his identity card and showed it to the young man.

*Welcome, sir. How can I help you?* Alessandro wondered if he had looked so anxious to impress when he started in the force, but he couldn't remember. He could only remember being a detective, a detective who had to balance the rigours of his job and the demands of the criminals he earned money from.

*I'm looking for Sergeant Davide Ruci. Is it possible to speak to him?* He smiled.

*Yes, he's in his office. I'll let him know you're here. Your name again, sir?* Once he'd mastered his name, he made the call. *Detective Alessandro Francesco from Florence is asking to speak to you, sir... Yes, I'll bring him to your office. Thank you, sir.*

Alessandro turned back from the wall of posters

informing those waiting for attention of the many jobs carried out by the Carabinieri and how best they might help you. Alessandro looked directly at the young man and smiled once again. *Excellent, young man. Lead the way.*

It wasn't a new building but it was well looked after. The light blue painted walls of the narrow corridors were clean and shiny. There were few windows, and the single white lights spaced evenly along the corridor caused the light to pool: darker, brighter, darker, brighter. They arrived at Sergeant Ruci's office. As Alessandro put out his hand, he noticed how tall and broad the sergeant was, a giant frame that seemed to fill the tiny office.

*Detective Francesco, welcome to Cesate.* The sergeant shook Alessandro's hand. *This is unexpected, but I'm guessing you're here about Diego Borroni's murder?* Alessandro was delighted the sergeant had made it so easy for him. *Have a seat.* And he pointed to a brown leather chair on the other side of his desk. Alessandro made sure he was sitting comfortably before he started.

*Yes, we know that Detective Borroni visited Cesate a week before his murder, and we wondered if he had visited the station when he was here. He left no notes concerning his visit, unusual for him. It seemed unlikely he was in Cesate simply to visit his parents; he would have taken a day off for that. Any light you can shed on his visit would be most helpful.*

Davide Ruci had good instincts after so many years as a policeman, and there were things about this man he didn't trust. Why wouldn't they have been informed of his visit? Why wouldn't he have called yesterday to say he would be coming? Why was he on his own? Detectives, in his experience, usually worked in pairs.

Alessandro was waiting for answers, and Davide needed to buy some time. *Before we get down to all of that, Detective Francesco, I'll get us some coffee.* Before Alessandro could reply, he had left the office and found an officer who could get a tray of coffee together. And while he waited for that to be done, he called the offices of the Carabinieri in Florence and checked Alessandro Francesco existed. And he did.

*

He returned to his office a few minutes later with a tray of coffee and a selection of small pastries. *You're no doubt wondering why I'm here without warning you and why I'm on my own? Well, the case is moving at a fast pace and we're all keen to conclude it as soon as possible, so lone working is the order of the day at the moment. I'm sure you'll understand that. You probably knew the family.*

Davide poured the coffee. *Yes, I know the family well. I worked with Diego's father for a number of years. He was an excellent man to work for. They are devastated, as you can imagine. I broke the news to them.* He paused. *Diego was here the week before his murder asking about an old case his father worked on many years before. It involved a young man called Paolo Bianchi who had killed a cat.* He let that hang there as Alessandro continued to make notes in his small black notebook. *He spent some time reading the file, had lunch with me, then headed back to Florence. He spoke a great deal about his girlfriend, Lesley. He seemed very happy.* Davide stopped speaking. He thought he might cry. In fact, he thought he might cry every time he thought about Diego.

*Would I be able to see the file on Paolo Bianchi?*
Alessandro waited.

*Yes, of course. I'll get it brought along for you to look at.*

Alessandro sat quietly, waiting for the instruction to be given before asking another question. *Can you tell me anything else about this man Paolo Bianchi?*

And so Davide launched into a brief history of Paolo Bianchi. And it was brief: he had lived in Cesate all his life, mainly with his mother, he attended the local schools and then Milan University, and he lived alone now since the death of his mother. And then the detail, *he's a loner, a bit odd. Eccentric might be the word. No doubt there is a term for his condition. Never been in trouble with the police apart from when he killed a cat one lunchtime at school. It's all in the file.* He paused. *And Piero Borroni's suspicions surrounding the murder of Father Rossi.* Alessandro was suddenly interested. *It was a brutal murder, never solved. Shocked the whole community. I'm not sure why Piero thought Paolo might have done it other than that he'd killed the cat. We had no leads, no forensics, and so Piero took to looking through all the cases of violent crime that had taken place in Cesate over the previous two to three years. And Paolo appeared on that list because of the cat. I can't imagine it was him who killed Father Rossi or anyone else.*

The young officer from the front desk delivered the file while Davide was speaking, laying it on the desk nearer to Davide than Alessandro. *As you can see, it's not a very thick file.* Davide picked it up and handed it to Alessandro, wondering, once again, if he was doing the right thing for both Diego and Paolo. But he didn't think he had much choice. *I'll leave you to read it, then we can have another chat.* He lifted the tray and left the room, closing the door quietly behind him.

There was little content in the file other than the statements given by staff and pupils who had witnessed the killing of the cat. And a statement from Paolo, who had murdered the cat *because he scratched me. I don't like being scratched. I don't like being touched.* And then there were Piero Borroni's notes following his visit to the Bianchi house after the murder of Father Rossi: a brief statement of facts from Paolo followed by a series of comments from Piero.

*Poor eye contact*

*Looking at the floor*

*Single syllable answers*

*No explanations*

*Mother silent on their movements in the evening.*

He noted Paolo's address, hoping this was where he still lived. He left the file on Davide's desk and made his way back to the front desk, where he thought he would find Davide. And he did. *Doesn't look like there's anything of interest in that file but thank you for letting me see it and for your hospitality. I'll be on my way now.* They shook hands, with Davide still wondering why a detective from the Florence Carabinieri would be sent to Cesate to look at a file of three or four pages when it could have been scanned and e-mailed to them.

Alessandro still wasn't convinced Paolo Bianchi was

of any interest, but he thought he should check it out.

*

Paolo had weeded half the driveway and was admiring his handiwork from the upper terrace, where he was eating his lunch, when he spotted the red Fiat Panda parked around 20 metres down the road. It was a car he had never seen before, and that worried him. No one parked in his road unless only briefly to answer a phone call or to urinate in the scrub at the side of the road. There were no pavements on his road, and generally, the only people he would see were those who walked their dogs in the woods at the top of the road or his neighbours as they came and went through their electric gates. Living on the quiet edge of Cesate had always suited him.

Paolo tried to ignore the car and the occupant of the car. He was enjoying his lunch and wanted to concentrate on that. He liked eating lunch when he was hungry, although he always ate his lunch whether hungry or not. It was a routine he couldn't break. Once every morsel had been consumed and everything had been tidied away, he returned to the weeding of the drive, a job he wanted to finish today. He knew the weeds were so small, most people wouldn't have seen them, but he could see them, and he could feel the irritation they always induced in him as they appeared amongst the stones. He had almost reached the last of the weeds nearest the gate when a man appeared on the other side of it and started speaking. *Excuse me, I think I've got myself a bit lost. I wonder if you could direct me back to the main road out of Cesate? I'm heading to the A1 and back to Florence.* Paolo could feel sweat in the palms of his hand as he stood up to look at this man. Florence, why was he mentioning Florence? He removed the straw hat he was wearing to protect him from the sun and looked steadily at the man for a few minutes before answering.

Paolo gave very clear directions, continuing to stare at the man, memorising his main features. Once he had given the directions, he stopped and said nothing. The man thanked him and waited, Paolo assumed, for more conversation. But there was none. Paolo put his hat back on his head, knelt down and started to weed once again, his black gloves moving gently across the stones in search of the weeds, his heart beating fast in his chest and a pounding returning to his head.

Alessandro thought he might now have his answer.

*

Rigoberto was still sitting in his Fiat 500 when the red Fiat Panda that had left many hours before drove up the street and stopped outside Alessandro's house. As the driver emerged from the car to open the gates, Rigoberto realised quite suddenly that his day had been wasted on watching a house not occupied by Alessandro Francesco. A novice error. An error he would have to admit to. An error he would have to admit to when he met Gianfranco and Violetta in a couple of hours.

## Thirty-six

Despite everything, Helen had a lovely Wednesday in Florence with Signora Conti. It was sunny again and having her own tour guide suited Helen very well. She found herself thinking of nothing but the beauty of the city and the freshness of the food. It was a relief not to be thinking of Lesley and death.

They visited the Duomo, climbing to the top — quite a climb — for a stunning view of the city. Then on to the Pitti Palace with its formal facade and stunning courtyard, the entrance to the magnificent Boboli Gardens. Signora Conti's knowledge of the city meant that walking between each site was itself a lesson in Florentine history. Like Lesley, Helen had always loved learning about history and imagining life long ago but felt grateful to have been born when she was.

\*

After walking the length and breadth of the gardens, they sat down on a small green bench close to the Forte di Belvedere, looking out over the vastness of Florence and its historic skyline. As she sat there, Helen could understand why Lesley had been so happy in Florence and why, with the friendliness of the Italians, she had never felt lonely. *Thank you, Signora Conti, for showing me around. It's been a lovely day.*

*Yes, I've enjoyed it very much. I hope you'll come back to Florence and visit me again.* The two women smiled at each other as they sat holding their small handbags securely on their laps, soaking up the last rays of the sun. Helen was certain she would come back.

\*

Generally, Alessandro didn't like to arrive home so early in the evening, but he was relieved to find his wife was still in her studio, painting. He knew that meant she either had a commission that needed finishing, or she was working on a project she had been thinking about for some time. Either way, it meant she wouldn't want to be disturbed. The house and garden were his for the time being.

After removing his tie and hanging his jacket back in the wardrobe, he grabbed a bottle of beer from the fridge and wandered out to his favourite seat on the terrace. The sun was beginning to set, and although not as warm as it had been earlier in the day, the smell of the camomile lawn filled the air as the cold beer moistened his dry throat. He'd make some pasta sauce in a while. He'd make enough for two.

Alessandro considered the events of his day and what they meant. He knew now he was definitely being followed. He had seen the young man in the Fiat 500 bang the steering wheel with his hand when he realised Alessandro had escaped him, and although he couldn't be certain Marco Poccini wouldn't be having him followed, he felt confident that the young man was a member of the Carabinieri, and more specifically, a member of Gianfranco Valdi's team. Although it was most likely Gianfranco would call the young man off once he learnt of his mistake, Alessandro wanted to know who he was. And he knew that wouldn't be too difficult to find out. Lorenzo, the car park attendant at the Carabinieri building, was always happy to make some extra money. Alessandro had used him on many occasions, and he would use him again.

As for Paolo Bianchi, that was a more difficult problem to solve. Alessandro remembered the small, slight figure on the other side of the gates: a man, it appeared, of no great stature or strength. A man who still displayed some of the behaviour recorded by Piero Borroni in his file — few words, fixed stare. A man who was wearing black leather gloves. It was the only link he could see to the man in the car with Lesley Hamilton and the man seen by Signora Conti when Pepe Poccini went missing, most likely killed. Could he be a killer? Was this detail enough?

He knew that as he had always done, he could simply give the Poccinis the information and leave them to deal with Paolo Bianchi, but then he remembered Franco. And more than that, he remembered his own part in the man's death. The photos in the papers of the burnt-out house and the details of his injuries had bothered him. Not because he objected to the Poccini's methods. He had lived with those for a very long time. But recently, he had started questioning many of his own decisions and the consequences of those for others. He had given them Franco's name. Alessandro wasn't sure why things had changed for him, why he could no longer pass on information and remove the implication of it from his memory. But he knew he wanted out, and he wasn't sure how he might do that.

The sky above the wall surrounding the garden was now red, filling the garden with hues of yellow and pink, and he knew he wouldn't give the Poccinis Paolo's name. Not yet. He would drive to Cesate on Friday night after his evening with Carla and see if he could find out more, maybe even get into the house. He had to be certain Paolo was the killer before doing anything. His fledgling conscience demanded it. Slowly, he made his way back into the house, ready to prepare their evening meal.

*

Violetta was glad to be back in Florence. Although she had found Diego Borroni's old team in Milan both helpful and sociable, she liked having her own space and her own routines, and those were difficult to find when living in a hotel and speaking to others as and when their routine allowed. It was something she knew she would have to work through and change if she was going to make progress through the Carabinieri ranks. They needed people who could adapt quickly to changing circumstances, and she found that quite hard to do. But she would keep working at it because in every other respect, she loved the work, the finding of solutions.

The office was in darkness when she came out of the lift apart from the single table lamp lighting up Gianfranco Valdi's corner office. She left her bag on her desk after removing her notebook from it, then made her way towards the luminous office. She knew she was early, she always was, and she wanted Gianfranco to know she was. The door was open.

*Good evening, sir, I'm a bit early. Should I wait at my desk until Detective Copelli arrives?*

Gianfranco looked up from the papers he was reading and smiled. *Yes, that would be fine, Violetta. Best all three of us are here before we start. I hope you were looked after in Milan?*

*Yes, sir, everything went very smoothly.*

*Good.* And he returned to his study of the papers lying in front of him.

As he emerged from the lift, Rigoberto saw Violetta sitting at her desk — catching up on e-mails, he presumed — and for a brief moment, he thought he was late. He looked quickly at his watch, which said 6.55 pm. He wasn't late; he was five minutes early. Relieved that at least he had got that right, he greeted Violetta warmly as he placed his jacket on the back of the chair at his own desk.

A voice from the corner office interrupted their greetings. *Let's get started, then. Sooner we start, sooner we can all get home.* Gianfranco remained in the chair behind his desk and invited his colleagues to sit in the chairs he had placed on the other side of his desk. He hoped they would have some sort of leads that would help with the case. He knew they were getting nowhere fast, and that usually meant a case might never be solved.

*Let's start with you, Violetta.* And he sat back in his chair, ready to listen.

*I'm afraid there wasn't a great deal to learn, sir.* Gianfranco continued to smile even though this wasn't what he wanted to hear. *Detective Borroni was much liked by his team. They described him as a fair boss who encouraged all members of his team to take a lead role. He made them feel part of every investigation, and although he always led from the front, he made sure everyone felt part of the end result. Everyone had contributed.* She paused. *Detective Borroni had a great deal of success in changing the face of the criminal underworld in Milan and was initially much admired by the public and his superiors.* She knew she could be describing Gianfranco Valdi. *Then came the Poccinis. There had been suspicions about their businesses for a long time, but nothing had ever been found to support those suspicions. More than that, they were friends with some of Diego's superiors and those in the city council of Milan. Powerful people who weren't happy with any aspersions being directed towards the Poccinis, frequent donators to local charities.* She looked up from her notebook at Gianfranco, wondering if he wanted to ask any questions. He didn't. He signalled with his hand that she should continue. *The team felt the Poccinis became an obsession for Diego. A convenient obsession, some said, since his home life wasn't as happy as it might have been and hadn't been for some time. Even when told to drop the case, he kept some of his team working on it, then Diego himself began following the Poccinis at weekends, and that culminated in the incident we know about at their Lake Como home. Detective Borroni then ended up here, and nothing linking the family to any criminal activity was ever found.*

*What specifically had the team been looking at?*

*Possible tax evasion, drug smuggling, people trafficking, extortion. No links to any of these were ever found.*

*Why did they think no links could be found?*

*Influence. Power. They still think the family are linked to organised crime, but there is no will to pursue it, either in the Carabinieri or amongst those who supposedly serve the city.*

*Thank you, Violetta. What do you think we should do now with this information?* Although she hadn't expected to be asked her opinion, she had considered what they should do next and was happy to give her opinion.

*I think we should look more carefully at the Pepe Poccini disappearance and speak to those who gave witness statements. There may be something that was*

266

*missed or something that links them to Lesley and Diego.*

*Excellent.* And Gianfranco passed on what he had found out from Helen Hamilton, and more importantly, Signora Conti. He suggested that he and Violetta speak to Alessandro Francesco tomorrow about the meeting he had arranged for the Poccinis with Lesley and Signora Conti. *I hope Detective Francesco will be able to remember the meeting he never recorded.* They sat quietly for a few moments, considering the implications of this statement and what it might mean. *Rigoberto. How did you get on?*

Rigoberto knew it was always best to come clean with mistakes, and as he stared at the man who had entrusted him with the job of following Alessandro, his disappointment in himself felt overwhelming. He didn't need a notebook to answer the question; there was nothing to note. *Tuesday, he spent the day here in the Carabinieri building, driving straight home after work. Today he left his house in his wife's car early in the morning and returned around five pm.* Silence.

*Where had he been?* Violetta asked the question before Gianfranco had a chance to.

*I don't know. I didn't spot he was the driver so have spent the day sitting outside his house assuming he was in there. He wasn't. A basic error, I know. My apologies, sir.*

Rigoberto had expected Gianfranco to be instantly angry, but he wasn't. He had turned his chair towards the window, looking out over the evening skyline, and he sat quietly for a few moments before speaking. *I thought he'd work out he was being followed. Tomorrow, Rigoberto, I want you to get the number plate of his wife's car and work with our colleagues in traffic to find*

*out where he went. He obviously had something to hide,
or he would have taken his own car. Well done, both of
you. We have something to work on now.* Gianfranco
stood up from his desk and shook both their hands. *We'll
meet again tomorrow about six pm for an update. None
of this information must be passed on to the rest of the
team. Understood?* They both nodded as he pulled his
jacket from the back of his chair and headed towards the
lift and home.

Violetta and Rigoberto smiled at each other. The
meeting had gone well.

\*

Paolo sat staring at his meal: rabbit and bean casserole.
He wanted to eat it, get tidied up and move on to his
reading of the newspapers, but his head wouldn't let him.
The man at the gate, he was sure, had been watching him.
Why else would he sit in his car for so long before asking
for directions? And why wouldn't he have gone to a
house nearer to where he'd parked his car? His home, a
place where he had never felt threatened by the danger of
his work, now felt different. He had tried sitting in his
mother's room, staring at her slippers placed neatly next
to the perfectly made bed, listening for her voice to help
him rationalise what had happened, but he couldn't hear
it. He couldn't make that connection.

And despite his determination to stick to his routines,
the pounding in his head wouldn't stop. He ate the food
slowly and deliberately although it was now quite cold,
then he tidied up. He read the newspapers. But all the
time, his head was hurting, pounding out the noise he
heard when he thought of Father Rossi, Lesley and

Diego. It needed action.

He assumed this man had found him through some connection with Franco, and he knew now that all ties with Franco and the flat in Livorno had to be broken. He would spend tomorrow preparing for his trip to Livorno on Friday, when he would destroy the flat once and for all. Then, he was sure, the pounding in his head would stop.

# Thirty-seven

For the first time since she had heard the news of Lesley's death, Helen woke feeling refreshed. She knew the fresh air and the walking she had done yesterday with Signora Conti had had the desired effect. She was sorry to be leaving Florence, and in some vague way, leaving Lesley. But she was equally keen to meet the Borronis, find out a bit more about Diego and be with people who understood and shared her pain.

She had decided to get a train that would get her to Milan at lunchtime, so she enjoyed her final buffet breakfast in the hotel before gathering together her belongings and checking out. A taxi took her across the city to the Santa Maria Novella railway station, with its modernist facade and large grass piazza opening up the city to travellers as they came out of the dark station into the clear blue light. The station was busy, busier than most stations Helen had been in, but the signage was good, and she soon found both her platform and the high-speed train that would take her to Milan before going on to Cesate.

The scenery sped by as the train quickly reached its top speed and silently took them through the mountains to the plains around Milan. The station at Rogoredo was, unlike her experience of high-speed trains in other European countries, some distance from the centre of the city and the next train station she needed to get to, but connections were abundant. She considered taking the subway to the station at Cadorna, but she wanted to see what she could of the city and decided instead to take a taxi.

Travelling above ground was something she always

preferred. She waited patiently in the taxi queue, watching the people in front of her grow increasingly impatient at how slowly the queue was diminishing. Helen didn't care. It was nice to be standing in the sun far from home. It almost made her feel young again. Young and free.

The station at Cadorna was, like the Santa Maria Novella, modern and well kept. The fountains and multi-coloured sculptures outside the main entrance made Helen smile and gave her the feeling she might be in a children's animated movie. Once inside, she found the departures board and decided she would take the 2.32 pm train to Cesate, giving her time for a leisurely lunch. Although she had eaten a hearty breakfast, Helen felt the need to eat, and for the second time since Lesley's death, she wanted to eat rather than simply knowing that she should eat. She texted Lucia with the time her train would arrive in Cesate, then selected a cafe.

The cafe she chose was small with tables squeezed close together to maximise the space. But she liked that. For those dining alone, they didn't feel alone. Animated conversations on either side of her kept her entertained even though she could understand very little of what was being said. The ragu alla Bolognese that she ordered was superior to anything she might have at home, and the small glass of house red went down very well. She had twenty minutes until her train, so she took out her phone and considered once again the text Kate had sent her the previous evening. It was, as always, a demanding text, which had Helen been at home, she would have felt the need to respond to immediately, but which at this distance seemed less urgent. Kate wanted to know what was happening, and more importantly, when her mother would be home.

Helen didn't want to give her too much detail since that would result in more texts and possibly phone calls, which she wanted to avoid at this point. So she explained that she had spoken to the police in Florence, who were continuing their investigation, and was now on her way to Cesate to meet Diego's parents. She promised to call on Sunday. She knew by then she would have made a decision about Lesley's funeral. She could break the news then.

Although painfully slow compared to the high-speed train, the trip to Cesate was short.

Helen had no idea what Lucia Borroni looked like, but she felt certain she would know her when she saw her. And she did. Lucia was standing close to the ticket barriers, eagerly scanning the faces of the people fussing with their tickets as they negotiated the machines that would let them out of the station. Helen waved, and the small woman in the neat navy suit waved back. They'd found each other.

*

Gianfranco arrived at his work feeling much more positive about the investigation and hopeful that today might give them a point from which they could make progress. He assumed Alessandro Francesco, like him, was at his desk early, and he called him as soon as he had arranged his jacket on the back of his chair and opened his blinds, letting the morning sun stretch across his desk and brighten the room. The phone rang several times before it was picked up. Gianfranco knew that the caller ID would show his name and extension, and he wondered if that was why Alessandro had taken so long to pick up.

*Good morning, Gianfranco.*

*Good morning, Alessandro. My apologies for bothering you so early in the morning.* Silence. He had expected a response. *I have some new information which I wanted to run past you and wondered when you would be free to meet today.*

*I have quite a few meetings today. Could it wait until tomorrow?* He didn't, but he wanted time to consider what the meeting might be about. He hadn't been followed into work today, but he knew Gianfranco was playing a subtle game in which he was the pawn.

*I'm afraid it can't wait, Alessandro; we have a couple of new leads and we want to move on them as soon as possible. I need you to cancel any meetings you have this morning and meet me here in my office at nine-thirty.* Gianfranco's tone had changed. Alessandro knew this was no longer a request; it was an order that he needed to follow. *I'm sure, like us, you're keen for the murderer to be found.* Silence.

*I'll be there at nine-thirty.* And the phone went dead.

\*

While Gianfranco and Violetta were preparing for their meeting with Alessandro, Rigoberto was already hard at work scouring CCTV footage to find out where Alessandro Francesco had gone in his wife's red Fiat Panda the previous day. Although he was aware of the value of CCTV cameras in the solving of crimes, he hadn't until this moment realised how many cameras there were in the city and how infrequently you could be out of their range.

The young officer sitting at the bank of screens next to him was adept at moving through each camera, looking only for the car in question, while Rigoberto found himself distracted by the many other things the CCTV picked up: Florentines walking home with their shopping, kissing couples, children riding their bikes, old men on sticks walking ponderously along the pavements.

*Found it.* The film had stopped; they'd found the car. Now they just had to follow it.

*

*Thank you for rearranging your morning, Alessandro. Do have a seat.* Alessandro sat down on the small leather sofa tucked in the corner of the office, once again feeling vulnerable. *You know Violetta; she was here the last time we talked.* Alessandro nodded in her direction. She smiled. Gianfranco continued to stand, moving towards the window as he spoke.

*I met with Helen Hamilton, Lesley's mother, on Tuesday afternoon. A lovely woman, very dignified. She'd brought Signora Conti, Lesley's neighbour, with her.* He turned to look at Alessandro. *She had some interesting information. I hope you can help us with it.* Violetta continued to scribble at speed in her notebook, only pausing to look up when Gianfranco paused.

Alessandro could feel his heart beating hard in his chest. His face remained blank. He said nothing.

*She described a meeting you arranged with Lesley and Signora Conti where Signor Poccini, the father of the missing ... or murdered boy, was able to speak to them directly and ask questions. An unusual thing to do, I would have thought, and ... more worryingly, you didn't record it.* He picked up the brown folder that had been sitting on his desk and slowly flicked through it. *I don't understand, Alessandro. I'm quite confused. You thought this boy might have been murdered and you arranged a meeting for his parent with two of the neighbours. Why those two? And then you didn't record the meeting. And then you didn't pass on the information to the homicide team. Definitely not procedure.* Gianfranco lowered himself onto the other end of the sofa, looking directly at Alessandro, happy to wait for a response. He knew now that he was in control.

Alessandro found his voice, although he was aware as he spoke it sounded unconvincing, even to him. *Yes, I appreciate it may seem unusual to do such a thing in a missing persons case. But ... the Poccinis were struggling to comprehend all the information I was giving them and I thought, when they suggested the meeting, they might believe what I'd been telling them if they heard it from the horse's mouth, so to speak. And, as I'm sure you'll agree, it's often good to speak more than once to witnesses since they may change their story or stumble on a new piece of information as they recall what happened. I thought it had advantages for both of us.* Momentarily, Alessandro felt he was on more solid ground.

*I agree it can be helpful, but not usually in the presence of the missing or murdered person's family.* He looked down at the file. *But why no mention of the man in the black gloves and black clothes observed by Signora Conti over a couple of days? That seems like a lead to me.* Alessandro remained silent. *It seems even more of a lead once you saw the footage of the man in the car with Lesley. I can see the connection; I'm surprised you can't. Can't you?*

Violetta had stopped writing. Gianfranco was sitting back on the sofa, thumbing the edge of the brown folder sitting on his knee. *I didn't think it was significant when Signora Conti told me about the man. He could have been anyone. A busy city, so many people. And I didn't remember about it when you showed me the footage of Lesley in the car. I didn't make the connection.*

*What about the Poccinis? What can you tell us about them?*

Alessandro was relieved Gianfranco had changed the subject. *Nothing, really. I knew Diego had had some problems with them when he was in Milan and that was the reason he couldn't continue with the case, but I'd never met them before.*

Very quietly, Gianfranco said, *I think you're lying, Alessandro. I have no way of proving that, but I don't think you could have made so much progress in the service if you were as incompetent as this case makes you appear. Thank you for meeting with us. I'll let you get on with your day.*

Alessandro rose slowly from the sofa, keen not to look too eager to leave but conscious he had said nothing in his own defence. Conscious that by saying nothing, he was confirming his own guilt. But he could think of nothing to say and simply left.

*Gather together all the information we have on the Poccinis, Violetta. I'm off to the lab to see if there are any DNA results on the black hairs found in Diego's flat and car.*

*

Sitting at the desk strewn with the remnants of food brought to them by colleagues throughout the day, Rigoberto and the young officer watched Alessandro Francesco get out of the red Fiat Panda and walk into the small police station in Cesate. Another new lead.

*

Doctor Brio Ricci saw Gianfranco come out of the lift and make his way towards the lab. He thought Gianfranco was walking more confidently than the last time they had met. He hoped that meant progress. As he unlocked the door to the lab and pulled it open, the two men smiled warmly at each other, shaking hands.

*You're looking a bit like the cat that got the cream, Gianfranco.*

*Things are moving; we're making progress. Not as quickly as I would like, but that is always the case, I guess. I'm hoping you also have some positive news for me regarding the stranger in the flat and in the car.*

Doctor Ricci opened his computer, typing in his 13-letter password before turning the screen towards Gianfranco. *We don't have a positive ID, Gianfranco, but... we have been able to link this same man to 10 other murders across northern Italy in the past 20 years. More than that, each of these murders has been recorded as most likely committed by a paid assassin.* Gianfranco patted Brio on the back and smiled. *I'm guessing that helps.*

*

Violetta and Gianfranco were already ensconced in Gianfranco's office when Rigoberto emerged from the lift. He knew he was late but was unconcerned on this occasion since he knew the information he had was more important than being on time. He nodded towards the sole cleaner noisily buffing the floor as she moved the heavy machinery from desk to desk, put his coat on the back of the chair, patted his hair with his hands and made his way to the meeting.

*Sit, Rigoberto. Coffee?* Gianfranco ushered him into a chair and poured the coffee he'd offered. *How have things gone today, Rigoberto?*

*It took a good while, hence my lateness, but we found where he went. He drove directly from Florence to the police station in Cesate, Diego Borroni's hometown. I guess we need to find out why now.*

*Excellent. Excellent. Do you know how long he was there?*

*About an hour and a half. When he left the station, we lost him when he entered parts of Cesate that have no CCTV. However, we know he remained in the town for some time since we picked him up again merging onto the motorway about two hours later.*

*Could he have been having lunch? I heard on the grapevine that he likes a long lunch.*

*Possibly, but we'd need to know why he was there in the first place. It could be a coincidence — that he was there following up on one of his own cases.*

*A coincidence? I don't really believe in coincidences, Rigoberto, but we'll give him the benefit of the doubt at this stage.* Gianfranco paused. They waited. *I want you to go to Cesate tomorrow, Rigoberto. I'll call the station sergeant first thing in the morning so they know to expect you. We need to know why he was there.*

Next, Violetta gave each of them a folder containing all the information she had managed to acquire on the Poccinis. It wasn't much and certainly wasn't revelatory. She summarised her findings, assuming they would both read the information in full later. There was nothing to connect the family to Alessandro Francesco.

*Thank you, very helpful, Violetta. An excellent reference point.* He placed the folder neatly on his desk before beginning. *I met with Doctor Ricci, and he was able to tell me that the hairs found both in their flat and Diego's car belonged to a man who has committed 10 murders across northern Italy in the past twenty years. Murders that are assumed to have been committed by a paid assassin. They have never been solved. I think it is now safe to assume that this man killed Pepe Poccini, and for some reason we are unaware of, killed Diego Borroni and Lesley Hamilton. Any thoughts?*

They sat in silence for a few minutes before Violetta spoke. *The Poccinis may have paid this man to kill Diego and Lesley because of Diego's work in Milan. But why, then, would he kill them in two separate places? And why would the Poccinis be so interested in speaking to Lesley and Signora Conti? No, that can't be it.*

Rigoberto, who had been staring at the pale blue linoleum floor while Violetta was speaking, suddenly spoke. *Could they have thought Lesley witnessed some aspect of Pepe Poccini's murder and that she might be able to lead them to the killer? They would have wanted to find whoever did it if they really believed he was dead. That's how they work. Revenge is everything.*

Violetta looked round at Gianfranco, who was now looking out of the window. *And if she did witness something, was the killer simply motivated to kill her in order to cover his tracks?*

Gianfranco enjoyed listening to their theorising, confident that these two officers were the future of his team. Then he spoke. *But why wait so long to kill her? Why not the day after killing Pepe? Why not blow her brains out the same way he blew out Diego's?*

Silence. Rigoberto finally spoke.

*Because he knew her.*

## Thirty-eight

Paolo knew he wasn't coping. When he was a little boy and was finding it hard to cope with the world, his mother would write out a daily timetable for him and he would focus on achieving each of the tasks scrawled on the page in her distinctive handwriting. And that was how he got through Thursday. He made a list of jobs to be done, punctuated by times for eating and sleeping:

Breakfast
Shopping at the supermarket
Weeding the border behind the house
Lunch
Preparing for the trip to Livorno tomorrow: black clothes, black shoes, black gloves, black balaclava, gun and silencer, accelerant in flask, small rag, lighter, matches, keys to the flat
Dinner
Prepare muesli and yogurt for breakfast
Reading
Bed.

It worked. He got through the day and slept well. But as soon as he woke, the anxiety returned, the memory of the man speaking to him at the gate overwhelming his thoughts. The fear of who the man was.

As he sat eating breakfast, he still wasn't sure whether he was making the right decision regarding Franco's flat in Livorno. He knew he wanted it gone and any evidence that might link him to it destroyed, but he wasn't sure whether burning it to the ground would achieve that. The man speaking to him at the gate, Franco's death and the files in the flat all contributed to his anxiety. He wondered now whether other evidence linking him to the many murders he'd committed might be found elsewhere, although he didn't know where. He wiped his sweating hands on his clean white napkin, then continued eating the muesli and yogurt he had prepared the night before.

Once tidied up, he placed his already packed bag in the boot of his car, changed the number plates for plates that would link the car to Rome, laid out his clothes on his bed for later in the day, then took himself to his mother's room in search of some peace. He sat down in the small red chair facing the narrow bed with its striped bed cover and plumped pillows tucked neatly underneath. He opened his favourite book, "The Cloudspotter's Guide", at page 62 and began reading aloud as if his mother were there in the bed enjoying him reading to her. The familiar words, predictable and certain, helped calm him. He would read until lunchtime.

"KALIDASA'S YAKSHA leaves his cumulonimbus messenger with one parting …"

Paolo's voice droned on in the silence.

*

Rigoberto was already on his way to Cesate when Gianfranco made the phone call to Cesate police station. He had earlier made enquiries regarding the name of the station sergeant and was able to ask directly for Davide Ruci. He waited on the line.

*Good morning, sir, Sergeant Davide Ruci speaking. How can I help you?*

*Good morning, I wanted to let you know that one of my team is on their way to your station.* He paused.

*Detective Alessandro Francesco?* Gianfranco smiled before replying.

*No, Detective Rigoberto Copelli. Alessandro Francesco isn't on my team.* He waited. *I'm aware he visited your station on Wednesday. Detective Copelli is on his way to find out why. We're investigating the murders of Diego Borroni and Lesley Hamilton and believe whatever Detective Francesco wanted to know may be of value to us. I trust we can rely on your silence in relation to this matter.*

Gianfranco waited for the sergeant to speak.

*I should have checked. I believed him, I trusted him. My apologies, sir. I should have known you would call in advance; that is the usual protocol.*

*Yes, it is, but I don't want you to worry about it, Sergeant Ruci. Just help my officer with his questions.*

*Yes, sir.*

The line went dead. It had been a long time since Sergeant Davide Ruci had felt so small and so stupid. A basic error.

\*

Helen woke to the sound of church bells chiming seven. She had slept well and felt better for it. The bedroom she was sleeping in was small but cheerful. The pink floral bedspread was now hanging half on the bed and half on the floor, and the pink cotton sheet which had been sufficient to keep her warm through the night was still tucked into the sides of the bed. She must have slept soundly.

Helen always enjoyed meeting new people, and although it didn't happen as often now that her life had become one of routines, meeting the Borronis had been a real pleasure. There had been a lot of tears as they sat chatting after dinner, managing to speak about their children's happiness despite Helen's Italian and Lucia's English being very limited. Helen's biggest regret was not having seen Lesley over those last few months, and she felt slightly jealous of the Borronis, who had seen both their son and her daughter quite recently.

Helen became aware of Lucia speaking to her husband somewhere in the house, and she suspected she had slept rather too long. Everything had been arranged for her comfort, and once showered and dressed, she headed towards the kitchen and the chattering voice. They both smiled when they saw her, Lucia ushering her to a seat at the kitchen table. Breakfast was light but filling: fruit, pastries, coffee, bread, cheese. Lucia continued her chatter, including Helen in the myriad of things she wanted to talk about. Mundane things. Piero watched his wife and listened attentively, occasionally filling a gap in the conversation with a one- or two-word response. Lucia's therapy for her husband, locked in a slow and almost silent world. Helen knew their marriage wouldn't have always been like this.

*I'm going to take Helen for a walk round Cesate this morning, Piero. We won't be gone long. You can sit on the terrace while we're away. Is that okay?*

He nodded and smiled.

*We'll go to the cemetery so Helen can see where Diego will be laid to rest.* She paused. *And you can see if that's where you'd like Lesley to lie.* They all had tears in their eyes now.

*That's an excellent idea.* Helen was sure it was what she wanted, and more importantly, after meeting the

Borronis, she was sure it was what Lesley would have wanted.

After breakfast, Piero took Helen's arm, and they made their way slowly out onto the terrace with its view of the garden and the surrounding houses. Helen helped Piero as he lowered himself slowly into his chair. As she turned to go back into the kitchen, he took her hand and held it tightly in his. *I'm so very sorry,* he said slowly and deliberately.

*I am also sorry, Piero. But they were happy, and happiness isn't something that comes along very often. We must remember that.*

Lucia, who was now on the terrace behind them, translated Helen's words for Piero, and they cried again.

Cesate was bigger than Helen had imagined, although it had that small-town feel since Lucia seemed to know and greet just about everyone they passed. It had a lovely array of shops and a large supermarket: no need to go into Milan too often, she thought. They passed a number of churches, finally stopping at the Parrochia San Alessandro e San Martino, the church attended by Lucia and her daughter. Its yellow exterior shone brightly in the sun, and the bell tower, with its ancient bell bare to the world, seemed tall and far above them as they stood at the bottom of the stairs staring up at this place of sanctuary.

They went in.

Helen sat down in the back pew while Lucia went forward to a small chapel on the right-hand side to light a candle for the dead and to pray, she suspected, for help in understanding why this terrible thing had happened. Helen liked the church. Its ornate ceilings and many frescoes gave you the overwhelming feeling that God was present and enjoying its grandeur, a complete contrast to the Church of Scotland she attended with its bare walls, single wooden cross and hard wooden pews. She wondered for a moment if being a Catholic would have been more pleasurable for her. Then she wondered, as she had on many occasions, if religion was about enjoying yourself at all.

Lucia slipped into the pew next to Helen, and they sat in silence, pondering the number of things that had happened to bring them to this moment.

The cemetery, Cimitero Pertusella, was the final destination on their tour of Cesate. Everything seemed white and black to Helen: white buildings, black stones, white stones. Birch trees surrounded the perimeter, moving slowly in the wind, brushing their leaves against each other. Swoosh. Swoosh. Helen felt momentarily queasy as they walked into the cemetery, the finality of putting Lesley in the cold ground suddenly striking her. Lucia walked with purpose to the far-right corner of the cemetery, stopping in front of a white marble stone with only one name on it. Helen stood next to her.

*This is where our first child, Giovanni, is buried.* Helen read the words on the stone and realised he had been two years old when he died. She took Lucia's hand. She couldn't imagine what it would be like to bury two children. *We want Diego to lie here too, and we would be very happy if Lesley joined them.* They both started to cry, and for a moment, Helen thought she might not be able to stop. The sun shone brightly on the white stones, in stark contrast to their combined sadness. As Lucia bent down to rearrange the flowers that had only been put there a few days before, Helen made her decision.

Lesley would be buried here. *I'd like that,* she said. *And I'm sure Lesley would too.*

*

Rigoberto took longer than anticipated to reach Cesate. A lorry accident on the A1 had held him up for three quarters of an hour, so it was nearly lunchtime when he parked in one of the visitors' spaces outside the front door.

The small entrance reminded him of his early days in the Carabinieri, manning the desk of a small police station on the outskirts of Naples, dealing with lost property, lost people, lost pets, local school parties on visits and a myriad of other mundane things that he had thought quite exciting at the time. The desk officer had obviously been told to expect him because as soon as he said his name, she asked him to follow her through to Davide Ruci's office.

When he went in, he was glad to see coffee and pastries laid out on a tray waiting for him. It had been a long morning. Davide Ruci and Rigoberto Copelli shook hands.

*My apologies for being so late. I got caught up in an accident.*

*It isn't a problem. You're most welcome.* Davide Ruci could see in this young man the enthusiasm he had once had for his job and the certainty of youth that things would work out. *I must start by apologising for speaking to Detective Francesco the other day without checking that his visit was legitimate. I didn't follow the rules.* It seemed odd to be saying this to a young man who could only have been in the service for less than ten years. It made his forty years seem a complete waste of time.

*That isn't a problem at all.* Rigoberto felt embarrassed and eagerly moved on to his list of questions while munching his way through a number of pastries and three cups of coffee. Davide detailed everything that had happened during Alessandro's visit, finally handing over the brown case file on Paolo Bianchi that both Diego and Alessandro had already looked at.

*What do you know about this Paolo Bianchi?*

*Paolo has lived in Cesate his whole life. Apart from the incident with the cat, he has never been in bother with the police. He lived with his mother until she died a number of years ago and has lived alone ever since, I think. I know his mother kept a very close eye on him and described him as autistic to others, but I don't know if that was a formal diagnosis.*

*Did he know Diego Borroni?*

*Yes, they went to school together, and I know Diego's mother, Lucia, used to have him round to the house on occasions to play with Diego. I don't think Diego enjoyed it, and he was certainly the only child in his year to have Paolo to his house.* He paused for a moment, thinking of his friend. *Lucia is very kind and always thinking about others.*

*Do you think he could be a murderer?*

Davide didn't answer quickly, and he realised in that moment that his opinion of Paolo Bianchi had changed over the past few days. *Maybe. But I have no evidence, and you'll find this file doesn't help either. Diego's father, Detective Piero Borroni, now retired, was always convinced Paolo had killed Father Rossi all those years ago, but there was no proof, no DNA, no witnesses. His mother was his alibi. And he was small, unlike Father Rossi. I don't know where he could have got the strength from to suffocate him.*

*Technique is more important than strength on most*

*occasions.* Rigoberto took a bite from a fourth pastry. *I'll read through the file now if you could get me Paolo Bianchi's address. I might just pay him a visit since I'm here.* And he began reading.

\*

Paolo's lunch had been a grand affair today since he didn't want to eat anywhere once he was in Livorno and would have to survive on this until he got home in the middle of the night. Minestrone soup, roast chicken, vegetables, tiramisu. Once tidied up, he donned his clothes, putting his morning clothes neatly in the washing machine before heading out for the drive to Livorno. He knew the drive would take around four hours, and instead of taking the most direct route which he had taken before, he decided to go via Genoa and the coast road. The sea always made him feel calm, and he knew that if he was too early, there would be plenty of isolated places to stop.

The car purred quietly as he locked the garage doors before driving through the gates, putting them back in place, then heading towards the Milan ring road and the A7. It was a lovely day for a drive, and now that he was on his way, he felt calmer and more certain that he was doing the right thing.

The A7 was quiet, and the first part of the journey to Genoa passed quickly. It wasn't particularly scenic, but Paolo enjoyed maintaining a steady speed and watching the many vehicles that passed him. Once round Genoa, he took the A12 towards Livorno and finally could see the Mediterranean Sea, blue and sparkling in the afternoon sunshine. Now and again, he left the A12 in order to maintain his view of the sea as well as ensuring his route was hard to follow if anyone wanted to find out where he had gone. He stopped once or twice to have a drink from his flask and to eat a muesli bar.

As he neared Livorno, it was starting to get dark. After his first visit, he knew that walking to the flat in Via Traversa would be easier than trying to find a space nearby. And so he parked in a tree-lined street behind the monument to Guiseppe Garibaldi and waited for darkness to envelop the city.

*

After a hearty lunch in the station canteen, Rigoberto found Paolo's house without any difficulty. He wasn't sure this was the right thing to do, but he wanted to impress Gianfranco, and he didn't want to come back to Cesate on another day unless it was essential. The file hadn't convinced Rigoberto that Paolo could be a murderer but given that others thought it was a possibility and all leads should be followed up, he was determined to do that before returning to Milan.

It was a quiet street, a dead end with fields and a small wood at the end of it. He parked directly outside the gates of Paolo's house and made his way through the side gate, walking quickly to its main entrance. The shutters were closed on all sides, and there was no sign that anyone was inside. He knocked anyway. No response. He knocked again. No response.

As he walked back to the car, he decided he would wait, certain that Paolo Bianchi would return to his house at some point today. He parked further up the street under a large beech tree next to the path into the forest. Paolo's gates were in view. More waiting.

*

It was dark now. The headlights of cars whose occupants were hurrying home to start the weekend flashed past, filling the car with light every few seconds. It was busy enough that he wouldn't be noticed. He knew the walk to Via Traversa would take only ten minutes if he took the direct route, but he wanted to be in narrow streets where he could hug the walls of the buildings and avoid as many people as possible. Crossing onto the island where Via Traversa was found was the critical point. He felt momentarily exposed as cars, bikes and people made their way across the bridge to or from the many restaurants that filled the New Venice district. Soon he was in Via Traversa, with its residential housing and no restaurants.

As he neared the main entrance to number 140, he donned his black gloves and put the black balaclava securely over his head, ensuring he couldn't be identified if he met anyone. He knew this was the crucial moment, the moment when luck would be needed. Slowly, he pushed open the heavy wooden door that took him into the central courtyard. Lights shone out from open windows as those who lived at 140 Via Traversa settled into their evening routines, some making dinner, others chatting, others watching TV. Most, he hoped, distracted from looking out onto the courtyard as he made his way towards the outside stairs that would take him to Franco's flat. The scent of herbs grown in the many tubs scattered around the central courtyard filled his nostrils. He placed his feet quietly and deliberately on each step until he reached the top floor. He met no one. His luck had held.

The flat was just as he'd left it. The two small lamps

that were timed to come on in the evenings were lit, but Paolo was confident the heavy lace curtains would obscure him from view. He went directly to the desk situated in the second room and took all the files out of the filing cabinet, scattering them across the top of the desk to ensure they would burn well. The phones, he realised, were a bigger problem. He would need to take them with him and dispose of them just as he had done with other phones over the years. So he put them in the bottom of his bag before checking the bottom drawer of the filing cabinet for any further papers. There were none.

In the small kitchen, he checked every cupboard and the fridge even though he had done that previously. He checked the small cabinet in the bathroom, looked inside the cistern and walked carefully over all the floorboards in case Franco had used a cavity under the floor to hide documents. He could find none. Satisfied he had checked everything, Paolo prepared to apply the accelerant to different areas in each room and finally be rid of the flat.

For a few moments, he considered whether what he was doing was the right thing to do. He knew now that those brief encounters with Lesley had changed his thinking. He had made a connection with another person, and he supposed he wondered if he could do that again. If he could, he wanted to be a better person. Although most likely, it was too late for that.

He thought he was sorry to be dragged once again into an act of destruction which might result in someone's death, but he knew he needed to eradicate any possibility of being found and his crimes being uncovered. It was what he had always done. His mother's voice echoed in his head as he considered these questions. *You have to go there and destroy all the evidence. It is the only way you can protect yourself. You wouldn't survive prison.*

Paolo took the flask of accelerant out of his bag, unscrewed the lid and began pouring it slowly and carefully in strategic areas around the flat, ensuring each area was joined to the next by a small trail of the fluid. The net curtains, the desk, the table lamps, the corners of each room, every door in the flat, the back of the front door, the rag he had brought in his bag. Every drop had been used. He screwed the lid back on the flask and placed it back in his bag. No evidence could be left.

Once he had taken his final look at the flat, he placed the sodden rag just inside the letter box, making sure it wasn't visible from the outside, then placed his ear against the door. Silence. As he exited, he closed the door quietly, ensuring both deadlocks were turned before lifting the flap of the letterbox and igniting the rag with the lighter. It caught quickly, the yellow flame licking the edges of the letterbox as it sought out the accelerant on the back of the door, which would in turn light up the rest of the flat.

Paolo moved quickly. Down the stairs, across the courtyard, momentarily looking up at the flat in the hope that the flames would now have reached the windows. They had. It was done.

## Thirty-nine

Carla's blonde hair was tied up in an elaborate bun, accentuating her pale skin and high cheek bones. She wore little make-up. Just the way he liked it. Alessandro rarely listened to what she had to say, and this evening was no different. He watched the movement of her fingers as she scooped the spaghetti on to her fork, rolling it round and round with the help of her spoon before placing it in her mouth and becoming silent for a few moments. He loved the contrast between the silence of their lovemaking and the endless chatter as they enjoyed their Friday night dinner in Trattoria Giovanni, where Alessandro could be certain of the proprietor's discretion. A policeman and a prostitute — discretion was key. As soon as she had finished that forkful, Carla began speaking again. Alessandro smiled. His meal had been finished long ago.

Once the meal was over, Alessandro walked Carla back to her flat, her work over for the day. She always took his arm as they walked along, and he remembered briefly the heady days when he and his wife would have walked like this, happy to be together, happy to walk in silence. The baby's death had changed all that. Once at the entrance to her flat, Carla kissed him lightly on the cheek. *You've transferred the money for this evening to my account?*

*Yes.*

*I'll see you next Friday, Alessandro. Have a good week.*

Alessandro turned away, back to the reality of his life and his trip to Cesate. The car was a few streets away, but he knew there was no rush. The drive would take him a few hours. And he wasn't sure what he was going to do once he got there, but he could make that decision later. Early summer evenings in Florence were to be enjoyed. The night was warm without being oppressive, and the beauty of the buildings drenched in white electric light drew your eye to their naked and ancient beauty. Alessandro enjoyed a cigarette as he walked. It was the only day in the week when he smoked. It was the only day in the week when he felt alive.

Just before getting in the car, he texted his wife: *Need to be at work all night. Will be home around lunchtime tomorrow. A*

He wondered whether she would believe him. He thought probably not.

*

Rigoberto realised he'd been asleep in the car for several hours, and he began to wonder if he'd made the wrong decision. Maybe he should have gone back to Milan and returned another day when he had more information and had discussed his findings with Gianfranco Valdi. He opened the door of the car and got out to consider his decision and get some fresh air to waken him up.

As he sat on the bonnet of the car, shielded by the branches of the tree reaching down towards him, he noticed someone walking up the street. The lighting was so dark, he couldn't make out any detail, but he was certain it was a man. He waited silently, watching to see where this person might go. They stopped outside the gates to Paolo Bianchi's house, looked around, then went through the side gate Rigoberto had himself used hours earlier.

As he emerged from under the beech tree, Rigoberto looked carefully around to ensure no one was watching from a nearby house. He thought his footsteps sounded loud as he walked towards the house and the open side gate. The tall metal lamppost positioned just outside Paolo's house spread no light onto the garden or the house, the small pool of light falling directly onto the road. Rigoberto pushed the gate slowly to one side, and balancing on the cobble edging, he made his way towards the steps up to the house. As he got closer, he noticed the garage had been opened at one end — forced open, he thought — and he could see lights going on and off through the closed shutters. He was certain it wasn't Paolo Bianchi in the house. He should call for assistance.

*

Alessandro had got to Cesate much quicker than he expected. The motorway had been quiet and the road conditions good. He always felt energised after seeing Carla, so staying awake wasn't an issue. Once in Cesate, he decided to leave his car two streets away from Paolo Bianchi's house. He didn't want to be noticed, and he wanted a walk to clear his head and help him decide exactly what he would do. He knew the decisions he was making weren't the ones he would usually make, and that puzzled him. He didn't want to hand an innocent man over to the Poccinis. He didn't want more blood on his hands. He wanted out.

Before leaving the car, he removed his regulation gun from the glove compartment and placed it in the holster under his jacket. Most policemen found driving with their gun nestled neatly against their chest quite comforting, but Alessandro had always found it distracting and worrying. Tonight was no different.

The streets of Cesate were quiet when he set out, walking between the dim pools of light as quietly and as quickly as he could. He met no one and was soon at the gates to Paolo Bianchi's house. It was in darkness, always a good time to catch people off-guard. He checked the street before donning a pair of blue gloves, opening the side gate and crunching across the pebbles towards the outside steps. He stopped momentarily at the bottom of the steps to listen for any unexpected noises. Silence.

Once at the front door, he rang the bell several times and knocked on the door. There was no response. He turned to look out across Cesate while deciding what to do. He had to get in.

The front door had two deadlocks; there was no way he could gain entry that way. The garage. It seemed a more likely entry point. And it was. A Yale lock, easy to breech. Once inside the empty garage, Alessandro felt more confident that Paolo Bianchi wasn't at home. Confident he could get in and out of the house without being noticed, he left the garage door, his exit route, slightly ajar, and using the torch on his phone, made his way across the garage towards the stairs in the corner, the stairs up to the house.

Alessandro felt strangely excited as he broke through the door into the house: breaking the law and breaking his own rules. He put on the light in the hall. Brown. Everything was brown or a shade of brown. The furniture sat neatly in its place, everything at right angles to each other. No adornments, no pictures hanging on the walls. Everything neat and tidy and clean. The smell of cleanliness was everywhere.

Alessandro made his way quickly from room to room, looking for clues that would link Paolo to crimes he couldn't imagine him committing. The kitchen, the dining room, the living room, two unused bedrooms, the bathroom and then the bedroom used by Paolo. He switched on the light and looked around. At the window, curtains and shutters were closed. Two brown wooden wardrobes filled one wall. Alessandro moved towards them. As he did so, he turned to look at the bed, and there, hanging alone above the headboard, was a drawing, a line drawing. It was hard to make it out in the dim light being cast by the central light, so he once again put on his torch and shone it on the paper. It was of Lesley Hamilton. The murdered Lesley Hamilton.

At that moment, he realised he hadn't expected to find any evidence linking Paolo to the murders, but he had now. He was disappointed. It left him again with another decision to make. He carefully peeled the piece of paper from the wall, where it had been attached with Blu Tack, folded it neatly in four and put it in his pocket. Time to go.

As he made his way back downstairs to the garage, he thought he heard a noise outside the garage door. A crunching noise. The pebbles being walked on. He stood silent and still in the middle of the unlit garage, watching the open door for movement. It seemed a long time before his eyes adjusted to the dark, and just when he thought he had waited long enough and it was safe to go out, the door began to slowly move. A hand could be seen pushing it towards Alessandro. He took his gun from his holster and pointed it towards the door. As soon as the door was far enough open and he could see the figure of a man staring into the darkness, he spoke.

*Come slowly into the garage, keeping your hands in the air. Slowly, remember.*

The man stopped, removed his hands from the door and put them in the air.

*Step forward, shut the door and put on the light switch.*

Suddenly the garage was flooded with light. Rigoberto almost gasped as he realised he was face to face with Alessandro Francesco.

Alessandro wished he hadn't asked him to put on the light. It meant now he had to do something. If he arrested the man, he would have to go to Gianfranco Valdi and hand Paolo Bianchi over to him. The Poccinis would never forgive him; he would be their next victim. He could kill this man and leave him here, leave Paolo Bianchi with a dead body to explain. Those were his choices.

As he pondered which choice to make, the man standing in front of him was speaking. *I'm Rigoberto Copelli, Detective Francesco. I work on Gianfranco Valdi's team. I think we're both here for the same reason.*

Silence.

A terror of being found out filled Alessandro's head, and pulling the trigger suddenly seemed the only option. The noise was deafening. Rigoberto Copelli fell backwards, hitting his head on the concrete floor while using his left hand to clutch his exploded stomach, which was oozing thick red blood through his several layers of clothes. He wasn't dead. Alessandro considered shooting him again, but he wanted out of this place, away from the same metallic smell he had encountered in Diego Borroni's flat. The blood was on the floor now, leaking all the life out of the young man's body. He would leave him to die.

Switching off the light, he pushed through the door, leaving it slightly ajar, engulfing Rigoberto in a terrifying darkness he would never escape from.

*

Paolo knew he had done a good job when he was able to see the flames rising from the building at 140 Via Traversa two streets away. The air was heavy with the smell of wood smoke and the clanging bells of the fire engines as they made their way through the narrow streets. People had come out of restaurants and buildings to see what was happening, and as Paolo looked at their shocked faces and listened to their exclamations of horror, he was satisfied that he would no longer have to worry about the flat in Livorno and what it might reveal. He stood amongst the crowds for a short time, ensuring his behaviour mirrored that of the people around him, before leaving them behind and heading to his car.

It was late now, and he wanted to be home. Home in the safety of his own house. The motorways were quiet as he made his way across northern Italy, back to Cesate. His car purred as he engaged cruise control, and he watched the miles disappear.

It was still dark when he got back to Cesate. The plan had worked perfectly, he thought. He was pleased. As he turned the nose of his car toward the gates of his house, switching off his headlights as he did so, he noticed the side gate wasn't quite on its latch. He hadn't left it that way. Momentarily, he was gripped by the same fear that had gripped him when the man at the gate asked for directions. Then he remembered it was Friday night, the evening when the supermarket distributed its weekly newsletter around the houses of Cesate offering money off coupons for items you rarely wanted. His breathing returned to normal. That would be the answer. He closed the side gate and opened the main gates, ready to drive in. He considered opening the garage doors so that he could drive straight in but decided it was best to be securely in the driveway before doing that.

He closed the gates quietly, a well-practised skill, and crunched his way across the pristine pebbles to the garage door. As his eyes adjusted to the night's darkness, he realised the door was unlocked, broken. Someone had been in his house or was still in his house. As quickly as he could, he returned to his car and took his gun and silencer from his bag.

Very slowly, he pushed open the end section of the garage door, putting his finger on the light switch and turning it on. Nothing happened. Silence. He waited. Just long enough to be certain that it was safe to go in and that no one was moving. The smell was the first thing to hit him. A strange smell, an unfamiliar smell. A smell he really didn't like.

Keeping his back against the garage wall, he eased through the door and looked around. If he looked straight ahead, everything was just as he'd left it, but when he turned to look across the garage, nothing was as it should be. There was a large pool of blood seeping across the garage floor, trying to get away from a young man whose rigid hand was gripping his stomach as his fixed eyes stared heavenward. He was dead.

The pounding noise of panic filled Paolo's head. He needed to check the house. Make sure no one was there.

The car couldn't come into the garage, but he needed to change the number plates. He had a body he had to get rid of. Too many thoughts. Too unexpected. Then he remembered his mother's advice: *just one job at a time Paolo. Just one job at a time.*

And as he thought of her and heard her whispering voice reverberating from every wall of the garage, he took control of the situation.

Slowly and deliberately, he worked his way through the list of jobs, leaving the cold dead body of Rigoberto Copelli until last.

# Forty

Alessandro sat in the car, still firmly clutching the gun that had killed Gianfranco Valdi's young detective, listening to the short, sharp rasps of his panicked breath filling the tiny space with the sound of death. In front of him, he saw all his plans unravelling. No retirement villa by the coast, no resurrection of his dead marriage, no escape from the underworld he had so successfully navigated for the past twenty-five years.

As his breathing settled, his grip on the gun lessened and he was able to place it back in the glove box he had taken it from only a few hours earlier. He put his hands on the steering wheel, resting his head on the cold leather between them. Decisions. Make a decision.

Go back to Florence?

Go back to the routine life of Detective Alessandro Francesco?

Go to the Poccinis?

Go to the Poccinis and give them the evidence?

Hand Paolo Bianchi over to the Poccinis to be murdered?

Go to the Poccinis, hand over the evidence and Paolo Bianchi, and then ask them to make him disappear?

He lifted his head from the steering wheel and decided the last one was the best option. He imagined starting again. Building a better life than the one he was now living. Building a simple life away from all the complications that his life in Florence encapsulated. He smiled at the thought of it.

He couldn't contact Marco Poccini right now, but he could drive to Lake Como, close to the Poccini's rural retreat, and wait for morning to break. They owed him for all the risks he had taken for them over the years. Paolo Bianchi's whereabouts would be his bargaining chip, his way out.

The car started first time, and he drove carefully and slowly out of Cesate, north to Lake Como.

*

Gianfranco hadn't thought about work or the murders of Diego Borroni and Lesley Hamilton for at least the last three hours. His entire focus had been on his family. An evening movie with popcorn and drinks served by Concetta as if she were the usherette in the cinema, followed by a game of Cluedo, Gianna's favourite board game. One the girls always won. He never did. A much-enjoyed family joke.

Concetta came back into the living room after making sure the girls were now sleeping, and the temptation he had to call Rigoberto for an update on his visit to Cesate faded as his wife snuggled in beside him on the sofa. It wasn't often that they had time alone to lie wrapped in each other's arms, enjoying the need to say nothing.

He'd call Rigoberto tomorrow. He was sure he would have called if he had any news.

*

Paolo had never had to get rid of a body before. Franco and his fixers had always taken care of such matters when required, and the smell of death had never lingered in his nostrils as it was doing now.

Paolo started by changing the number plates on the car, ensuring it wouldn't draw any attention from passersby when morning broke. Then, after bolting the garage door from the inside and reattaching the Yale lock, he moved on to the phones. The ones he had brought from the flat and the one he found on the body. He broke them up, smashing them into as many pieces as he could before putting them in a small black bag, ready to be taken to the landfill along with the shredded SIM cards. Then he placed a chair in the middle of the garage, sat on it and considered what he would do with the body. Whether he would do anything with the body.

The pools of blood had now congealed, making a pattern of circles across the floor. It would be difficult to remove, he thought. The body lay with its head to one side, eyes staring in shock at the ceiling, its left arm bent rigid where the young man had grabbed his stomach as the bullet entered and tore through his skin. His legs were the only bit of him that was straight.

The smell of the wood burning stove floated down from the house to the garage, and Paolo was content that all the evidence of this man's identity was burning to nothing as he continued to ponder what he would do with the body. His police card, his wallet, photos of a family (probably his family), a linen handkerchief (unusual, Paolo thought), a small mandarin. He hoped he had stoked the fire well enough that it would burn to nothing. The ash would then join the other debris he piled on his compost heap, and soon it would be soil.

The fact that the man was a policeman worried Paolo, not because he thought it made his death worse than any other person's death, but because it made his own position more vulnerable and probably meant he would have to leave his home for good when he removed the body. He felt certain he must have been found out. As he sat in the cold, quiet garage, he was struck by the fact that the pounding in his head had not reappeared. He felt calm, a feeling he could rarely identify. Certain that leaving the house was most likely the best thing he could do. A new life somewhere else seemed attractive.

After locating the largest tarpaulin he had, he placed the chair back in its position against the wall of the garage and laid the tarpaulin on the floor, ready to receive the body. Paolo headed back up to the house in search of his boiler suit, some blue latex gloves and all the bleach he had stored under the kitchen sink. In his bedroom, Paolo found the boiler suit neatly folded and placed in the bottom drawer of one of his wardrobes. He had begun to consider what he would take with him or whether he would take anything at all when he noticed a small piece of Blu Tack on the floor. Puzzled, he looked up, ready to speak to the drawing he had done of Lesley, only to find it wasn't there, the marks made by the Blu Tack staring back at him from the pale wall. He sat down on the bed.

Once again, his head was pounding. His hands began to sweat as he realised that the young policeman didn't have the picture. Whoever had killed him did. The only item taken from the house. The link between him and the murders. So many murders. He would have to leave before daylight broke. Even then, it might be too late. The body would have to remain exactly where it was.

*

Alessandro understood why Italians and tourists alike flocked to Lake Como, with steep mountains falling dramatically into the blue lake and the picturesque towns and villages evoking a past life that wouldn't have been as comfortable as people might imagine. It was daylight now, and he knew Marco Poccini would be up. He didn't sleep well; he'd often commented on it. He made the call.

*Ciao.*

*Ciao, Marco, it's Alessandro Francesco. I have evidence and information for you, Marco. I need to see you as soon as possible. I'm here at Lake Como. Can I come now?*

*Yes, of course you can, Alessandro. I am always happy to see you.*

The phone went dead. Alessandro knew he had said too much. Marco Poccini was always careful to say as little as possible on the phone just in case his calls were being tapped. Paranoia had kept him alive and out of jail this long, and he didn't plan for that to change.

As he drove through the electric gates towards the house, Alessandro could see Marco Poccini waiting for him on the terrace looking out over Lake Como and its dramatic landscape. Standing beside him was Leonardo, his bodyguard and confidante. The man Alessandro was certain would have killed Franco. The man who might kill him if he didn't play his cards right.

# Forty-one

*It's a beautiful morning, Alessandro, is it not?*
Alessandro nodded, aware Marco Poccini couldn't see his
response but knowing his response was irrelevant. It was
simply a way for Marco to start the conversation. *Let's sit
down, Alessandro.* Leonardo moved towards them as they
walked towards the small bistro table and its two chairs
placed strategically at the corner of the terrace to take full
advantage of the lake views.

As he sat down, Alessandro was aware of Leonardo's
presence directly behind him. He wondered for a moment
if he should have brought his gun with him from the car.

*So, what is this evidence and information?* Alessandro
began his story, telling Marco about his visit to the police
station, the details regarding Paolo Bianchi and his visit
to Paolo's house. When he'd finished, he removed the
paper with the line drawing of Lesley Hamilton from his
pocket and handed it to Marco Poccini, aware that he was
also handing over a death sentence for Paolo Bianchi. It
still felt wrong. Too close, too calculated.

Marco looked at it carefully, then handed it to
Leonardo to look at. *It's her,* he confirmed.

*His address, Alessandro?* Alessandro removed a
second piece of paper with Paolo's details written on it
and handed them over. *Lock them in my desk, Leonardo.*

As Leonardo walked away, Alessandro decided it was
time to tell Marco about the policeman. When he had
finished, silence. *I need to disappear, Marco, start a new
life somewhere else with a new name etc. I've worked
hard for you over the years, I'm sure you can do this for
me. I have money I can access, but I need new papers,
somewhere new to live and a degree of protection. Will*

*you do this for me?*

Alessandro could hear the pleading in his voice, and suddenly his plan seemed uncertain. Marco Poccini didn't like loose ends, and Alessandro was making himself a loose end. As he started to get up from his chair, in need of movement to dissipate his panic, he felt Leonardo's hand on his shoulder, pushing him back down into his chair.

*Get the men to remove the car from the driveway, Leonardo, take it up into the hills and destroy it.* A pause. Leonardo spoke quietly into a radio he carried hidden under his jacket, and from the back of the house two men appeared, jackets on, and drove the car out of the driveway. Gone. *I have a safe house at Bellinzona in Switzerland. Leonardo, use the boat and take Alessandro to Gravedona ed Uniti. I'll make sure Pietro is there to meet you and take Alessandro overland into Switzerland.* Marco Poccini stood up and looked at Alessandro. *Thank you, Alessandro, you have done an excellent job.* He started to walk towards the house. *I will be ready to go to Cesate when you get back, Leonardo.*

Leonardo took Alessandro's arm and started walking him towards the lake and the boat that would take him away from the life he had lived to a new unknown life far from everything he knew. Leonardo barely spoke to him as they got on the boat, and still he wondered if Marco Poccini would allow him to live.

\*

Paolo was ready to leave. He'd always been ready to leave: multiple passports, multiple identities, multiple bank cards, 5,000 euros in cash, a few clothes, all in a bag he could carry onto a train away from Cesate, away from Italy. Away from his home.

The sun was rising and he wanted to be away, but he needed to stand once again beside his mother's bed and be sure that this was what she would have wanted. He stood in the silence looking at the bed, her slippers, her Bible, and for the first time in his life, he couldn't hear her voice. The only voice resonating in his head was his own repeating 'leave' over and over. And so he did.

As he drove slowly out of the drive, returning to close the gates once his car was safely out, he wondered if he would ever see the house again. He hoped he would.

*

As Helen lay awake in her bed listening to the sounds of Lucia and Piero Borroni coming to life for the start of another day, she felt content that the arrangements she had agreed to yesterday with the funeral director were the arrangements Lesley would have wanted had she been there to agree to them.

The funeral would be on Thursday: Mass in the Parrochia San Alessandro e San Martino followed by a graveside ceremony at the Cimitero Pertusella. Although she had few of Lesley's possessions, Gianfranco Valdi had given her, along with the manuscript of Lesley's first and only novel, her diary. And in there, Helen could read and hear Lesley's voice. Her joy at living in Florence. Her excitement after meeting Diego. Her contentment with the life they had started building together. The feeling Lesley had been deeply loved and had loved deeply. Something rare.

Helen sat up slowly and placed her feet on the cool

tiles, ready to start another day. The sun was once again shining, and Helen wondered what they would do today, what she would learn about Lesley today and what she would learn about herself. She knew she should phone Kate to tell her about the funeral arrangements, but she'd said she would phone on Sunday, and she thought she would leave it until then. Maybe, hopefully, it would be too late for Kate to get a seat on a flight to Milan before Thursday. Helen thought that's what Lesley would have wanted.

*

It was unusual for Sergeant Davide Ruci to be on duty on a Saturday morning. It had been like that for some time. But today, as he walked up the short flight of steps into the station, he hoped the young officer he was covering for would have a lovely wedding. It was a perfect day for it. The station was much quieter at the weekend, which he liked, and as he greeted the front desk officer, he hoped he might be able to get through the large amount of paperwork that seemed to accumulate daily on his desk.

Since the news of Diego's murder and the dealings he had had with the Milan Carabinieri, he'd found it more difficult to concentrate on the mundane and wondered more than once a day if it was time for him to retire. He would consider it in a few weeks.

As he turned the handle on his blind to let the early morning sunshine flood into his office, his phone rang. An internal call from the front desk.

*Sergeant, I've had a call about an abandoned car on the outskirts of Cesate. A man out walking his dog noticed it when he came out of the woods. He said it has*

311

*its windows down. He thought it looked a bit strange. He's given me the registration number. Should I go out and check it?*

Davide looked at the paperwork and decided it could wait for another day. *No, no. I'll go and check it if you check the number plate. I wouldn't be very good at running the front desk, I don't think. I trust you got the man's name and contact details?*

*Yes, sir.*

*Excellent.*

It wasn't far from the station to the narrow street on the edge of Cesate, with the woods a favourite haunt of dog walkers and teenagers alike. It was difficult to see the car, which was parked discreetly under a beech tree on the edge of the woods. As he walked towards the car, he realised it looked familiar to him. He was certain he'd seen it before. He looked at the number plate and knew then that it was the car belonging to the young detective from Florence who he'd met with yesterday. But there was no sign of the young detective.

Davide called the station and asked the young officer what he'd found out about the car.

*It appears to be from Florence and belongs to a man called Rigoberto Copelli. He's from Naples originally.*

*Look in the visitors' book from yesterday, early morning. Did someone called Rigoberto Copelli visit me at the station?* He knew the answer would be yes, but he needed it confirmed.

*Yes, he did, sir.*

*I need a team of officers here to secure the site. Contact Milan central and let them know we have a missing policeman. They'll send a team.*

*Is there a body, sir?*

*No.* Silence. *I'll wait here until they arrive. I need to contact Gianfranco Valdi and the homicide team in Florence. Once you've contacted Milan, get me Valdi's number asap.*

*I'm on it, sir.* The line went dead.

*

Leonardo was standing outside the black Range Rover, waiting for the arrival of his boss. The engine purred quietly as he looked at his phone, waiting for a message from Pietro that the job had been done.

Marco Poccini kissed his wife gently on the cheek before descending the stone stairs to the waiting car. She had wanted to go with him, but he knew it was best she knew simply that the job had been done rather than witnessing it.

Ping. *The job is done. Thank you for the work. I enjoyed it. Pietro.*

*Any news, Leonardo?*

*The job is complete, sir. One loose end gone.*

*Not quite, Leonardo. The job will only be complete when Paolo Bianchi is dead.*

They got in the car and started the journey to Cesate.

*

Gianfranco had tried calling Rigoberto several times, but the phone was dead. No ring tone. Nothing. He was worried. Worried enough that he was considering going to the young detective's house to check on his whereabouts. He knew it wouldn't go down well with the family, but he felt something was wrong.

*You're not listening, Gianfranco.* Concetta was used to her husband not listening to them, preoccupied with a case or a clue to solving a case, and she enjoyed teasing him about it.

*Sorry, I was just ...* His phone rang. It was the office number.

*We have a call for you, sir. A Sergeant Davide Ruci. He said he needs to speak to you about Detective Rigoberto Copelli. We've checked the number he's calling from and it's definitely him. Do you want to take the call?*

Gianfranco stood up from the table and walked through the open French doors into the garden and the warmth of the early morning sunshine.

*Yes, thank you.*

*You're through now, Sergeant Ruci.*

*Thank you.*

*What news, Sergeant Ruci?*

*We've found Detective Copelli's car abandoned on the edge of Cesate but no sign of him. I've called in a team from Milan to secure the area, but I thought you'd want to know.*

*Do you know why he would have been there, Sergeant Ruci?*

*I think I do, sir. He took the details of Paolo Bianchi just as Alessandro Francesco did. And the house is 100 metres down the road.*

*Okay. Are you going to check the house?*

*Yes, sir, as soon as back-up arrives. It shouldn't be long now. But I passed the house after parking my car and it looked just as it always does.*

*But you will check it?*

*Yes.*

*I'll leave in the next five minutes. I'll get helicoptered in. Is there somewhere we can land?*

*I'll text you the co-ordinates, sir, if you give me your number.*

And he did.

As he prepared to leave, donning once again his formal work clothes, he decided he would take Violetta Morelli with him. She could meet him at the helipad.

## Forty-two

Paolo felt he had been driving for a long time when he finally reached Ventimiglia and its glorious views over the Mediterranean. Normally, he enjoyed driving, particularly when it involved skirting the majestic Mediterranean coast, with its sharp blue light bouncing off the sea and leading the eye out to an endless horizon. But today he continued to feel anxious, wondering if the body had been found and if he was being followed. He knew he had little control over what would happen next, and he knew that second guessing the actions of others was not a capacity he had. He could only think about himself. Franco would have known what to do. Franco would have made him disappear. But Franco was dead. Dead. He knew now he should have appreciated him more.

Once parked in the long-stay car park close to the railway station, he checked he had left nothing in the car that he might need and headed to the station and a train into France. It was warm now as he walked through the automatic doors tucked under the five arches that made the station so recognisable. He scanned the main hall for a ticket machine; he didn't want to speak to anyone. He didn't want to be remembered.

He decided to take the shortest journey over the border. Menton. He would pick up a car there and head up into the hills, away from the coast and its noise. There was a train for Menton due in five minutes. He bought his ticket and waited on the platform, his back against the wall of the railway station building, ensuring he could see everyone who was waiting for the train. Ensuring he was out of the light, unnoticed.

The train was busy; he'd expected that. It was Saturday, a rest day for the majority of the population. A day for taking a trip. People eager to get a seat on the top deck of the train bustled forward as soon as the doors opened, but Paolo waited. He wanted to get in last, to remain in the small area at the end of the carriage, standing directly under the CCTV camera that was nestled in the corner of the ceiling.

Twenty minutes later, he was in Menton and was first off the train and out of the station. Although opened in 1869, none of the station's grandeur remained. Instead, a building of rectangular windows, rectangular doors and flat roofs led you out into a small square taking you down into the town and towards the bright blue sea, the destination for the majority of those travelling on the train.

Paolo saw the AVIS car hire office first and headed straight for it, ensuring the passport he used to secure a car gave him a new identity — Stefano Esposito. As he stood at the desk while the girl — Amelie, her badge said — took his details and his money, he wished he hadn't relied so heavily on Franco during his working life. He wished he had made other contacts because now it would have meant no risks, no revealing yourself in public, no speaking to others, no answering questions. Beads of sweat were forming on his forehead despite the air conditioning in the office, and he could feel panic rising, fogging his brain.

*Is a Peugeot okay for you, Monsieur Esposito?*

He nodded.

*Excellent. I'll just print out the paperwork and get the keys.* She turned away from him, searching in a small cupboard for the correct set of keys. *It's a lovely day again.*

*Yes.* Silence. He knew she would expect him to say more, but he could think of nothing to say and he didn't want to speak. He didn't want to be remembered.

*There we are. I can come out and go over the car with you.*

*No.* He was too quick. He was drawing attention to himself.

*Okay. Enjoy your trip, Monsieur Esposito. We'll see you in a month.* He said nothing, knowing she wouldn't see him again.

Once in the car, Paolo removed his black leather jacket, got a map up on his phone and headed out of Menton, unsure where exactly he would go. It was early in the day. He thought he had plenty of time.

He left the busy town by the D6007, a meandering road that would take him along the coast, giving him time to think.

\*

Gianfranco hated trips in helicopters. It wasn't something he did often, but it always made him feel vulnerable and anxious. Violetta, in contrast, looked energised and excited as they flew low over the Tuscan countryside towards Milan. She smiled at him, and although he knew he should have smiled back, he found it impossible to do.

It was a ten-minute ride in the Carabinieri patrol car to the site in Cesate where Rigoberto's car had been found. As they reached the edge of the town, the road was suddenly blocked off with yellow tape and two Carabinieri officers barring their path and the path of any others who wanted to walk this way. The patrol car stopped to let them out. Gianfranco and Violetta made their way on foot towards Rigoberto's car and a house that seemed now to be swarming with people: plain clothes officers, Carabinieri officers and forensic teams in their white paper overalls and blue plastic shoes examining the car still tucked neatly under the beech tree leading into the forest.

Gianfranco knew now the news wouldn't be good.

*Detective Chief Inspector Valdi?* The voice was familiar, and the outstretched hand that shook his was strong. *I'm Sergeant Ruci.*

Gianfranco said nothing, waiting for the man who towered over his small frame to say something. There was a moment's pause.

*I'm afraid Detective Copelli has been found. In the garage of Paolo Bianchi's house. Shot. Murdered.*

Violetta gasped and thought momentarily that she might cry. She felt stupid for not realising as she made her way past the yellow tape, watching the forensic teams busy about their business, that this would be the outcome. She could tell from Gianfranco's face that he hadn't made that mistake.

*Can I see the body?*

*Yes, sir.* They started walking towards the house when Gianfranco remembered Violetta. He thought he should say something to reassure her, but he couldn't think of anything. There was nothing reassuring to be said. The death of a fellow officer brought home the reality of your own fragility, and he thought it best that she be reminded of this early in her career. It might make her more careful. More careful than Rigoberto had been. He could hear her footsteps crunching across the gravel close behind him.

The garage door was half open, giving forensic teams access to the house. *Can I introduce you to Detective Chief Inspector Manelli from Milan, Detective Chief Inspector Valdi?* The formality of the introductions seemed ludicrous to Gianfranco. He wanted to see the body, to see what had happened to Rigoberto. And he knew Manelli; no introductions were needed.

*Where's the body, Manelli?*

*This way.* Davide Ruci was left standing in the driveway as the three detectives walked towards the open door of the garage.

Violetta walked behind the two men, unprepared for the sight that would greet her. Unprepared for the smell. The smell was the first thing to greet her. Metallic, pungent. Then the rigid, lifeless body of her colleague, with his eyes wide open in shock, futilely clutching his stomach where the bullet had entered. She gasped and covered her mouth. No one looked at her; no one said a comforting word. Procedures needed to be followed, evidence found, and the murderer located. She dropped her arms and took out her notebook. She knew Gianfranco would want notes taken. She could at least do that.

Gianfranco had been here before. Other colleagues, other murders. But this one felt different. He knew Rigoberto shouldn't have been there. He should have visited the Cesate police station, then returned to Florence with the information gathered. Then they could have decided together what to do next. But he knew the pressure detectives felt working for him. The pressure to succeed, to gather evidence, to solve crimes quickly. They wanted to impress him, but they didn't need to. And he knew that had Rigoberto's wife and young family been living in Florence, he would have gone home from Cesate. Gianfranco once again felt sorry for the part he felt he had played in this death just as he felt he had played a part in the deaths of others.

*Is someone informing his wife?* That was always Gianfranco's priority. He never wanted Concetta to be the last to know if the same fate ever befell him.

*Yes, we contacted Naples and they're sending out family liaison officers to tell the family.* Gianfranco would call her tonight. It needed to be more personal.

*What do you know so far?* Violetta was poised, ready to write down every word uttered by Manelli.

*He has, as you can see, been dead for a number of hours. He was shot in the stomach, and at the moment, we think he bled out rather than dying immediately. It's quite a pool of blood. No attempt to move him has been made. The garage door has been tampered with; we don't know if he broke in or not.* Gianfranco knew he wouldn't have. *There is no evidence in the car to lead us to any further conclusions.*

*Where is Paolo Bianchi? The man who lives here. Have you located him?* Manelli wondered how Gianfranco Valdi, so far away in Florence, would know of Paolo Bianchi.

*No, we haven't located him. The neighbour over the road saw him leave early this morning, but she thought this wasn't unusual. He tended to go out when others weren't about.*

*Are you trying to locate him?*

*Yes.*

*I assume DNA has been collected from the house?*

*Yes.*

*Do you know anything about the bullet?*

*No, we won't know that until the postmortem is done. We didn't want to move him until you got here.*

*I'm here now; he can be moved.* The two men looked at each other. Violetta felt the tension. *I'm going to call our pathologist, Doctor Brio Ricci, and let him know the body is going to Milan. He'll be able to keep in touch with the team in Milan so that we have all the forensic evidence we need. Can I have a look around the house?*

*Of course.* Manelli could have refused, but he knew Gianfranco would look round it anyway. *What is your interest in Paolo Bianchi? He seems to be a man with no history and certainly no criminal history.*

*He's a suspect in the killing of a Florence detective and his girlfriend. We would like to speak to him.* Gianfranco and Violetta headed towards the stairs in the corner of the garage and up into the house.

\*

Leonardo asked Signor Poccini if he wanted to stop in Milan and pick up his sons.

*No, Leonardo. But thank you for asking.* Marco Poccini would normally have taken his sons with him, but on this occasion, he wanted to carry out the deed alone. Leonardo would ensure his wishes were carried out.

Pepe's disappearance and the conclusion that he'd been murdered weighed heavily on Marco. He had done everything to keep Pepe out of the family business and far away from the many crimes committed by and on behalf of the Poccini family. Yet still he had been unable to protect him.

The countryside, villages, towns and cities merged into one as they headed towards Cesate, and he hoped, the murder of the man who had killed his son. Mozart's Andante con moto filled the car as he stared blankly out of the window at the passing scenery.

## Forty-three

Paolo remembered Cagnes-sur-Mer. It had been many years since he had last visited with his mother, but he remembered the holiday as if it were only yesterday. Franco had rented them a flat at the stunning Marina Baie des Anges, with its uninterrupted sea views and private beach. They had spent ten days exploring the coastal towns and mountain villages nearby. Although they had been impressed by Antibes, Vence and St Paul de Vence, Tourettes-sur-Loup had been their favourite. High in the mountains, it provided panoramic views of the coast as well as allowing his mother to enjoy wandering in and out of the craft shops that lined the tiny car-free streets. Nothing was bought, but seeing the handiwork of real craftsmen took her back to the early days of her marriage when collecting the unusual had been their hobby.

Paolo would sit quietly at any nearby cafe enjoying a dark, aromatic espresso while she explored the tiny streets. He particularly enjoyed sitting in the Cafe du Midi looking over the Place de la Liberation and its many comings and goings: drivers struggling to get in and out of the tight car park, villagers greeting friends as they bumped into each other while out shopping, people walking dogs tired from the hot sun. It looked a nice life, a life he thought he might like if only he could learn how to be part of it.

And so Paolo decided to head inland from the sea, up into the mountains and the village he remembered so well. He was hungry now, and as he passed the large Carrefour supermarket, he wondered if he could risk going in there. No. He drove on until he passed a roadside boulangerie with an empty car park. He drove across the dusty car park, ensuring the car couldn't be seen from the side of the road, and ventured into the empty shop. It was just before 1.00 pm and they would be closing in a couple of minutes. A good time to go in. He bought six sandwiches and six bottles of water. The assistant seemed surprised.

She laughed. *Are you collecting the picnic for everyone?*

*Pardon?*

*Are you collecting the picnic for everyone? We don't usually sell so many sandwiches in one go.* She smiled, then looked up as she carefully placed the last of the sandwiches in the brown paper carrier bag.

*No, I'm just ...* Paolo stopped speaking. He didn't know what to say. He handed over the money, took his change and left carrying the bag laden with brie sandwiches that he hoped would keep him going for a couple of days.

She smiled at him again in the same way many people had smiled at him throughout his life. Confused by his responses but wanting to be kind. He hated that. He hated not knowing what he should do.

*Au revoir.* Her voice faded as the automatic door swooshed open and took him once again into the warmth of the sun.

The road was quieter now, most people having left the hurly-burly to enjoy a long lunch with family and friends. The car park in Tourettes-sur-Loup was busy, almost full. Too busy for Paolo, so he drove a short distance out of the village, stopped in the entrance to a field, climbed the gate and settled down behind the stone wall to enjoy some food and a sleep. He was tired now, hungry and anxious. Never a good combination. He would decide what to do next when he woke up.

*

*It's all so brown, sir. So orderly. So bare. He didn't leave in a hurry.*

*Maybe he did, Violetta. Maybe it's just always like this. Maybe this is how he lives.* The forensic teams had finished their work in the house, leaving Gianfranco and Violetta to look around the house, with its air of pervading sadness and general emptiness. Gianfranco had been in the homes of other assassins and knew that order and organisation was often the prevailing theme. He understood that when much of your life was controlled and dictated by others, you had to find a way of regaining some sense of order.

They could find nothing of interest in any of the rooms. No diaries, no records, no paperwork. It was as if no one lived there at all, even though they knew that wasn't the case.

*Come in here, sir.* Violetta was in the bedroom of Paolo's mother, staring at the narrow bed with its striped bed cover and plumped pillows tucked neatly underneath. In the corner, a small red chair faced the bed with a pair of slippers sitting side by side next to it and a well-worn Bible waiting expectantly on the bedside table for someone to read it. *Whose room is this, sir?*

*His mother's, I guess. A museum to his mother.* The cupboards still contained her clothes, but little else, and the Bible, with its brown leather cover, had only her name inside it, nothing else. He was glad now he'd read as much information as he could about Paolo Bianchi, although Detective Francesco had been reluctant to give it to him. He now had a sense of who this man was.

They made their way out onto the terrace, looking down at the neatly tended garden and the white-clad forensic teams busying themselves trying to gather as much evidence as they could. Gianfranco knew it would most likely be a thankless task. Order on this scale often left few clues. A match between this man's DNA and the DNA found at the murder sites of Diego and Lesley was all he needed. He would have his man and the murders would be solved. He would speak to Doctor Ricci this evening; maybe Milan would have sent through a match by then.

*Have you got everything you need, Gianfranco? We're winding up here. We'll put a guard on the house, and I'll keep you up to date with any progress we make. Are you heading back to Florence now?* His phone rang ... *Thank you, that's great. We'll be there as soon as we can.*

*They've found the car. Ventimiglia railway station. He's probably in France now. An easy escape route. I'm going to head there and see what we can find ...* Another phone was ringing, not the phone still clasped in his hand. *Excuse me.* Manelli turned and walked away from them, down the stairs into the garden and towards the gate. Gianfranco stayed exactly where he was, waiting to see what would happen next.

Detective Chief Inspector Manelli removed a second phone from an inside pocket and began speaking. He walked out of the drive and down towards the yellow tape still being guarded by the two Carabinieri officers. As he ducked under it and continued to walk down the road, Gianfranco spotted a black Range Rover parked diagonally across the street, ensuring no other car could pass. Manelli was walking straight towards it. *Get the registration of that car, Violetta.* She ran down the stairs and out into the street while Gianfranco Valdi watched Manelli speak to the person in the back of the car.

\*

*What's going on, Manelli? Why are you here? We're looking for Paolo Bianchi. Is that his house?* Marco Poccini sat squarely and firmly against the beige leather upholstery, ensuring his face could not be seen out of the car window.

Manelli was confused by the questions but knew he could not risk lying to Marco Poccini. Nor could he ask too many questions. His fate would be the same as many others if he stepped over those lines. *A policeman from Florence has been murdered in Bianchi's house.*

*Have you got Bianchi?*

*No.*

*Do you know where he is?*

*No. We've found his car but ...*

*Where?*

*Ventimiglia railway station car park. I'm heading there now to see if we can find out where he's gone.*

*I need to find him first. He murdered my son. Make sure you keep me informed of everything you find out. We'll see you in Ventimiglia. Remember... keep me informed.*

Leonardo drove off as Signor Poccini pushed the button to raise his window.

*Milan, Leonardo. We'll take the helicopter; it'll be quicker.* Marco Poccini wondered if his opportunity to kill his son's murderer had been lost. It saddened him to think that might be the case.

*

Gianfranco and Violetta waited until Rigoberto's body and his car had been removed from the scene. It seemed the right thing to do. It also meant that Gianfranco could speak to Sergeant Ruci and find out exactly what Rigoberto had discovered on his visit to Cesate.

*I need to know what Rigoberto found out, Sergeant Ruci. Is that possible?*

*Of course, sir. Come back to the station and I'll let you see the file we have on Paolo Bianchi. There isn't much in it, but there must have been something that made your young officer risk coming to the house alone. And we'll get you something to eat.*

Violetta was already on the phone to Florence getting a trace on the car number plate.

## Forty-four

It was almost evening when Paolo woke. The warmth of the sun had sent him quickly to sleep, and the stress of the last twenty-four hours had induced a deep sleep, the type of sleep he usually only enjoyed at home. As he looked out across the hills, down towards the Mediterranean shimmering blue and yellow as the sun began to set, he realised decisions would have to be made. But he was ready to make those decisions now.

He started considering the facts:

*the body would have been found by now and the police would be hunting for him*

*the person who killed the policeman was also probably looking for him*

*the person who killed the policeman could, with the drawing, link him to Lesley Hamilton's death, and as a consequence, to Diego Borroni's death*

*DNA would have been gathered from his house, and they would now be able to link him to many other unsolved cases as well*

*his car would have been found, and they would soon make their way to Menton and the car hire shop and have the registration number of the car he was now driving*

As if it was a new thought he could control, Paolo knew now that he should never have followed Lesley Hamilton. He should never have imagined she could be his friend or even possibly more than a friend. That was his mistake. His mother would have known that was a mistake. He should have stayed in the shadows, certain in the knowledge that he couldn't have the life he saw others having.

Now he considered his choices:

*he could continue running in the hope he could disappear and never be found (most likely impossible given he knew no one who could help him)*

*he could hand himself in to the police in Vence and confess to his crimes (it would end the chase, but prison would follow, and he would never survive it)*

*he could return to Cesate and ...*

Paolo sat very still considering his options and listening for his mother's voice, when he noticed, hopping up the tree in front of him, a short-toed treecreeper in search of insects. In search of food. A simple life, as simple as Paolo's had been before he saw Lesley. Before he'd wished for a different life. A life he could never have back.

His decision was made.

*

Sergeant Ruci had just finished retelling the story of Rigoberto's visit to the police station when Violetta's phone rang. She excused herself and went out into the corridor. Although the sergeant hadn't told Gianfranco anything he didn't already know, he was interested in the way the information was conveyed. Sergeant Ruci had obviously never considered Paolo Bianchi to be a danger to anyone, just an odd fellow protected by his mother, living a simple life with no friends. But now he thought he had been wrong. And more than that, he thought he had been wrong to persuade Piero Borroni to leave Paolo alone when investigating the murder of Father Rossi so many years ago.

*Do you think it would be worth my while visiting the Borronis and speaking to Piero? Would he have more information?*

*No, he wouldn't know any more than what is written in the file.* He paused. *He had a stroke a few years ago. His speech was affected. He would find it very hard to ...* Sergeant Ruci stopped speaking and stared at the floor, imagining the upset and stress such an interview would cause his friend. *I don't think it would help.*

*Okay, we'll head back to Florence now and await the DNA results. There's no need to speak to the Borronis just yet until we're sure Paolo Bianchi is the murderer. And we'll leave Detective Chief Inspector Manelli to do the chasing.*

Violetta was back in the room sitting next to him. Gianfranco stood up.

*If you hear anything, Sergeant Ruci, or you think of anything else that might be useful, please call me. You have my mobile number now.*

There was a pause.

*I was wondering, Sergeant Ruci, do you think Paolo Bianchi would consider coming back to his house?*

*He might. I can't imagine he has anywhere else to go. We have two officers on the gates.*

*Thank you.*

Gianfranco and Violetta made their way out of the station and climbed into the back seat of the unmarked police car that would return them to the helicopter and Florence. Violetta wasn't sure why she didn't want to say out loud what she'd been told in her phone call, but she knew Gianfranco would want to know. So she texted.

Ping. *The car we saw in the street belongs to Marco Poccini*

Gianfranco read it carefully. He would need to speak to Alessandro Francesco. He would contact him as soon as they returned to Florence.

*Thank you, Violetta.*

＊

They knew now that Paolo Bianchi had travelled to Menton, hired a car and left the town. It was an easy trail to follow. Now they just had to find the hire car. How hard could that be?

Although Detective Chief Inspector Manelli had all the necessary information and was working with the French police to find the car as he had done on other occasions, he couldn't stop thinking about what Marco Poccini had said. If Paolo Bianchi had murdered Pepe Poccini, Paolo Bianchi was no ordinary murderer. He was an assassin. Quite a different ball game. That meant Paolo Bianchi may have left this trail to be found but would by now most likely be out of the country. These guys always had contacts.

He pulled his phone out of his pocket, ready to call Marco Poccini with the facts he knew rather than the suspicions he harboured. He would head back to Milan after this and wait; there was nothing else he could do here.

＊

It was dark by the time Gianfranco and Violetta got back to Florence. As they drove towards the Carabinieri building, they said little, staring out at the people walking amongst the many ancient buildings lit from several angles to accentuate the beauty of their architecture and their ancient masonry. People were out enjoying life in the ancient city, with its many trattorias serving Tuscan ingredients to locals and travellers alike. Violetta was hungry thinking about it and asked if she should order them a pizza carry-out. She knew if she did it now, they wouldn't have to wait long for it to arrive once they were in the office.

*An excellent idea, Violetta. I've already let Concetta know I won't be home tonight.*

She wondered when he'd done that, but she knew that she'd been so wrapped up in her own thoughts that she wouldn't have noticed even if he'd spoken to his wife. She made the call.

The building was silent as they sat in Gianfranco's office eating pizza. They hadn't spoken yet about what they would do next; sustenance was the priority. As she ate her pizza, Violetta wondered how many pizzas had been delivered to detectives and officers working late into the night to solve crimes that they hoped wouldn't be repeated but always were. Too many to count, she thought. Gianfranco finished first.

*I'll call Alessandro Francesco and ask him to come into the office. We need to know what is the connection between Paolo Bianchi and Marco Poccini. He and Manelli are the only people who can answer that question. Do you agree?*

*Yes, I think you're right.* Once the last piece of pizza was in her mouth, Violetta gathered up the two boxes and the empty water bottles and took them to the bin next to the lift. She knew the stale smell of pizza would distract them as they grew more tired from lack of sleep, and a general feeling of nausea would overcome them. As she turned to go back into the office, she wished Rigoberto were there with his keen mind and endless enthusiasm.

But he wasn't. Gianfranco was speaking to Alessandro's wife as she took out her notebook and sat in the chair opposite him at his desk.

*Signora Francesco, I'm sorry to be bothering you, but I'm trying to get in touch with your husband. I've tried his mobile several times, but there is no response.* He listened. *No. No ring tone at all. I thought he might be at home with you and have it switched off.* He listened. *Do you know where he is? It's very important that I speak to him.* He listened. *When did you last see him?* He listened. *He didn't tell you where he was going?* He listened. *Thank you, Signora Francesco. If you hear from him, please let him know I need to speak to him.* The line went dead.

*She last saw him on Friday morning, Violetta, and has no idea where he might be.* Gianfranco was silent for a moment, surprised at what he was about to say. *She said he always sees his whore Carla on a Friday and that he might still be with her, but she thought that unlikely since he didn't like spending money.* Violetta looked up from her note-taking. *Telling me didn't seem to upset her. Find her, Violetta. We need to speak to her.* He paused. *I hope Concetta would be more upset if she didn't know where I was.* Violetta was confident she would be. *I'll call Brio and see if we have any DNA evidence that will help us.*

Violetta returned to her desk, unsure exactly how she would find Carla, but she knew there would be a way.

*How do you always know, Gianfranco? You must be telepathic; I was just about to phone you.* The two men laughed. *I've got some information that I think you will find both interesting and helpful. Let me find the document on my computer. I'll send it over so we can both see it and talk at the same time.*

Gianfranco could hear the buttons being firmly pressed as Brio made sure the correct document was sent. *It's here, Brio. Talk me through it.*

*Firstly, Rigoberto Copelli did not die immediately from the gunshot wound. It ripped through his stomach and he bled to death.* Neither of them spoke. Gianfranco would have preferred he had been shot dead. No suffering, no waiting for death to creep up and grab you. *They say it's a peaceful way to die, Gianfranco.* He wondered for a moment if that was true. *The bullet was retrieved, and it belonged to a police gun. He was shot by someone carrying a police weapon. It might have been his own gun, but there is no evidence to support that, although they haven't yet been able to find his gun.* Neither of them spoke. *Secondly, the DNA retrieved from the house does match with the DNA we retrieved from the chair in Diego Borroni's flat and the passenger seat in Diego Borroni's car. The owner of that DNA is the murderer of Lesley Hamilton and Diego Borroni as well as being the murderer in the unsolved cases I alluded to in our previous conversation. It is safe to assume the DNA belongs to Paolo Bianchi given he lives alone in the house, but we can't definitively say it is his until he is found. We can also assume he is an assassin since there is no clear link between all the other murders except that they all involved someone known to be or presumed to be linked to the criminal underworld. Lesley and Diego don't fit that criterion: he must have had another reason for killing them. I'll put all the details together and send them over with my thoughts. It's definitely a step forward.*

*Yes, it is, Brio, but it also throws up more questions that I fear I won't be able to answer. I'll contact Manelli and see how they're getting on with finding Paolo*

*Bianchi. Thank you. Thank you.*

*Always a pleasure, Gianfranco. We must have dinner soon.* The phone went dead.

When he looked up from the computer, Violetta was in his office, pleased to report that she had located Carla and sent a squad car to pick her up and bring her to his office. Gianfranco thanked her and noted how readily she used her initiative. *Coffee, sir?*

*Yes, please. But before you do that, get Alessandro Francesco's car number plate circulated to all forces across the north and get the tech guys to trawl CCTV and see if we can see when he left Florence and where he went. Thank you.* Gianfranco swivelled round in his chair until he was facing the window looking out across the Arno towards the Pitti Palace, carefully lit to accentuate its rigid structure. How did all the pieces fit, he wondered. And what would he do next? If he couldn't contact Francesco, he had to speak to Manelli. They would have to return to Cesate and make sure Manelli was there too.

\*

Paolo knew it would be a long drive back to Cesate avoiding the motorways and main roads. But he was certain he could get back by tomorrow night if he set off in the next couple of hours. It would be dark soon, so he ate one of the sandwiches he'd bought earlier, drank one of the bottles of water and planned his route. He would have to memorise the route since the charge on his phone was unlikely to last that long. But he liked that. He liked having a focus.

## Forty-five

Gianfranco knew it was hard to justify, but he needed to question Detective Chief Inspector Manelli about Marco Poccini. He thought it likely now that Pepe Poccini's disappearance must be the link to Lesley Hamilton and therefore to the murder of Diego Borroni. He trawled through the back of the diary lying idly on his desk and found the number of the generale di brigata. He would be able to give the order for Manelli to be taken to Cesate as long as he could justify the need for it.

*She's here, sir, Carla. Are you ready to speak to her?*

*Five minutes, Violetta. I need to make a call. Close the door. Thank you.*

She closed the door, and Gianfranco made the call.

*

Helen, Lucia and Piero had finished dinner and were now sitting quietly in the living room watching television. Helen understood nothing that was happening on the screen, but the familiar noise of the television was strangely comforting. She wondered if either Lucia or Piero were watching it or simply, like her, taking up a practised position that was somehow reassuring.

Helen hated to say it, but she had had a lovely day with Lucia and Piero. Some gardening in the morning, lunch on the terrace, a walk with Lucia in the afternoon, then dinner. And she didn't feel guilty although she knew she probably should have.

She would have to phone Kate tomorrow and tell her about the funeral arrangements, a task she wasn't looking forward to. She wondered momentarily how Detective

Chief Inspector Valdi was getting on with his investigations. She knew she was meant to want answers, want justice, but all she wanted at the moment was to remember Lesley and make sure her life was celebrated, untainted by its terrible end. She didn't want her death to be what she was remembered for. She turned back to the television and allowed the noise of the voices to wash over her.

*

*Carla, I am Detective Chief Inspector Valdi.* He shook her hand, conscious of her apprehension in such unfamiliar surroundings. She smiled. *Do sit down.* And he waited until she had made herself comfortable, as comfortable as she could be. Violetta sat in the chair next to her, notebook in hand. *We are trying to contact Alessandro Francesco but have been unable to do that. We know from his wife that you were probably the last person to see him.* He wondered if her expression would change. It didn't. *You saw him on Friday?*

*Yes, I see him every Friday. Have done for years. He comes round about five, we ... spend some time together, then we have dinner at Trattoria Giovanni. He walks me home, then leaves.* It was clear she had no intention of protecting Alessandro Francesco; he was simply a client.

*Did he say where he was going?*

She paused before answering. *No. We never discuss his work. I asked if he'd transferred money to my account and then he left.* Suddenly, Gianfranco felt sorry for Alessandro: a wife who didn't care he spent his Friday evenings with a prostitute and a prostitute who cared nothing for her client.

*Did you see him get in his car?*

*Oh, no, he always parks some distance from my apartment. It isn't good for a policeman's car to spend many hours outside the home of a prostitute.*

*Has he ever spoken to you about a man called Paolo Bianchi?*

She thought for a moment. *No, we never talked about his work. In fact, we rarely talked. I spoke and he didn't listen. It suited us both.*

Gianfranco nodded. *Thank you, Carla. Would you like a lift home?*

*No, thank you.* She stood up. *Never a good idea to be seen with the police.*

Violetta walked Carla to the lift with the officer who had brought her in, then returned to Gianfranco.

*We'll have to hope the tech boys trace the car. In the meantime, we're going back to Cesate. They're bringing Manelli to the station in Cesate. We'll question him there. I'm going to have a shower in the changing rooms before we go. It'll waken me up, I hope. Make sure the tech boys know to keep in touch with us and organise the helicopter. Give me an hour. Thank you.*

As he walked away, Violetta wondered why he wanted to return to Cesate. She knew he often worked on hunches, and she thought he might be working on a hunch now.

\*

The dark night sky was clear of any clouds as Paolo meandered along country roads, twisting and turning, climbing up hills and descending into valleys. He drove slowly, not because this was the way he liked to drive, but because he couldn't afford to have an accident or draw attention to himself. He stopped every three hours to eat another sandwich and drink another bottle of water. They tasted stale now, but he knew he had to keep himself alert, and the need to eat all of them rather than throwing anything out overwhelmed him.

After crossing the French border, he headed north through Piedmont, driving north of Turin. Once through Ivrea, he stopped for the last time. The sun was almost up, the dark night sky slowly changing colour, the bright stars diminishing as the morning light took over. He needed to sleep now and finish his journey to Cesate as soon as darkness had enveloped the world once again. The large forests east of Ivrea afforded him the opportunity to drive off the road and find barely used tracks to hide the car from any passing traffic. He knew someone might see him, but it was the best he could do. He was soon asleep, tired from the driving and the endless activity in his brain.

# Forty-six

Helen woke early, earlier than she had any other day. Her sleep had been fitful, with vivid dreams of life when Lesley and Kate were young, happy moments suddenly interrupted by Lesley's death repeating itself over and over as she slept. She felt tired and drained and wanted her conversation with Kate to be over sooner rather than later. She would call her now. Kate's voice sounded upbeat.

*Mum, hello. How are you?* Helen was surprised and pleased that this was the first question she asked.

*I'm fine, dear, being very well looked after by the Borronis. They are lovely people.*

*When will you be home?* Helen could feel the disappointment of the question in the pit of her stomach. No questions about the investigations, no questions about the funeral. No questions about Lesley. No apparent sadness at her sister's death. She remembered Kate as a loving child who had looked out for her younger sister, making sure she was safe from others. But that had all changed when her sister found her own way in the world, with her own expectations and views. They hadn't matched those Kate had for her, and tensions had developed. Tensions Kate refused to ignore, tensions she exacerbated by questioning and condemning her sister for her choices. Lesley understood that falling out with Kate wasn't the best option, so she began telling her little of her life and even less of her hopes. She heard the barbed comments but chose to ignore them. Kate had changed and found herself locked in a life she didn't really want, having abandoned her own hopes and dreams through the fear of what might happen if she followed them.

Helen chose not to answer her daughter's question. *I was just calling to let you know the funeral arrangements. After experiencing Lesley's life in Florence, speaking to those who knew her and spending the last few days with the Borronis, I've decided that Lesley will be buried with Diego here in Cesate.* Silence. She continued to talk, making sure she didn't stumble over her words or cry. She could show no weakness. *So the funeral is on Thursday in the church Diego attended as a boy, and they will both be laid to rest beside Diego's little brother who died when he was two.* Silence. *If you want to come out for the funeral, there's a flight from Edinburgh on Wednesday. I'm happy to pay for your fare. We could fly back together at the weekend. I'm sure David could manage for a couple of days on his own.* She was certain he could.

For a moment, Helen hoped that Kate was silent due to grief. *How could you? How could you? I'm here on my own with the children. Struggling on my own.*

*You aren't alone, Kate. You have David. He's an excellent father and is always helping you. You have friends. Lots of friends. They will be happy to help if you ask them.*

*But they don't understand me. They don't know me. You know me.* Helen wondered if she knew her at all. *I want you to come home.*

*I'll be home next weekend. You'll need to get on with things yourself until then.* Silence.

*I can't leave the children. I won't be at the funeral.* The line went dead. This wasn't what Helen had wanted, it wasn't what she'd hoped for, but it was the reality she had to live with.

For the first time in his life, Gianfranco had slept through a flight, the flight to Cesate, his irrational fears the least of his worries and the many hours without sleep finally taking their toll. Violetta found sleep hard to come by. She felt alert, as if a current of energy were passing through her, keeping her brain active and her senses alive. She wondered as they landed what would happen when this feeling left her.

Waiting at the helipad with an unmarked car was Davide Ruci, who had abandoned his weekend in the hope that he could help solve this case and bring some peace to his friends Lucia and Piero. He knew now that Piero had probably been right about Paolo Bianchi all those years ago and that he, along with others, had persuaded him against pursuing the boy for the murder of Father Rossi. A poor decision he would now have to live with.

As they drove through the streets, slowly coming to life as the light of the new day began to envelop the world in sunshine, there was silence in the car. Davide had let them know that Detective Chief Inspector Manelli was at the station in a cell. It was the only way they could contain him given the extent of his anger. Gianfranco was considering his questions. Violetta was considering what would happen if they were wrong. And Davide just wanted things to move along.

Before questioning Manelli, Gianfranco made sure everything was set up for the interview to be filmed without Manelli's knowledge, while in the small interview room, Violetta would, with her trusty notebook, ensure every word uttered was recorded. He would need concrete evidence if he were to ensure Manelli was found out.

The interview room was at the back of the station, far from the hustle and bustle of the front desk. The shuttered window offered a limited view of the small courtyard garden at the centre of the station, while the four comfortable chairs placed strategically around a small round coffee table with a tray of pastries and coffee sitting squarely in the middle seemed deceptively cosy and friendly. Gianfranco and Violetta waited in silence for Manelli to arrive.

They heard him before they saw him. Davide Ruci opened the door and Manelli entered, tired looking and angry. *I thought it would be you,* Manelli said as he slumped down in the chair next to Violetta and poured himself a coffee. *I don't know what's going on, and no one will tell me anything.* He paused. *I hope you've cleared this with someone further up the chain, Gianfranco.* He smiled as he said it, confident, Gianfranco thought, that he would win the day and Gianfranco would be the one being interviewed before long. It was a pattern he'd seen with other colleagues whose corrupt activities were eventually exposed. A certainty they should never have been certain of.

*Yes, I have permission to interview you from those at the highest level.* Manelli looked up from the pastry he was now devouring, momentarily surprised. *You are entitled to a lawyer, Manelli. I need to make that clear. I'm happy to wait until that is organised if you want.*

*I don't need a lawyer; I've done nothing wrong.* It sounded defensive.

*Detective Morelli will take some notes.* Manelli nodded, still oblivious to the bombshell about to break.

*Is there any news from the French police on Paolo Bianchi?* Gianfranco always liked to start with questions that would seem, to the guilty, the least likely question to be asked.

*They hadn't located him or the car, the last I heard.*

*Do you think there is a reason why he's so hard to find? It seems unusual to me.*

*I don't know.* Manelli understood now that the great Gianfranco Valdi probably knew far more than he'd anticipated him knowing.

*I want to tell you what I know first, Manelli.* Before speaking again, Gianfranco leaned across the table and poured himself a cup of coffee, leaving Manelli to ponder what might come next. *Many years ago, Paolo Bianchi, the man we are all keen to find, was a suspect in the murder of the local priest, Father Rossi. Detective Piero Borroni, father of the murdered Detective Diego Borroni, was convinced Paolo Bianchi had been the murderer. But no evidence could be found to link him to the case. I guess it was a hunch. We all have those.* Gianfranco sipped his coffee and paused. *Paolo Bianchi lived a quiet life here in Cesate, never drawing attention to himself, living alone once his mother died. No friends, no relatives, a solitary life. Then Pepe Poccini disappeared in Florence.* Manelli continued to stare at him, expressionless. Violetta continued writing, hoping this series of hunches being verbalised by Gianfranco would pay off. *Diego Borroni, a man demoted because of his investigations into the Poccini family, was sent to interview Pepe's neighbours, one of whom was Lesley Hamilton. Once Detective Alessandro Francesco took over the case, Diego asked Lesley out and they became a couple. But, unbeknown to any of us, Lesley knew something about the disappearance, and Paolo Bianchi was someone she got to know. Only briefly.*

Gianfranco stood up, turned towards the window and looked out at the green leaves of the camellia plants shining brightly as the morning sun moved slowly round the courtyard. He wanted to leave his last words hanging for a few moments. He hoped his guesswork wouldn't be found out.

*Detective Alessandro Francesco, a friend of the Poccinis, was now in charge of the Pepe Poccini disappearance. Pepe's blood had been found on the stairwell in the flats, but it wasn't reported to my team. To homicide. An unusual decision, I think you would agree, for Detective Francesco to make unless he was covering something up, or worse, letting the Poccinis find the murderer and kill him. The Poccinis interviewed, in the presence of Detective Francesco, Lesley Hamilton and Signora Conti. An unusual thing for a detective to do, don't you agree?* Manelli moved in his chair, the first time he'd moved since Gianfranco started speaking, but his face didn't change. *Diego Borroni is then found murdered in his flat and Lesley Hamilton is drowned in the Arno. Both by the same killer, a man in black gloves. The same man noticed by Signora Conti, another neighbour of Pepe's and Lesley's, at the time Pepe disappeared.* He turned to look at Manelli. *There had to be a connection. Too many loose ends. I don't like loose ends.* Gianfranco sat down once again, maintaining eye contact with Manelli as he stared straight ahead.

*Detective Francesco had already visited Cesate to find out about Paolo Bianchi, so we knew then that someone else suspected this man of being a murderer. But who could that be? The Poccinis?* He didn't wait on a

347

response. *And so I sent Detective Copelli to Cesate in search of what Francesco had found out. I regret that now.* And once again, he saw in his head the shocked face of Rigoberto Copelli hoping to cling to life by holding his stomach. A picture he had not conveyed to Rigoberto's widow when he spoke to her last night. *He too appears to have believed Paolo Bianchi could be the murderer, and as you know, he remained here when he should have returned to Florence. And was killed.*

*I think you probably know the rest of the story, although I'm not sure you'll know that Paolo Bianchi's DNA links him to the murders of Diego Borroni and Lesley Hamilton and many murders that have taken place in the north of Italy over the past 20 years. Murders with links to the criminal world. Interesting, don't you think?* For a moment, Manelli looked like he was going to respond, but he didn't. Gianfranco knew now he had the upper hand.

*We'll continue after lunch. I'm quite hungry now.* He opened the door and asked the young officer to return Manelli to his cell.

As he left, he turned toward Gianfranco and said, *I think I want a lawyer.* Gianfranco nodded. Unlike his arrival, Manelli's return to his cell was silent. Gianfranco was certain he'd got most of it right.

Violetta placed her pen in the fold of her notebook and smiled at Gianfranco.

## Forty-seven

Leonardo, following instructions, had pulled into the parking bay close to the helipad. Nothing was said for several minutes.

*I've changed my mind, Leonardo, take me back to Lake Como. He won't be in France; there's no point in going.* Marco Poccini thought the best he could hope for now was that some time in the future, Paolo Bianchi would resurface and Detective Inspector Manelli, or one of his many other contacts, would give him his location and the murder of this man who had taken the shining light from his life could be undertaken.

*Are you sure, sir?*

*Yes, Leonardo. Thank you.* Marco leaned back in his seat, resting his head against the cold leather of the head rest, and closed his eyes. He wondered what he would tell his wife, whose anger at the death of her son, he knew, could not be extinguished.

\*

It took several hours for Manelli's lawyer to be located and to get to Cesate. Gianfranco and Violetta spent the intervening hours discussing the case, eating lunch, getting some fitful sleep and deciding on the questions they would ask in the next interview. The filming of the interview no longer had to be hidden, so with the help of Davide Ruci and his team, the room was made ready for Manelli's return.

Gianfranco had experienced, on several occasions, the success of revealing a corrupt policeman, but it rarely felt satisfying. Just another story to erode the public's opinion of the force and the work they did on behalf of the nation every day, the often-tedious work carried out by people like Davide Ruci who had devoted their life to the job and their community. People who wanted to get things right. Gianfranco had always been one of those people.

At 3.00 pm the door to the interview room opened and Manelli entered, accompanied by his lawyer. A young man. Tall, slim, no grey hairs and a black suit with an open-necked shirt. Unusual? No, just a sure sign Gianfranco was simply getting older. The young man extended his hand towards Gianfranco and introduced himself. *Nice to meet you, Detective Inspector Valdi. My name's Matteo Esposito. I'll be representing Detective Inspector Manelli today. Shall we sit at this side of the table?* Gianfranco nodded. Violetta and Gianfranco sat at the opposite side. There were no pastries, no coffee this time.

*My client has brought me up to speed with this morning's interview, and although it seems to me it would be unfair to call it an interview since there weren't many questions asked by you, my client is happy to answer any further questions you might have.* He paused. *I like questions, Detective Inspector Valdi, not hunches.* Violetta thought he looked rather smug when he said this. Unwisely, she thought, given they were now on more solid ground, and facts rather than hunches would be the basis of this interview.

*Of course, Signor Esposito. Lots of questions. Let's start with this one.* He looked directly at Manelli, whose morning arrogance had disappeared and said, *what is your connection with Signor Marco Poccini, the Milanese businessman?*

It was clear as the silence hung gloomily in the room

that neither Manelli or Signor Esposito had expected this to be the first question.

*I have heard the name of Marco Poccini, but I do not know the man. He is well known in Milan, but I have never met him.*

*Detective Morelli.* Gianfranco leaned back in his chair as Violetta began.

*On Saturday, when Detective Chief Inspector Valdi and I were looking round Paolo Bianchi's home, we took time to stand on the terrace and look out at all the police activity. Detective Copelli's death had been a terrible shock to us; we needed time to process it.* She was unsure why she'd added that. *When we were standing on the terrace looking across the driveway, we saw you take a phone from your inside pocket — a phone we now have in our possession, I should add — and answer it. It was a very brief call: 48 seconds, we now know. Then you walked away from the house toward the yellow taped cordon and spoke to someone in a black Range Rover. I ran a trace on the number plate and discovered it belonged to Marco Poccini.* She paused, looking down at her notebook as if she were about to read something from it. But she didn't. *How odd you would take a call from a man you didn't know, then go and speak to him. Can you explain that?*

Signor Esposito touched Manelli's arm and nodded.

*Could I have a few minutes with my client? We'll return to his cell.* The recording was stopped.

*Of course.*

As they sat alone in the room, waiting for Manelli's return, nothing was said. An air of satisfaction replaced the gloom. Gianfranco pondered how many hours he'd spent just waiting while doing his job and assumed it would be far too many to count. Violetta was simply pleased.

*Ah, you're back, Detective Inspector Manelli and Signor Esposito. Sit down. We'll start recording again. Would you like Detective Morelli to repeat her question?*

*No, my client would prefer to start by making a statement. I suspect you will have further questions once he's made it, but we think it might be helpful if we start from this point.*

*Go right ahead.* Violetta admired Gianfranco's patience, the certain knowledge he had that he would win the day.

Manelli began. *I do know Marco Poccini. So, when I received the call, I was not surprised. He has called me on many occasions. However, I was surprised that he was in the street. I had no idea how he knew I was there, and I had no idea why he would be interested in this case. He asked me to come to the car, so I did. There was so much activity going on, I didn't think I would be noticed.* Gianfranco nodded. *When I got to the car, he asked me if the house belonged to Paolo Bianchi. I was surprised that he knew Paolo Bianchi. I told him it did and asked how he knew him. He said Paolo Bianchi had murdered his son and he needed to find him before the police in order to ...* He didn't finish that sentence. *I told him Paolo had been traced to Ventimiglia Railway station, and he said he would go there. I don't know if he did.* He paused. *He asked me to keep in touch and give him any information I had regarding the whereabouts of Paolo Bianchi.*

*And did you?*

*I called him some time later, once I realised, like you, that Paolo Bianchi must be a paid killer. It seemed to me unlikely that Marco Poccini's son would be randomly killed. And the fact that his body had disappeared probably meant a professional job. Although I was working with the French police to find the car, I couldn't stop thinking about Marco Poccini's words. If Paolo Bianchi had murdered Pepe Poccini, Paolo Bianchi was no ordinary murderer. I thought Paolo Bianchi may have left this trail to be found but would, by now, most likely be out of the country. I thought Marco Poccini should know my thoughts. I haven't spoken to him since then.*

*Thank you, Detective Inspector Manelli. Your statement has been very helpful, although it has not made finding Paolo Bianchi any more likely. Do you think Paolo Bianchi killed Detective Copelli?*

*No, I don't. There is no evidence to link him to that murder even though he seems to be the obvious candidate. I would be surprised if he carried or owned a service revolver.*

*I agree, it seems unlikely.* He paused before he spoke again. *I thank you for your honesty, Detective Inspector Manelli, although I know it wouldn't have been your preferred option to give us all that information. I think it will put you and your family in direct danger.*

*I'm unmarried. I'm the only one in danger.*

*Ah. You will be charged with perverting the course of justice in relation to this case, but I know there are others who will want to speak to you in relation to Marco Poccini and his activities.* Gianfranco paused, lowering his head, then lifting it once again to look at Manelli. *Diego Borroni spent many years trying to find out exactly what Marco Poccini and his sons were involved in. There would be some form of justice if you were able to help that to happen. You will be taken to Milan for further questioning and for your own protection. I have no further questions, Signor Esposito. Paolo Bianchi needs to be found, and I intend finding him.*

The two men left the room. Arrangements for Manelli's transfer to Milan had already been made. It would be someone else's job to question him and hunt down the Poccini family. He hoped Manelli would live long enough to make that happen.

*

Paolo had slept a very long time, but he felt better for it. His head was clearer, and he was more certain that his decision to return to Cesate was the right one. He ate the last sandwich and drank the last bottle of water before starting the car and his final journey back to Cesate. Back to his home. It would be dark when he got back.

*

Davide Ruci took Gianfranco and Violetta to his home for something to eat. They needed to speak to the Borronis and let them know about Paolo Bianchi, but he knew they needed to eat before they did that. The early evening streets were quiet as the three of them walked silently to Davide's home and a spell of normality that had been lacking for the past two days.

While Davide prepared the food, Violetta asked if she could watch television. She found a soap opera that she had never seen before and began watching it, immersing herself in the unreality of it. She'd had enough reality for one day. Gianfranco took himself outside to the garden, enjoying the fresh air that replaced the dank air of the police station, and found a wooden seat from which he could phone Concetta. He relaxed when he heard her voice, and just as she always did, she told him all about what she had been doing with the girls over the past few days and asked no questions. He listened intently, imagining all the fun he had missed. He said he hoped he would be home soon. *We'll look forward to that, darling. Ciao.*

Davide turned out to be an excellent cook, much to the delight of Gianfranco and Violetta. The first proper meal they had had in the last few days. A meal eaten at leisure rather than speed. Violetta helped with the tidying up, then they were ready to visit the Borronis.

*Gianfranco, I think I should tell them about Paolo. They are my friends, and I think it might be easier coming from me.*

*As you wish.*

*Lesley Hamilton's mother is also there, so we will be able to let her know as well. Always best to tell people in person, I think. Will you be able to help with the English?*

*Of course.* There was nothing else to say.

It was dark now as they made the five-minute walk to the Borroni's house.

*

Paolo parked the car on the outskirts of Cesate on the opposite side of town from his house. A quiet street of residential housing with only a few lampposts that pooled the light, taking him from circles of illuminated orange to dark tarmac as he walked. He knew the walk would take him about forty minutes and had, while driving, planned the safest route he could think of to get him back to his home without being seen. He passed familiar sights, places he had known all his life, places where he felt safe.

The final part of the walk took him up the lane behind the Parrochia San Alessandro e San Martino church and the house that had been Father Rossi's home when Paolo committed his first murder. It was a murder he tried never to think about since he found it hard to understand why he had done it. He had no real reason for killing him. He knew people often cried, and he'd heard his mother cry before, but Father Rossi's lack of concern at his mother's anguish had triggered an anger that he knew now simmered just below the surface all the time. He stopped to look at the back of the house, remembering how purposefully and without fear he had entered that house of silence and murdered the man in his bed. The tight squeeze as he made his way along the narrow gap at the side of the house, the placing of his shoes for a quick exit, the creaking of the stairs, the smell of sweat from a man whose weight made all tasks burdensome, and the muffled cries of Father Rossi as he slowly pushed the life out of him.

It had been easier to commit all the other murders, the murders of people never known, never part of his life. A contract between him and Franco. Do this, get paid. He didn't need to know the reason. The reason belonged to someone else, and he was happy with that. Until Pepe Poccini. He often wondered why Pepe's murder had been so difficult for him, and although he could list reasons, none of them seemed to fit.

Thinking of Pepe took him back to thinking about Lesley. He knew he couldn't regret the botched murder of Pepe Poccini because without that, he wouldn't have met Lesley Hamilton. He wouldn't have experienced the joy of knowing her even for such a short time. She gave to him, in their few short meetings, a feeling of joy that had left him when his mother died. He remembered again the ease with which she had let him push her face into the cold flowing water of the Arno, and he knew that she had been ready to die. There was no life for her without Diego. He knew now that he too was ready to die. There was no life left for him other than being hunted for his crimes. No life.

When he came out of the path, he noticed immediately the bright yellow tape surrounding his house. And, although he couldn't see the main gates from where he was standing, he was confident that the house would be guarded. His only way in would be through the narrow gap in the hedge at the back corner of the garden. Momentarily, he wondered if there would be policemen in the house, but he was happy to take the risk.

As he pushed his way through the hedge, he placed his black bag across his front to protect him from the sharp branches of the hawthorn and held one hand across his face to prevent any scratches. The noise as he pushed through seemed loud and intense to Paolo, and he wondered if those guarding the house would hear him and kill him before he could make it to the sanctuary of his home. Once through the hedge, he stopped immediately to get his bearings and assess the situation. There was no light shining on that part of the garden from the streetlights; he was safe.

Across the garden and past the house, he saw two men standing in front of another line of yellow tape that hung across the gates, the entrance to the house. He couldn't see their legs, so he knew they were on the road side of the gates. Their voices carried across the silence as they spoke about mundane matters to pass the time and keep each other awake. The smell of camomile filled the air as Paolo walked silently across the lawn to the steps leading up to the house. He had already removed the front door key from his bag, and when he reached the steps, he removed his shoes to ensure silence as he climbed up to the front door, where he knew he would no longer be able to see the two men. And no longer be able to be seen.

The door opened easily. He was in. Familiar smells. Familiar sights. Nothing looked out of place. Surprising. He placed his black shoes next to the doormat and went directly to his mother's room. It was just as he'd left it, as if it was waiting for his return. He removed his black leather jacket and hung it on the back of the small red chair. Next, he removed his book from his bag and placed it on the chair, ready to read the words that always calmed him and that he so enjoyed. He thought he would miss those words, if you were still able to hear words when you were dead. Once settled in the chair, he placed the gun, with its silencer attached, neatly on his lap, switched on the lamp next to his mother's bed and began reading aloud as if his mother were there enjoying his company.

*Chapter Eleven: The Other Clouds*
*The accessory clouds, supplementary features, and stratospheric and mesospheric clouds*
*The ten main cloud types ...*

## Forty-eight

Visiting the Borronis reminded Gianfranco of visiting his own parents. The outside and the inside of the house were organised and tidy, and the politeness shown even in the darkest of times gave them an air of dignity it was hard to find in the young. Tea and coffee were made before any talk of the case took place, and Lucia Borroni made sure everyone was comfortable. The tension felt by Helen Hamilton and Lucia Borroni dissipated in their busyness to ensure the visitors were properly catered for. But Piero Borroni sat upright and rigid, his tension far more visible. Gianfranco sat next to Helen on the small sofa to ensure he could translate Davide's words quickly and quietly. Violetta sat in the corner with her notebook in one hand and a cup of coffee in the other, while Lucia placed her chair next to Piero so that she could hold his hand and give him some of her strength. They were ready. Gianfranco began. In Italian then in English.

*Thank you for seeing us at such short notice, but I thought you would want to know what progress has been made in our enquiries, and I wanted to see you personally before I returned to Florence. Davide is going to give you the update so that I can translate his words for Helen.*

*How kind.* Lucia always found kindness even in the darkest of moments. *Davide.* They all turned to look at him.

*There has been significant progress since we last saw you. Detective Chief Inspector Valdi sent one of his men to meet with me on Friday regarding a suspect in the case. Paolo Bianchi.* Lucia gasped and opened her mouth as though she was going to speak then didn't. Piero squeezed her hand tightly, allowing a solitary tear to roll down his face. He said nothing. Helen looked confused. Davide looked at her. *He is a resident in Cesate and went to school with Diego. Piero investigated him in relation to a murder committed in Cesate many years ago, but no evidence to link him to the case was found.*

Piero stumbled out his words, unable to remain silent any longer. *It was a hunch.*

*Yes, it was a hunch. And we think now you were right.* Davide lowered his head, ashamed that he hadn't supported his friend at the time. *The policeman who visited me, unbeknown to both me and Detective Chief Inspector Valdi, remained in Cesate, visited Paolo's house under some pretext and was murdered while there. We do not know who murdered him, but we do not think it was Paolo.* He paused. *However, the DNA we got from the house has confirmed that he murdered both Diego and Lesley and that he has committed a number of murders over the past twenty years across the north of Italy.*

*An assassin?* Lucia had found her voice.

*Yes.*

*He was contracted to kill Diego and Lesley?* Piero squeezed his wife's hand, knowing that she would ask the questions he now found so hard to formulate.

*No, we think Lesley witnessed something in relation to another murder in Florence that was contracted and knew too much. Diego had also visited Cesate to see Paolo's police file, so we assume he also suspected Paolo of having committed one or more murders. These are our hunches. None of this we can confirm, but it seems the most likely explanation.*

*Where is he now?* Helen could think of nothing else to

ask.

*We don't know. We know he drove to the French border, took a train to Menton, hired a car and went on his way. We are working with the French police to find both the car and Paolo Bianchi.*

*You'll never find him.* Lucia's demeanour had changed. *You didn't support Piero when he could have stopped him, and now he will have disappeared. These people have contacts. I know how these things work. All those times I ...* She started to cry, unable to contain her anger. *We had him in our house. I felt sorry for him. Sorry for him and his mother. Please can you leave.*

Gianfranco continued to speak to Helen, explaining what he knew about Paolo's connection to the Borroni family. She looked shocked but not upset, and he admired her capacity to deal with distress.

*Thank you, Detective Chief Inspector Valdi. I think you should go. We need time to process all this information. Grief is a complex thing.*

Gianfranco, Violetta and Davide stood up. *I will be back with more answers once I have them, and I can assure you we will find him.* Piero Borroni stretched his hand out towards Gianfranco and shook it. He would do now what his wife would normally do.

*Thank you.*

Once they reached the street, Davide asked them what they wanted to do now. Did they want to stay?

*No, there is no reason to stay now. We need to get back to Florence and see if we can get more answers to the unanswered questions. If you could organise a car to take us to the helicopter in an hour, that would be great. I want to have one more look around Paolo's house in case there's anything we've missed. Can you do that, Davide?*

*Yes, I'll let the officers at the house know you are coming, and I'll get everything else organised. I hope we will see you back in Cesate again.*

They shook hands.

*

He reached the end of the chapter and placed the book next to his mother's Bible on the bedside table. He sat back down in the small red chair, lifted his gun and placed it at his temple, ready to fire it. It felt cold in his hand, and momentarily, he thought about the suddenness of death and his part in bringing death to many others.

He squeezed the trigger gently and the gun popped, showering blood and brains across the pale pink paint on the walls.

It was over.

*

Gianfranco and Violetta arrived at the house and spoke to the two police officers before entering the garden and walking towards the house. Everything was silent. No cicadas chirping, no breeze blowing through the hedges. The key turned easily in the door and they were in, immediately on their guard as a dim light shone under the bedroom door on the left. At first, Gianfranco wondered if it had been left on by accident, but he thought that unlikely. He reached for his gun. Violetta already had her gun in her hand, prepared to use it if need be.

Gianfranco placed his finger across his lips and indicated that Violetta should go to the other side of the bedroom door. He pushed the door open violently and moved quickly into the room, his gun out in front of him, ready to fire. And then he saw him. The face of the man they had been seeking torn apart by a single bullet, his gun still in his hand trailing on the ground.

It was over.

\*

Concetta had never been to Cesate. Her first trip a funeral. Gianfranco had never asked her to come to a victim's funeral with him before, and she wondered why on this occasion. She felt sure it was because he felt less certain, more vulnerable given the level of corruption he had now uncovered and the number of murders Paolo Bianchi had been able to commit without being found out.

Over in the far corner of the cemetery, they could see a crowd gathered tightly together, mourning the deaths of Diego and Lesley, crying at their young lives lost and the joy they had found gone forever. In stark contrast, Gianfranco and Concetta were the only two people watching Paolo Bianchi's internment in a lonely grave with only his mother for company. No words said.

They would travel back to Florence this afternoon, stopping on the way for a long lunch.

\*

Marco Poccini sat quietly on the terrace eating his breakfast with his wife, looking out over Lake Como, pleased to be there away from the pressures of life in Milan. Determined to mend the rift their son's death had caused in their marriage.

The gates to the estate were opened by the security guard and two police cars made their way towards the house and its extensive gardens, ready to take Marco Poccini back to Milan to face his reckoning.

It was over.

## About The Author

Laura Jane Smith began writing seriously in 2019 when she took early retirement after a 34-year career in education. She lives in Perthshire in Scotland, where she enjoys gardening, walking, theatre and going to the cinema, as well as cycling and cross-stitching.

Her interest in writing came not just from her own reading but also from the process of teaching others about reading, writing and understanding the written word. The ideas for her first novel came from her experiences in education and travelling in Europe, as well as her enjoyment of a well-told psychological thriller. She focuses on human behaviour and individual motivation when faced with life-changing events and difficult decisions. Relationships are at the heart of the novels. The decisions made by the characters and the relationships they develop drive the plot.

The inspiration for this first novel, *Listen to Mother*, came initially from a trip to Florence in 2011. However, the main inspiration was a desire for others to experience the world from the viewpoint of someone with high-functioning autism whose struggles with the reality of life result in his joining a world in the shadows.

www.blossomspringpublishing.com